# THE LADY AND THE ORC

FINLEY FENN

## ALSO BY FINLEY FENN

### ORC SWORN

The Lady and the Orc

The Heiress and the Orc

The Librarian and the Orc

The Duchess and the Orc

The Midwife and the Orc

The Maid and the Orcs

Offered by the Orc (Bonus Story)

### THE MAGES

The Mage's Maid

The Mage's Match

The Mage's Master

The Mage's Groom (Bonus Story)

Visit www.finleyfenn.com for free bonus stories and epilogues, delicious orc artwork, complete content tags and warnings, news about upcoming books, and more!

# ABOUT THE LADY AND THE ORC

*He's the most feared monster in the realm. And she's what he needs to win his war...*

In a world of warring orcs and men, Lady Norr is condemned to a childless marriage, a cruel lord husband, and a life of genteel poverty—until the day her home is ransacked by a horde. And leading the charge is their hulking, deadly orc captain: the infamous Grimarr.

**And Grimarr has a wicked plan for Lady Norr, and for ending this war once and for all.** She's going to become his captive—and the perfect snare for Lord Norr.

There's no possible escape, and soon Lady Norr is dragged off toward Orc Mountain in the powerful arms of her greatest enemy. A ruthless, commanding warlord, with a velvet voice and mouthwatering scent, who awakens every forbidden hunger she never knew she had...

**But Grimarr refuses to accept half measures—in war, or in pleasure.** And before he'll conquer Lady Norr's deepest, darkest desires, she needs to surrender *everything*.

Her allegiance.

Her wedding-ring.

Her future...

And with her husband's forces giving chase, Lady Norr can't afford to play such a dangerous game—or can she? **Even if this deadly orc's plans might be the only way to save them all?**

# PROLOGUE

Lord Norr was leaving. Again.

Jule sprinted down the road, her light slippers sliding in the muddy wheel-ruts, her heavy skirts catching on her ankles. "Astin!" she shouted. "Wait!"

She could see her husband's slim shoulders tensing, his booted feet nudging at his horse's sides—but several of the uniformed men riding with him had already turned to look, fixing Jule with kindly, indulgent smiles.

"My lord," one called. "Your wife."

Astin didn't even turn his head, and for an instant, there was the grim, terrifying certainty that he'd make Jule chase him all the way to Wolfen. Or wherever the hell he was off to now, only the gods knew where, or for how long.

"Astin!" Jule shouted again. "A moment, please!"

His men had started to slow, pulling up their horses and loaded wagons, and finally Astin was obligated to do the same, lest he ride straight into the wagon in front of him. Meaning that Jule finally caught up with him, grasping for his horse's bridle, dragging in gulping, shuddering breaths as she looked up at Lord Norr's face.

And even in this, in her husband of five years blithely riding away from Norr Manor without a single word of farewell, Jule still felt her breath catch at the familiar, thrilling sight of him. He was dressed impeccably, as usual, his riding-clothes perfectly tailored to fit his tall, slender body, and his wavy brown hair was swept back from his forehead, accentuating his straight nose and blue eyes and sensual bowed mouth. And even though he was now nearing forty—more than a full decade older than Jule—he still looked every bit the young, strapping, handsome lord one heard about in fairy-tales.

"Yes, wife?" he said, his voice crisp, his eyes flicking up and down Jule's messy, sweaty form. "This had better be important."

Jule's heart was thumping unpleasantly, and she shoved back the haphazard mess of her own brown hair, and mopped at her too-hot forehead. "You haven't," she began, her thoughts frantically catching and discarding at words, "left a guard at the house. We have no defense."

"And?" Astin asked, gazing blandly toward her, and Jule gulped for air, put a shaky hand to his horse's warm, silken neck. He was a lovely new gelding, entirely unsuited for long journeys like this, and—the realization belatedly slammed at Jule with invisible, staggering force—Astin hadn't left a guard at the house, and he *knew* it. He'd done it on *purpose*.

"B-but," Jule protested, her voice coming out far more plaintive than she meant, "but the *orcs*, Astin."

Astin only raised an eyebrow at her, as though the orcs were an entirely novel concept. As though he'd somehow forgotten the horde of brutal, vicious beasts, squatting in their massive, impenetrable mountain, only several days' ride away. Orcs were huge, hideous, dangerous, deadly, constantly raiding for goods and women—and if a woman were unfortunate enough to be taken, she would be trapped, broken, and carelessly used by the mob. Filled with wicked orc-seed again and again and again, until their huge orc-sons took hold, and tore free of her womb, and *killed* her.

"The *orcs*," Jule gasped again, as her heartbeat thumped louder, echoing almost painfully through her skull. "They're getting worse, Astin. They've attacked every town in Yarwood but ours this spring. We *need* a guard. A few armed men. *Something*."

Her voice had risen sharply as she spoke, and she could see Astin casting an uneasy glance behind him, toward the dozen-odd armed men in his entourage. "Watch yourself, wife," he said, under his breath. "I can't afford to waste any more of my coin on those stupid beasts. If you want a guard so badly, you can go hire one yourself."

Jule felt herself flinch, the anger twisting and curdling, and she raised her chin, met Astin's flinty eyes. "Then give me access to my father's trusts," she said, "and I will."

It was the wrong thing to say, she already well knew—Astin had mortgaged away those trusts years ago—and she didn't miss the sight of his slim, gloved fingers clenching around the handle of his ever-present horsewhip. More of a bullwhip, really, long and snakelike and vicious, and Jule felt herself take a swift, reflexive step backwards. He'd only fully used it on her once, after she'd gone riding alone with a handsome visiting lord from the north—but it had been more than enough, and Astin damn well knew it.

"You'll be just *fine*, wife," he said now, with a grim, satisfied smile. "You still have the manor's tower, don't you? If the orcs attack, just lock yourself up there, and wait for the Talford regiment to come."

Jule's thoughts were sputtering again, casting in all directions at once. Should she argue, beg, make promises and declarations, point out the utter unlikeliness of escaping to the tower in time? What did Astin want from this, what would sway him—

"Please, Astin," she said finally, helplessly. "We *need* a guard. If not for me, at least for your house, or your servants. Surely you don't wish anything to happen to *them* while you're gone?"

"Oh, they have their orders," Astin said airily, and that meant he'd at least managed to inform *them* about this trip in advance, damn him. "And those orders include keeping an eye on *you*, wife dearest. No going into my rooms, or sneaking *anything* from my house to sell for coin. And especially"—he flicked his fingers toward Jule in a come-here gesture, and she went without thinking, close enough that he could grasp her chin with his gloved hand—"no other men while I'm gone, wife. You keep your legs closed, and stay faithful to your lord. Or else."

Jule felt herself give an unwilling shudder, caught on his handsome face, his lovely eyes, the feel of his warm gloved fingers against her skin. And even on those words, hinting that he truly cared, perhaps, or wanted her for his own—but dragging also at misery, and loneliness, and her shameful, compulsive terror at that bullwhip, still clenched tight in his other hand's fingers.

"Yes, my lord," Jule heard her hollow voice say, even as she cursed herself for speaking, for falling into his slippery grasp once again. "I'm always faithful to you, and you know it."

The smug smile on Astin's mouth had tilted up, slipping into something infinitely more dangerous, almost like affection. And without warning he leaned down, abruptly drew Jule's face to his, and then—for the first time in weeks—he *kissed* her. His mouth warm and familiar, his tongue tangling deep and powerful against hers, and *gods* he tasted good, gods it had been so *long*, and despite everything Jule felt herself moan against his lips, her hand coming up to slide into his cropped hair. Her hunger rising and madly swerving, knocking against her chest, maybe it was good after all, maybe it was *fine*—

When Astin pulled away Jule was still gasping, her face flushed and hot, and he was still smiling, his gloved hand gently patting her cheek. "I don't know what you're so worried about, wife," he said, his voice soft, almost tender. "Everyone knows orcs only want whole women anyway. Women they can actually knock up with their foul orc-spawn. They'd never want to take *you*."

The words felt like a slap, even as his hand kept patting her cheek, even as he kept giving her that smile. Colder now, brittle, speaking of the ever-curdling bitterness between them. Five years of marriage, any number of illegitimate children on Astin's part, and not a whiff of a single true heir, despite his countless attempts, and demands, and threats.

Jule could feel her shoulders sagging, her eyes casting downwards, and above her Astin actually chuckled, his shining boot coming to nudge at her flat waist. "There, there, wife," he murmured. "You relax here in your beautiful home while I'm gone, and if you're good, maybe we'll try again when I'm back. Now smile for me, like a good wife, and wish me safe travels. Loudly."

The retorts were lurking on Jule's lips—*you won't, you've barely touched me in a year, Norr Manor isn't my home, it never will be, what about the orcs*—but she choked them back, and nodded, and even contorted her mouth into something that might have passed for a smile. Maybe they really would try again. Maybe it would be *fine*.

"Safe travels, my lord," she said, her voice loud, carrying, a lie. "I shall eagerly await your return."

Three days later, the orcs attacked.

The alarm came not from the surrounding village of Talford, like Jule had expected—but instead in the form of a familiar, bone-chilling male shout, rising straight from below.

The orcs were *in the house*.

"To the tower!" Jule screamed, charging at full tilt down the second-floor corridor, toward the servants' quarters. "Now!"

Some of the servants were already running, leaving their slower counterparts to straggle behind, and Jule grasped at Cook's waist, and dragged her up one set of stairs, and then the next. All the while searching and desperately counting, it had been the butler's voice she'd heard shouting downstairs, the groom and stable-boys were outside and hopefully escaping, she'd seen Kate and Lou, please gods—

Norr Manor's tower was at the very top of its fourth floor, accessible only by a single trapdoor through the stone ceiling, and Jule dragged Cook into the room, shoved her up onto the rickety rope ladder. "Is Elise up there?" she shouted at the wide-eyed faces of her servants already above. "And her babies?"

There were swift glances, shaking heads, and Jule spat out a curse, whirled around, and took off again. Last she'd seen, Elise had been mending on the second floor, her children playing around her feet, surely she'd have heard, *surely*—

"Elise!" Jule shouted, as she leapt down one staircase, and then another. "Where *are* you?"

There was no reply. Only the rising, terrifying sounds from below, boots stomping, steel weapons clanging, the crash of breaking crockery. And above it all, the harrowing screams of Norr Manor's doomed butler and footman, as the invading orcs hacked them to their deaths.

But Jule couldn't think about that, couldn't bear to, and she dragged in another heaving breath. "Elise!" she shouted again, sprinting through the corridor, holding up her cursed full skirts. "Stefan! Ame! Where *are* you?"

She was almost to the next staircase when she heard it. A strangled little sob, coming from the long-empty nursery, and Jule whirled around, and dashed inside. Going straight for the room's heavy closed wardrobe, with that telltale whimpering sound behind it.

She yanked the door open, and thank the gods, they were there. Her serving-maid Elise, and her two small children, twins, still too young to speak.

"You can't stay here," Jule gasped, dragging at Elise's hand. "The orcs will smell you. Find you."

Elise let out a strangled moan, and she frantically swatted Jule away, and clutched at the children. Her eyes were bulging with terror, and for good reason, because the orcs would know she was fertile, would smell it, take her away, and...

"You *have* to come," Jule choked out. "To the tower. The others are already there. It's safe."

Elise kept shaking her head, shrinking back into the

wardrobe, and after an instant's jolting panic, Jule grabbed for the children instead. Dragging them away by the waists as they fought and screamed, but Jule didn't care, because the sounds of bloodshed below had ceased, and had been replaced with the thud of boots, coming up the stairs. Coming closer.

Hoisting a wailing child under each arm, Jule pitched off toward the door, and back up the staircase. Ignoring the shouts from Elise behind her, but a frantic glance backwards showed her following, chasing them, thank the gods.

"Stop!" Elise shouted, but Jule kept running. Down the corridor, up the next flight of stairs, toward the tower room, children squirming and screaming, while the sounds of heavy boots and clanking metal grew louder and louder behind them—

"Put down the ladder!" Jule hollered, bursting through the tower room door, but the servants above were already doing it. Lowering the ladder through the opening above, and Elise was finally here, finally helping. Grabbing at her children, thrusting them upwards, while Jule held the bottom of the ladder taut, and the thunder of boots came closer, closer...

The servants above pulled at the climbing children, dragging them up, and now it was Elise climbing, tripping over her heavy skirts. Almost there, *please*, but the boots were so close now, and with them that sickening smell of blood and death.

"Pull up the ladder!" Jule shouted at the staring faces, at Elise, finally safely above. "Close the door! That's an order!"

They obeyed, thank the gods, pulling the ladder's rungs up hand over hand, and slamming the steel trap-door shut. Just in time, because something huge and powerful grabbed at Jule's shoulders, and hurled her across the room.

The orcs were here.

## 2

J ule had seen orcs before, of course. Everyone had, what with the seemingly endless, brutal raids on every human settlement within a week's journey of Orc Mountain.

But she'd never seen orcs this close. Had never smelled them this close. And looking up at them now—three orcs, *here*, in this small room with her—Jule's knees were actually knocking, her heart a hammering thunder-beat in her chest.

They were *huge*. Jule had never been a small woman, but they were still a good head taller than she was, and perhaps twice as broad. Carrying scimitars as big as saw-blades, still dripping red with her servants' blood.

The fear in Jule's chest pounded against a surging miserable rage, and it was enough to make her lift her chin, and look into the nearest orc's hideous face. Grey, leering, scarred, with glittering black coals for eyes.

"You won't get them," she said, though her voice came out wobbly, high-pitched. "Not before the Talford regiment comes."

The orc's grey lips broadened, showing a row of sharp,

deadly white teeth. "No," he agreed, in a low, guttural voice. "But we have you."

Jule backed up, her feet scrabbling on the stone floor, and she gave a helpless glance upwards, toward the closed steel trap-door above.

"Y-you don't want me," she stammered. "I'm—I'm *barren*."

Never in her life had she thought she'd be so grateful to speak those words, even as the vivid, painful vision of Astin juddered through her thoughts. *Orcs only want* whole *women. They'd never want to take you...*

The huge grey orc had stepped closer to Jule, looming over her, staring at her with those glittering black eyes. And then— Jule flinched all over—he leaned in, and *smelled* her.

He was far too close, terrifyingly so, and the reek of blood surged through Jule's nostrils, powerful enough to make her retch. A sound that the orc didn't miss, judging by the way he snapped backwards again, his grey lip curling over those pointed teeth.

"You lie, woman," he said, in that thick guttural voice, as he abruptly grabbed her shoulders, and thrust her toward the other two orcs behind him. Who were even more hideous than he was, with their pitted faces and unruly black hair, and smirking sneering mouths.

"Smell," the first orc ordered them, and they did, both leaning in too close. Leaching that scent of blood so strong that Jule had to cover her mouth this time, squeeze her eyes shut, try not to sob, or scream.

"Yes, Captain," one of them said, his voice deep and grating. "She lies, as all humans do. She is ripe and hale. She would make you a good mate, and bear you strong sons."

Mate. *Sons.* Jule's entire body seemed frozen in place, trapped here, pinned by the weight and grip of that huge hand on her shoulder. This couldn't be happening. She was barren, they couldn't want her, it *wasn't possible...*

"Do not fear, woman," said the voice behind her, the captain. "I shall not force you to this, or bring you to harm. But"—that hand on her shoulder tightened, its claws pressing sharp against her skin—"neither shall you escape. You are mine now."

His. It was so appalling, so audacious, that Jule somehow found the courage to look up, to meet those glittering black eyes. "But I'm already married," she gasped. "I already have a husband. And my husband is a very, *very* powerful man."

Those black eyes looked down at her, and she almost wanted to cower under the strange, inexplicable weight of them. Looking at her, through her, deep into her soul.

"I see no powerful husband," he said, and the words seemed to stop the breath in Jule's throat, the whirling screeching terror in her thoughts. He saw no powerful husband. Here, at Norr Manor? Or inside her? Part of her?

"Lord Norr is away," she said, weakly, and the orc's lip curled again, showing that row of sharp white teeth. With the two canines longer than the rest, looking not unlike wolf-teeth, and Jule felt another shudder wrench down her back.

"Lord Norr," the orc said, and that was contempt on that mouth, in those eyes, "left you no guard."

Jule swallowed, drew a hard breath through her too-thick throat. No. There'd been no guard. And though she'd frantically spent the last three days searching for coin, for goods or services to loan or sell or barter, she'd made little headway. She'd needed more time, more money, a husband who actually cared, a *home*—

But Jule had none of those things. And the huge, hideous orc staring at her knew that, saw that, and smiled.

"You are mine," he said. "And you will come."

J ule should have fought. Should have kicked, and screamed, and made the orcs spill her blood. Should have joined her servants in the afterlife with her honour unbroken, her head held high.

But it would be gruesome. There would be grunts and shrieks, and perhaps desecration of her body, afterward. The orcs might make an example to leave there, for when the soldiers came, for when Elise and Stefan and Ame finally climbed back down that ladder.

So Jule bowed her head, and went. Followed the two orcs down the staircase, down the corridor, while that first orc—the captain—kept his hand clamped hard to her shoulder, his huge bulk close behind.

There were no new voices yet, no sound of frantic towns-people or soldiers, and Jule's hurtling thoughts couldn't under-stand why, or how. The orcs would have had to break Norr Manor's not-insignificant gate, or tunnel under it, the manor was surrounded by the village of Talford with its smattering of cottages and shops, there should have been witnesses, some-one, *something*—

"How did you get in?" a voice asked, and too late Jule realized it was hers. "The cellar?"

The orc behind her made a grunting noise, perhaps indicating his agreement, and the truth of it was confirmed once they reached Norr Manor's bottom floor, and the kitchen. Which had two horrifying, blood-soaked bodies lying in the middle of it—the butler and footman—and Jule had to put both hands to her face, and drag in choked, heaving breaths.

"Did you," she gasped at the orc, "really have to *kill* them?"

"Yes," came his reply, deep and immediate. "They attacked us with knives. They died bravely, with honour."

Dear gods. A hoarse noise had escaped Jule's throat, but the orc didn't seem to notice, or care. Just kept marching her toward the back of the kitchen, to the narrow, circular staircase that went to the cellar.

The cellar itself had been raided, Jule saw now, casks and barrels broken and smashed, and stores of meat and vegetables gone. All the food Jule and her servants had worked so hard to save, pinching every copper, knowing full well that whenever Astin left, Norr Manor's funds would always go with him.

And here in the cellar, of course, were more orcs. Carrying torches and milling about around the back corner, where there should have been a solid stone wall, but now—there was a massive, rough-hewn hole. A tunnel. Through which yet more orcs were carrying away stores, barrels of dried fish and salted meat and tallow and ale.

The orcs seemed to collectively halt at their approach, a dizzying sea of hideous grey and green faces in sparking fire-light—and suddenly there was a shout. And another, and another, until the noise was deafening in the closed room, a horrifying grating miasma of orc-screams and clanging weapons and huge stomping feet.

The grip of the orc captain's hand on Jule's shoulder had gone even tighter, and she flinched at the feel of his other hand, clamping on her other shoulder. Holding her out toward the screeching sea of orcs, as if brandishing her toward them, and in a hurtling flood of terror she realized that they were screaming for *her*, because she was their captain's plunder.

"We have gained our prize," announced the deep voice of the orc behind her, once the shouting had finally, blessedly subsided. "Sken, come, see her. Ezog, bring me chains."

*Chains.* Another hard shudder rippled down Jule's back, but the hands on her shoulders held her firm and still. While another orc hobbled over, an older-looking one, with a bent back, a shock of white hair, and filmy whitish eyes.

"Your name, woman," he said, his voice a painful grating croak, as he reached a wizened, mottled grey hand toward Jule's chest. Making her flinch, and try to scrabble backwards, but that huge captain orc behind her held her still, his claws sinking against her shoulders in a not-so-subtle warning.

"Obey, woman," the captain's voice ordered behind her. "Speak your name."

The old orc's hand was touching Jule now, pressing flat at the base of her bare neck, and she dragged in a strangled breath around it, against it. "Jule," she gasped. "Lady Norr. And you are?"

The old orc's filmy eyes flitted up to hers, perhaps disapproving, but behind her she could feel the huge orc shifting, the heat of him prickling against her back. "This is Sken," his deep voice said. "And I am Grimarr, of Clan Ash-Kai."

*Grimarr.* The shock was like a living thing, screeching inside Jule's bones, and her head whirled around to stare at the hideous orc behind her. *He* was Grimarr? The notorious new captain of all five orc clans, and the sole ruler of Orc Mountain? The callous murderer of hundreds of men, the scourge of the entire countryside, a brutal killing fiend who attacked in the night and haunted children's dreams—was *here*? In Jule's *cellar*?

"*You,*" she said, her voice faint, "are *Grimarr*?"

"Yes," he replied, without hesitation, before fixing his black eyes back on the old orc before them. "What do you see, brother."

The old orc—Sken—had finally taken his hand from Jule, and his filmy eyes looked up toward Grimarr behind her. "She is strong," he said. "Brave. Clever. Ripe. She shall be the boon that you seek."

The watching assembled orcs launched into shouts again, the sound clanging painfully against Jule's beleaguered senses, and she squeezed her eyes shut, fought to find purchase in her strange, slippery thoughts. *Strong. Brave. Clever. Ripe.* No, no she was not, she was barren, beaten, terrified.

"Yes," said the voice—Grimarr's voice—behind her, and Jule didn't imagine the long exhale of hot breath against her neck, the very slight squeeze of those fingers against her shoulders. "She hid away her servants, and met me alone."

There was something almost approaching pride in his deep voice, and another strange shudder crept down Jule's back. This was what she had become? Lady Norr, loathsome to men, to her very own lord *husband*—and pleasing to *orcs*?

Another orc had scuttled over, this one carrying a clanking length of heavy steel chain, and Grimarr's huge grey hand released Jule's shoulder long enough to grasp at the chain, and fold it double. And then his big hands spanned her waist, slinging the chain around it, and yanking tight.

"I do not wish to bind you," he said to her, his voice sounding almost regretful, as he wound the chain's other end up his thick, veined grey forearm. "But you will seek to run."

Jule had to close her eyes again, while her trembling fingers went, almost unconsciously, to grip at the steel chain. It was cold, powerful, orc-forged, thick enough that there would be no escaping it. Not unless she were to somehow knock out this bastard, drag him with her, or perhaps cut off his arm while he slept...

"Come," he said, pulling rather than pushing her this time, and Jule went, staggering on her unsteady feet. Walking through Norr Manor's familiar cellar, over its familiar stone floor, toward this travesty the orcs had carved into it.

It was pitch-black inside the tunnel, smelling of damp and earth, and Jule put out her hands, in an instinctive attempt to keep from floundering straight into a wall. But instead, her fingers brushed against solid heat and shifting muscle—Grimarr's *back*, dear *gods*—and though she snatched her hand away, she was certain he'd noticed it, his big body hesitating in the blackness.

"Ach, women cannot see," Grimarr's voice said, confusingly—and suddenly there was a warm, strong arm, gripping tight around her shoulders. Drawing her close against him, deep into that bitter-salt smell of blood, and though Jule tried to shove away, he was far too strong, and his other hand on the chain just pulled her harder, closer into his side.

Gods *curse* the bastard, and for perhaps the first time today Jule felt her eyes smarting, and fought to swallow down the telltale lump rising in her throat. She would not weep. She could not. Not where Grimarr would see, and perhaps mock her, or make an example of her, or worse.

But the more she fought the misery back, the more it sought to escape. Filling the blackness before her eyes with images of those bloody bodies in the kitchen, Elise's screaming babies, the taste of Astin's beautiful mouth, the sight of his straight, uncaring back as he'd ridden away. *Orcs only want whole women. They'd never want to take you...*

A single tear streaked down Jule's cheek, and with it a betraying sniff from her nose, but she fought to keep walking, keep up. Think of other things, think of her father, the late Lord Edgell, who'd been a captain too, a true lord. Hard and demanding of his soldiers, of his family too, but generous with his coin and his praise. *Good girl*, he would say, clapping Jule's back, or pulling her to his chest. *You honour me.*

Another tear escaped Jule's eye, but if Grimarr noticed, he didn't comment. Only kept walking, his strides long and sure of themselves, his big arm still close and heavy over her shoulder. His muscles shifting through cloth against her—gods only knew what he'd been wearing, Jule hadn't even noticed—and his chest filling and emptying silently, without a single grunt from his mouth.

The same couldn't be said for the orcs clattering along behind them, huffing and snorting, speaking excitedly among themselves. Their words were entirely unintelligible, all harsh and guttural grunting, and Jule realized dully that they were speaking in the orcs' awful old Black-Tongue, said to be all that remained of the elves' high speech, after the orcs had stolen and destroyed it.

"We near light," said Grimarr's rumbling voice beside her, his heavy arm moving away to push at something—and suddenly, somehow, there was fresh air again, and sun so blinding that Jule had to shield her eyes.

"Where are we?" she asked toward Grimarr, without thinking—but then she went stock-still all over, because she was looking at him, and he was looking at her. And here, standing in the bright, unforgiving daylight, the infamous captain of the orcs was truly, thoroughly *hideous*.

His skin was a deathly shade of grey, latticed over with scars, one almost bisecting his long, crooked nose. His eyes were sunken and black, framed by stringy black hair that was tied back in a matted mockery of a braid, and his neck was thick and corded, angling down to sloped, bulbous shoulders.

And the *clothes*. His tunic was made of mismatched fabric stitched together, barely covering his huge barrel chest, and his filthy, blood-stained trousers literally hung around his waist, tied up with what looked to be rope. The mud-splattered leather boots looked to be the only thing made to fit him, and Jule pitied the poor cobbler, who'd probably been forced to make them at knifepoint.

"North of Beghol," Grimarr said, incongruously, in that rumbling low voice, and it took Jule too long to realize he was answering her question. They were north of the next town over. Moving due west. Toward Orc Mountain.

"You are going home, then," Jule said, her voice cracking, and her eyes moved from Grimarr's hideous face, to the tips of his pointed grey ears. They weren't swollen and tattered, like many of the other orcs' were, and they were perhaps the only non-hideous thing about him, hinting again at the long-gone elves who had supposedly fathered the orcs, ages ago.

"Yes," Grimarr said, and again, he was answering her question. Making Jule blink at him, briefly, while her thoughts digested the truth of that. He was taking her to *Orc Mountain*. The orcs' longtime lair, the highest summit of the Sakkin Ridge, buried deep in Sakkin Province's dense forest. A dangerous, impenetrable place, teeming with tunnels and mines, almost certain death for any human who ventured near.

And a place that would be near impossible to escape.

The panic seemed to strike again all at once, clanging against Jule's entire being—and without thought, without intent, she was running. Sprinting toward the east, back toward Norr Manor, needed to escape before they trapped her in Orc Mountain *forever*—

But the chain, of course there was still the *chain*—and even as the awareness of that bloomed through Jule's thoughts, she was yanked backwards by the waist with violent, painful force. Back toward *him*, Grimarr, the hideous orc captain who'd *kidnapped* her, taking her to *Orc Mountain*, and Jule kicked and shoved and shouted against it, against him, no, no, *no*—

But it was like fighting a boulder, huge and hard and utterly unyielding, and Jule felt a large, powerful hand snap close and threatening around her wrist. "Stop this, woman," hissed that voice, deep and commanding against her ear. "You are mine now. You shall not run from me."

Jule tried for another kick, aiming her knee straight toward his flat stomach, but he twisted out of the way with surprising ease, and gave a hard, tooth-rattling jerk of the chain, still clamped tight around her waist. "Stop," he growled again, deeper this time. "You shall not escape me, or your new home in our mountain. And if you keep fighting me thus, I shall hogtie you, and haul you there over my shoulder."

The words finally sank through the chaos swarming Jule's skull—he would *hogtie* her, no doubt while all these awful orcs leered and laughed—and she felt her body go slack against his grip, even as her furious eyes glared at his hideous, pitted face.

"*Curse* you, orc," she spat at him. "You lying horrible *beast*. I am *not* your newly acquired property. And your awful mountain will *never* be my home!"

The orc's glittering black eyes only looked at her, as that big hand around her wrist yanked her closer, back against his side. "Speak all you wish, woman," he replied. "You are yet mine. And you shall not run from me."

Jule's cheeks were burning, the heat again threatening to escape from behind her eyes, and she turned her face away from him, toward the tall trees all around. This couldn't truly be happening, she couldn't be trapped with an *orc*, dragged off to Orc Mountain, she would *never escape*...

"Captain," interrupted a voice, sharp and guttural, and when Jule glanced over it was another orc, standing beside Grimarr. Looking even more hideous, his skin tinged a deep puce, his nose a mashed swollen mess. "What next. Too slow. Men will pursue."

The orc's black eyes darted balefully toward Jule, and she distantly realized that their raiding-party had been travelling slowly, thanks to her. Orcs almost always seemed to be running, barging from one place to the next, and Grimarr's slow walk through the dark tunnel had, perhaps, been meant as a kindness.

"Camp at Kentnek," Grimarr said, finally, his heavy black eyebrows furrowed together. "I will carry my woman."

What? Jule blinked at his horrible face, and opened her mouth to protest—but already Grimarr had reached down, and swiftly snatched her bodily up off her feet. Hoisting her in both arms, close to his chest—and then he took off due west, at a full-tilt run.

Jule belatedly kicked and squirmed at him, but it only served to clamp his iron grip tighter, clutching her even closer to his massive chest. "You shall not escape me, woman," he said again, his hard voice barely even out of breath. "The sooner you learn this, the more content you shall be."

Jule huffed out a miserable groan, but she reluctantly stopped struggling, and in reply Grimarr's grip loosened, and his mouth did something that might have been intended as a smile. "Better," he said. "Now rest. I shall keep you safe."

It was ridiculously absurd, and deeply infuriating, being told she was safe in the arms of a hideous hulking orc, who was currently *kidnapping* her, and dragging her against her will to *Orc Mountain*. But then, his grip shifted and softened again, repositioning Jule to better see around them—and for a stilted, fleeting moment, it felt like she was in another world, wearing a stranger's skin. Watching stones and trees race by, feeling the smooth rolling gait of Grimarr's feet beneath her, hearing the even exhales of his breath, the steady thud-thump of his heartbeat.

It wasn't unlike riding horseback, her detached thoughts pointed out, with the strong, solid body beneath her, and what the hell kind of thought was *that*? And a good look over Grimarr's shoulder disabused it entirely, because charging behind them was a motley, truly hideous mess of gasping, salivating orcs, most of them rolling huge barrels, and one of them—Jule winced—wildly swinging a long string of sausages around his head, and smacking his neighbour straight in the face.

The sausage-smacked orc nearly lost his footing, but swiftly regained it, and then hurled himself toward the first orc, swinging a huge fist at his already-mangled face. The blow landed with an audible crunch, a howl of pain, to which several of the neighbouring orcs cheered, and then jumped in.

It was a melee in an instant, perhaps a half-dozen orcs brawling at once, while the rest shouted and jeered and laughed. A scene so thoroughly appalling that Jule almost didn't notice that Grimarr had stopped running, until he dumped her unceremoniously to her feet, and then turned and strode straight toward the melee. Leaving Jule to lurch and stagger awkwardly after him, dragged by the chain still around her waist.

"Who began this," Grimarr growled, his deep voice reverberating through the air, and in response there was an unintelligible chorus of shouting orc-voices. So loud that Jule put her hands to her ears, but somehow Grimarr had made sense of it, because he reached into the mass of hideous orc-bodies, and yanked out the first two orcs, one in each huge hand.

"You first," he said, to the one who'd swung the sausages, and there was a chorus of shouts and groans—and Jule stared as the surrounding orcs came together, and collectively held the first orc still. While the second orc stepped closer, wound up his fist, and pummelled the first orc straight in the face.

There was spurting red blood, the shrill sounds of screaming, and even more bloodcurdling orc laughter. And then—Jule covered her eyes this time—the orcs held the second orc still, while the now-bleeding one launched his fist toward him.

There were more screams, more shouts and laughter, but Jule just felt sick, exhausted, miserable. Even as Grimarr bodily picked her up and took off again, racing up a steep rocky hill, sweeping trees and sky and a slowly sinking sun, the steady sound of his heartbeat thumping under Jule's ear.

She must have dozed, somehow, because when Grimarr put her down again it was dusk, and they were deep in the forest. Well off the main roads, in a place she didn't at all recognize, and she allowed Grimarr to prod her toward what appeared to be a solid rock wall—which, upon further inspection, was yet another tunnel, disappearing into blackness.

"Where is this?" Jule managed, her voice thick. "Kentnek?"

She didn't recognize the name, but it was what Grimarr had said earlier, and if she wasn't mistaken, that was an approving flash of his sharp white teeth in the darkness.

"Yes," Grimarr said. "Old camp. Dry. Safe."

Well then. At least it wasn't the mountain, not yet—though it was well on the way there, without question somewhere deep in Sakkin Province. And this awful orc was taking her into this unfamiliar tunnel, leading only gods knew where, and Jule shrank back, staring at its yawning black emptiness.

"Wait," she said, and her face suddenly felt hot, her hands clammy and cold. "First I need to—uh—relieve myself."

She couldn't look at Grimarr as she said it, or at the orcs milling all about, rolling their stolen barrels inside. But she caught the wave of his big hand, the deep sound of something like mockery in his throat.

"Then do so," he said, and now Jule did look at him, her mouth dropping open of its own accord. "*Here*?" she demanded, voice wavering. "In front of you? And *them*? No. I am a lady. I require at least some semblance of privacy. *Please*."

She could feel Grimarr's eyes on her, even if she couldn't see them, and the low, hurtling dread was here again, too strong. What if he forced her. What if he humiliated her. What if he watched…

But then, to her surprise, he turned, and pulled her on her

chain through the nearby brush. Taking her deeper and deeper into the trees, until—she blinked—he actually stopped and turned his back away from her, a silent silhouette of broad shoulders in the darkness.

It was better than nothing, and Jule swiftly managed her business, and then remained crouching, hands feeling desperately at that chain around her waist. While the rest of her listened and looked, gauging which direction was north, which was home. She had no weapon, nothing to break the chain with, but perhaps a stone, perhaps—

"Come," Grimarr's voice interrupted, a low order in the darkness, with a warning tug at the chain. "Now, woman."

Jule went, finally, bowing her head, because of course it was futile. Even if she did escape this cursed chain, she was surrounded by dozens of huge, fully armed orcs, hell bent on taking her to their home. And what else was she supposed to do, how else did one flee such a fate? Death, perhaps—but even now that would be in Grimarr's hands, held by this grotesque, primitive, hateful mockery of life.

She was trapped. She was doomed.

"I will never stop cursing you for this, you horrible *beast*," Jule said, the words quiet but sure. "I will never, *ever* forgive you."

There was more silence, and the sound of Grimarr's breath, coming in and out, harsh and low. While those huge shoulders rose and then fell, almost like a sigh.

"Yes," he said. "But you are yet mine, woman. And now"—he turned, and his eyes seemed to flash in the darkness—"you shall spend this night with me."

# 4

---

Jule would spend the night with him.

"B-but," she stammered, her voice gone thick and hoarse. "You—you said—you wouldn't—"

The tales were swarming her thoughts again, vivid and unrelenting, leaving her shaking, sweating, breathless. Orcs took women with brutal force, to the point of sometimes killing their victims. Swiving into them with their beastlike cocks, while biting their necks and drinking their fill, tearing them apart both inside and out.

And then. If the woman lived through the initial mating, and the subsequent attempts, there would be a child. An impossibly powerful orc-son, appallingly large, complete with deadly claws and teeth, just waiting to tear its way out of its helpless mother's womb...

"You need not fear, woman," came Grimarr's harsh voice, and Jule blinked at his shadowy face, the glint of his eyes in the dark. "I said I should not force you or harm you, and I shall keep my word. But I must yet treat with you this night. Now come."

He had to *treat* with her? That bizarre claim was accompanied by a purposeful yank on Jule's chain, and finally she drew in a helpless, bracing breath, and went. Following Grimarr toward that gaping hole in the rock wall, and then down into the earth itself.

It was entirely disorienting inside, cramped and twisty and damp and dark. And it was like the ongoing horrors of the day were sharpening, suddenly, converging in close black tunnels and rising echoing orc-voices, while Grimarr marched her down, and down, and down.

There seemed to be even more orcs here than had been in their original party, many more shouts and grating laughs, and the awful, chilling awareness of big, sweaty bodies, crowding too close. And when someone finally lit a torch, Jule flinched all over at the shocking sight of what seemed to be hundreds of orcs, all crammed into the low-ceilinged, rough-hewn earthen tunnel.

Grimarr hesitated before the throng, and then shouted something in black-tongue, deep and carrying. Earning an almost deafening roar in return, while the mass before them parted in front of—Jule's breath caught—a door. An honest-to-gods proper oak door, placed way down here in the earth, as though some errant human had gotten lost, and installed it.

The sight of it was enough to keep her shaky feet upright, even as Grimarr bodily turned her around, and gripped those hands once more to her shoulders. Showing Jule to the orcs, while they shouted and cheered, and the unease and the fear burned her cheeks, her thoughts, her dignity. Whatever the hell this was, it was without question a statement. A claim. A threat.

Grimarr again shouted something in black-tongue, a dreadful grating scrape in Jule's ears, and then he abruptly pulled her backwards, by the chain, toward that oak door. Dragging her inside it with him, alone.

Jule should have fought it, but instead found herself

standing there, shivering, and staring at an actual—room? Yes, a room, with a proper brass bed in the middle of it, covered in what looked to be animal-skins, and lit by the flickering light of a tall, single candle.

"What is this?" Jule's voice asked, cracking on the words, and she realized that Grimarr had closed and latched the door behind them, dulling the still-shouting voices to a low hum.

"It is mine," his low voice said. "Now that I am Captain."

Right. This Grimarr was a relatively new captain, and Jule distantly recalled the tales of the orcs' previous captain, an equally horrible old butcher named Kaugir. An orc who hadn't been killed by men, in the end, but had instead been found chopped to death by orc-scimitars, and left to rot in a field.

"How long have you been Captain?" Jule heard her voice ask, as she gave a furtive glance toward Grimarr's hideous face. "A year?"

Those black eyes were gaping hollows in the dim light, staring at her, through her. "I have led my brothers for the better part of my thirty years," he said. "But the name Captain, I have held this for nigh unto two hundred days."

Jule blinked at him, and felt her eyebrows rising. "Two hundred?" she echoed. "You can *count*?"

She didn't imagine the twist on his grey lips, the brief glimpse of bared white teeth. "Yes," he said, voice flat. "Orcs are not fools, woman."

Jule couldn't help a grimace—how the hell was she supposed to know that?—and she belatedly pulled herself taller, frowning at those black orc eyes. "Well, you've already made quite the name for yourself, haven't you, *Captain*?" she said. "Killing hundreds of innocent people, terrorizing the countryside, running a new raid every second *night*."

"Yes," Grimarr replied, without even a hint of hesitation, or remorse. "But my raids take goods, not women. And we do not seek the lives of men, unless they are thrown away in folly upon our swords."

Jule's stilted thoughts briefly considered that—*had* there in fact been fewer women taken, fewer total lives lost, these past months? But then her hands clenched on the chain, still tight around her waist, while visions of her dead servants marched past her eyes.

"Rubbish, orc," she shot back. "You killed two men today. You took *me*."

Grimarr didn't speak this time, or even acknowledge the words. Just stood there, looking at her, his hulking body dark and looming in the faint candlelight, and Jule felt her heartbeat pick up, pounding faster, stronger.

"And now," she said, her voice badly wavering, "here you are. Trapping me alone in this room with you, so you can *treat* with me, whatever the hell that means. No doubt you're planning to *force* me, and drink my blood, and"—she dragged in more air—"and then likely throw me to your waiting horde outside."

The vision of it was suddenly almost overwhelmingly horrifying, and Jule felt herself shrinking backwards, her arms crossed tight over her chest. She was at his mercy. She was trapped. She was *doomed*.

But before her, Grimarr had given a hard shake of his head, his heavy brows furrowing together. "Ach, no, woman," he said. "I shall not force you nor bite you. And neither shall I give my brothers leave to touch you. I am here to treat with you"—his big form seemed to grow even larger, his eyes piercing into hers—"for your hand, and your troth. I wish to ask you to be my mate."

His—*mate*? Jule could only seem to gape at him, while her thoughts spun and churned, deep below. Yes, there had been tales of orcs taking these so-called *mates*, women to keep as their own, hidden away in secret dens, bearing only that orc's children. Like a mockery of marriage, a travesty of affection, a concession made only in the interest of keeping the line pure.

But now, staring at this Grimarr, of course it made sense that this was what he would want. He was a captain. He would want sons of his own. He would want to create his own progeny, to continue his own lineage. Just like Astin.

"So it's sons you want, then, orc?" Jule said, because perhaps the longer she spoke, the longer she could prevent any of this from happening. "To help establish yourself as captain?"

"Yes," came his immediate answer. "A captain must have a mate, and sons. He must have strength at his back."

Right. *Sons are a matter of life and death for orcs*, Jule had often heard people say, and at the time that had rankled, because sons were life and death for many humans, as well. For Astin.

"Then why have you waited until now to seek a mate?" Jule's wavering voice continued. "Despite your pretty claims otherwise, we both know you orcs have stolen women away for *years*. Wouldn't it have been to your advantage to be well prepared with plenty of whelps before you took the captaincy?"

There was silence from the hulk of Grimarr's shadow, and then it came a swift, alarming step closer. "I have made attempts," he said finally. "It is not easy."

Jule's heartbeat kept clanging, battering away inside her chest, and her mouth let out a sound that could have been a laugh, or a sob. "How in the gods' names is it not easy?" she demanded. "You kidnap a poor unsuspecting woman at knifepoint, chain her to you, drag her under a mountain, and force her to carry your *children*!"

There was more silence, the sight of those huge shoulders going up, and down. "I have learned," his voice said, "that this is not the way. When a woman is taken thus, she will run back to the men, and her babes shall meet death. There is no joy in this."

It almost sounded like grief in his voice, but Jule had no sympathy, no patience for the murdering kidnapping *swine*. "So what happened to your previous *attempts*," she snapped. "They ran?"

"Yes," came that low, regretful voice. "One with my son still small in her womb."

Jule's body took another abrupt step backwards, and she was trembling again, because yes, this was what he wanted here. What he was doing here.

"And what happened to her," she managed. "You killed her."

There was an abrupt, convulsive-looking twitch of Grimarr's shaggy head. "No. I did not. She now lives with a new husband, and I have left her be. I would not harm a woman. I do not wish to harm you. I have sworn to keep you safe."

If that was supposed to be comforting, it failed miserably, and Jule raised her chin, and glared at his ugly shadowy face. "You *would* harm me," she said. "You're asking me to be your *mate*. To bear your *sons*. Orc sons *kill* their mothers."

There was more silence from him, his hulking body unmoving in the shadows. "Not all sons," his deep voice said. "Not if the woman is well cared for, and not if she is large and hearty and hale. And you are this, woman. You are strong. You are brave."

Jule's cheeks felt oddly hot, the wetness smarting suddenly behind her eyes, and she took another unsteady step backwards. "I am not," she said, maybe because she just had to disagree, to counter everything this orc said. "You know nothing about me."

That huge body came a slow step closer, moving silently in the darkness. "You hid your servants away," he said. "You met me alone. Even now, you do not plead or beg. You stand tall, and defy me."

His voice on the words was warm, perhaps even approving,

and something strange seemed to dip in Jule's belly. "I'm terrified of you," she corrected him, sharply. "I've never been so bloody afraid in my *life*."

There was another instant's silence—and then a dusky, rolling sound from his throat that might have been a laugh. "Yes," he said, his voice even lower, warmer than before. "You are a good woman. You shall make good sons."

Jule's breath came out sharp through her throat, her eyes briefly squeezing shut. "I can't make sons, orc," she said, gritting out the words. "I told you, I'm barren."

"You shall have sons, should you choose," came the reply, firm, immediate. "If you could not, Sken would have seen this. His magic is strong."

Oh. Jule's thoughts flicked reluctantly back to that moment in her cellar, with the old orc touching her, with the way Grimarr's breath had felt on her back. "Well, what if he *had* seen that. What if he'd told you I *was* barren."

She could see the rise and fall of Grimarr's huge shoulders, but there was no sound with it, not that she could hear. "I would yet have brought you here," he said. "But I would not now seek your troth as my mate."

Of *course*, and Jule's mouth let out a strangled laugh, hard and bitter. "So magnanimous of you, orc," she said, before she could stop herself. "So damned *typical*. Women are only good for one thing, right? For both men *and* orcs, apparently."

Grimarr's dark head tilted, and she could *feel* those eyes, boring through her, into her. "Were I not captain," he said, slowly, like he was weighing every word, "and thus in need of sons, I should yet seek your hand. A woman such as you is good for many things."

Jule stared at him, at that awful face in the shadows. At this orc—this *beast*—who was flattering her. Complimenting her. Being *kind* to her.

"Well," she said, because what else was there to say, "there's a man in Yarwood who would deeply disagree with you."

Grimarr's big hand went briefly to his side, closing on nothing, and Jule vaguely noted that he must have removed his scimitar, left it somewhere else. And maybe that was why he didn't smell of blood anymore, why the scent in the room had somehow become low and earthy and warm.

"The man who gave you no sons, and left you no guard?" Grimarr said now, the contempt clear in his deep voice. "That man is weak. And a fool."

There was a curious lurking bubble in Jule's throat, because in all her five years of marriage, so many people had seen this, known this—but none of them had ever dared say it. *Lord Norr is consumed by responsibilities*, they would say. *Lord Norr was mistreated as a child. Lord Norr is unwell.*

"That man is very powerful," Jule said bitterly. "He is one of the highest-ranking nobles in the entire realm. He has five thousand armed men at his call."

Grimarr came another silent step closer. "Yes," he said, with undeniable satisfaction. "And now his woman is mine."

Jule twitched, and then stared at those shadowed eyes. "You chose me on *purpose*?!" she demanded, her voice gone sharp, shrill. "You're—you took me to make some kind of fucked-up statement to Astin? To start a *war*?"

And gods, how had she not seen it. Of course it hadn't been a random attack, of course there was a reason, and despite herself Jule was looking at this orc—this captain—with new eyes. He'd *planned* this. And from the outside, she could admit, it was clever. Perhaps even brilliant.

"I have started naught," Grimarr's rumbling voice said. "Men have waged war on orcs since the days of old. I only defend my own."

Jule was ready to protest—to point out the raids, the kidnappings, the gruesome bodies left in the orcs' wake—but somehow, the words wouldn't seem to come. Caught, perhaps, in her memories of the constant attacks on Orc Mountain, the poisoning of the lake at its base, the longstanding bounty on those pointed orc ears. And most strongly of all, the bloody public massacre, a few years back, of a handful of unarmed orcs who had been promised a peaceful hearing without bloodshed.

That last mess had been on Astin's orders, as so many of them had been, and Jule knew very well that Astin found the orcs useful. That there was nothing quite like the havoc of a bloody orc-raid to distract from his people's too-frequent hunger, or their uneasy discontent under his distant, indifferent rule.

"Look, I don't want to be your pawn in all this," Jule told the orc, helplessly, foolishly, because it wasn't like there was a choice, was there? "I don't want to be just your—your *revenge*."

She couldn't explain why it bothered her so much—what difference did it make if she'd been taken because of Astin or not?—but it did, maybe because everything always went back to Astin, trapped always under the weight of his shadow.

"And you supposedly wanting me for your *mate*—that goes straight back to Astin too, doesn't it?" Jule continued, quieter now. "It's another advantage. A bragging right. Stealing away Lord Norr's wife, in every possible way."

The words felt heavy in her mouth, heavy in the air between them, and she could hear Grimarr's sigh, heavier still. "I shall not deny this, woman," he said. "Earning you for a mate should be a great boon to me. Not only before the men, but also before my brothers. It would grant me strength on all sides."

Well, at least that sounded like truth, and Jule felt her feet shifting, her mouth grimacing at the floor. Even an orc didn't *really* want her, beyond what benefits she could bring him. And why was that such a lowering thought, why in the gods' names did she even care...

"But you are not just this, woman," continued Grimarr's voice, so low now that it almost seemed to vibrate the air around her. "I have watched you. I have wanted you."

The breath caught, oddly, in Jule's throat—he had *watched* her?—and he came another slow step closer, that smell of earth and heat rising in her nostrils. "You are able," he said. "You ride well. You hunt for game. You know these lands. You trade your goods wisely. Your servants eagerly follow you."

Jule was staring at him again, because how the hell did he know these things, since when had orcs acquired the skills to track and hide and spy? But then the thought had gone, vanished entirely, because his big body came another step closer, near enough to touch.

"I have hungered for you," he said, his voice almost a purr between them. "I wish to make you my own."

His hot breath on her skin was strangely sweet, and too late Jule caught herself inhaling it, deep. Smelling that scent of earth, of rich warmth, of *life*.

"I will not force you," that voice continued, deep rumbling heat in Jule's thoughts, her belly. "I wish to earn your troth, woman. I wish for your hand, freely given. I wish for you to hunger for me, as I hunger for you."

Ha. Hunger for an orc. That was impossible, ludicrous, he was the most hideous thing Jule had ever *seen*, a beast, a monster, he had *kidnapped* her...

"I hunger to touch you," he purred, soft. "I hunger to taste you."

His voice was doing inexplicable things to her, inside her, and Jule gulped for breath, for sanity. "You hunger to gain a tactical advantage, you mean," she snapped at him, but her voice came out lower, huskier, than it should have. "And you hunger to make me carry your *sons*."

There was one of those deep, rolling laughs, making Jule's body go taut and warm all over. "Ach, yes," he said, softly. "I wish to fill your empty womb. I wish to see you blossom with my seed."

It was a thoroughly appalling statement—wasn't it?—but it felt more like a caress, thrumming low in Jule's ears. And somehow there was the hurtling, incongruous image of it, herself, round and full, her breasts heavy, her ripe belly blossoming with new life...

"I'm not fertile," she gasped, and that was true, it *was*—but Grimarr only gave that laugh again, low and hungry, sweet-smelling heat on her skin.

"You are," he murmured, and Jule twitched at the feel of his big hand, coming to rest warm and heavy on her shoulder. "With my seed, you are."

Gods. Jule had to swallow, shake her head, what was she *thinking*. Orcs were beasts, monsters, bloodsuckers, kidnappers, death, she did *not* want to carry his sons, his sons would be *orcs*...

"My seed hungers to fill you," his husky voice continued, and Jule twitched again at the feel of his other hand, settling large and gentle on her other shoulder. "My seed hungers to flood you, and flower deep inside you."

Gods curse her, because Jule's breath actually choked this time, the heat pooling hard in her groin. What the hell, what in the actual fuck, he was an orc, an honest-to-gods hideous bloodthirsty *orc*...

"I long to touch you," he said, so smooth, so quiet. "Will you give me leave to do this, woman?"

Would she. Jule tried for a snort, but it came out more like a gasp, thick and heated in her throat. "Would it actually make a difference," she managed, "if I said no?"

"Yes," came his reply, more decisive than Jule would have

expected. "I shall not force you, woman. And naught shall change if you refuse. I shall yet guard you with my life."

As if. But those hands on Jule's shoulders weren't moving, were just waiting there, warm and heavy. And his gaze on her felt just as heavy, watching her, waiting for her answer.

And Jule's answer was—what? No, of course, *no*, but—was it? Perhaps? It had been so long since she'd been touched, and even longer since it had felt—*untainted* like this, free of the dragging jealousy or shame or fear. And what *would* it feel like, to have those big warm hands caress against one's skin? To be truly wanted, desired, longed for?

"Will you give me leave, woman?" he asked again, so soft. "May I touch you?"

The question set something inexplicable flaring in Jule's gut, and she took a slow, shuddering breath. Could he touch her. Maybe? Perhaps? Maybe—yes?

"Yes," she heard her shocking voice whisper. "For a moment."

There was a ragged, rumbling growl from Grimarr's throat, and then those big hands—now somehow with their claws pulled back—were moving. Sliding slowly, inexorably, down from Jule's shoulders, over the front of her now-filthy dress, until—she gasped aloud—they had found her breasts, and curved softly, gently around them.

Jule should have taken it back, yelled at him, fought for her honour, *something*—but she only stood there, *feeling* that, her breaths coming short and shallow. While those fingers tightened, caressed, and she could feel the betrayal of her too-hard nipples, jutting against the fabric, against the heat of his huge palms.

"Should you mate with me, these teats shall fill with milk," that voice murmured, purred, promised. "My sons shall suckle them, and grow fat and strong."

Jule's mouth gasped again, her body giving a convulsive

shudder, and she felt him lean in closer, warmer. "And this belly," he breathed, as those hands slid downwards, hotter, slower, "shall swell as my seed blooms inside it. It shall grow my sons strong and hearty and hale."

Gods curse him, because Jule had gasped again, her eyelids fluttering, and she almost didn't notice one of his hands hesitating, plucking a little at that chain around her waist. Because she was still *chained* to him, she had been chained to him throughout all this, he had *trapped* her here in this room—

It was enough to bring a semblance of sanity back again, and Jule roughly, belatedly shoved those big warm hands away. She was a lady. She was a prisoner. And Grimarr—Grimarr was an *orc*. The *worst* orc. A brutal, conniving *monster*.

"You *kidnapped* me, orc," Jule hissed. "You brought me here against my will, in order to start a war with my *husband*. And now you expect me to actually—agree to this? To offer myself—my body, my freedom, my *future*—up to you on a silver *platter*? On my very first *night* with you?"

Those big clawless hands remained still, hanging now at his sides, and for a twisted, ridiculous instant, Jule's traitorous eyes lingered on them, wishing them back again. "I expect naught," he said finally, so low, so smooth. "I ask for your troth, freely given. I wish for your regard, and your hunger. And in return, I shall offer you my sword, and my fealty, and my favour. I wish to bring you joy, woman."

Jule's chest heaved, and she forced her own hands back to that thick chain, still tight around her waist. He was lying, he was manipulating her, how in the gods' names could an orc be offering anything but misery and pain and death?

But as Jule watched, Grimarr slowly, purposely raised that huge forearm, and unwound his end of the chain from around it. And then he dropped the chain to the earthen floor, allowing the rest of it to go slack, sagging against her hips.

He was letting down his guard, Jule's thoughts shouted.

Finally. And she should absolutely be trying to escape right now, should be bolting for that door, the tunnel, the open air. She should be running back to Norr Manor, to Astin.

And Astin would be furious, Jule knew. Not just at her, but at what this meant for his own name, his reputation. *Lord Norr's wife was stolen by orcs*, his people would whisper. *The orcs breached Lord Norr's own manor. What if Lord Norr's barren wife conceives an orc-son?*

"You lie, orc," Jule choked out, as her hands shoved at that sagging chain, thrusting it down to fall at her feet. "You can't earn my affections, or bring me joy. You're"—she pulled in a hard breath—"a looting, murdering, bloodsucking *beast*, and what you're proposing is unnatural, and evil, and *wrong*."

"It is not wrong," came Grimarr's reply, smooth, inexorable. "It is the way of things. It is as the gods decree."

Jule's mouth barked out a hoarse, high-pitched laugh. "What, the gods decree that orcs have to kidnap women, and make them bear their sons? You can't honestly *believe* that?"

"No," he said, and one of those big hands slowly lifted toward her again, this time settling warm and heavy against her hip. "This—*kidnap*—you speak of, this was from the war. From men who deny us women. Who deny us our sons, and our freedom."

Oh, so now it was all the *men's* fault, but Jule's retort was silenced by the feel of Grimarr's other hand, coming to spread flat and warm against her belly. "But it is the gods' decree that orcs mate with women," he murmured. "If it were not so, there would be no sons. No pleasure in the mating."

Jule had to close her eyes, fight to block out the feel of him, the succulent rich scent of him. "There *is* no pleasure in the mating," she snapped. "Orcs *ravage* women. You leave them bloody and broken and miserable and *terrified*."

There was another one of those low, rolling laughs, a replying clench deep in Jule's belly. "That is the tale your men tell to keep you away," his voice purred. "In truth, an orc gives his mate deep joy. Deep hunger."

He was lying, he had to be, and Jule swallowed hard as one of those big hands slid upwards again, until it was once more cupping her breast. "Your hunger rises for me now, does it not?" he breathed, as his thumb brushed at her hard nipple through her dress. "I will give you great joy, woman. I pledge you this."

It wasn't possible, it wasn't, but Jule still wasn't moving. Wasn't running. Was just standing here, feeling the heat of those big hands, and gasping a little as the one on her hip slid slowly, surely, around to cup at her arse.

"You can't give me anything," she protested, weakly, even as her back arched a little at the touch, as that huge, strong hand tugged her a little closer. "I'm a lady. You're an orc. And you're *hideous*."

"Then do not look at me," he whispered back, almost in her ear now, and how had he come so close? "Listen to me. Smell me. Feel me touch you."

And yes, yes, Jule could do that, because gods, he smelled so good. Felt so good. His hands so big, so warm, sliding slow and smooth and powerful against her, and the scent of him was like a hidden truth, a flickering hope, a long-forgotten memory...

"You are ripe," Grimarr whispered, his breath low tickling honey in her ear. "You are rich with sweetness. Your hunger lights you as a flame."

Jule's head had tilted back, somehow, and he came even closer, those fingers now coming up to spread warm and gentle on her cheek. "I long for you," that voice murmured. "I long to fill you. I long to make you flower."

He chased the words with a soft brush of his mouth, hot and jolting against her skin, and Jule couldn't stop the sharp little groan that escaped from her lips. Making him chuckle in reply, the sound rumbling down to her bones, and then his mouth tasted her neck again, harder this time, sweeter, with just the slightest nip of too-sharp teeth.

"You're an orc," Jule insisted, or tried to, but the words came out like an admission, perhaps even a defeat. "You're an *orc*."

"Yes," came the smooth, rumbling, mouthwatering reply. "And I shall fill you. I shall ripen you. I shall please you like no man has before."

His mouth was pressing kisses up her neck, up her jaw, and now his lips were here, only a breath away from hers. While his hands drew her closer, tighter, all against the hard muscle of his huge solid body, and—Jule gave a harsh cry—against a shocking, swollen, pulsing hardness, jutting out strong between his legs.

"I shall give you this," that mouth breathed, promised, firing blinding hunger in Jule's thoughts, "if you stay. If you pledge me your troth as my mate."

If she pledged her troth. "And if I don't?" Jule's mouth gasped, her breath so close to his, her body all but wrapped against him, pressing that thrilling hardness closer. "What then?"

The world was this, hanging on his answer, and his mouth gave a low growl against hers, husky and glorious. "Then I shall not stop you," he said. "You shall run back to that big, hollow house. Back to that weak fool man, who did not keep you safe."

The words almost seemed to wrench out Jule's breath— there was no way she could truly go *back*, was there?—but Grimarr's big body slowly, purposefully moved away from her, and those hands against her went still, slack, quiet. Enough that she could push them off, if she wanted to. Could actually jump up, and run away, and out that door.

She could still go back. Back to Astin. That weak fool man. Who had not kept her safe.

And this was important, even the idea of not going back

was foolish, ridiculous. Astin would give chase, there would be attacks, retributions, revenge. It would be a mess, it was already a complete and utter disaster, Jule's breath was his, his breath was life...

"What is your wish," came that rumbling voice, that firing heat, that damned impossible *salvation*, so close. "Will you run. Or will you stay? Will you be my mate?"

Grimarr's body remained unmoving, waiting, and Jule gathered her courage, and looked into his shadowy eyes. She wouldn't stay with an orc. She couldn't be his *mate*. Would she?

And with a shuddery, gasping breath, she closed the last space between them, and kissed him.

## 5

Never in her life would Jule have imagined herself voluntarily—willingly!—kissing an orc. A beast.

The truth of it still shocked her, even as she was in the midst of it, as that warm, liquid mouth met her, drank her. As it let out a deep, fundamental growl, vibrating her lips, her breath, her soul.

"You are mine, woman," it breathed, and there was triumph in it, sparking hard and powerful. "I will have you."

Jule should have protested, should have found the space or sanity for it, but she was too caught in drinking him back, finally tasting that sweetness at its source. Soft lips, warm breath, a tongue that was far too large and strong, sweeping against her, inside her, oh *gods*.

"I will have you," he said again, as if hearing the words for the first time, and then he laughed, a deep rolling thrill of pleasure in Jule's ears. Enough to make her chase that laugh, that mouth, tasting its bounty, and making it her own.

He growled again, dragging her up and closer, his big hand coming behind her head, tilting it back. Angling his mouth deeper, harder, against her, how could *anything* taste so good, how could one swirling tongue be everything at once...

"I wish to see you," he said, suddenly pulling back, putting both hands to her face. "To touch you."

He was asking again, Jule realized, waiting for her answer, and she couldn't look at him, couldn't speak—but her head had nodded, somehow, against the touch of those hands, and he let out another one of those laughs, straight streaking pleasure deep to her groin.

"Brave woman," he whispered, and those hands were already yanking up on her dress. Hard enough to tear it, damn him, and it was her only one at the moment, and Jule swatted his big hand away long enough to unfasten the buttons, to pull it off properly.

It left her standing there in her faded white shift—in her underclothes, with an *orc*—but those hot, hungry hands were back again, sliding the loose fabric upwards. Over her hips, over her breasts, her head, what the hell was she doing, this couldn't actually be *happening*—

But it was, Jule was standing here naked in front of an orc, and not quite breathing. While said orc looked at her, and looked at her, and looked.

It was enough to send a convulsive shudder down her back—why was he silent, what did he see—and then again as he reached out, not to caress her, but to tug a little at her still-braided hair. Saying, too clearly, what he wanted, so with fumbling fingers Jule pulled the braid out, let the long dark waves tumble down over her shoulders.

There was another sound from Grimarr's mouth, not quite a growl this time, and that hand reached out again, and raised her chin. Making her look at him, she realized, while he looked at her, and his long, slow exhale of breath was almost a living thing.

"My woman," his voice said, finally, so low that it was almost a sigh. "My own fair one. My mate."

The words were their own streak of pleasure, a gasp of colour in the darkness, and suddenly, he was here. His big hands on Jule's skin, gripping and caressing, sliding the length of her bare back, curving over her bare arse. And then coming up her front, circling around both breasts at once, pushing against her hard nipples, dragging a ragged hungry gasp from her throat.

"Yes," he said, husky, as one of those hands slowly slid downwards. Over her belly, into her coarse dark hair, and—Jule gasped again—down to cup close and protective against the curve of her, all raging dark hungry heat.

"Such ripe fruit," he whispered, his hand pressing a little harder, rubbing back and forth, exposing her swollen, clenching wetness against it. "So rich with its juices."

Jule's entire body was arching into him, against that impossible, audacious feel of him, and he gave that low, rumbling laugh of his. Making her too-wet body pulse against him in response, and in reply he laughed again, tinged now with no small trace of triumph.

"You yearn for me, woman," he said, and though Jule should have resented that smug satisfaction in his voice, she truly didn't care. Especially when one of those big fingers broke from the rest, sliding with more pressure, delving soft, inexorable, deep into her swollen slick wetness.

Jule cried out, her traitorous body clenching hard around him, and he gave that laugh again, torturing her, that finger sliding ever deeper. "You long for me," he whispered, and he chased the words with a kiss, slow succulent heat from his tongue against hers. "Your womb grows rich and fat for me."

The answering gasp from Jule's mouth might have been a protest, but he silenced it with another kiss, another sweep of that hot, delectable tongue between her lips. "I will fill you," he breathed, promised, as his finger pressed in harder, deeper. "I will plough you and plant you. I will drench you with my seed."

Gods curse him, his voice his words that finger, because Jule's entire body was trembling, and her hands had somehow, finally, found the courage to touch him. To cling to those broad, warm shoulders, feeling the shift of hard muscle beneath his tunic as that finger went deeper, exploring her, invading her.

"I wish you to ask me," he whispered now, his breath hot and hungry against her ear. "Ask me for my seed."

Jule's mouth gasped again, definitely in protest this time, because there was no way in hell she was asking this shameless orc for anything—but then that single finger pulled out, away, what the hell, why.

"Ask me, woman," he said again. "Beg me to fill you."

Damn it, damn him, Jule would not beg—but now those big hands had both come to her bare arse, bodily lifting her up like she weighed nothing, and—oh *gods*—shifting her legs so they were around him, so her hungry open wetness was pressed directly up against that huge, straining bulge through his trousers.

"Fuck," she gasped, and he gave a low, approving laugh. Making Jule's too-exposed body clench up against his trousers, and—she gasped again—he'd felt it, he *knew*, because that huge hot hardness actually pushed itself back against her, all jolting furious shouting pleasure.

"Yes," he murmured, as his hands went tighter on her bare arse, pulling her closer, wider against him. "You long for my ploughing, woman. Ask me."

Jule still wasn't, she wouldn't, but her traitorous legs had somehow tightened around his back, too. Helping him, bringing that hardness ever tighter, if his trousers were off they'd be fucking, he'd be inside her, oh *hell*.

"You cannot deny it, woman," he said, and there was another throb of that hardness against her, like it was alive, a beast of its own. "Your hunger soaks me. Its scent fills this room. It clings to my prick."

Jule's breath was coming in ragged gasps, her hands sliding against those strong shoulders, and her hips had somehow circled a little against that hardness, more firing twirling pleasure. But her mouth had stayed silent, and that was something, maybe the one thing, he didn't have everything...

"Stubborn woman," his voice whispered, those hands pulling her even tighter—and now there was movement, swift and smooth, and before Jule had quite realized it, she was down on her back, on the bed, with her legs still locked around his waist. While Grimarr leaned over her, both hands to the bed on either side of her head, a looming hulking shadow in the candlelight.

"You shall ask me," he said, like it was a pact, a promise—and he backed away, standing up. Those big hands going to the front of his trousers, and—Jule gasped, groaned, stared—bringing that hardness out.

It was—*huge*. Larger than any man she had ever seen, as big around as a young tree-trunk, or perhaps a drinking-cup. And it was wet, slicked over, and with a gasp Jule realized that that was because he was dripping copiously out the tapered grey tip of it, a thick pale ooze of shining wet orc-seed.

"Ask me, woman," he said, commanded, the words a breathless thud in her thoughts. "Beg me for this."

Jule's throat swallowed, her tongue coming out to wet her lips, but she still wasn't speaking. She couldn't possibly beg for this, couldn't even imagine how this would possibly fit inside her...

"Beg me," he said again, and now those hands pulled her legs up, closer. Spreading them apart, preparing her for this, exposing her most secret places to his eyes, to that slick hungry heft of him, so close.

"I—I can't," she managed, and yes, that was true. She was

human, he was an orc, there was no way this was working, even though she could actually hear her traitorous body's wetness, clenching, begging, pleading.

"You can, woman," he breathed, and he stepped a little closer, that huge orc-prick straining to meet her swollen, soaking-wet heat. "If you yet wish for this. Do you wish me to stop?"

No, he couldn't *stop*, and Jule frantically shook her head, even as she gulped for air, for thought. She wanted this, she had to at least *try* to have this, what would that *feel* like, sliding inside...

"Ask me," came his voice, smooth, sure, inexorable, liquid pleasure in Jule's ears, her thoughts. "Beg me, and I shall fill you."

He'd brought that hardness even closer with the words, and as Jule gasped, stared, his big hand came and stroked up it, once. Thickening that dripping ooze to a smooth steady stream, and—Jule gave a sharp little cry—drizzling it down onto her still-clenching wetness.

It felt hot, sticky, slippery, glorious, and the sight of it even more so, that leaking cock now connected to her with that thick band of white. While that big hand pumped out even more, oh *fuck*, coming even thicker, pooling hot and hungry against her, into her.

"You wish for more," he whispered. "Beg me."

Jule's breath was still gasping, making her breasts heave and jiggle, and her thighs had somehow spread wider, her wetness open and exposed and desperate. Drinking up his seed, fighting to suck him inside, and she couldn't not have this, not now...

"Fine," she choked out. "Yes. Do it."

There was an audible gasp, a visible twitch of that seeping hardness, and now another one of those laughs, low in his throat. "I said beg, woman," he breathed, but as Jule watched, he pulled her up a little more, brought himself closer. And—

Jule's entire body convulsed—that hot, dripping tip of him finally touched her, just brushing up against her swollen gasping heat.

"Beg," he said, but the word came out ragged, his own chest rising and falling heavy under his tunic. "And you shall have it."

*Beg.* He was heady, thrilling, alive against her, and Jule could somehow *feel* that hardness straining to reach inside. While her body strained to meet him, to draw him further in, but he was holding her still, waiting, the bastard.

"Please," Jule said, because there was no other thought but the need for him, pounding furious and desperate over everything else. "Please. Fill me."

He groaned aloud, the sound a swirling firing shock of pleasure, and that cock against her swelled, twitched, pulsed. "By name," he gasped. "Please, woman. Jule."

*Please. Jule.* And it was that last, single word, tilting her over the edge, because it was him doing it first, him giving that to her, rather than just taking. Him wanting it just as much as she did.

"Please, Grimarr," Jule's voice whispered, pleaded. "Please, fuck me. Fill me. Make me your mate."

The sound from his throat was thick, rumbling, alive—and finally, finally, he was there. Pressing that hot, leaking hardness against her, into her, delving it between her wet lips, spreading them apart, oh *fuck*.

Jule's mouth cried out, too loud, but there was no pain, not yet. Just slick hard heat, sliding slow and purposeful inside, and Jule could already feel it thickening, broadening. Spreading her wider around it, stretching her open to fit him.

And gods, it felt huge. And tight, and close, and trapped, and there was resistance now, dragging him slower. But he wasn't stopping, just kept pushing, piercing, invading, and how the fuck was there so much of him, how could she possibly take any more...

"Good woman," gasped that voice, and it made Jule's body clench up even tighter, all around him. "Is it pain."

It took Jule's spinning, screeching thoughts too long to follow, to shake her head. "No," she breathed, and somehow, miraculously, that was true. Even with that tree-trunk cock wedged halfway up inside her, there was only pleasure, only the sharp shouting craving. "Don't you *dare* stop, orc."

He gave that laugh again, tinged with something like relief this time, and there was more heat, more pressure. Pushing harder, deeper, wonderful, impossible, and Jule could almost feel that cock breathing, vibrating, shuddering base to tip as it pumped out more of that thick rich seed deep inside her, oh *hell*.

There was one more hard push, one strangled-sounding gasp from his throat—and there, oh gods, he was in. Their bodies wedged tight together, her spread thighs flush against his hips, the bulging weight of his bollocks pressing huge and thrilling below.

*Gods.* Jule's entire body was sweaty and gasping, stuck like a pig on a spit, the entire world condensed to that massive cock jammed up between her legs. Filling her, just like he'd promised, seeping out that seed inside her, and in her shouting, flailing thoughts, something seemed to shift and jolt and change.

She felt—*wonderful.*

"Fuck," she gasped, and she didn't care anymore what she said, what he heard. "It's so *good*, Grimarr."

In reply he groaned aloud, his big chest shuddering, that heat flailing up hard inside her. "Yes," he whispered, ragged, firing warmth deep in her belly, her thoughts. "You sheath me whole, woman. My prick has never tasted such a thing."

He was comparing her, Jule's dazed thoughts realized, to

whatever unfortunate women he had taken before—but rather than feeling sorry for them, at the moment, Jule almost felt smug. Relieved. And perhaps, ridiculously, even a strange surge of jealousy, because had he done this often with them, had he gasped like this, throbbed like this inside them...

It made her push down harder, closer against him, her legs tight around his hips, sucking him in, claiming him. Needing that huge strength inside her, needing that still-seeping seed, and he seemed to feel it, giving another one of those glorious, breathtaking groans.

"You wish for more, woman?" he whispered, and Jule desperately nodded, clung to him. While those big hands came to span her hips, gripping her tight, and—she cried out—holding her still while he dragged himself out, slow. Not all the way, but enough that Jule was clinging harder, silently begging, needing it again, please—

He sank back in with a single driving thrust of his hips, oh *fuck*, and Jule's mouth let out something alarmingly close to a scream. It was impossible, so good, especially when he let out another one of those rumbling, breathtaking groans, jagged fraying pleasure through Jule's still-screeching thoughts.

"Again," she gasped, but he was already there, already doing it. Holding her still, dragging backwards, and then—then—slamming hard inside, so huge and full and shocking, like a punch to the gut, a blast of screaming shattering ecstasy.

"Oh *gods*, Grimarr," she choked at him. "More. Harder. *Please*."

He did, thank the gods, that huge cock driving and swiving into her, ploughing her. Ramming her, battering her, with a frenzy that matched her own, huge punching heat again and again. Swelling and pumping, hot orc-seed seeping every-where, the wetness the fullness expanding her, ballooning inside her, filling her so full she was going to break—

And then she did break. Shuddering jolting shouting

ecstasy swallowing her whole, drowning everything. Throbbing again and again and again around that huge hardness, milking it out of him, spinning gasping relief everywhere, oh gods, oh gods, oh *gods*.

His answering groan was a shout, almost like a war-cry—and his entire big body arched, straightened, fired. Pummelling his seed straight out that huge invading cock, driving it into Jule's body like a geyser, a cannon, liquid gushing spraying everywhere, leaking, filling, drenching.

When it finally stopped Grimarr was dripping wet all over, his clothes stuck to his skin, his big chest heaving with his breath. His eyes were closed in the dim light, his eyelashes thick and black against his shadowed cheek, and for a brief, hanging instant, there was only this. Only Jule and an orc, locked together, breathing as one, alone and drifting in the universe.

And when those eyes finally looked up, settling steady on hers, the heat flared strong enough to be another touch, another lock, deep and quiet and impossibly powerful. He was her orc. Her mate. *Hers*.

"Have I gained your troth, woman?" he asked, so soft it nearly brought tears to her eyes. "Are you my mate?"

Was she his mate. And Jule felt herself nodding, her eyes blinking back that inexplicable wetness, and she brought her trembling hands up, touched them to his scarred, hideous face.

"Yes, Grimarr," she whispered. "I am."

His replying growl seemed to shake the room, the entire world, and that dark head bent down to hers, his lips brushing hers in a quiet, reverent, powerful kiss. Confirming it, sealing it, and Jule felt herself moan into his mouth, her entire body rippling, trembling, aflame with the sheer, primal power of it.

"Then in return I shall pledge you my troth, my fair Jule," his voice said, so quiet, so raw. "I grant you my favour, and my sword, and my fealty. I shall keep you safe, and fed, and filled, so long as I am able, and so long as you shall wish."

It felt like a pledge, like words once learned and never forgotten, and in that hanging, stolen moment, it was—*everything*. It was truth, it was assurance, it was a promise that Jule could lean against, and rely upon, and make her own. It was the safety of a wild, powerful, untamed orc, bending the knee, and offering himself as her own.

For a long moment Jule could only breathe, digest that, revel in the strange swarming peace of it—but then his eyes finally fluttered closed, and that hot hardness still filling her slowly pulled out, drawing away from her. Releasing its hold with a loud, humiliating noise, and—Jule gasped—also releasing his thick white seed like a pent-up fountain, splattering over her, over him, the bed, the floor.

He'd pulled back to watch, Jule realized, even spreading her legs wider to see it, and once the worst of it finally subsided, she could still feel it seeping from her, oozing thick out onto the bed. And her mate—her *orc mate*—was *still* watching, and pressing her legs apart even wider, and then flashing her an affectionate, if rather terrifying, sharp-toothed smile.

"You enthrall me, my fair one," he said. "You have brought me joy beyond compare. I shall forever mark this night."

But there was something different in the words, something changed, from just a moment before. And when Jule frowned at him, pulling up a little to better look at those eyes, he immediately stepped backwards, with almost unnatural speed. While also pulling up those trousers, and swiftly hiding himself away again.

It left Jule alone, exposed, debauched on that bed, and when she slowly sat upright, she felt achy, tingly, sore. Like a woman who'd just been mated to an orc, perhaps, and she blinked up toward where he was still looming over her, huge and grey and hideous. Watching her with an odd, glittering intensity, his head tilted, his big hands in tight fists at his sides.

"What?" she heard her voice say, scratchy and unsure. "Is something wrong?"

He gave a jerky twitch, and one of those big hands abruptly reached out, and cupped her face. "Naught could be amiss with you, my fair one," he said, though his voice sounded rough and hard, not nearly as smooth as before. "But I must beg your forgiveness for what I do next."

He'd reached for her tattered shift as he spoke, tossing it over toward her, while she blinked at him, tried to follow this. "You will dress," he said, "and come."

Jule kept blinking at him, but she was already obeying, pulling on the shift with shaky hands. And now he was here, so close, his big hand gently gripping at her arm, and guiding her up to her feet. And she was still complying, even though her legs were jelly beneath her, and it was only that solid strength holding her up.

"You must come," he insisted, in that strange harsh voice, and Jule still wasn't following, not in the least, even as he half-guided, half-dragged her toward the door. Too powerful to argue, to even try to resist, but then Jule's dazed thoughts finally, suddenly understood.

He was taking her—outside. To the orcs. Like this.

Too late Jule flailed back against him, fought to kick and scrabble and flee—but she was weak, exhausted, and he was far too strong. And already he'd knocked aside the latch, and kicked the door open before her.

The shouts outside it were almost deafening, suddenly, and it was a living, teeming mass of darkness, of orc limbs and bodies and eyes, lit only by faint torchlight. All too close, smelling of blood and death, and Jule gagged as that huge hand shoved her weak, shaking, barely clothed body out toward them.

"Behold," came a loud voice from behind her, Grimarr's voice. "My new mate. Smell how she bears my scent, and my seed!"

The orc-shouts rose, swelled, and Jule could feel their greedy stares, almost like a touch. Leering at the mess Grimarr had made of her, still leaking down her thighs, and this couldn't be happening, he couldn't be doing this to her. It was all a dream, the worst dream she had ever had in her *life*—

"This woman begged me for this," Grimarr's voice continued, deep, powerful, arrogant. "She called me by my name. She swallowed my prick whole, and spewed my seed like a *flood*."

The noise was everywhere, everything, the mass of eyes and laughter and bodies far too near in the small space, and Jule couldn't move, couldn't breathe, couldn't be real, please gods. Had to be a dream, had to be...

"She spurned her human husband," his smug voice continued, gloated. "She chose to abide here with me instead. She chose to become my mate!"

With the words, that big warm hand came down to grasp hers. Not kindly this time, but hard, purposeful, yanking her hand up, showing it to the still-shouting orcs. Showing them—Jule's breath caught, broke—Astin's gold-and-diamond wedding-ring, still glinting on her finger.

"Behold," Grimarr said again. "The sign of her spurned husband, Lord Norr. He is the humans' captain. The man who kills our sons. The man who blights our water and burns our home and grants *riches* for our deaths."

The orcs' shouts had turned angry, vicious, and Jule flinched as Grimarr yanked her wedding-ring off, and brandished it out toward them. "Behold," he said, his voice gone hard, cold, "what fate soon befalls Lord Norr!"

And before Jule could think, or react, Grimarr had thrown the ring up into the air, and caught it in his waiting, gaping-open mouth. The mouth that had so gently kissed her, said those quiet beautiful things to her, was now chomping down on her wedding-ring with an audible, awful *crunch*.

The orcs laughed as one, raucous jangling noise blasting through the air, and Grimarr chewed the ring once, twice, three times. And then tossed his big head back, swallowing the ring with a visible gulp.

"You know where that will end up!" one of the orcs shouted shrilly, just in case they didn't all get the joke, and the laughs seemed to swell even louder. Some of them complete with obscene farting noises, and Jule was beginning to feel truly ill, and faint, and wretched.

"Lord Norr's wife is mine," announced Grimarr's terrible voice beside her. "Lord Norr's wife is mated to the captain of the orcs!"

The orc-roar was deafening, drowning Jule's ears and her thoughts, and she only distantly noted her legs shaking, her body trembling all over. What was happening. What had she done. *Why*.

And when that big, menacing hand pulled her again, back toward that room, Jule's legs finally gave out altogether, and the world blessedly, mercifully went black.

## 6

W hen Jule awoke again, she was in a soft bed, and the sky was dark.

For a moment, it was her bed at home, and soon Elise would be in, opening the curtains. Saying, *Good morning, my lady, where would you like your tea, in your bed, or in the breakfast-nook?*

But then Jule remembered the dream. A dream so real that it hadn't been a dream at all, and when she snapped up to sitting, blinking into the darkness, she was still trapped inside it. Still in this same cursed room, and—she yanked the flimsy blanket up to her chin—still with this same cursed orc.

"You," she breathed, blinking in the faint candlelight toward where Grimarr was sitting on the floor, leaning against the wall opposite. As far away as he could be from her, while still in the room, and Jule's distant, jolting thoughts noted that she was very sore, very tired, and—she shifted, and winced—still very wet.

"Yes," came that deep voice, and Jule winced again at the sound of it. The memory of that voice, saying those horrible things to those shouting, leering orcs. *This woman begged me for this. She spurned her human husband. She called me by my name.*

Jule dragged in breath, courage—and before her thoughts had even decided it, she was already out of bed, and sprinting for the door. Making good time, despite her staggering legs, and her hand reached out, grasped the latch—

But then Grimarr's huge, powerful body crashed into her, knocking her aside. While big, strong hands clamped onto her wrists, pulling them up above her head, pinning them hard to the wooden door behind her.

It left Jule gasping for breath, the room spinning slightly, and Grimarr was here, only a hands-breadth away. Smelling distinctly of blood, with just a faint trace of sweetness, and Jule spat toward it, just missing that scarred hideous grey face.

"What the *hell*, orc," she hissed at him. "Let me go!"

He didn't move, those huge fingers flexing even tighter against her wrists. "No," he said. "You are my mate, woman. You wished to stay."

Like hell. "I wished no such thing," Jule shot back. "And if ever I did, it was *before* you showed me off to your horde, and mocked me like a cheap trinket, and—and *defiled* me, and my wedding-vows!"

Those black eyes briefly closed, and she could feel his breath, hot and harsh on her skin. "It brought me no joy to do this, woman," he said, his voice very steady. "I held no wish to bring fear or shame upon you, so soon after we spoke our vows. But it was a burden that had to be borne."

"What, by *you*?" Jule demanded, and she spat at him again, straight in his face this time. "That was hard for *you*? You lying *prick*. I want to leave. *Now*."

There was a strange satisfaction in watching her spittle drip down his scarred cheek, off the grim line of his heavy square jaw. "Yes," he said, his voice weary now, almost resigned. "You are as fickle as all humans are. You will deny your pledge to me, and seek to run."

With the words, he shifted both her wrists into one hand, and reached for his waist. For the chain, that was now tied loosely around him, and Jule closed her eyes, tried to choke back the rising sob in her throat. Of course. She was still a prisoner, still his captive, she had been this entire damned time, and he'd just been sitting here, waiting to chain her up again.

"Of *course* I want to run," she said, because it was all that was left of her freedom, her pride, her dignity. "I *hate* you, orc. You conniving *swine*."

The chain was already around her waist, pulling tight, and the hand on her wrists let go, down to wrap the chain back around his forearm again. "I sought your pledge without anger, or threat," his even voice said. "I even gave you leave to run, and had you chosen this, I would have honoured my word. And yet, you freely chose to grant your troth to me."

The words left Jule breathless, staring at him, at that repulsive scarred orc-face. "You *lied* to me," she shot back. "You—you *cursed* me, or something. I would never, *ever*, voluntarily choose to stay with a monster like you!"

"You did," came the orc's reply, cold, implacable. "I did not speak false to you. I did not curse you or use magic against you. You yearned for my touch, as all women do. As you will again."

The presumptuous arrogant *bastard*, and Jule actually laughed, the sound coming out bitter and incredulous. "In your dreams, orc. I will *die* before I voluntarily touch you again."

There was an instant's stillness, and then he pulled the chain around her waist a little tighter. "Then shall it be," he said, and it came out low, menacing, a threat. "I shall not force you, woman. But neither shall I release you. I have marked you and claimed you, before the eyes of a hundred orcs from all five clans. I have given much to set this snare for Lord Norr."

Jule's heartbeat had picked up pace, but she glared up at

him, at that huge looming shadow of him. "I couldn't care less about your plans. And I will *not* help you kill my husband!"

There was a low growl from his throat, and damn if Jule's traitorous body didn't give a strange little lurch at the sound of it. "He is no longer your husband, woman," came that menacing voice. "You chose me as your mate. You pledged me your troth. I swore the vows. You *will* abide by this."

Jule's head was shaking back and forth, this couldn't truly be happening, what had she done. Given up her *life*, her body, *everything*, to a callous, vicious, brutal *tyrant*.

"I won't," she gasped. "I *won't*. You shamed me and humiliated me. You used my weakness as a weapon against me. You were cruel, and manipulative, and *awful*. You're a beast. A *monster*."

That big body twitched, and Jule could almost feel the air shift, growing colder around her. And then—she flinched, flailed—Grimarr thrust her back against the door, and one of those big, clawed hands came up to circle around her neck. Not hard enough to be painful, but his fingers were huge, his claws scraping sharp against her bare skin, his threat very, very real.

"You *will* yield, woman," he growled. "On this wagers my life, and those of all my brothers. I do not wish to cause you pain, but if I must, I will. I will do all within my power to gain this."

Jule's breath was too thin to speak, gasping against that huge hand, and he wasn't even looking at her, his eyes squeezed shut. "I will bind you and gag you," his menacing voice said. "I will starve you. I will keep you from the sun for the rest of your days. I swear this, woman."

Jule's body was sparking and trembling now, very near to full-on panic, and abruptly Grimarr let go, stepping backward. Leaving her to gulp for air, bending double, both hands pressing clammy to her throat. What was she going to do, what was there to do, what was left...

"So this is how an orc treats his mate?" she managed. "The woman he expects to bear his sons? You confine me and threaten me with misery and *starvation*?! No wonder your other women ran from you. You are a *monster*. You are the sickening, ravenous beast that haunts our *dreams*."

Grimarr was very still before her, his big body an inscrutable block of blackness, and she could hear the harsh exhale of his breath. "It matters naught what you think of me," he said finally. "You will yield, woman. You will honour me before my brothers, as a true mate should. You will come with me to your new home, and hold your head high."

Jule's breath choked on a sob, and her thoughts had scattered, shouting all at once. She should fight him, she should try again to run, she should find his scimitar and drive herself onto it. But then he would catch her, he would do all those horrible things, he would starve her, bind her, keep her from the sun...

No. *No.*

Jule was better than this. Smarter than this. And she knew full well, from hard-won experience, that there was nothing to be gained by fighting back, by being beaten and broken. Not when she was so overpowered and outnumbered. Not yet.

But if she were truly wise, she would wait. Listen. Bide her time. Perhaps even gain the odious orc's trust.

And then when Astin's men came—they *would* come—Jule would be there. She would help them rid the world of these cursed orcs. She would gladly watch—she would cheer—as this orc was impaled on the sharp end of a spear.

So Jule pulled herself tall, and raised her chin, even as the wetness streaked from her eyes, and dripped off her jaw. She would do this. She would have her revenge.

"Very well, orc," she said, though her voice wavered, far too close to a sob. "I will yield."

## 7

When Grimarr marched Jule back out of that room, with that chain still around her waist, it was to the sight and sounds of more orcs, more cheers, more incomprehensible chaos in Jule's head.

But her face was dry, her head held high, her eyes looking straight ahead into the tunnel's blackness. And at least Grimarr had allowed her to properly dress, and braid her hair back, though he had propped his big body against the door the entire time, and watched.

The chain was still around her waist, and her body still felt tired and sore and miserable all over. A state that was most certainly not helped by the scattered words she understood in the clamouring orc-shouts, things like *wedding-ring* and *good strong ploughing* and *show her to us again, Captain*.

Grimarr didn't, at least, just kept prodding Jule along before him, and already she could hardly bear it, the fear and the shame pounding under her skin. She would escape. She would find revenge. Astin's men would kill them all.

The blinding light of the sun was almost painful, after all that time spent underground, and Jule blinked at its brightness through her fingers. Halfway up the curve of the sky, it was mid-morning, and had Grimarr kept his whole band waiting here all this time, just for her?

"Do you hunger," came Grimarr's curt voice beside her, drawing Jule's unwilling gaze—and then she squeezed her eyes shut, breathing hard. Gods, he was *hideous*. Absolutely repulsive, in the light, like a grey rotting corpse whose face had been carved into by maggots, and had she truly kissed that mouth? Had she welcomed the touch of those hands? Had she sworn to make him her mate? What the *hell*?

"Do you hunger," Grimarr said again, his voice deep and menacing, and despite herself Jule took a small step back, her hand coming to touch reflexively at her throat. "No," she said. "But—I need to drink. And relieve myself. Please."

She hated asking, hated giving this orc even more power over her, but he nodded, and led her into the nearby trees. Toward where Jule could hear the rush of a stream, and Grimarr once again turned his huge back while Jule drank, and then dealt with her morning needs in the bushes. Including mopping up some of the mess down there, and she tried not to think of why, of what had done this to her.

When she finished, Grimarr led her back to where there was a growing, waiting mass of orcs, clearly readying to depart. Most of them the same ones who'd come here with them the day before, thirty or so, and Jule swiftly counted them, compared them to the numbers she'd seen the night before.

"Where are the rest?" she asked, reluctantly, but better to know her surroundings, to plan properly for her revenge. "Will they follow?"

"Some will," came Grimarr's immediate reply. "Some came from away. They heard of my feat, and wished to witness it."

Oh. Of course. Meaning that word of this—of Jule standing there, half-dressed and humiliated, leaking Grimarr's seed— would no doubt travel to all corners of the realm. To Astin.

"We are pursued," Grimarr's voice said. "We must depart. Do you wish to walk, or be carried."

Jule's legs were still shaky, but she recoiled at even the thought of touching this orc, of letting him touch her. "I'll walk," she said, and he nodded, thank the gods. And maybe if she walked slowly enough, their pursuers would catch up, she would be rescued, taken home, the men would impale this orc on their spears...

They set off through the forest, with Jule and Grimarr at the head, and the thirty-odd orcs clattering and chattering behind. Through an uneven rocky path that Jule couldn't see or follow, full of roundabout twists and swiftly running streams. Intended, no doubt, to throw off their pursuers, and Jule had to admit that Grimarr was doing a damned good job of it, because if not for the sun above, she herself would have been hopelessly lost.

It didn't help that Grimarr kept up a punishing pace, dragging Jule along behind him by her chain, and by noontime she was already exhausted, her body drenched with sweat, her light leather shoes scuffed and soaked through. And when Grimarr finally stopped at the edge of a large clearing, Jule didn't even look up at him, just sank down onto the nearest rock, and buried her face in her knees.

"We shall eat," Grimarr's voice announced, earning a cheer from the orcs behind them. "Silfast, lead a party, and bring us that buck I smell, to the north. He who makes the kill gets the first cut of meat."

There was more yelling—gods, why were orcs so *loud*—but thankfully some of the sound began travelling off, due north. No doubt warning the hapless deer that they were coming, but Jule didn't care, didn't want to ever move again.

"Drink," came an abrupt voice from beside her, and Jule flinched, and turned toward where Grimarr was holding out a waterskin. And since when did orcs have waterskins, and it was probably filthy, but Jule took it anyway, gulped the blessed cold liquid down her throat.

"You are weary," his voice said, quieter now. "Are you in pain?"

Jule thankfully wasn't, for the most part, but she was still too exhausted to move, or speak. And finally Grimarr stood, chain jangling, and Jule lifted her head long enough to see him wrapping his end of the chain around the huge trunk of a nearby tree, and fastening it tight before striding away.

"Watch her, Baldr," he said over his shoulder. "Tell me if she moves."

One of the huge, hideous orcs who was still nearby rose to his feet, loping over toward her, and Jule turned her face away from the sight, and tried to stop the frantic pace of her heartbeat. He wouldn't touch her, would he? Grimarr had said he wouldn't share her, hadn't he?

"Greetings, woman," said the orc, in a strangely melodious voice, and Jule blinked, and turned to stare. Yes, he looked like every other orc here, perhaps a little younger, and perhaps even more repulsive due to the deep greenish pall of his skin— but he was smiling at her, showing her a set of sharp white teeth.

"It has been long since we have had a human among us," said the orc, still in that light, incongruous voice. "How fare you, woman?"

How fared she. Jule blinked at him again—he was really asking this?—and then let out a bitter laugh. "How do you think I'm faring, orc?" she demanded. "I've been stolen from my home, and mocked and humiliated, and dragged across half of Sakkin Province without the slightest regard for my wellbeing or wishes, by a company of *deeply* horrifying and hideous orcs!"

The young orc winced, and his dark eyes dropped, down to where his big hands had curled tight together. "Ah," he said.

"Yes. That. It must all be very trying. And I know we orcs are very loathsome to human eyes. Could I offer a gift to help with your comfort? A blindfold, perhaps?"

Jule felt an unwilling stab of regret, and then squeezed her eyes shut, gave a shake of her head. No, no. She had said nothing wrong, she was *not* going to apologize to a fey green orc, this could *not* be her life now...

But another glance at the orc showed him looking truly crestfallen, his bulky shoulders sagging pathetically, and it was so comically ridiculous that Jule sighed, and rubbed at her swollen eyes. "No, but thank you for asking," she said, without at all meaning to. "I'm just very tired right now, and Grimarr—"

She couldn't seem to finish, because suddenly her throat was choked, her eyes dangerously full again. Enough that she had to put her hands to her face, try to breathe, try not to break down sobbing while this strange orc watched. He had probably seen her humiliation last night, had been one of those in the clamouring crowd, she didn't need to give any of them any more power over her...

"You are sad," the orc's voice said, sounding almost grave, and Jule blinked at him again, at his nodding greenish head. "I know sadness too."

"You do?" Jule's voice asked, challenged, because her experience so far suggested that orcs felt very little, apart from self-serving hunger, or murderous glee—but that green head kept nodding. "When I think of my mother," he said, "I feel sadness."

His mother. It was surprising enough that Jule sat up a little, and frowned at him. "Wait. You actually *knew* your mother?"

His green head nodded again. "I loved my mother," he said. "She was kind, and generous, and brave. I grew up speaking her common-tongue, and hearing her many tales. She taught me much of humans."

"How?" Jule demanded. "I mean, when? And where? I thought"—her thoughts floundered—"I didn't think any women stayed. Or survived."

The orc gave a shrug of his bulky shoulder. "There have been no women in the mountain for many years," he replied. "But many others hide away from humans, and bear their sons in secret. Most give their sons to their fathers to raise once they are weaned, but my mother wished to keep me. She raised me in a cave by the eastern sea."

"And what happened to her?" Jule asked, tentative now, and there was the sadness, etching into the orc's green face. "We were found," he said. "By armed men. She was killed trying to protect me, and I was wounded and left for dead. But the captain came, and took me."

The captain. "Recently?" Jule asked, but the young orc shook his head. "Many moons past," he replied. "The captain has worked long to find and guard the many hidden orc-sons. To offer us protection, and sanctuary."

Well. Jule glanced up toward the trees, in the direction where Grimarr had disappeared. "How lovely for you," she said thinly. "In my case, I have been offered the generous choice of either compliance and servitude, or captivity and starvation."

The orc's head tilted, his black eyebrows furrowing—but before he could speak, the rest of the orcs barged back into the clearing, now carrying the bloody carcass of a massive brown buck. Which they hacked into with gusto, sending blood spattering onto one another, and Jule put her swimming head back to her knees, and choked back the almost overpowering urge to gag.

"Here," said a too-familiar voice, a little later, and when Jule looked up there was Grimarr, holding out a still-warm, still-dripping chunk of raw deer-meat. "Eat."

Jule stared at it, and then she shook her head, put it back to her knees. Away from that awful face, from the sudden surge of anger that jolted and screamed in her thoughts from even the sight of it. She would have her revenge. She would.

"Eat," he said again. "You are faint."

But even the thought of eating raw meat was making Jule feel ill, and she shook her head again. Earning one of those low, threatening growls from Grimarr's throat, but at the moment she couldn't seem to muster the wherewithal to care. Even if he did starve her, or bind her, or whatever fresh hell he was planning next.

For a moment there was silence, broken only by the sounds of clattering orcs, but finally she could hear Grimarr standing again, and then the sound of him unwrapping the chain from the tree. "I shall carry you," he said. "We must reach the mountain tonight."

The mountain. Jule gave a hard shudder, but she didn't speak, and when Grimarr's big hands picked her up again, she didn't resist. Just let him press her close against that massive chest, with that slowly thudding heartbeat beneath it.

There was movement, speaking, foreign words in the black-tongue that Jule couldn't comprehend. And then, once again, the swift rolling gait beneath her, the smooth rising and falling, the sharp exhales of his breath against her too-tired body.

Jule should have traced their path, tracked coordinates and landmarks, but it was so much easier to simply do nothing. To just be there, in those arms, feeling the hair whip around her face, watching the sky and trees flash by, until sleep finally came.

But then, of course, some time later, Jule awoke. And this time it was in pure blackness, and the world was filled with screams.

Jule jolted against the solid warmth holding her, and stupidly clung to it, buried her face against it. While the screams become louder, cackling close deafening shouts, and above them all was Grimarr's voice, booming strong and deep through his chest.

"I have won my prize!" it announced, and Jule felt herself being bodily lifted, brandished, in the darkness. "I have taken Lord Norr's woman as my mate, and claimed her with my pledge and my seed. I have overcome Lord Norr and his weak men, and shall do so again, and again, and again!"

There were dozens of screams, hundreds, deep pounding dread in Jule's aching head. Made even worse by Grimarr yelling back, in the black-tongue this time, thick sharp words that raised more cheers in their wake, and then the distinct, hooting sounds of orc-laughter. No doubt mocking Jule further, shaming her, exposing her weakness for their amusement.

She didn't look, just kept her face safely hidden, while that big body moved again, striding strong beneath her. Going somewhere, through the crowd of clamouring orcs, moving upwards, deeper into the darkness.

There were more voices as they moved, more rumbled replies in the black-tongue through Grimarr's chest, but at least it was quieter here, with no more shouting. And when the movement stopped entirely, those legs beneath her finally gone still, and Jule stirred, and blinked. Finding an actual glimpse of light behind her eyes, and she blinked again, tried to refocus the strange stilted slowness of her thoughts.

They were in a room. Another dark room, with another bed. And this one was very dimly lit by a shaft of moonlight, pouring through a small opening in the stone of the room's wall. A window.

Grimarr's body shifted under Jule's, putting her carefully down to her feet, and then pulling the chain off from around her waist. And instead of running for the door, like she should have, Jule's wobbling legs made straight for that little window. Where she could see the stars, glittering on a level with her eyes, and then the steep expanse of jagged rock sloping down below to blackness. She was in Orc Mountain.

"*Damn* it," she breathed, rubbing at her face, because gods, how had she let this happen. Why hadn't she been fighting, paying attention, why the hell did everything important vanish into nothing when this awful orc so much as *touched* her?

Her eyes darted around the room, searching for an exit, but there was only this tiny window, and the door they'd come in through. Which seemed to be covered by a curtain of some sort, rather than an actual door, but the bulk of Grimarr's form was in front of it, blocking her escape.

"You shall stay here, woman," he said, all too easily following her thoughts. "This is your home now."

*Home.* The word felt like a hammer-blow, striking deep into Jule's chest, and she backed away from him on trembling legs, her head shaking back and forth.

"No," she breathed. "No. This is not home, orc. *Never.*"

The image of Norr Manor had flashed through her thoughts, wrenching up even more misery in its wake, and Jule kept backing away from Grimarr's watching black eyes, toward the stone wall behind her. "Don't pretend I don't know what this is," she said, as her eyes darted compulsively toward the bed opposite. "This is a *prison*. A place where you'll keep me trapped and at your mercy, and make me give you whatever the hell you want!"

She could see Grimarr's eyes close, briefly, and open again. "I will not force you," he said. "And I did not. You freely swore your troth. You *begged* for me."

Gods curse the bastard, and Jule backed further away, toward the corner. "Yes, and I was a fool!" she said, her voice choked, strained. "I was alone and confounded and *terrified*, and I believed your whispered honeyed *lies*!"

"I did not lie," came the immediate reply, sounding almost stubborn this time. "I spoke only truth."

Jule let out a sharp, strangled laugh, her body pressing itself back into the cold stone. "Oh *rubbish*, orc," she snapped. "You said I could run if I wished, you said you would give me pleasure and purpose and *joy*. You said you would"—she had to stop, gulp for breath—"please me like no man before you. Yet in truth, you threaten to *strangle* me, you shame me publicly, you trap me against my will, you promise to bind me and imprison me and *starve* me!"

The last came out as a sob, the first in an uncontrollable shuddering series of them, and Jule sank down the wall, buried her face again in her knees. Gods, she was a fool, she was trapped in Orc Mountain, what in the gods' names was going to happen to her next.

"I ought not to have done this," came Grimarr's voice, finally, and when Jule glanced up, wiping her eyes, it was to the sight of his big body kneeling, still across the room, his mouth frowning down at the stone floor. "I ought not to have spoken to you thus, or raised my hand against you. I have made you fear me."

Jule took a gasping breath, and was about to point out that she'd feared him long before that—but then she closed her mouth, pressed her palms hard to her eyes. Because she *had* feared Grimarr before that, yes—but it had been fear for her dignity, her well-being, not her one and only existence upon this earth. Because she'd *believed* him, for some unfathomable reason, when he'd said he would keep her safe.

"Yes," she said now, wearily, to the floor. "I am terrified of you, orc. You win the day."

Grimarr's throat gave one of those rumbling growls, his low body shifting in the dim light. "I do not win," he said, slowly, "if my mate fears me. I have walked this path before."

Before. Jule couldn't help a furtive glance at him, despite herself. "What do you mean."

One of his hands pressed to the stone floor, his claws

scraping loud against it. "My other mates feared me," he said, even slower. "My last carried my son in her womb, yet still cowered at each sight of me. As you do now."

Jule swallowed hard, scrubbed her eyes with her hand. "Yet you still expect me to believe," she shot back, "that you didn't force her?"

"I did not," he replied, quiet. "Each night, without fail, without prompt, she begged me to lie with her, even through her fear. She did not face me with bravery and call to me with her eager hunger, as you did."

Gods, this was fucked, that poor miserable woman, and yet Jule's appalling, traitorous breath had caught in her throat, coming out shaky and slow. Call to him. Did he truly think that was what she had done?

"I did no such thing," she said, but her heartbeat had picked up pace, hammering fast and strange in her chest. "Again, you *lie*, orc. Last night was all you. Not me."

He didn't deny it this time, and for some ridiculous reason that almost made it worse, made Jule's eyes linger on his in the dim light. "And now you're going to do it again," she hissed, lower than she meant. "You're going to force yourself on a terrified trapped prisoner who *hates* you."

Those shoulders rose and fell, the sound of his breath heavy in the room. "I have never forced a woman. I would not force you. I would never harm my mate."

"Rubbish," Jule spat. "You would, and did, and you *will*. You'll trap me, and starve me, and threaten to *choke* me to death!"

She could feel those eyes on her in the dark, quiet and close, despite the distance between them. "No," he said finally. "We shall alter this, woman. From henceforth, I shall do only as you wish."

Jule blinked at him, and then laughed, the sound thick and

mocking in her throat. "Good," she said. "I wish for nothing. I wish you to leave me."

She didn't know what she expected, perhaps for him to speak, or argue—but it wasn't for him to stand, abrupt and graceful, to his feet.

"As you wish," he said. "I shall go."

# 8

In Jule's mental list of all the awful things Grimarr could have done, leaving her alone and unchained in a room was not one of them.

But once he had gone, his bulky form slipping out silently past that curtain, Jule couldn't seem to stop glowering after him, her thoughts repeating his words again and again in her head.

*We shall alter this. As you wish. I shall go.*

He could have at least said when he'd be back, Jule's irritated thoughts pointed out, but no, no, she should be welcoming this. She should be taking advantage of this. Plotting her revenge, and enjoying the blessed relief from his looming, growling, near-constant presence.

She began by exploring the room, tentatively at first. Studying the steel-framed bed and its bare mattress—it had a Grimarr-shaped divot in it, and smelled like him, too—and then the odd sight of several human-made tapestries, hanging on the wall opposite the bed. One with the usual images of lords and horses and victories won, and the other—Jule's head tilted—a scene of murderous black orcs, hacking the terrified humans apart, spilling blood beneath their feet.

Now that Grimarr was gone, Jule could almost appreciate the irony of an orc captain displaying such a tapestry, and she went back to the bed, and lay down upon it, in the hollow Grimarr had made. Confirming her suspicion that this tapestry would be the chief object in his vision, when lying upon this bed, and why would anyone want that? As motivation? Gratification? Something to impel one's dreams at night?

The bed smelled even stronger of Grimarr, once one was lying upon it, and without thinking Jule rolled over, and let herself breathe in that low musky sweetness. There was no way orcs were supposed to smell so good, and that was part of why she'd been so foolish the night before, she was sure of it...

And now here were the memories of that, so strong, so present in Jule's thoughts. Those warm hands touching her, stroking her with such intent, such reverence. That hungry mouth on her skin, the taste of that clever tongue on hers. The sight of that huge swollen hardness, with that thick string of white leaking from the tip...

Gods curse her, and Jule lurched up and off the bed, and made a swift circuit of the room. There was nothing else in it, just the bed and those damned tapestries, and she stalked over to the window, and stared out of it. It faced south, judging by the position of the moon, and it was far too small to climb out of, but maybe if she tried, Grimarr would come back and yell at her, and she would yell at him, and then—

She scrubbed at her face, and then reached her hands for the window itself, feeling along its thick edges. The stone was smooth and rounded, like it had been worn away by long weathering, and there were no cracks, no weaknesses to be seen. Even a forceful kick of her foot at the most promising-looking corner achieved nothing but a sharp pain in her leg, and she huffed out an irritated breath, and then made for the room's stone walls instead.

But beyond the curtained door, which Jule carefully avoided, the walls were just as smooth and seamless, without so much as a crack, a leak, or a mouse-hole. Even the steel frame of the bed was without a single seam or rivet, as though it had been forged in one piece, and Jule felt herself glowering down at it, her foot tapping on the stone floor. Perhaps the bed could be taken apart somehow, perhaps she could call Grimarr back and ask, and then...

She groaned aloud, pulling at her hair, and paced across the room again. No. She needed to watch, and plan, and plot her revenge. She needed to track the orc population here, learn names and positions, make a mental map of the mountain's tunnels. Find a way to get out a message, somehow, maybe she could ask Grimarr to give her some paper and charcoal, and while he was here, he would—

She let out a muttered string of curses this time, and then finally stalked for that curtain at the door, and yanked it aside. Expecting—hoping?—to see Grimarr waiting there, but no, instead there were—other orcs. Yes, two other huge, hulking orcs, leaning against the wall opposite with weapons drawn, and looking at her.

Jule's body went very still, but nothing happened, and she frowned between the two orcs in the near-blackness, catching sight of a vaguely familiar nose. "Baldr?" she demanded. "Is that you?"

There was a flash of white teeth in reply, and the shirr of metal as Baldr sheathed his scimitar. "It is indeed," he said, in that light, melodious voice of his. "How fare you, woman?"

Jule glared at him, and at the other orc too—where was Grimarr?—and had to shake her head, try to think. "I've been better. Look, Baldr, did you"—she hesitated, took a breath—"did you, uh, hear all that? Before Grimarr left?"

"Indeed I did," Baldr said, with what seemed to Jule an excessive amount of cheerfulness. "And so did Drafli, here."

He'd nodded toward the other orc, who still had his huge scimitar drawn, and Jule eyed this one, tried to remember if he'd been in the raiding-party or not. "Right," she said. "Hello, I'm Jule."

Drafli gave a curt nod, but didn't speak, and Baldr flashed Jule more of his white teeth. "Drafli doesn't speak out loud like we do," he said. "But he listens, and sees much. He is the captain's Right Hand, and I his Left."

He spoke this with no small trace of pride, and Jule eyed him, and then this Drafli. "So if I try to leave this room right now," she said, as conversationally as she could, "what happens?"

Drafli immediately snapped up his huge scimitar, in a silent but very clear answer, and Baldr reached over a familiar hand, rested it on Drafli's muscled forearm. "You will not run," he said. "We will stop you. The captain deserves our loyalty."

There was a hint of reproach in his voice, hinting that perhaps Jule was similarly obliged, and she crossed her arms over her chest, and leaned against the doorway. "Yes, well," she said irritably, "Your captain has actually been *kind* to you."

"He has also been kind to you," Baldr replied, again with that reproachful tone in his voice. "Very few orcs would have tolerated that tongue-lashing you gave him just now. Not from another orc, and most certainly not from a human woman."

"Yes, because human women are obviously the lowest of the low," Jule snapped back. "Only good for giving you your precious sons, right?"

Drafli had made to raise his weapon again, but Baldr's hand was thankfully still there, holding his arm still. "We do not all believe so," he said firmly. "Before my mother's passing, the captain treated her with respect, and listened to her views. And while I did not meet his last mate, I know he sought to do the same with her. He mourned her for a full twelvemonth, after she left."

Jule opened her mouth, and then closed it again, because that was not—*not*—jealousy, prickling low in her gut. She wasn't jealous of that woman, what about her would possibly have made Grimarr mourn, perhaps she had been very petite and blonde and beautiful—

"Did Grimarr happen," Jule said loudly, trying to escape that rather alarming trail of thought, "to leave any food, or a chamber-pot of some kind?"

Baldr once again flashed her that row of teeth, and—Jule blinked—reached down behind his hulking form, and pulled out a small sack, and a gurgling waterskin, and what indeed looked to be a porcelain white chamber-pot, complete with a well-fitting lid.

"Oh," Jule said, numbly, and then grasped the items from Baldr's hands, and stalked back through the curtain without another word. Being unquestionably rude, she knew, but gods damn it, she was supposed to be plotting, planning, but she couldn't even *think*—

She opened the bag of food first, dumping the contents out onto Grimarr's bed, while her stomach audibly grumbled. There were fresh-looking apples, and berries, and a few carrots, and even—Jule lifted it, sniffed—fresh roasted meat. Some kind of fowl, and had Grimarr arranged to have it cooked, for her?

Maybe Jule was just hungry, and exhausted, and that was why she wasn't thinking properly. So she carefully ate what she could, without upsetting her long-empty stomach, and then drank, and made use of the chamber-pot. And then tried to lie down on the bed, to find some semblance of sleep, but it absolutely did not come, not with that too-strong, too-sweet scent of Grimarr all over the mattress.

*You begged for me*, he'd said, and maybe, lying here alone in the moonlight, Jule could look at that, could finally touch at the truth of it. She *had* begged for Grimarr. She had wanted him, in that moment. She'd longed for his touch, his words, his promises of safety and joy.

And perhaps, she could admit, that was in part because of Astin. Handsome, smiling, smooth-talking Astin, warm one day and viciously cold the next, in an endless, exhausting cycle that had left Jule increasingly desperate and lonely and miserable.

But it had been a safe alliance. And a crucial one, if Jule's lord father were to ensure his people's continued protection once he was gone. Not just from orcs, but from his neighbouring enemy lords, including the powerful, unpredictable Lord Norr. And thanks to Jule's marriage to Astin, the path had been neatly smoothed for her father's heir—Jule's cousin Frank, Lord Otto—to step into his new role and lands uncontested, with Astin as an ally, rather than an enemy.

*Just grin and bear it, my girl*, Jule's father had said, during his endless final illness. *Take what you can get from Norr, and give him a child or two. And then cuckold the swine afterwards to your heart's content.*

But the children had never come. And neither had the cuckolding, because both Jule and her father had underestimated Astin, and the lengths to which he would go to ensure that if Jule would not bear him children, she would bear them to no one.

And Jule could admit, in this dim, sweet-smelling silence, that she'd wanted children. Not just for Astin, but for herself. To make a little family of her own, once her father had gone. To have something else to love.

*I wish to fill your empty womb*, Grimarr had promised, in that low, husky voice of his. *This belly will swell as my seed blooms inside it. It will grow my sons strong and hearty and hale.*

Even the thought of it brought the heat to Jule's face, her

breath inhaling deep that sweet, heady smell of Grimarr's bed. And she wondered how often he slept here, what he would think of as he lay here, was he as lonely as she was, he'd mourned his last mate a full twelvemonth…

Gods *curse* her, curse this steaming pile of filth in her head, and Jule shoved herself off the bed, and stalked in circles around the room. Grimarr had kidnapped her. Killed two men. Dragged her off to this mountain. He had threatened her, shamed her, mocked her in front of a *horde*.

"Baldr," Jule snapped, too loudly, as she flung the curtain open again, and glared at his hideous face with its surprised blinking eyes. "Could you explain to me, please, what this is, between orcs and women?"

"What it is?" Baldr asked, still blinking at her, and Jule took a breath, let it out. "Yes. What it *actually* is. Not this rubbish about it being decreed by the gods."

Baldr's head tilted, perhaps hedging, and Jule stepped a little beyond the doorway, earning an unpleasant rattle of Drafli's huge scimitar. "Please," she said. "You will help your captain by telling me. I don't understand it, we have no concept or explanation for it among the humans, and it is all quite deeply alarming. I have no idea whatsoever why I would ever feel even the slightest—um, *interest*—in a person like your captain. *Please.*"

Baldr's eyes darted toward Drafli, who had lowered his scimitar slightly, and Jule could almost see him relenting, his big body leaning against the wall behind him. "The captain does not speak false," he said finally. "Human women are drawn to orcs. If the tales are to be believed, you always have been, as long as we have walked this earth. Our scents and forms and voices are appealing to you."

That wasn't promising, at all, and Jule took another deep breath. "And can this, um, *appeal* be resisted? Or broken?"

"Do you see any other women here?" Baldr countered, his

voice tinged now with bitterness. "And have you not seen our faces? This—*appeal*—is all we orcs have to offer you. And as you can see, even this is not nearly enough."

Oh. Right. The women always ran, always went back to the men, and Jule tried to cast her thoughts backwards, to recall if she'd ever actually met one of those escaped women. She'd heard the tales of them, of course, and it had indeed seemed that with enough distance, said women could recover, and return to their old lives. Once the orc-leavings had been expunged, of course, and properly disposed of.

The thought sent a strange twist through Jule's belly, and she studied Baldr's face in the dim light. Yes, he was hideous, but he was also helpful, and kind. *Had* Grimarr been kind?

"But it—it *feels* as though this should be enough," Jule said, and braced herself, brought up truth. "My mind, it seems—*consumed* with your captain, though I barely know him. And what I know, I do not like."

"You are his mate," Baldr said, without hesitation. "You accepted his vows, and his seed, and so the mating bond is complete. The union between an orc and his mate is very strong."

There was an instant's silence, in which Jule stared blankly at Baldr, and then gave a violent shake of her head. "Your captain and I are not," she said, "*mated.*"

Drafli rattled his scimitar again, but Jule felt somewhat inured to it by now, and kept her eyes on Baldr, who was frowning back toward her, and looking almost confused. "Yes," he said, "you are. No orc could mistake this. You carry the captain's scent and his seed, and your form all but shouts his name. For a human, perhaps, it is like this wedding-ring you wore, but"—he frowned, as though truly considering it—"instead of a small ring, it is a large placard, balanced atop your head."

He gave Jule a hopeful smile, as though his analogy might

be construed as comforting, rather than thoroughly appalling, but once again she could only seem to stare, and chase after her scattered, blown-about thoughts. "So if I keep resisting this—*bond*, will it get better with time? Or worse?"

Baldr was probably duty bound to tell her whatever Grimarr would want her to hear, but she saw him scratching his dark head, almost as though he were again truly considering her question. "I cannot say for certain," he said. "But I think proximity has much to bear upon it. I know when my father was still alive, my mother did not mourn when he was gone. But when he was near, even within a half-day's journey, there was no keeping her away until they'd mated. Every night."

His voice had the dry sound of one who had seen far more than he should of such things, and Jule fought to objectively consider his words, and compare them to her own observations. She did feel this—*bond*, toward Grimarr, just as she had last night. But then, afterwards, had she felt it quite so strongly? Before Grimarr had gone and ruined everything, had she not felt—peaceful? Sated? At ease?

Jule's heartbeat had quickened, slightly, because what if that was the only way? *Just grin and bear it, my girl*, her father had said about Astin. And this was just the same, wasn't it? With stakes just as high, wagering her very *life*?

And the more Jule considered it, the more it seemed the only way. She could waste her time and energy resisting this odious orc's odious appeal, or she could make a logical, tactical decision. Please the orc, appear invested in the orc, give in to the orc's temptations. And then...

"Thank you, Baldr," Jule said, and she meant it. "You have been very helpful. And for what it's worth, I think your face very striking."

"You do?" Baldr asked, his voice gone high-pitched. "Truly, woman?"

Jule nodded, and couldn't help a reluctant smile at the broad, delighted grin on his mouth. But her heart was already hammering faster, she wasn't really going to do this, or was she, but those warm hands, the heat of his voice, that huge dripping cock...

"And so," Jule said, and gathered air, where was the air. "I was hoping"—she tried to smile—"that you could find Grimarr, and bring him back to me."

## 9

This was a bad plan.

The worst plan, in fact, because what kind of revenge was it on a murderous kidnapping orc if you actually gave him his way? What the hell was Jule thinking?

But Baldr had already rushed off, clearly all too willing to drag Grimarr back here, and Jule's heartbeat was thundering so loudly she could hear it. Yes, she would make this sacrifice. She would submit to this orc, for future gains, future revenge. It wasn't a bad plan at all.

But when Grimarr strode back into the room, all hulking looming coiled shadow, Jule found herself somehow back in the far corner, and breathing hard. Why had she done this. What was she *thinking*.

"Baldr says you ask for me," he growled. "For what do you wish, woman."

There was no kindness in that tone, or in that look on his face, and perhaps Jule had truly angered him, earlier, or insulted him beyond repair. Perhaps a true orc's mate would seek to make amends.

"I wished," Jule ventured, "to thank you. For the food. And the—other things."

Grimarr's black eyes briefly flicked to the chamber-pot, now perched innocuously in the opposite corner. "I accept your thanks," he said flatly. "Is that all."

He had already half-turned to leave—he couldn't *leave*— and Jule stepped forward, too quickly. "And," she said, oh gods, "I—wished to hear you speak."

It was true, curse her, and she could feel the heat rising in her cheeks as Grimarr turned back, and looked at her. Looked *into* her, with those bottomless black orc-eyes.

"You wish to hear me speak," he repeated, slow. "And say what."

Jule thought about backing down, but she was in this now, he was here, the scent of him already swirling just slightly through the air. "Um," she said, and she fought to ignore the awareness of Baldr and Drafli, no doubt still listening just beyond that curtain. "Whatever you wish."

Something shifted, changed in those eyes, and Grimarr came a slow, prowling step closer. "What if," he said, that voice pitched lower, "I wish to speak of last night."

Oh. Jule's breath gasped, both at the words themselves, and at how that voice seemed to sink straight to her groin. While that sweet smell circled ever closer, and she closed her eyes, inhaled it from its source, deep, slow.

"Then I," she began, swallowed again, "would not wish to stop you."

She could feel the fullness of Grimarr's attention, now, the hulk of his form stepping closer. "What if," he murmured, more sinking firing heat to Jule's groin, "I wished to speak of you on your back, with your legs open wide, begging for my prick."

Gods, of course he would go straight there, but Jule's choking breath betrayed her, all the same. Bringing up that low, husky laugh of his in reply, and he came another step closer, almost enough to touch.

"Or what if," he continued, "I were to speak of the joy I found between your legs. How I could scarce set eyes on you today without thinking of this. Of how you sheathed me whole, and spurted out my seed."

Jule's whole body twitched, and he was absolutely making a point, but right now she couldn't seem to make herself care. Could only look at him, and breathe, and wait for what he said next.

"Or," he continued, even softer, and now here were his fingers, warm, tilting up her chin, "what if I were to speak of tasting you. Of putting my mouth deep between your thighs, and lapping up your sweetness."

Fuck. Jule groaned aloud this time, the shuddering heat racing hard down her spine, while her own shaky, traitorous fingers went to him, to touch against that so-close solid warmth of his broad chest. "Then I would say," she shot back, husky, because gods, the *thought* of that, "you're full of it, orc."

Grimarr replied with one of those growls, deep and guttural and utterly thrilling—and in a sudden, swift movement, he'd grasped Jule by the waist, and half-dragged, half-thrown her onto the bed. The bed that smelled so strong of him, but he himself smelled even stronger, and Jule leaned into it, drew it in, even as strong hands thrust up her skirts, and shoved her legs wide apart to the air, to his eyes.

"Mark this, woman," he breathed. "What I do with a mate who pleases me."

There was the thought, warm and sudden, that this meant she'd pleased him—had she?—but then it was gone, shot through into nothing, because Grimarr's tongue was between her legs, and *licking* her.

Jule cried out, too loud, and belatedly tried to clamp her legs together—but he was far too strong, and if anything he pushed her thighs harder, wider apart. Exposing everything, *everything*, and Jule's entire body was trembling, twitching, quivering. He couldn't actually be doing this, Astin had never, *ever* done this, it was appalling, and grotesque, and—

And Grimarr licked her again. This time starting from the back of her crease, oh *hell*, all the way up, and up, and up. His tongue flat, hot, slick, powerful, and Jule desperately squirmed under it, he couldn't possibly be doing this, he *couldn't*—

But he only did it again, another deep, slow lap of her, all hot sweet choking friction, all of her exposed and panting under his mouth. And fuck, how had Jule been missing out on this, she'd been pacing around this damned room all alone when she could have been having *this*—

"This pleases you, woman?" Grimarr's voice demanded, and Jule had to blink at him through dizzy eyes, fight to focus on his shadowed face. "Yes," she breathed. "Yes. *Gods.*"

He gave that low, rumbling laugh, his sharp smile crooked, challenging, smug. "Then beg me."

Beg him. And were they really going to do this whole stupid rigmarole again, and as Jule blinked at him, at those gloating dark eyes, she realized, suddenly, that she still didn't care. That if he wanted begging that much, then for this, he could damn well have it.

"Please," she said, and she didn't miss the brief look of astonishment, and then pleasure, that flashed across those eyes. "Please. Don't stop."

She was rewarded with another low laugh, another slow, thorough lick of that tongue. Lingering even longer this time, delving deeper into places it absolutely was *not* supposed to go, and Jule still didn't care, because it felt so damn *good*.

"Again," Grimarr murmured, now flicking his tongue against the top of her crease, bringing out her breath in sharp, choked gasps. "By name, woman. Loud."

Such an arrogant fiend, so damned transparent, and Jule

glared at him, even as her gasps indeed came louder, harder. He was making a statement, making her pay, saying, *My woman sent me away, and now she's begging for it, screaming for it.*

"Again," he ordered, promised, "and the louder you beg, the deeper my tongue will go. I shall lick you clean from the inside out."

Gods damn the bastard, but Jule's resistance was gone, vanished, drowned deep in those words, that voice. What the hell, what did it matter, if she meant she got to have more of this. She would think about revenge later, after, some other time...

"Please, Grimarr," she said, louder, and her cursed legs had spread even wider, her swollen wetness pulsing, gaping open, begging for that tongue. "Please, give this to me."

There was another swift, approving glance from those eyes—and then, oh gods, he did it. His tongue licking and lapping in just that one thrilling place now, and then sinking a little inside her, oh *hell*.

"Please, Grimarr," Jule gasped again, even louder this time, and she was immediately rewarded with another lick, plunging even deeper into her. And gods, his tongue was strong, and *huge*, and she writhed under it, against it, around it, *oh*.

"Don't stop," she breathed, her hips and thighs straining, trying to escape the shocking thrilling torture of it, while still trying to take it deeper. Feeling how far he was inside, how that tongue kept flicking and licking, how his lips had actually begun *sucking* on her, holy *hell*.

"Fuck!" she choked out, and that had definitely been too loud, but so were the sounds of his mouth, sucking and slurping and licking. Drinking her, feasting on her, the sight of it almost shockingly obscene. An orc's hideous grey maw, buried deep between her thighs, being soaked with her juices, while Jule spread her legs even wider, welcoming it, revelling in it, craving it more than she'd ever craved anything in her life.

"Oh gods," she gasped, and she felt almost giddy, lost, frantic, all her limbs tingling, her thoughts spinning, shouting, screaming at once. "Oh gods, Grimarr, oh gods, oh please, fuck me, *please!*"

His groan rumbled against her, deep inside her, and in a single lurching movement he was above her, looking down at her, his ugly face still slick with her wetness. "Again," he growled, his voice just as desperate as hers felt. "With my name. And I shall do it."

And was this about revenge, or was it something else entirely, because Jule stared at that face, met those glittering black eyes, felt her chest heaving hard for air, her heartbeat thundering inside it.

"Please, Grimarr," she said, and her voice was a caress, a low spoken heat. "Please, Grimarr, take me. Fuck me. Fill me with your prick and your seed."

His harsh, guttural growl was a pleasure all its own, curling up deep in Jule's belly, and just as strong was that look in his eyes. Like Jule was the only other being on this earth, like she was water to one who had long been starving of thirst.

"Yes," he whispered, his big head bowing a little, thick black eyelashes fluttering against scarred grey cheeks. "I will, woman."

And without warning, without conscious thought, he was there. That huge, hard head of him was there, nudging slow and hungry between her legs. Pumping out its thick, sticky seed already, and Jule cried out, spread her thighs wider. Sank whole into the impossible, shocking feeling of that expanding, thickening pole, ramming sure and strong and deep inside her.

"Fuck," she was gasping, chanting, and he wasn't even halfway in yet, oh gods. "Fuck, Grimarr. More. *Gods.*"

He gave an answering thick grunt, low in his throat, and that invading hardness plunged deeper. Splitting her, owning her, wringing out more of that hot seed deep inside, and it was truly like being impaled, like being taken by the blunt wooden end of a gods-damned *spear*.

"My orc-prick pleases you," his voice purred, sweet melting syrup in her thoughts. "Do you wish to sheath it again?"

In reply Jule's hands clenched on his tunic—when had she begun touching him?—and pulled him tighter, closer. Because yes, yes, he couldn't stop, not now, but of course he had, the bastard. Holding himself there, still, with almost all of him now inside, but for one last, impossibly thick-looking fingers'-width, still visible to Jule's eyes.

And maybe she hadn't quite seen this last night—maybe she'd been too caught in the rest of it—but now that she was looking, she couldn't stop. Her thighs obscenely spread, as wide as they would go, her hips angled up toward him. And coming out of her, jamming into her, was a huge grey orc-prick, and as Jule watched—shouted—it briefly, visibly thickened, and she could *feel* more of that thick orc-seed, pumping out deep inside.

"Yes," she groaned, her eyes fluttering at the sight. "Sheath you. All of you. *Please*, Grimarr."

Another one of those laughs, husky and low, his big grey hands gripping tighter on her thighs. "Then mark this, woman," he breathed, and as he watched, as she watched, he drove himself deeper, deeper inside. Until their bodies were flush, Jule's pink swollen heat split open as wide as it would go, stretched tight all around the huge base of him.

There was another deep shudder of that hardness, huge and otherwise stilled inside her—and it seemed to break something, release something, because suddenly Jule's arms and legs were clutching, frantic, pulling, craving.

"Please," she gasped, one hand digging into his silken tangled hair, the other scraping at the broad heat of his back. "Please, don't stop, oh gods, I *beg* you."

His big body seemed to hear, to obey, his growl fierce and

trembling as he finally moved, thrust, drove. Leaning against her, holding her still as he slammed inside, again and again and again. He couldn't stop, Jule needed this more than *life*, needed everything everything *please*—

She came with a shout, perhaps even a scream, her body thundering hard around that still-swiving, still-invading cock. Her arms and legs dragging him closer, her face buried into his sweaty neck, and now it was him arching up, tightening, aiming, firing.

The seed filled her like a flood, an expanding swelling rush of almost unbearable pleasure, and Jule did scream this time, her hands clinging around his back, pulling him down hard and close against her. Hearing that deep guttural groan in her ear, long and low and powerful, matching those long shuddering pulses inside, fuck, *fuck*.

When it finally stilled, quieted, it was to the realization that Jule had all but pulled Grimarr's full weight on top of her, and that her face was still buried in his hot, sticky neck. And there was no reason to move, her thoughts distantly noted, because he still smelled *so* damn good, the richest most beautiful thing she'd ever smelled in her *life*.

"Do I crush you, woman," his voice said, vibrating through his neck against Jule's mouth, and she actually smiled into it, shook her head.

"No," she whispered. "It's lovely."

And curse her, she wasn't supposed to be saying these things to an orc, she was supposed to be planning revenge— but then he pulled up a little, propping himself on those huge muscled arms, and looked at her. And he was an orc, he was still hideous, but his slow, sharp smile still pulled at something deep inside her, and so did that unmistakable glint of warmth, of approval, in those eyes.

"Good," he said, low. "This pleased me, woman."

There was more warmth, firing from Jule's face to her groin, making her body clench again around that still-invading hardness. Bringing something else, perhaps, to those black eyes, and Grimarr raised his big hand, traced it almost reverently down her cheek.

"Will you give me one more gift?" he asked, his voice so husky, so unbearably soft. "May I show our joy, and my seed, to my brothers?"

Jule felt her head nodding, tilting into his touch, because in this quiet, close, wonderful moment, she still didn't care. Whatever he did, whatever he wanted—for what he'd just done, he could have it.

"Brave woman," he purred, his smile gone almost thrillingly wolfish, and he pushed himself up a little more, and glanced sharply over his shoulder, toward that curtained door.

"Baldr," he called. "Drafli. Come, mark this."

Jule blinked, her body gone strangely stiff under him, her thoughts suddenly all shouting at once. He couldn't have meant—or wait, he *did*, because here were Baldr and Drafli, still with scimitars drawn, striding through the curtain, and into the room. The room—Jule stared, frozen—where she was still lying spread-eagled on the bed, her skirts thrust up around her waist, with Grimarr's huge cock still jammed up inside her.

He was going to show them—*that*. Himself drawing out of her, after he'd pumped her so full of his seed, and then...

"No," Jule croaked, the panic suddenly clanging wide under her skin. "No. *Please*."

And thank the gods, Grimarr heard, and hesitated. His brows furrowing together, his hand clenching on Jule's bare knee, his eyes searching hers. "No? You do not wish my brothers to witness this proof of our joy?"

"No!" Jule replied, almost a wail, and finally Grimarr turned toward a still-watching Baldr and Drafli, and began speaking in unintelligible black-tongue, while Jule clutched her hands to her burning cheeks. This couldn't be happening. This couldn't be happening...

Finally Baldr and Drafli left, clanking out of the room, and only once they were safely outside did Grimarr finally draw himself out of her. So swift and sudden that Jule cried out, at both the humiliating sound it made, and the empty feel of him, gone—and then again at the mortifying sight he had wanted them to see. Her gaping, swollen, pumped-full body, spurting his seed out of it like a geyser.

It spattered on him, on the bed, on the floor. And all the while Grimarr kept staring, his greedy eyes held to the awful, traitorous, still-clenching core of her, until the spurting white seed finally slowed to a steady, oozing stream.

Jule finally seemed to gain the presence of mind to wrench herself away from him, yanking down her skirts with shaking hands. And then turning away from him, and curling her trembly, rubbery-feeling body into something small and safe on the bed. She would have her revenge. She *would*.

But she could still smell Grimarr, could still *feel* him, still standing close beside the bed. "What vexes you, woman?" he asked, his voice back to guttural again, scraping rough and unpleasant against Jule's ears. "I did naught that you did not wish for."

Jule twitched all over, and shot a furtive, furious glare over her shoulder. "Honestly, orc?" she demanded, before she could stop herself. "You really think I would *wish* to be stared at and mocked by you and your friends as a—a cheap parlour trick?!"

Grimarr's dark eyes blinked at her, and his hands had gone down to where—why did Jule notice, *why*—his too-large, too-wet prick was still hanging pendulously out of his trousers. "I would not have mocked you," he said, as he tucked himself away again. "I would have honoured you, woman."

Jule's throat convulsed, and she shoved herself up to her wobbly feet, away from his huge bulk. "You would not," she shot back. "It was just like last night. You were trying to trick me, and shame me, and use my weakness for you as a *weapon*!"

Grimarr remained still by the bed, his face no longer visible in the shadows, but Jule could still feel those eyes, watching. "This is not a weapon," that guttural voice said. "You are my mate. This means you are not shamed if I show you bared and claimed. You are honoured. Praised. Protected."

There was no way Jule was swallowing that, and perhaps Grimarr saw it in her eyes, because he came a large, alarming step closer. "Then grasp this, woman," he said. "There are no secrets among orcs. You do not think my brothers could not hear our mating? Or that the scent of it does not colour this entire passage? I would have shown them naught that they did not yet know."

Jule took a step backwards, felt her hands clench into fists at her sides. "That's not an excuse, orc," she hissed. "Seeing is *entirely* different from hearing and smelling, and you know it!"

That shaggy head tilted, outlined in white from the window's streaming moonlight. "I do not know this," he said slowly. "For orcs, these are much the same."

The words sounded almost genuine, enough to catch Jule's waiting retort in her throat, while he came another slow, silent step closer. "And to show my fair, eager mate," he continued, "so deep in my thrall, so full of my seed"—she could almost feel the slow, shuddering heat of his sigh—"this is a joy I have longed for all my life."

Oh. He—*meant* that. And Jule's mouth had gone oddly dry, and she took a breath, about to speak—but just then, Baldr burst back into the room, the whites of his eyes gleaming in the moonlight. "Captain," he said, breathless. "They are here."

*They.* Jule's heart suddenly leapt, kicked into double time, because he had to mean their pursuers. Talford's principal regiment, one hundred good fighting men.

They were here for her. To *rescue* her.

"What are your orders?" Baldr asked, with a meaningful, sidelong glance toward Jule. "Should we hunker down, block the passages? Wait until they've left?"

There was an instant's silence, during which Grimarr looked at Jule, his eyes black holes in his harsh, unreadable face.

"No," he said, the word gruff and clipped on his tongue. "We will fight. And we will win."

## 10

Only moments later, Jule was once again being dragged through a pitch-black tunnel, with a chain tied tight around her waist, and orcs clattering and shouting all around her.

"Don't fight these men because of me," she gasped, toward the hard pull of that chain. "Please, Grimarr."

His pace didn't hesitate, and here was the feel of big, strong fingers, closing around her forearm, pulling her faster. "I do naught because of you," his deep voice said. "These men attack our home. We will defend it."

Jule's feet staggered under her, and she silently cursed the bastard, and his transparent orc lies. If this truly had nothing to do with her, why hadn't he left her up in that room, with its comforting little patch of moonlight? Why was he dragging her about through what felt like leagues of pitch-black corridors, with this deafening band of armed, shouting orcs?

"Half of you will stay in the mountain, and wait!" called Grimarr's voice, louder this time, rising above the rest. "You will not come out until my command!"

There were more shouts of affirmation, the harsh clank of

weapons, the overpowering sound of crunching rock. And abruptly there was fresh air again, and moonlight, as half of Grimarr's band—perhaps twenty-odd orcs—crowded out onto a little stone outcropping, near the bottom of the mountain.

"There they are!" rose a shout from below, and when Jule whirled around, there was Talford's regiment of one hundred men. Beautiful, wonderful, smooth-skinned men, wearing proper clothes and armour, carrying proper swords and longbows. Some of them were familiar in the moonlight—Jule had hosted the regiment's captain for dinner on several occasions, and had sometimes ridden out to watch the men drill—and even the sight of them standing there was a breathtaking, head-swarming reminder that the world had not been consumed by orcs, after all.

"They have Lady Norr!" shouted one of the lieutenants, and this, of course, was why Grimarr had dragged Jule out here. To show her off, to make a statement, and she flinched at the feel of his strong arm, circling around her waist, and yanking her up against him.

"I have a new mate," his voice called back, deep, carrying, authoritative. "I have marked her and claimed her as my own. She will bear me many strong orc-sons."

The orcs around them shouted, because that was apparently what orcs did when Grimarr spoke, and Jule closed her eyes against the racket, the oddly disorienting feel of that hard chest, rising and falling against her. These men were her allies. They were here to rescue her. But there was no way they could truly succeed, was there? Not with only the one regiment, and all the black tunnels at the orcs' back, and many more orcs inside?

"Is Lord Norr with you," growled Grimarr's voice behind Jule. "Does this weak fool man have the heart to face me."

None of the men replied—it was doubtful that anyone had even been able to reach Astin yet, to tell him the news of Jule's capture—and in the dim light Jule could see the captain glancing at his lieutenants. Giving orders now, *You go that way we'll go here*, but Jule's heartbeat was thundering in her ears, her body twitching against Grimarr's chest. There was no way. The men would never win. Good honourable men turned to corpses, because of her.

"There are more orcs hiding in the mountain!" a voice shouted, and too late Jule realized it was hers. Making all the orcs whirl at once to face her, their snarls and growls rising all around, and behind her Grimarr's body went strangely, suddenly hard, his arm very tight around her waist.

There was a horrible instant's stillness, during which the orc-growls around them grew even louder, and Jule squeezed her eyes shut, waiting for Grimarr's retaliation—but it didn't come. Only a sharp rise and fall of his chest against her, a brandishing of the huge, terrifying scimitar in his other hand.

"There are more orcs hiding in the mountain," his deep voice called out, repeating Jule's words, almost as though he had endorsed them. "Will you run in fear? Will you prove as weak as your fool lord? Or will you stay and fight?"

The orcs shouted again, their attention fully back on the men, who were now quietly conferring with one another. Several of them casting wary eyes on the band of orcs, on the jagged, rough rock of the mountain.

"We fight," called the captain, more to his men than to Grimarr, and Jule's mouth had opened to shout out again, to say, *No, don't, this isn't the way, run*—but suddenly here was Grimarr's huge hand, clamped hard over her mouth, yanking her head back tight against his shoulder.

"You will not betray me again and live, woman," he breathed, hot and deadly in her ear. "Do you understand?"

His hand was pressing harder, threatening to break her jaw or her neck, and Jule gasped against it, tried to think. There had to be something she could do, something else, some kind of hint, or warning—

Grimarr's body under her suddenly moved, dragging her away, and with a powerful, angry jerk of his hands he almost hurled her back toward the opening they'd come out of. "Baldr, you watch her," he barked out, over his shoulder. "Keep her inside. Bind her if you must."

He strode away without looking back, and already here was Baldr, looming over Jule, his greenish face grim and disapproving in the moonlight. "Come," he said. "Quickly, before a stray sword finds you."

Jule's staggering feet went, though her eyes kept searching frantic behind her. The men were going to fight, they were going to die, Grimarr was striding to the head of the orcs now, raising that huge scimitar, a blood-curdling bellow rising from his throat—

"Get in," Baldr snapped, more curt than he'd been with her yet, and Jule lurched back into the mountain, into the encroaching blackness. Feeling Baldr's hand grip around her elbow, pulling her through the tunnel, around one corner and then another, and another, until—Jule blinked—there was light.

They were in a huge, cavernous room, and the light was from a fire, crackling away in a massive, open fireplace at the far end. There was an unfamiliar orc kneeling by the fire, perhaps tending it, and a variety of others scattered around it, perhaps ten or fifteen of them. Many of them looked older, with bent backs and white hair, and almost all of them gave curious glances over their shoulders toward Jule and Baldr.

Baldr didn't take any notice, and dragged Jule over toward the closest corner, thrusting her still-shaky body into it. "I would prefer not to bind you," he said, as he hovered between her and the rest of the room, his arms crossed over his chest. "But if you make one move to run, I will."

He was truly angry with her, Jule realized, and she dragged in a heavy, shaky breath. "Those men are going to die," she said, her voice cracking. "Because of me."

"No," Baldr countered, his black eyebrows furrowing. "They will die because they are foolish enough to attack us on our own mountain with only one hundred men."

It was the twisted orc logic again, and Jule dug her palms into her eyes, hard enough that she saw stars. "But don't you see, Baldr," she said, "these men know if they fail to chase me, they'll lose their positions, perhaps be imprisoned or charged with desertion. At least this way, even if they die, their wives and children might get a measly pension, and stay out of the poorhouse!"

There was only silence from Baldr, and when Jule dropped her hands he was still frowning, his head tilted. "It was still not your place to warn them," he said. "Grimarr is captain, and your mate. It is your place to support him."

"And his place to threaten me with *death* if I don't?!" Jule shot back. "To say I wouldn't *live* if I betrayed him again?!"

Her voice had cracked again on the words, and Baldr's head tilted even more, his mouth pursing. "He would not have meant death at his own hand," he said. "He would have meant at the hands of one of our brothers, likely claimed as an accident. Why do you think he had me take you away, woman? Betrayal is no small matter among orcs."

"So Grimarr would just let them *kill* me?" Jule asked, her voice gone increasingly shrill. "I thought he was supposed to *protect* me!"

She couldn't understand why it even mattered—she was supposed to be thinking only of revenge, wasn't she?—but it did. Grimarr had claimed so many things, said so many honeyed words, they had all seemed so genuine—and now *this*?

"The captain *did* protect you," Baldr said, his voice stubborn. "He could not easily guard you in a battle he is meant to lead, with so many of our brothers caught in the bloodlust's thrall. So he sent you away. It was a kindness, in the face of your betrayal."

Gods curse him, curse them all, and Jule put her hands back to her eyes, breathing hard. She could hear very faint clangs and shouts from beyond the room's door, no doubt the orcs killing all those poor men, tearing all those fathers away from their innocent children...

"If you truly feared for the families of men," Baldr's voice said, quieter now, "you would not bring shame upon your mate by calling out to warn them on a battlefield. Instead, you would be wise, and prove yourself worthy of your mate's trust. And then, when you spoke of your fears to him, he would listen."

He would listen. Jule had a very hard time believing that, and looked up to tell Baldr so—but suddenly, barging through the door, there was Grimarr himself.

He was surrounded by his shouting, terrifying orcs, and his big body was half-covered with blood, his tunic a torn-up mess. But his face was grim and satisfied, and both his hands were raised in the air, one of them still holding his giant, dripping-red scimitar.

"We have won!" he announced, to the room at large. "All our brothers yet stand, and the men are defeated. Those who did not run from our strength are dead!"

Dead. Jule's heart skipped, and she bowed her head, folded her fingers tight together. Fighting in vain to block out the sounds of cheering orcs, the curdling image in her head of beautiful, smooth-faced men, lying broken and bloodied on the mountain.

"Our brothers fought bravely," rumbled Grimarr's deep voice. "Olarr killed four men alone. Silfast killed two with his axe at once. Abjorn broke his leg leaping to the scree wall, yet killed his man with honour!"

All the surrounding orcs shouted in unison, the awful sound echoing in waves through the room, and Jule reflexively clapped her hands to her ears, blocking it out. No. Too much death, too many broken families, broken men. Killed, because of her.

It was almost like Grimarr had heard her thoughts, because now he turned, huge and bloody and horrifying, and stalked toward her. His eyes were hard and glittering in his face, and here was the heavy, sinking awareness that he was furious with her, and that the sight of Jule standing here like this—cowering into the wall, with her hands pressed over her ears—was most certainly only making it worse.

"And this defeat," he growled, loud enough that it reverberated through Jule's hands, "was in spite of my headstrong mate, and her betrayal of me to her own kind. What do you say to this, woman?"

Every orc in the room was staring at her now, all with critical and accusing eyes, and Jule dropped her hands, tried to step backwards, but found only wall behind her. "It—it wasn't fair," she managed, her voice wavering, her eyes dropping to Grimarr's tattered, blood-soaked trousers. "They were only doing their *jobs.*"

A hard, disapproving growl rumbled from Grimarr's throat. "They attacked our home," he said, his voice loud, authoritative, echoing. "Their numbers were twice our own. And I gave them leave to run. They did not."

Jule couldn't help glancing at all the watching faces—was this a trial? A public judgement?—and she swallowed, dragged her eyes back up to Grimarr's. "They didn't have a *choice,*" she shot back. "If they'd refused to fight, they'd have been punished. Their families would have suffered."

Grimarr gave another of those deep growls, rumbling through the room. "If they had no choice, then why did you call out to warn them. Why did you betray me for naught!"

Jule swallowed again, looked at those furious black eyes. Why *had* she done it, when there had been no chance of it truly helping her revenge, and it had been certain to only make her plight here worse? Stubbornness? Anger? Madness?

"I wasn't trying to betray you, orc," she said finally. "If anything, I was betraying Astin. Lord Norr."

She hesitated briefly at the words, her eyes fixed blankly to those filthy trousers again, because was that true? Perhaps?

"Not to *undermine* him," she added, too quickly, glancing up at Grimarr's eyes, and why was she telling him this, had the mating-bond truly infected her so much? "But don't you see? Those men dying at your hands, on such a pointless, hopeless mission, for Lord Norr's stolen wife—it makes them the heroes, and you the villains. It gives Lord Norr reason to use more men and more resources against you. It gains him even more support among the humans to destroy you all for good."

The orcs' murmurs began to rise again, filling the room—until Grimarr raised a sharp hand, and the room filtered back down to silence. "You think we do not know this, woman?" Grimarr said, his voice low, deadly. "You think I did not weigh this, when I chose to fight this battle? You think we are not already the villains in each tale the humans tell?"

Jule couldn't seem to find an answer to that, and he came a step closer, almost near enough that the scimitar dripped its blood on her shoe. "Tell me, woman," he hissed, with pure fury in those glaring black eyes, "what Lord Norr's men would do to a band of orcs who walked up to his gate? Would he give us clean, honourable deaths, like the ones we have given these men?"

Jule flinched, pressing herself flatter to the wall, her thoughts trapped and darting and futile. What would Lord Norr do, why did it matter, why the hell did she even care?

"No," she heard herself say, her voice gone oddly weary. "Lord Norr would eviscerate you. He would torture you in the town square. He would give your bodies to the dogs and pigs, and your heads to the children as prizes."

It was true—Jule had seen it done, once, to an orc who'd been captured in Yarwood's forest—and even the memory of it was horrifying enough to bring bile to her throat. Astin had been showing his strength, one could argue, reassuring his people of their safety—but even then, Jule had known there was no excuse. No possible justification. Not even revenge.

"You know, I even begged for your orc's dignity, when I saw Astin do this," Jule heard herself say, bitter now. "No one listened, just as none of those men listened to me today. Just as *you* don't listen to me now, when I tell you I was only trying to *help* you!"

Grimarr's mouth grimaced, and there was another heavy growl in his throat, almost like a sigh this time. "I listen, woman," he said. "But I hear many words, and no offers to make amends to me, or my brothers. What will you give me, to atone for what you have done."

Jule's eyes dropped again, and she felt her thoughts stutter, her body gone cold. What would she give him. And why was she even considering it, why did it matter, these orcs were monsters, she was supposed to be getting revenge. Wasn't she?

But she couldn't seem to lift her eyes, and she squared her shoulders, took a breath. She could still have revenge. There was still time. Astin's men would regroup, reconvene, and come back with a real plan. Not a rubbish one like this, that only led to suffering and death.

And when they came back, she would be ready.

"Very well, orc," Jule heard herself say. "I will yield to you, for this."

There was silence all around, strange and suddenly oppressive, and when Jule looked up, Grimarr's eyes on hers seemed even harder than before. "Yes, you will yield. You have already vowed this, woman. I ask, what else."

What else? Jule's heart was hammering, her eyes darting between the watching orcs. What could Grimarr possibly want, beyond the yielding? Information about Astin, perhaps? Details on Yarwood's other forces, or their locations? Things that would only hurt more humans, and jeopardize Jule's plans for revenge?

The surrounding orcs were still silent, staring, and Jule lifted her chin, fixed her eyes back on Grimarr's face. "I will— I'll make you an excellent meal. From the choicest foods in your larder."

She had no idea if there even was a larder here, but orcs had to eat somehow, didn't they? And perhaps this *had* been a legitimate thing to offer, because a few of the orcs were nodding, and Grimarr didn't look *more* angry, at least, did he?

"I will take this," he said flatly. "But it is not enough."

Not enough. Jule's eyes desperately searched the surrounding room, with all these orcs, all clustered here close to its crackling fire. "I will—I'll make you a supply of candles," she said. "So you are not always in the dark."

There were more murmurs, but Grimarr's hard eyes didn't change. "Very well, woman. What else."

Jule dragged in a slow, shuddery breath, because what else did he want? What else *did* Grimarr like? Did she even have to ask?

"I will"—she began, and squared her shoulders, met those eyes. "Next time you wish to take me to bed, I shall lie you down, and serve you, and worship you as a king."

The murmurs rose all around, most definitely with approval in them this time, and finally, thank the gods, Grimarr's head gave an almost imperceptible nod.

"I will take this," he said. "You will do this now, woman."

Now. And honestly, what else had she expected, and Jule swallowed hard, and even tried for a smile.

"Very well," she said. "Then please, take me to your room."

## 11

G rimarr was still furious with her.

It was surprising, and perhaps rather disconcerting, to discover that Jule was very aware of this fact, and perhaps even unsettled by it. And that when his big hand had closed tightly around her wrist, drawing her out of the room and through the twisty pitch-black corridors, she almost felt—*sorry*.

"Did you sustain any injuries in the battle?" she heard herself ask, into the silence, but Grimarr only replied with a snort, and kept moving. The anger almost rolling off him in waves, and why did that feel so unpleasant, why did it even matter?

"Thank you for obliging me," she said, and then made a face in the blackness, because was she really *thanking* him for this? For raging at her in front of a room full of armed, threatening orcs until she agreed to *worship* him? In *bed*?

Grimarr still didn't reply, and finally he thrust her back into that room, with its blessed patch of moonlight. Which had grown brighter in their absence, tilting now toward dawn, and

Jule turned to look at him in the faint light, at his blood-soaked clothes and his flat, furious eyes.

She could do this. She could touch a murdering angry orc, and pretend to want him, and care for him. Gods knew she'd done far worse for Astin, hadn't she?

"Well?" Grimarr snarled, and Jule realized that she was still standing frozen, staring at him. As if any of this was going to do itself, and she made herself clear her throat, and stand up straighter.

"Right," she said, with a glance down Grimarr's huge, bloody frame, and back up again. "Um. Perhaps I could—wash you? To begin?"

She braced herself against his reply—perhaps orcs didn't wash, perhaps he would take the offer as an insult—but he gave a curt nod, a commanding wave of his hand toward the curtained door. "Then ask for what you need."

Jule blinked, but obediently went to open the curtain. And here, incredibly, were Baldr and Drafli again, and where in the gods' names had they even *come* from?

"Do orcs not sleep?" she demanded at them, and there was a brief flash of Baldr's white teeth in the dim light. "We do," he said. "Just not as much as you weak humans. Now, what do you need, woman?"

The cheerfulness was back in his voice, almost like he approved of her again, and Jule gave a quick glance over her shoulder, to where the look on Grimarr's face was the total opposite of approving. "Well," she said, cautiously, "perhaps I could have a basin of water, and a clean cloth? And a clean change of clothes for him? And"—she felt her face heat, but said it anyway—"do you have any oil? And perhaps a comb?"

If Baldr considered such items unusual, he didn't let on, and gave a satisfied little snort before trotting off down the corridor. Leaving Drafli still there, still with that ridiculous scimitar in hand, and Jule tried not to think of the last time she had seen him, and swiftly dropped the curtain.

Grimarr behind her still hadn't moved, just standing there glaring at her, and Jule squared her shoulders, and stepped back toward him. "May I," she made herself say, "may I undress you?"

She fought to hide her grimace at the words, because—despite the several times they had done *things* so far—she'd only ever seen the essential parts. She hadn't yet been subjected to the frightful sight of a hideous, fully naked orc, a nightmare that was sure to haunt her for the rest of her days.

"You undress first," Grimarr snapped, bringing another surge of heat to Jule's face. But in this moment, perhaps undressing herself *was* a superior choice to undressing an orc, so she took an unsteady breath, and did it. Pulling off her grimy dress, and the shift beneath, and then made her naked body walk over to the bed, and drape the clothes over the end of it.

She could feel Grimarr's angry eyes on her the entire time, sending a curious prickle down her spine, and when she stepped back toward him she intently avoided looking at his face, and instead focused on his bloody, shabby tunic. It could barely even be called a tunic—more like a badly sewn tent—and Jule touched a tentative finger to the nearest seam, which was stitched together with large thread that looked suspiciously like gut.

"Where do you get your clothes?" she asked, without thinking, and an unwilling glance up at his eyes showed them just as forbidding, just as furious, as before.

"We make them," he said curtly. "From those of men."

The tunic really was a disaster—Jule could see now the lines of the original shirt, many times smaller, likely stolen from some poor dead soldier—and frowned at the thought of it. "You can't make your own shirts to properly fit you, like everyone else?"

She knew it was petty, even as the words came out her mouth, and wasn't at all surprised by Grimarr's hard, answering growl. "Tell me where I am to get this cloth, woman," he hissed. "From the sheep that the humans will steal? From the flax or the mill that the humans will burn? From the trader or the tailor who will seek to *kill* me if I so much as *ask* to trade for this?!"

Right. Jule couldn't help a wince, and she forced her eyes—and then her shaky, fumbling hands—down to the hem of that bloody tunic. Awkwardly pulling it up, and up, and then standing on tiptoes as Grimarr silently raised his arms, and let her pull it off over his shaggy head.

Jule felt her heart thudding faster as the tunic fell to the stone floor—she could do this, she'd seen worse things than a half-naked orc, surely—and she took a breath, and braced herself, and looked.

And. Perhaps it was the mating-bond again, that very faint sweet smell curling through the air, just now distinguishable over the salty scent of blood. Or perhaps it was the fact that Grimarr's torso was actually still bleeding, dripping from several ugly but shallow-looking cuts, adding to the chaos of awful-looking scars that marred his grey skin.

But whatever it was—Jule's eyes angled up to his angry face, and then back down—the sight of him standing here, stripped to the waist, was bringing a strange flutter to her heartbeat, a deep pull in her belly. And an entirely inexplicable greed to her cursed betraying eyes, because they just wanted to look, and look, and look.

Grimarr was bigger than any man she'd ever seen, and powerfully built, with those huge sloped shoulders, that broad chest. And rather than the flabbiness Jule might expect of someone his size, it was all hard muscle, every line and ridge visible, from his thick corded arms to the flat ripples of his waist.

His skin was all that disconcerting grey, of course, and covered with all those scars, but it also looked supple and smooth. Untouched by hair, but for the thatch of black that peeked out from under his arms, and for some reason Jule's eyes lingered there, and then to the deep grey circles of his nipples, almost on a level with her mouth. And what would he do, what would it taste like, if she were to lean forward, touch her lips to one, taste it with her tongue—

She squeezed her eyes shut—it was the bond, it was madness, he'd *murdered* all those men—and her hands blindly reached for his filthy bloody trousers, shoving them downwards. Not looking this time, not even as she could feel that hardness bobbing out, could even smell it, that heavy hot sweetness now unfurling through the air.

At precisely that unfortunate moment, Baldr strode back into the room. Not even knocking, or announcing his highly unwelcome presence, and one of Jule's hands immediately snapped to cover her breasts, the other gone down between her legs. Earning for her trouble a look from Baldr that was almost amused, as he set a bowl of water at her feet, and beside it a rag, a comb, a pile of clothes, and a small metal flask.

"Here you are, woman," he said lightly, as though the sight of Jule and his captain both standing there naked—with his captain's huge cock standing half at attention—was an entirely unremarkable one. "Is there anything else you need? Or you, Captain?"

Grimarr replied with a negative-sounding grunt, thankfully, and Baldr trotted out again, dropping the curtain behind him. Leaving Jule red-faced and flustered, enough that her traitorous eyes glanced downwards, toward where—her breath caught—that huge grey hardness was shuddering, just a little. Filling, swelling, lengthening.

Jule had to force her gaze away, and abruptly fumbled for the cloth, kneeling as she dunked it in the bowl of water.

Keeping her eyes on her hands wringing it out, rather than on Grimarr, or on that strangely enthralling part of him. Why had she agreed to this, why did she care, he was an orc, a hideous murdering *orc*...

"Why *did* you fight the men today?" she made herself ask, out of sheer desperation for distraction, as she stood up again, and gingerly dabbed at the worst-looking of Grimarr's wounds, a gash across his collarbone. "If you knew it would only give Astin more motive to fight and destroy you in return?"

Another growl rumbled from Grimarr's throat, seeming almost to vibrate the air around her. "It is not your place to question me, woman. It is your place to serve me, in this."

It stung more than it should have, and Jule glowered at the wound under her cloth, at how the grey skin already seemed to be knitting itself back together. "How is it not my place?" she shot back. "I *knew* some of those men, my husband paid their *salaries*, they were only here because of *me*, and now they're *dead*, and I can't even ask you *why*?!"

Her voice sounded shrill, her fingers gone slack on the cloth, her eyes blinking down toward it. And now here was the sight of Grimarr's big hand, minus claws, closing around her fingers, guiding them down to the next cut, much lower on his torso.

"I did this to show that I am a true threat," he said finally, voice flat. "One that the men cannot dismiss or ignore. There are but a thousand orcs yet living in this realm, and I shall not stand by while we are winnowed to naught."

Jule's cloth was now wiping dangerously close to *that*, and she kept her gaze carefully averted until she'd finished, and then sidled swiftly away, around to his back. Only to be confronted by—she took a breath, let it out—the powerful width of his shoulders, the rippling muscles of his scarred back, the high, hard curve of his arse-cheeks.

"There are only a thousand of you left?" Jule managed, as

she wiped at a cut on his scarred grey shoulder. "That can't be right, aren't there orcs all over the realm?"

The shoulder gave a shrug, the muscle shifting beneath her hand. "Orcs hide in many places," his curt voice said. "But we are less and less with each season. There are few new babes, and many deaths."

Oh. Jule's hand kept wiping, now smoothing against an old, curving scar on his back, looking unnervingly like the line of an axe-blade. She'd gotten most of the blood at this point, and though she'd expected to also find dirt and grime all over him, there was no evidence of it on her cloth. Just the blood, and perhaps orcs *did* bathe after all, how else would his skin be so burnished and smooth and clean?

"To hear the humans speak," Jule said, and was she already thinking of them as something separate, somehow? "There are thousands upon thousands of orcs in hiding, just waiting to steal all the women, and kill all the men."

Grimarr's back under her fingers tautened, his shoulders rising stiff. "Humans think *us* crude and foolish," he hissed. "Yet they cannot count, or recall their own cruelties, or hear their own women's tales. They *choose* to live in darkness."

Jule didn't seem to have an answer to that—*had* she ever heard a firsthand tale of another woman's encounter with an orc?—and after an instant's stilted silence, she dropped her cloth, and reached instead for the metal flask Baldr had brought. It was indeed oil, just as she'd requested, and she poured some into her palms, and then—she took a bracing breath—reached up, slow and careful, and ran her slick hands against Grimarr's broad, scarred grey back.

The muscle twitched slightly at the touch, but his skin was so warm, so smooth. Enough that Jule's fingers spread a little wider, increased the pressure, rubbing the oil into that silken, scarred skin. While it occurred to her, incongruously, that Astin had had no scars. His back had been pale and smooth, his shoulders narrower across than her own. And again, here was that memory of those orcs who'd sought an audience without bloodshed, and how Astin had so blithely ordered their deaths. How Astin had smiled afterwards, cold and smug and satisfied.

Jule had thought it loathsome then, and was distantly surprised to note that she found it even more loathsome now. And that her hands had gone, seemingly on their own volition, up to those tense shoulders, rubbing and kneading against them. Working to uncoil the tension, to feel them relax just slightly under her fingers.

"Will you lie on the bed?" she asked, before she lost the nerve. "So I can reach you better?"

There was an instant's stillness, but then Grimarr nodded, and did it. His huge naked form striding away from her, the muscles rolling and rippling with every step, until he dropped himself facedown on the bed, his messy head buried in his arm.

He had to be tired, Jule thought now—he'd just led a battle, and despite what Baldr said, orcs must have to sleep some-time—and there was an odd twist in her stomach as she picked up the oil-flask and the comb, and padded over toward him. Looking again at the sight of him, lying there silent and still, his only movement the slight rise and fall of his scarred back with his breath.

Jule couldn't seem to stop looking as she put one knee to the bed, and then the other. And then used her oddly trembly fingers to pour the oil liberally over his back, where it pooled into the deep line of that awful curved scar.

It felt easier to touch him this time, to slide the oil over that smooth silken skin. And then to knead harder into the muscle, working it with palms and fingers, while her body leaned lower and lower over him. Breathing in the sweet scent of the oil, mixed deep with the sweet muskiness of his skin.

"Does this please you?" she murmured. "Shall I continue?"

"Yes," his muffled voice said back. "You are to worship me as a king."

Right. And if Jule were truly treating him as a king—she couldn't help a heated glance downward, to that hard muscled arse—she would oil not just his back, but his entire body, right? There was really no alternative, was there?

Her hands felt almost eager as she slicked them with more oil, and then slid them slow, all the way down to the smooth curve of that hard arse. Making it twitch with her touch, and Jule took a shuddery breath as she cupped it, kneaded it, spread her fingers wide. While her eyes watched, drank in the sight of pale fingers against grey skin, smoothing just slightly over the cleft of him, not quite daring to delve too deep.

Next she went to his powerful thighs, just as smooth and muscled as the rest of him, with a glimpse of more black hair deep beneath them. And then to the backs of his knees, his muscled calves, his huge feet, surprisingly well-formed but for their disconcerting claws, which, just like those on his hands, retracted once she came too close.

She took her time going back up, leaving the skin behind her supple and glistening. And then she lingered again on his broad back, tracing carefully over that awful scar, until she finally rose to his neck, to that matted black hair.

A tentative touch at the hair showed that it was smooth and silken too, despite the tangles, and in a flash of daring Jule straddled herself over Grimarr's back, her bare body spread wide and exposed above him, as she carded her fingers through his hair, pulling it away from his pointed grey ears. It was a mess, but one that seemed to improve as she worked, and she reached for the comb, and began teasing out the knots, brushing it smooth.

And like the rest of him, it was surprisingly, strangely appealing. The strands thick and silken and black, sliding soft against her fingers, and the more she combed it the shinier it looked, rippling over his shoulders in waves. Coming almost down to his middle back, in parts, and Jule vaguely wished she'd asked for scissors, to cut it straight, to make it as lovely as it should be.

Instead she braided it properly, smoothing oil into that as well, and after looking for something to tie it off with, went to collect a strand of thread—or perhaps gut—from his torn shirt on the floor. Making that head lift to look at her, for the first time since he'd lain down, and the sight of him like that—with the smooth hair and pointed ears, the rippled muscle and shining skin—made the heat pool sudden and hard in Jule's naked groin.

"Your hair is really rather passable," she said, as she went back to kneel beside him, and tied off the end of the braid. "Rich men would pay quite a sum to have a wig of it."

Grimarr's lip curled in obvious distaste, and he propped himself up on his elbow to frown at her. "I have seen these men in their silly wigs," he said, with such firm, decisive scorn that Jule couldn't stop her mouth from twitching. "They *pay* for these?"

Jule's hands twitched, and she choked back her chuckle into something resembling a snort. "Wigs are fashionable," she managed. "Astin often wears one."

"Lord Norr is a fribble and a fool," Grimarr replied scathingly. "In a wig he should be taken for a young child, or a broom."

With that, he dropped his head back to his hands, as though the matter were entirely settled, leaving Jule to bite at the inside of her cheeks, trying desperately not to laugh. "You should see him in his fawn breeches, and his yellow silk topcoat," she heard her wavering voice say, and far too late clamped her mouth shut, because why was she saying such things about her husband? To an orc, who she'd just massaged all over? *Had* she gone mad?

But it was too late, because Grimarr had actually flashed her a smug-looking smirk over his shoulder, and with a push of his hand he rolled over, dropping onto his back. Showing her that broad chest, that rippled abdomen, and—Jule swallowed—that swollen, still-leaking hardness. Jutting out of a mass of thick black hair, lying flat against his muscled belly, looking too huge, too obscene, to be real.

The scent of him had risen as he'd turned, that heady sweet muskiness swirling through the air, and Jule couldn't keep her tongue from coming to wet her lips. A movement that Grimarr clearly didn't miss, his black eyes narrowing as his gaze lingered on her face, and then dropped lower, to her bare breasts and peaked nipples, the clenching, traitorous heat between her legs.

"You wish for this," he said, with no small trace of satisfaction. "You wish for a strong, powerful mate who does not wear a wig. You wish to worship me, woman."

Gods, he was so full of it, how did Jule keep forgetting that? And perhaps she should have pointed out, fairly, that Astin didn't always dress like that, and that the sight of his tall form in riding-boots and rolled-up shirtsleeves had always wreaked madness in her thoughts—but the vision of it had already vanished, replaced by the sight of her own audacious fingers, brushing almost eagerly against the silken skin of Grimarr's bare torso. Which now, incredibly, seemed to show no discernible trace of where his injuries had been.

"My only wish in this, orc," Jule said, belatedly, "has been to avert your rage over my perceived betrayal of you. And that's *all.*"

Grimarr's smile was sudden and wolfish in the early morning light, and one of his big hands went down, and—Jule couldn't help a choked gasp—curved around his hard, leaking cock. And then that hand slid upwards, brazen and tantalizingly slow, milking out more of that slick liquid, making it spurt and dribble down over the smooth head of him.

"You lie, woman," he murmured, and maybe he was right, because Jule's eyes were trapped on the sight, his shameless muscled bulk tensing a little as his hand slid up again, more white liquid pooling down into his fingers. "You wish to fill your hungry womb with my seed."

Jule swallowed hard, searching uselessly for some kind of retort, and Grimarr laughed again, all thrilling rumbling heat in her belly. "Even as you still leak from your last use," he continued, and suddenly his other hand was there, *here*, cupping soft and suggestive against the curve of her. "You beg to be used again. You beg to be split wide again around my prick."

Jule could only seem to stare, far too distracted to argue, and even more so when—her breath cut off in her throat—he dropped those massive thighs wide open, insolent and flagrant. Showing her more rippling muscle, more dark hair, and the appallingly arousing sight of those huge, swollen bollocks, nestled deep between his legs.

"I will do this," he promised, and she could feel his fingers between her own legs pulling her a little apart, rubbing up into her wet, shivery heat. "But first, I wish you to taste me."

Taste him. Jule's breath choked again, even as her betraying body clenched against those delving fingers. She couldn't possibly, of course not, it was abominable, he was an *orc*—but her eyes were still watching, latched to that huge, shuddering hardness. To that huge hand still milking it, coating it with rivulets of slick sticky white.

"A true subject would wish to taste her king," purred his voice. "She would suckle him like a babe at a teat."

Oh *gods*, he was such an appalling impossible *beast*—and even more so when he moved a finger to touch that oozing smooth head, slipping it deliberate and familiar into that leaking slit. And then, oh *hell*, he brought his finger back up, now dripping with white wetness, and slid it, slow, between Jule's gasping, parted lips.

She should have shoved him away, should have said, *This is grotesque, immoral, wrong*—but she was still trapped in the sight of it, the heady sweet smell of it, the feel of that thick finger delving into her mouth. And *then*, sudden and shocking, flooding her, drowning out all the rest—was the taste. Thick, rich, sweet, warm, *wonderful*.

Jule's eyelids fluttered, her mouth suddenly sucking on that invading finger, and Grimarr gave another one of those low, rolling laughs. "This pleases you," he murmured, as he tugged the finger free, and went back down, pooling more of that thick sweetness onto it, and then bringing it back to Jule's mouth. "How do I taste, woman."

Jule should have lied, but her swirling tongue would have betrayed it, and her gaze was trapped in those watching, half-lidded eyes. "Sweet," she managed, around his finger. "Like honey."

"Good," Grimarr replied, and his hand came to curve around the back of her head, guiding her downwards, toward that huge, dripping heft of him. "Come. Drink. Fill your hungry belly with my seed."

There seemed to be no way to refuse, not with the source of that taste so close, smelling like that, looking like that, spilling out even more of its bounty, just for her. And with a hard, bracing breath, Jule drew herself closer, and—tasted him.

It was just the slightest touch of tongue, a single jolt of heady sweetness, but Grimarr gasped at it, his muscled body coiling under her, his thighs clamping close around hers. "Yes, woman," he whispered. "More."

More. Again there was no refusing, not even a thought of it, and Jule's tongue darted out again, tasting more of that impossible rich warmth. Bringing another gasp to Grimarr's mouth, and that was a strange twitch of pleasure on its own, enough to make her do it again. Letting her tongue linger a little more this time, feeling his silken hot hardness trembling against it.

"Yes," Grimarr breathed, and that strong hand clenched behind her head, pulling her closer. "Suckle me, woman. I shall give you a feast of good seed, and grow you fat and hale."

Jule glanced again at those eyes, and there was the distant awareness that she should protest that, point out that this was not in fact food, *something*—but that inexorable hand on her head only guided her closer, his other hand aiming that thick length toward her, those eyes on her intent, determined, in control—

And when that hard, oozing tip met her mouth, Jule could only gasp, and watch, and take it. Watch that big grey hand guiding that huge, delicious cock deeper, invading her mouth, spreading her lips wider and wider around it. Until they were stretched nearly as open as they could go, hot tight friction as he kept sinking deeper and deeper, finally settling the smooth leaking head of him deep against Jule's convulsing, almost-gagging throat.

"Yes," he whispered again, and even the sound of it made Jule groan around him, made him give a half-laugh, half-growl in reply. While that heft between her lips seemed to swell even further, shuddering from base to tip, leaking more hot sweetness down the back of Jule's throat.

"You please me, woman," he said, soft, and another glance at those eyes showed that he did look pleased, and perhaps even proud. "I have never before had a woman take me so deep."

So his other women *had* done this, then, and once again there was that strange, inexplicable surge of jealousy. Wondering what they had looked like, whether he had ever looked at them this way, with that pride and pleasure and perhaps even awe glimmering in his hungry black eyes.

And without at all meaning to, Jule held those eyes, took a breath—and then sucked on him, hard. Pulling him so deep into her throat that it brought water to her eyes, but it had been well worth it, because his muscled body flailed under her, his mouth letting out a rough, guttural groan as he pulsed out even more of that rich sweetness, in almost astonishing quantity, swarming her mouth with its pleasure.

Fuck, it was good. Better than cakes, than sweet wine, than fruit fresh from the vine. And suddenly there was no other thought but drinking more, filling her mouth and her belly, sucking harder and deeper, because she could already see how that brought out the most of it, dragging it up from those huge bollocks below.

And if one of her hands went to those bollocks, cupping against their swollen fullness, and the other to the huge base of that cock, curving only partway around it, Grimarr didn't comment, didn't complain. Only spread his thighs wider, the groans from his mouth almost steady now, his fingers carding deep and powerful into her hair.

"Yes, woman," he gasped, between groans, his eyes dark and hazy on hers. "Good woman. Yes."

It was utterly glorious, and quite possibly the most arousing thing Jule had done in her *life*, and time around them seemed to vanish, plucked away into thin air, even as the light through the room's small window kept brightening. Showing off every muscle and scar of Grimarr's huge taut body, every contortion of his face, every movement of his throat. While his cock just kept pouring, shuddering out its sweetness in a delicious heady stream, and Jule kept sucking, audibly now, making wet, slurping noises that should have been humiliating but only seemed to drive the hunger higher, harder, hotter.

When Grimarr's hands on her head finally pulled her up, she actually fought it, tried to reach him again—but his hold was firm, his eyes perhaps just as drunk and dazed as hers felt.

"You will be sick," he rumbled, soft, as one of his fingers came to trace almost reverently against her swollen, sore mouth. "And your womb yet hungers, does it not?"

Jule's only answer was a helpless groan, and those strong hands reached down, and dragged her up. Maneuvering her with surprising ease, spreading her legs wide over his hips, bringing her hot hungry wetness dangerously close to that slick, leaking prick.

"I wish you to ride me," he murmured, as one of those hands slipped down between her legs, spreading her apart with sure, strong fingers. "I wish to feel you sit deep upon my prick."

Jule couldn't even pretend to argue, and the first touch of that hard, slippery cockhead made her cry out, her body clenching tight, craving more. And when he raised his hips just slightly, easing that slick tip just a little deeper into her dripping-wet heat, she moaned and sputtered, her eyelids fluttering furiously, gods he felt so good, he had no right to feel so fucking *good*—

His eyes angled up to hers, from where they had been watching, very intently, to his cock nudging between her legs. "I yearn to see this, woman," he murmured. "I have long wished to know the joy of a woman seated full upon my prick. No other woman has done this in all my days."

Gods, Jule couldn't *think*, and here were the visions of other women doing this, trying to do this. And she could do better, of course she could, and she angled her hips, settled herself a little deeper upon him, her shaky hands steadying themselves on that scarred, silken chest.

"Yes, woman," he purred, and there was the weight of those big hands guiding her down, spreading her wider. "Suck me deep into you. Just as you sucked me into your throat."

Jule replied with a strangled groan, her body bearing down now, sinking with effort onto that hot driving pressure. Feeling herself being thrust apart, split in two, as that thick hot wetness shuddered out inside, oh *fuck.*

He kept pushing up, too, his black eyes rapt, greedy, intent on the sight. His huge cock, wedged halfway up inside her, driving deeper, slower, slower. Until it stopped entirely, not quite all the way up inside, and there was no way Jule could take him any deeper, not like this, she couldn't—

"More, woman," said Grimarr's heated voice, but Jule's head was shaking, saying no. She already had her full weight on him, he was already everywhere, filling her body her thoughts her world, gasps in her breath and stars to her eyes—

Grimarr's fingers were there again, gentle and warm between her legs, pulling her wider apart around his stuck, invading orc-prick. But there was no movement, no way, he'd have to fulfill his stupid fantasy somewhere else, with some other woman, and why did that feel so awful, what the *hell* was wrong with her?

"Woman," Grimarr's voice said, softer now, and when Jule blinked up, his eyes were here, solid, safe. Looking into her, touching deep inside, feeling almost as strong as that cock, bound tight between her legs.

"You please me," he whispered, and here were those big hands, cupping close and protective over her shuddering breasts. "You are ripe and rich and sweet. Your mouth and your womb are bright gifts to me from the gods."

The gods had a sick sense of humour, Jule rather felt, but the thought disappeared as swiftly as it came, replaced only by the feel of strong hands, stroking soft and warm at her peaked, too-sensitive nipples. "I long for you," he murmured. "I long to sire many strong, hale sons upon you. I long to see you flower with my seed."

Jule's mouth let out another helpless groan, her breasts arching into the touch of those hands. And in response she could feel that prick shuddering out more slick wet heat, perhaps slipping just a shade deeper inside her.

"Good woman," Grimarr breathed, and those hands slipped down to span her waist, to smooth against her bare hips. "Seat yourself full upon me. Teach yourself to welcome this gift."

The words were ridiculous, audacious, but the tone and the heat of them were far too strong to ignore, driving that pulsing hardness higher, deeper. So close now, his coarse hair tickling at hers, so tight and full and spread apart, he was everywhere, everything—

And with one last push, one last shout from Jule's mouth, he was there. Buried all the way inside her, stretching her taut around the huge base of him, pressing skin to skin, trapped.

"Fuck," Jule gasped, everything shaking, her body fighting the invasion even as it craved it, welcomed it. As Grimarr's breath gasped too, his heft flaring and pumping inside her, his long eyelashes fluttering over glazed hungry eyes.

"Yes," he breathed, his hands settling to her hips, tilting her a little backward, giving himself a better look. Seeing how there was nothing left to see, no sign of his engorged cock, only Jule's swollen, stretched-open body, taking it all inside. "You honour me, woman."

There was no replying, only Jule's ragged gasping breaths, only the feel of that invading heat shuddering out more thick liquid within her. And at the moment there was nothing left to do but rock against him, just enough to make herself cry out, to bring another rumbling gasp from Grimarr's corded throat.

"Yes," he said again. "Ride me, woman, and I shall fill you with good, strong seed. I shall fill you with my sons."

And surely it was just the mating-bond, but the promise of it still seemed to light up inside Jule's belly, burning away the last of the hesitation. Leaving only the frantic craving frenzy in its wake, the need to fuck him, to show him, to keep him here inside her. To prove to him that she could take him whole, she was the only woman who'd ever done it and now he would give her his seed, he would give her *sons*—

Their bodies were grinding in unison, Grimarr's hips canting up as Jule's came down, his hands on her pushing hard, making her meet him. And fuck it felt good, Jule's head her whole body arching backwards, that cock circling and filling inside, he would, he had to, holy fuck *almighty*—

His shout seemed to shake the room, his body curling up taut toward her, and she could feel his hardness inside her tense, and then fire. Spurting up into her like a flood, filling her full, even as Jule's own body finally wrenched, and froze, and then relented. Thundering out its release all around him with impossible, aching ecstasy, oh gods, oh fuck, *oh*.

When it finally faded again, Jule found herself sweaty, shivery, and still pinioned on a massive invading orc-prick. And escaping it would be—should be—the best plan, but that was where things had gone so wrong before, wasn't it? And when those big warm hands drew her down to lie against that slick warm chest, Jule didn't refuse, just let herself collapse into the strangely reassuring feel of his rising and falling breath, his heartbeat slowly thumping under her ear.

"Good woman," rumbled his voice, as those hands caressed slowly up and down her back. "My fair mate. This pleased me."

And it shouldn't matter, it didn't, but Jule still felt her body relaxing deeper into him, sinking into his solid heat. She'd pleased him, and made amends. She'd given him what they'd both wanted. She was tired, and sated, and *safe*.

"Sleep," that silken voice whispered, as strong arms circled around her, cocooning her in their safety. "I shall hold you."

It was all Jule had needed to hear, in this moment, so she closed her eyes, and let sleep come.

## 12

J ule woke to the brightness of early afternoon sunlight, and the feel of something cold around her ankles.

She leisurely yawned and rubbed her eyes, blinking blearily downwards—and then felt a shudder hurtle down her back. She was in Grimarr's bed, she was naked and alone, and she was—*shackled*.

She sat up so fast the room spun, and she put her suddenly shaky hands to the cold steel on her ankles. Yes, they were full-on shackles, orc-made, their thick unpolished cuffs clamped close and hard around her anklebones. The steel chain connecting the two shackles was perhaps the length of Jule's forearm, enough to allow her to take small steps, if not for— the shudder rippled down her back again—the fact that it was linked to a second chain, one that was clamped firmly to the steel bedpost.

Jule stared at it for what felt like an age, while her heartbeat seemed to hammer more wildly with every breath she took. Where was Grimarr? Why had he shackled her? Had he—had he *planned* to do this when he'd told her to sleep? When he'd said he would hold her?

A frantic glance around the room showed that Grimarr's clothes were gone—both the dirty ones, and the clean ones Baldr had brought—and so were the comb, the bowl of water, the oil. The only things still here were Jule's shift and dress, still draped on the end of the bed where she'd left them, and the chamber-pot, which—the first low flare of anger surged in her belly—had been moved close to the foot of the bed, clearly for her use.

And she did need to use it, curse the bastard, not least because she'd been left an utter mess, her lower half still sticky and sore, and drenched with his copious leavings. And how had Jule wanted that, how had she actually craved that, why in the gods' names did the sight and the smell of it still set her body clenching, the memories whirling through her head—

She made swift use of the chamber-pot, cleaning herself up as well as she could without water or a rag, and then snatched for her clothes, yanking them on over her head. And then sat on the side of the bed, folded her hands tightly together, and looked at the curtain across the door.

"Baldr," she said, her voice sounding thin, strained. "May I speak with you? Please?"

But there was no answer, no sign of movement, and Jule fought down the rising panic, and took another shaky breath. "Baldr," she called, louder this time. "Are you there? Is anyone there? Hello?"

There was still silence, still no movement beyond the curtain, and Jule took one more heaving breath. "Help!" she hollered. "Baldr! Grimarr! Anyone?!"

Her only reply was more silence, feeling oppressive, empty, cold. Grimarr had shackled her, chained her to his bed, and left her alone. He'd said he was pleased with her, he'd pretended to be kind to her, they'd done what they'd done—and now this?

Jule's eyes had begun prickling, stupidly, her breath giving a sharp little sniff from her nose, and she shook her head, clenched her hands into tight fists. No. She knew better. Grimarr had manipulated her, lied to her, used her. Again. And what Jule had done last night—what she was doing now—was planning her revenge. She was watching, waiting, learning. Pretending. Making Grimarr think he was getting his way. And that was all.

It was enough to keep her eyes dry, enough to keep her sitting there, still and silent. Presumably not even Grimarr would intend for his mate to starve, so there had to be some kind of time limit on this, some planned reappearance at some point. Didn't there?

The wait felt interminable, sitting there alone with nothing to do or look at, and the angle even prevented Jule from seeing out the window. Instead, she repeated her plans, over and over, fighting to burn them into her brain. She would wait. Watch. Learn the orcs, their mountain, their resources, their weaknesses. Learn the escape routes. And then run, and tell Astin's men everything she knew.

Distraction finally came, perhaps an hour later, in the form of Baldr, his hulking greenish body striding through the curtain. "Hello, woman," he said cheerfully. "Did you sleep well?"

Jule bit back the first retort that came to mind, and instead waved down at her ankles. "I've been shackled," she said, her voice betraying only perhaps a shade of her anger. "To a bed."

Baldr's eyes avoided hers, suddenly, and he went to the bedpost, where the chain was clamped. He'd pulled out some kind of tool, not unlike a key, and stood there and fiddled with the chain until it snaked away, pooling toward the floor.

"There you are," he said, though he still wasn't meeting her eyes, perhaps because the shackles themselves were still very much present, binding Jule's ankles together with that too-short length of chain. "Come along, now."

He'd turned toward the door, and Jule stood on her

unsteady legs, and tried to follow—but even her first tentative step was too much, jerking her leg up short against the chain, and she lost her balance, and very nearly pitched straight into the wall.

Thankfully Baldr had spun around in time, catching her arm with a strong grip, and pulled her back upright again. "Small steps," he said brightly. "Perhaps best to use the wall to steady you."

The anger lurched again, but Jule choked it back, and obediently took small, shuffling steps as she followed Baldr out of the room. Back into the dark corridor, which swiftly became darker and darker, until Jule was staggering along in pitch blackness, holding one hand to the wall, and clinging to Baldr's solid arm with the other.

"Where are we going?" she asked, as Baldr nudged her around a corner, into more inscrutable blackness. "Outside?"

The word came out sounding undeniably hopeful, and Baldr gave an easy chuckle, as though even the idea was absurd. "No, woman," he said. "To the kitchen. You're to make us all a human meal, remember? And candles."

His voice sounded decidedly chipper at the prospect, and Jule blinked toward it in the blackness. A human meal. And candles. For *them*?

"Uh, Baldr," Jule said, moving one foot too far and very nearly tripping, "I said I would do those things for *Grimarr*. Not *all* of you."

There was an instant's quiet ahead of her, and Jule could almost feel Baldr's attention on her in the dark. "No, woman. You betrayed all of us last night when you shouted to warn those men. Therefore, you must make amends to us all."

What? "Grimarr absolutely did *not* specify that," Jule countered. "And I clearly meant for it to apply only to him. As if I would lie you *all* down and worship you as kings?!"

She could hear a funny little growl from Baldr's throat, and too late she realized that that was probably an insult, as so many things were with these blasted orcs. "Of course that part was meant only for your mate," Baldr said back, his voice curt. "But the rest is for all of us, and I assure you, it is what the captain expects. I would suggest you do as he wishes. For your sake."

*For your sake.* It felt like a threat—even *Baldr* was threatening her now?—and Jule once again blinked back that highly unwelcome prickling behind her eyes. She was faking this. Watching. Planning revenge.

After what felt like endless twists and turns in the darkness—despite her best efforts Jule was once again hopelessly lost—they entered a high, cavernous room that had to be the kitchen. There was a fire at one end of it, crackling in a large fireplace, and Jule gritted her teeth, and held her eyes on the light. She would do this. She would make the orcs their damned supper. It was another chance to learn, another possible advantage. Right?

There were two orcs already in the kitchen, working over a single long table, and around them the walls were lined with shelves and barrels—many of them her own cellar's barrels, she noted with misgiving—and there there was a steel contraption next to the open fireplace that looked like a large oven. There were also a variety of tools and cauldrons lying haphazardly about, and while the room seemed to lack any kind of proper organization, it was also not as filthy as Jule might have expected, without a single vermin in immediate view.

"So what am I to do?" she asked Baldr, glancing between him and the two unfamiliar orcs, who were now assessing them with narrow black eyes. "Just—start cooking?"

"Yes indeed," Baldr replied. "Gegnir is our Head Cook, and Narfi is his assistant. They will guide you."

Jule looked at the two orcs, and their staring unfriendly faces. "But," she said helplessly, "but how many do I need to cook for? And when does it need to be served? And what should I make, what do orcs even like to eat?!"

She could hear her own panic rising in her voice, but Baldr only waved again at the two staring orcs. "They will guide you," he said again. "And orcs like to eat everything. Human food is always a treat."

With that, he turned and trotted off, leaving Jule alone in this strange kitchen, with these strange orcs staring at her. And Jule knew very well that having an outsider in one's kitchen was often an insult, especially if said outsider was expected to make food better than one's own—so she squared her shoulders, and shuffled over to the orc Baldr had called Gegnir, the head cook. He was the older-looking of the two, with a reddish face, and grey-streaked hair that was pulled back into a tight, messy knot on his head.

"Hello," Jule said, with an attempt at a smile toward him, and then toward the other orc as well. "I'm Jule. Thank you for helping me."

Neither orc replied, only looked at her with unfriendly black eyes, and Jule took another breath. "I was wondering if you might kindly give me a tour, and explain how you do things here? I wish to work within your ways."

Gegnir gave a little grunt, but finally nodded, and waved Jule toward the nearest wall. And then began explaining, in a gravelly, heavily accented voice, where the various kinds of stores were kept, how the fire had to be kept always burning, how the stove had to be brought to a certain temperature before cooking.

"So what is the best way to manage this?" Jule asked him, once he'd finished his admittedly informative tour. "Maybe we could use some stores from my cellar—some root vegetables and pork, perhaps? We could prepare them the way humans usually do, and I could make pies for dessert, if you have some kind of filling?"

It would be a simple meal, but in Jule's experience males generally preferred simple meals, and she was gratified when Gegnir gave a curt nod, and asked how best to season the pork. And soon the three of them were standing in a row at the long table, Gegnir pounding and marinating the meat, Narfi chopping vegetables, and Jule with several sacks of flour from her own stores, a barrel of sweetened berries that had clearly been stolen from somewhere, and an unnerving pile of something like two dozen pie-plates.

"How many orcs do you usually feed?" Jule asked Narfi, who was closest beside her, as she began kneading her pie-dough. "A lot, I take it?"

Narfi nodded, giving Jule a quick, shifty-eyed look. "We feed all the mountain's orcs the evening meal each day. Sometimes it is six tens, sometimes twenty."

Feeding up two two hundred orcs per day seemed like a lot of work for two cooks, and Jule eyed Narfi, who seemed rather smaller than most of the other orcs, with hair that was cropped short to his egg-shaped head. "How did you end up doing this work?" she asked. "Is it because you like cooking?"

Narfi's eyes narrowed, as if that was an inappropriate question, so Jule punched down at her dough, and tried again. "I mean, did my mate give you this job? Does he assign work according to his brothers' interests?"

Narfi visibly relaxed, and that was something to note, that just as with Baldr, he seemed to better accept her questions when framed around Grimarr. "Yes," he replied. "He asked for my choice. He knows I am weak in battle."

He said the words matter-of-factly, but not without regret, and Jule watched him out the corner of her eye as she rolled out her dough with a rusty rolling-pin Gegnir had found. "Does Grimarr have many orcs who are weak in battle?" she asked, perhaps too casually, because Narfi's eyes immediately went narrow again. "No," he snapped. "And I wish you would stop asking questions. You are here to work."

Jule obliged, but it made for a slow, tedious afternoon. Rolling out endless pies, while trying to surreptitiously watch what Gegnir and Narfi were doing, to make sure they prepared the food properly. They'd also begun talking to one another in the black-tongue, meaning that Jule had no clue what they were discussing, but they glanced at her often enough to suggest at least one of the subjects.

The room also became very hot, once they'd started with the oven, and as soon as the smell of frying meat began wafting through the air, a variety of orcs began to wander into the room. Making a haphazard queue, right in front of the damned table, chattering loudly and staring openly at Jule as her aching arms made pie after pie.

Grimarr was nowhere to be seen, not even when Narfi finally began serving the orcs what somehow, miraculously, seemed to be a halfway decent meal. One good enough for orcs, at least, judging by how many of them asked for more, only to be curtly told by Gegnir that they had to go back to the end of the line.

It meant that the line seemed never ending, the work never ending, and as the hours passed, the shackles around Jule's ankles felt heavier and heavier. She kept trying to pay attention, to count the total number of orcs, to pick out names and roles, and to greet the watching faces with smiles and deference rather than disgust. But so many of them were so very disgusting, a sea of staring black eyes and nonstop chattering voices, and gods Jule felt exhausted, and overwhelmed, and more and more trapped with every orc that passed.

She was on her forty-second pie, and had counted 137 total orcs, when her head snapped up, her eyes focusing at the door. Because—she gripped hard at her rolling-pin—there was Grimarr. Striding into the room with Baldr and a few other orcs, talking and laughing together, and the sight of him there, wearing a clean tunic, with his hair still neatly in the braid she'd made, sent a hungry, involuntary clench to Jule's groin, and set alarm-bells ringing in her head. No. No. He'd lied and manipulated her. *Shackled* her. She would have her revenge.

She forced her eyes downwards, focusing on her pie, and ignored the too-sharp awareness of Grimarr coming closer, and closer. Waiting his place in the line with the others, part of her grudgingly noted, even as the other part of her cursed his foul presence, and carefully considered whether poisoning the orcs' suppers could be a legitimate future possibility.

"Woman," Grimarr's voice said, once he was near enough to speak, and Jule gave a brief glance up, and then down again. Twitching despite herself at the sight of his stupid face, she did *not* like his face, he was thoroughly, breathtakingly hideous—

He didn't speak again, though she could feel his eyes on her as she worked, as her strangely shaky hands rolled out another pie. And why didn't he say something else, maybe *I'm sorry I left you alone and shackled*, or *thank you for sharing your food with me and my hundred friends*—but manipulative males like him never apologized until they were at risk of losing what they wanted, and Grimarr was getting exactly what he wanted right now, wasn't he?

"You neglected to inform me," Jule said finally, using excessive force with her rolling-pin, "that I would be making supper for well over a hundred orcs, rather than just yourself."

Grimarr made a sound like a snort, barely audible in the surrounding din. "You offered this, woman," he said. "You betrayed my brothers to the men who attacked our home. You must make amends."

The anger rankled, and Jule shot him a black, furious look. "Is being left alone and shackled in your bed also part of my amends, too? Or is that just how you orcs treat your mates?"

The orcs immediately around them had gone quiet, clearly

listening in to every word, and Grimarr's eyes on her were wary, disapproving. "Last night, you showed yourself as an enemy. I must treat you as such."

Jule's mouth gave a bitter laugh, her hands all but hurling her flattened dough into the nearest pie-plate. "You mean to say that wasn't what you were already doing before?" she demanded. "What with the threats, and the *kidnapping* me, and trapping me here in this *prison*?"

She could hear Grimarr's breath, hissing out of his mouth, and he leaned over the narrow table toward her. "Do not speak to me thus, woman," he said. "I will not warn you again. You agreed to yield."

The unease lurched up sharp in Jule's throat, but the cold rage was still stronger, still drowning all sense under its wronged righteous exhausted fury. "Of course I did," she snapped. "I was under threat of being gagged, and starved, and kept from the sun for the rest of my days! Do you think I would ever voluntarily *choose* to obey you, or stay trapped in this hell-hole? Let alone help you monsters *reproduce*?!"

The words rang through the room, over the sound of the rapidly quieting voices all around, and perhaps that was precisely what Jule wanted. To openly declare that she wasn't beaten, she wasn't their servant, she was better than this, she was a *lady*...

"You shall not speak of my brothers thus," Grimarr said, his voice deep, dangerous. "You will beg for our mercy, woman. Now."

He stood there, looming, waiting, but the anger kept shouting in Jule's head, wrenching with pain and misery. How dare this orc make her apologize, she was toiling away in his kitchen like a *servant*, he'd put her in gods-damned *shackles*—

"I won't," Jule heard herself say, her eyes challenging on his. "It's all true, you're all brutal *beasts*, I mean, just look at what you're doing to me right now, I'm working shackled to serve you supper from my own stolen goods, under threat of my own *starvation*—"

But Grimarr's eyes suddenly flashed with rage, and without warning he was here, leaning too close over the table. And one of his hands had come to grip painfully to Jule's shoulder, the sharp claws pressing against her skin, his breath hot in her face.

"I shall not starve you," he said, his voice cold, menacing. "But I shall do this, woman. I shall burn your clothes. I shall forbid you to hide yourself. I shall make you walk bare among my brothers for the rest of your days."

*What?!* He wouldn't, or would he, but his other hand had already come to the neckline of Jule's dress, his claws deadly and sharp. And one claw was pulling down on the filthy fabric, tugging hard, almost enough to tear.

"I shall plough you before their eyes," Grimarr continued, even lower. "I shall make you scream and leak and spurt for them. I shall make them laugh."

Jule shuddered so hard she nearly staggered, and she searched desperately around at the watching, listening mass of orcs, her heart suddenly hammering with sheer shouting terror. "What?" she breathed. "No. You can't."

Grimarr's shadowed eyes were grim, hard, triumphant. "I can," he said. "I will. If you *dare* speak thus to me again, one more time, I will."

Jule felt herself sagging backwards, her eyes dropping to her flour-covered hands, because he had her, the bastard. Once again, this conniving swine was using her weakness to manipulate her, and why had she ever even let on that any of it mattered? How had she so rapidly lost sight of her plans? Her revenge?

"Of course, sire," she said, finally, to the table. "I shall do as you wish."

He made a noise like a satisfied grunt, and the listening orcs slowly began talking again, their voices rising back into cacophony. But not loud enough to overpower the pounding in Jule's head, the curdling miserable fear. Grimarr lied. Grimarr threatened. Grimarr was a monster.

Finally she began rolling out pies again, though she worked slower now, shaky and exhausted and miserable. Fighting not to notice, or care, as Grimarr turned away, with a full plate of her food in his hand, and walked out of the room, and didn't look back.

## 13

T he rest of the evening passed in a haze of cleaning, and exhaustion, and silence.

Jule had angered the orcs again, she realized, to the point that Gegnir and Narfi didn't meet her eyes, or speak. Only ignored her entirely as they began tidying up, washing endless dishes in a stone basin of filthy water, and sweeping up the mess of crumbs from the tables and floors.

Jule tried to help, though it was made clear that her help was entirely unwelcome, and finally she stopped altogether, and sank down against one of her barrels, her head to her knees. She was exhausted, unusually so, and all but covered in flour, and she just wanted to sleep, to escape, to be alone.

It wasn't to be, of course, because after an all-too-brief amount of time, there was the sound of someone approaching. And when Jule glanced up through unnervingly wet eyes there was Gegnir, holding a large roll of something that looked suspiciously like Jule's own beeswax, from her own cellar.

"Next, woman," Gegnir said in his gravelly voice, "you are to make candles."

Jule stared blankly at him, before barking out a sound not

unlike a laugh. "You expect me to make candles *now*?" she asked, the incredulity too clear in her voice. "Sorry, but I can't. I'm too tired. I'll do it tomorrow."

"It is the captain's wish," Gegnir insisted, and beneath Jule's exhaustion the anger flared up again, so visceral it was almost painful.

"I of course wish to honour Grimarr's wishes," she gritted out, "but if I try to make candles right now, I'll probably fall straight into the pot of hot wax, and die."

That shut Gegnir up, and sent him scurrying away, and out the door. A development which should have been welcome, but only served to bring up more dread in Jule's belly, more misery in her thoughts. Where was he going? To tattle on her? To Grimarr, who would burn her clothes?

She was soon spared any further conjecture by the inevitable sight of Grimarr himself, striding into the room, with Gegnir at his heels. And once again—Jule shrank back toward the barrel—Grimarr looked furious.

"What is this, woman," he demanded at her. "I am told you again refuse to keep your word. And instead, you vow to bring yourself to harm to escape me?!"

Gods, Jule felt broken, raw, but she somehow forced her head up, made herself meet those angry black eyes. "I didn't refuse," she said tiredly. "I said I would do it tomorrow. Candle-making can be dangerous, and I'm exhausted, and therefore I'm liable to make stupid mistakes, which is all I meant."

There was a low growl from Grimarr's throat, his hands in huge fists at his sides, his big bulk looming far too close. "You say far too much, woman," he hissed. "And after, you turn and say you mean these things in the other way. This angers me. This brings shame upon me before my brothers."

Jule brought shame upon him. And perhaps this was where Grimarr would punish her. Perhaps now he would make good on his threats to burn her filthy clothes, and degrade her, while Gegnir and Narfi watched, and laughed.

A full-on shudder ran down Jule's back, her eyes squeezing shut, and she distantly noted that her heart was racing dangerously, her breath coming far too fast and shallow. Making her head feel light, the room slowly starting to spin, what would Grimarr do if she went into hysterics, if she collapsed at his feet, if she begged, bartered, made promises, anything—

And without warning, without mercy, here was the memory of Astin, surging vivid and unrelenting into her thoughts. His tall, handsome form looming close and powerful over her, his horsewhip tight in hand. His blue eyes watching impassively as she'd begged and bartered and sobbed—

But in the end, it had changed nothing. Astin had still done what he'd meant to do, but perhaps with even more vindication, more enjoyment, than before. And afterwards, when he'd come to Jule in bed, and held her bandaged body against his, whispering promises to hire the best healers in the realm, she'd even begged his forgiveness, while he'd smiled with the supreme satisfaction of one who had done nothing wrong.

And perhaps Jule had been seeing this orc as separate from Astin, different from Astin—when in truth, they were very much alike. And if Jule could have reversed time, and gone back to that horrible day with Astin, she would have refused to beg, or sob, or plead. Instead, she would have given him nothing. Only a distant, indifferent emptiness.

It was something she'd worked on afterwards, like a mask taken on and off, with varying degrees of success. But it had helped with Astin, and thank the gods, it was here now, enough to make her eyes look up, past Grimarr's hideous face, to the flickering stone wall beyond.

"Of course, sire," she said, her voice carefully, politely distant. "I await your punishment."

She could almost feel Grimarr's big body twitching, stepping closer. "You will look at me when you speak to me," he growled, so Jule did, keeping her eyes unfocused as she blinked at his blurry, still-hideous face.

"Of course," she said again. "As you wish, sire."

Grimarr replied with another growl, and his hand circled tight around Jule's arm, dragging her up, and then toward the door. Making her exhausted, shackled feet slip and stagger, but he didn't slow down, didn't even look.

The maze of black corridors passed in a haze, Jule's thoughts entirely focused on staying upright, on keeping her thoughts distant and cool. She would give him nothing. She would bide her time, and have her revenge.

Even so, when Grimarr finally dragged her back into his room, Jule's eyes caught on that blessed little window, and its tiny patch of moonlight. Strong enough that she wrenched herself away from him, and half-shuffled, half-staggered toward it, and put her hands out into it, into real air and real light, oh gods.

The scent of fresh cool air in her lungs only seemed to harden her mask, her resolve. And when she felt Grimarr's big body walk up behind her, his heavy, warm hand coming to rest on her shoulder, Jule didn't turn, didn't even flinch.

"Woman," he said. "I wish you to look at me."

Of course he did, because that was no doubt how his orc-bond worked best, but Jule managed to keep her eyes carefully blank as she again turned, and looked. Seeing not him, but only blurry shadow, smelling too strong of musk and sweetness.

And that was another way he did it, with the smell, so Jule breathed carefully out her mouth, keeping her breaths short and faint. Not speaking, or allowing any expression onto her face, because that was just more fodder for his fucked-up, self-serving game.

"You do not look at me," his voice finally said, rumbling

into the silence, and Jule shook her head, blinking at his unfocused face. "Of course I look at you, sire."

"You do not," he snapped back. "And I do not wish you to call me *sire.*"

Jule fought back the sudden urge to scream at him, and instead gave her blandest smile. "Of course. What is your preference, then."

There was an instant's silence, a tilting of that huge head, almost as if he were considering it. "You may call me Grimarr," he said. "Or mate."

*Mate.* Jule's mouth gave a bitter little grimace, but she forced it back into the bland, distant smile. "Of course," she said again. "Mate."

She managed to make it sound flippant, somehow, a note that Grimarr didn't miss, judging by the sound of yet another growl from his throat. "You will speak to me with honour, woman. As I am due."

The threat was there in his voice, as real as Astin's whip—he might burn her clothes, take her in front of his friends—and another hard, unwilling shudder ran down Jule's back. "Forgive me, Grimarr," she said woodenly. "I shall seek to improve."

His blurry face contorted, with meaning that Jule couldn't identify. "You again speak words you do not mean, woman. They are empty of truth."

Jule's stomach flipped in her gut—he wasn't supposed to pinpoint that so quickly—and without meaning to, she took a deep, full breath. Filling her nostrils and her thoughts with the scent of him, with that musky warm sweetness, low and hungry and close.

"I wish you to speak with your actions, woman," he said, his voice flat, sure of itself. "I wish you to offer amends to me, as you did last night."

Jule's thoughts twitched, going straight to those mouthwatering memories, with that swollen hardness leaking into her mouth, driving up between her legs. And the hunger was still there, still so close, and why couldn't she escape this, how was this craving still so strong?

"Why do you wish this," she said, unsteadily, as her eyes dropped to those broad shoulders, and then lower, to the bulge already visible at his groin. "If I bring you such grief and displeasure. If even a whole day of my labour on your behalf, without being offered so much as a meal or a bath, serves only to shame you."

The words were a betrayal of her supposed indifference, but Grimarr again seemed to consider them, his blurry black eyes feeling intent enough to be a touch. "I wish to forget the shame," he said finally. "I wish to think of your hunger for me, and the joy you bring me."

Well. At least that sounded like a truthful answer, because it admitted that it was all about him, after all. And it was enough, perhaps, to make Jule lift her head, and attempt a mockery of a smile.

"Of course, Grimarr," she heard herself say. "I shall do whatever you wish."

## 14

J ule had never known that something could feel so good, and yet so empty.

Because objectively, repeating what she'd done the night before, following the exact same course, felt wonderful. Like she was being swarmed with pleasure, like Grimarr's delectable body leaked pure magic, his rumbling gasping breath the only sound in the world.

And Jule was so hungry, suddenly, after not eating a single bite of food all day, and perhaps there was some truth to his comment the night before about the feeding, after all. Because once she'd finished sucking him she did feel full, and sated, and when she was finally riding him, feeling him shudder her with hunger from the inside out, it was again ecstasy unlike anything she'd ever felt with Astin, with any man, ever.

But when she finally pulled herself off him, ignoring the requisite mess, it was to the realization that beyond her gasps, she hadn't said a single word the entire time, and neither had Grimarr. That his eyes watching her had gone darker and stranger, and now—Jule swallowed hard, and wiped at her wet face—they were looking at her with something not unlike disappointment, or regret.

Jule couldn't bear to see it, to endure any more of his unmet unattainable expectations, and she moved herself away from him, dropping her body to the side, facing toward the wall. Fighting to keep her breaths steady, to keep more of the wetness from leaking out her eyes.

She could feel that big body shifting behind her, still much too close. And then—she flinched—there was the feel of a warm hand touching her ankle, and carefully turning the cold shackle around it.

He'd yanked off the chain binding her ankles earlier in this—once he'd realized that it actually prevented her from properly riding him—and now she could feel the shackle's cuff finally snapping open, exposing her rubbed-raw ankle to the cool air.

Grimarr's hands lingered on her foot, and she could hear his breath, a slow quiet exhale. "This hurt you," he said, into the silence. "You ought to have said this to me."

The threat of his promised punishment surged sudden and sickening in Jule's thoughts, and she fought for the mask, for the distance. "Forgive me, Grimarr," she said, though her voice wavered. "I shall seek to improve."

In reply he gave a hard growl behind her, but Jule didn't look, or move. Just waited while he lifted her other ankle, and did the same, snapping the cuff off with surprisingly gentle fingers.

There was the sound of the cuffs clanking on the stone floor, and then silence. Broken only by the quiet sniffles of Jule's unsteady, ragged breaths, coming out too hard through her nose.

"This did not please you," Grimarr said finally, quietly. "You did not truly wish for this."

Jule could no longer seem to speak, so she remained silent. Blinking at the wall in the dim light, fighting and failing to control the erratic pace of her breath.

"I ought not to have done this," he said now, his voice low and strained, enough that it almost sounded like he meant it. "I have never done this to a woman."

It sounded unnervingly close to an apology, something Astin would never have done, but maybe he was seeking some kind of validation, or forgiveness? Reassurance that he could freely proceed and punish her, after all? Whatever it was, Jule was not providing it, and she kept blinking at the wall, saying nothing.

She could hear Grimarr's breath again, a heavy long sigh, and then felt him moving, getting off the bed. And despite everything Jule didn't want him to go, and that was shamefully ridiculous, leaving was another thing Astin had always done, just another way to manipulate and control.

"Wait for me here," he said. "I shall return."

It wasn't like Jule had a choice, since there were sure to be more orcs in the corridor, and she squeezed her eyes shut, pulled in deep breaths. She would wait, and wear her mask, and have her revenge. She would.

Grimarr returned quickly, and with him was the unexpected sound of sloshing water. "You said that you have not bathed," his voice said behind her, still oddly strained. "I wish to wash you."

Jule still said nothing, and could hear him moving closer, then a soft thunk as he perhaps set a basin nearby. And now—her whole body flinched—there was the feel of a damp cloth touching her, sliding cool and gentle down her back.

"If you wish me to stop," Grimarr's low voice said, "I wish you will say this."

Jule didn't say anything, didn't turn to look at him, just

remained still and let him do what he wanted, his hand smoothing the cloth gently, carefully over her skin. He felt guilty, perhaps, and so he was trying to assuage his guilt, for his own benefit. It changed nothing.

"I mean this when I ask you to speak truth, woman," he continued, his cloth sliding further down, over the curve of her bare arse. "I do not wish to take what is not freely given. With this, or aught else."

The anger was suddenly hot and close, charging up with startling power, and Jule couldn't stop her mouth from giving a hard, brittle laugh. "You might as well stop lying to yourself, orc," her wavering voice said. "Once you shackle and imprison and starve a woman, and then publicly threaten her with exposure and humiliation, nothing afterwards is freely given, is it?"

The hand that had been washing her abruptly snatched away, and she could feel those eyes, intent and prickling on her back. "You chose to come to our home, woman," he said. "You chose to do this today. You wished for this. Just as you have wished for my touch, and my prick."

And this was so damn typical too, making as though this was all Jule's doing. And she needed to keep her distance, remember the whip, she was biding her time, getting revenge, and that was all...

"Of course," Jule said, her voice weary, blank. "Whatever you say, Grimarr. I wished for this. I wished to leave my comfortable life as a lady, with my lovely servants and horses, to come here to this hovel and be berated and mocked and threatened by orcs."

She was already saying too much, rising to his bait, and she gritted her teeth together, breathed out hard through her nose. "I mean," she said, "forgive me, Grimarr. I shall seek to improve."

There was no mistaking his growl this time, low and

guttural behind her. "I said, I wish you to speak truth to me, woman."

The anger lurched again, swarming Jule with a sharp scrabbling desperation, and her body suddenly snapped up, and whirled around to face him. "You don't want my truth, or my questions, you just want my silence and my *lies!*" she shouted, to those watching black eyes. "Just as you don't want a mate, you want a *servant!* You want a mindless *puppet* that you can control and manipulate and *use* at your whim!"

Those eyes kept staring at her, the wet cloth slack in his fingers, and she saw him blink, once. "This is not what I wish," he said. "You judge me harshly, woman."

Jule's hands briefly went to cover her face, her mouth letting out a sound not unlike a strangled scream. "Can you even *hear* yourself, orc?" she demanded. "You really think I'm judging you harshly? Do you not recall, down while I was making supper for you and your hundred friends, how you publicly threatened to burn my clothes and *force* me while they *laughed?*"

Grimarr's eyes blinked again, and Jule leapt to her feet, not caring if she was still naked and filthy, just needing to get away, as far from him as possible. "*You* are the one who brings shame to *me*, orc," she gasped. "And to all your fellow orcs as well. You have shown me that in comparison to you, my husband Lord Norr, who I believed to be one of the cruelest men I have ever known, was in fact a patient and generous soul. And if ever presented with the choice"—she gulped in a breath, glared at those eyes—"I will immediately reject you, and run back to Norr Manor, and thank the *gods* for my blessed good fortune!"

She was fully hollering at the end, finally abandoning all semblance of control, of composure, of distance. Of not caring, pretending that it didn't hurt, because it did, so much, for reasons that she couldn't understand or explain. And hurting this orc in return was the only recourse left, and she was almost gratified at that look on his face, distaste and unease and perhaps even pain.

"I will ride Lord Norr's prick," Jule said, promised, even as she flinched at the image, fought to shove it back. "I will tell him he's the best fuck I've ever had. I'll drink his seed and use it to make a toast to the gods in his favour. I'll get on my knees and beg and *plead* with him to finally give me his son."

That seemed to alight something new in Grimarr's black eyes, so Jule kept at it, striding closer to his still-naked bulk. "I won't have your sons, orc," she breathed. "I will never, *ever* have your sons. And if I do, if your constant swiving ever makes such a disgusting travesty inside me, I'll—"

Grimarr's whole body lurched toward her, and with alarming, horrifying speed he clamped his huge hand over her mouth. So tight and close that Jule couldn't breathe, and she flailed and kicked under him, trying to bite and scream at him, because it didn't matter now, it didn't...

"Stop," Grimarr's voice bellowed in her ear. "STOP!"

It was so loud the room rang, the teeth rattling inside Jule's mouth. "You will not say such things," Grimarr gasped, and Jule could feel his chest rising and falling against her, his fingers trembling oddly against her lips. "You must not. I beg you this."

He looked desperate, he felt desperate against her, and Jule felt just the same, her body still twitching, trapped under his huge hands, trapped in those strange pleading eyes.

"You must not say this," he whispered. "Not about our son."

His huge hand had dropped from her mouth, and if Jule had been able to find air, she might have breathed again. But there was nothing there, nothing at all left in the space between them, because that hand had gone to her belly. Spreading wide, flat, protective against it, while an awful, terrible understanding seemed to pierce Jule straight in the heart.

"*What*?" she choked out. "No. No. You're lying. It hasn't even been a week, there's no possible way—"

But there was, the look in his eyes proved it, and Jule felt her legs slowly crumple beneath her, while the room finally filled with the sound of her sobs.

## 15

Jule was supposed to be barren.

That was the one thought, the one truth, that kept rising and rising, breaking through her desperate horrified misery. It was supposed to be decided. Done. An utter impossibility.

And yes, Grimarr had said things, and under the orc-bond's spell, Jule had found those things alluring, or perhaps arousing. Never an actual possible reality, not really, because it had been *years* with Astin, years and years of nothing but disappointment.

"It can't be true," Jule gasped, between sobs, at those unreadable black eyes. "Not after a *week*. You're lying."

"I do not lie," Grimarr replied, his voice hard and flat. "Orcs know this truth before women do. Your scent betrays it."

Jule refused to believe it, refused to listen, and finally Grimarr threw her shift toward her, and reached for his own trousers. And once they'd both dressed he stalked for the door, and reappeared an instant later, dragging Baldr behind him. And Baldr, after giving a series of uneasy glances between them, leaned toward Jule, took a long inhale, and nodded.

"The captain speaks truth, woman," he said. "Your son's scent is upon you. It is faint, but undeniable."

*Undeniable.* It was a shocking word, a shocking thought, and a loud, guttural wail rose from Jule's throat. How in the gods' names would she have her revenge if she was pregnant, if there was an orc-son, what the hell would she do with it, how would she ever escape—

Baldr had leaned toward Grimarr, murmuring something in the black-tongue, and after an instant's hesitation, Grimarr backed toward the door, his eyes shuttered and distant. "I shall return," he said. "When you wish for me."

*When.* Such a presumptuous infuriating bastard—that bastard was the *father* of her *child*?!—and Jule's mouth made a sound that was half-growl, half-scream. And finally Grimarr did leave, thank the gods, his repulsive form finally out of Jule's vision, but now he was inside her too, it couldn't be true, it *couldn't*—

Baldr's hand was on her arm, warm and perhaps almost friendly, and it tugged her toward the bed. And suddenly Jule was far too tired to resist, or to do anything but sink onto the bed, and cover her face with her hands, and keep sobbing into them.

She was trapped. Ruined. Doomed.

"Is it truly so terrible?" Baldr's quiet voice cut in, as he sat down beside her, the bed sagging a little under his weight. "To have a son?"

The sobs kept wringing from Jule's mouth, her hands trembling over her face, and beside her Baldr huffed a quiet, strange laugh. "It is because it is an orc-son," he said. "If it was a man-son, you would not weep so."

The unfairness of that brought Jule's head up, even as the wetness kept streaking down her cheeks. "You don't know that," she said, but the look on Baldr's face was taut, pained. "I do know this," he replied. "We orcs all know how our mothers truly felt about us."

Jule dug her palms into her eyes, and pulled in a shaky, ragged breath. "For your information, orc," she ground out, "mothers can love their children, while hating the circumstances that made them. And the fathers that made them."

She could feel Baldr's eyes on her, his weight shifting again on the bed. "You hate your son's father? Your own mate? But why?"

Oh *gods*, these *orcs*, and the lurching fury was enough to bring Jule to her feet, making a swift, unsteady circuit of the room. "How are you orcs so deliberately obtuse?!" she demanded. "Have you not *seen* how your beloved captain treats me? He is easily angered, he uses my weaknesses as weapons against me, he continually reads the worst into my words and actions. He insults me and embarrasses me and treats me like a prisoner and a *servant*!"

Baldr's eyes on her were unblinking, his big body unmoving, and Jule walked over to stare blankly at Grimarr's mocking tapestry, all raging orcs and human agony and death. "No child should live a life of this," she said toward it. "I do not want my son to learn to treat me like this."

Baldr remained silent and still, so Jule kept talking, perhaps more to herself now, or to those raging orcs before her eyes. "It was just the same with my husband. I wanted children so much, but perhaps it was a mercy that they never came. Astin would either have ruined them, or used them as more weapons against me."

There was the sound of the bed creaking behind her, of Baldr perhaps standing to his feet. "The captain I know would not use his children, or ruin them," his voice said. "He would cherish them."

Jule held her eyes on the tapestry, on the huge orc at the lead of all the rest, trampling bodies beneath his huge clawed feet. "The captain you know is not the one I have seen," she said wearily. "He has shown me very clearly how he treats those weaker than himself. And if he treats me this way, he will surely treat his children this way as well."

It was the truth, and somehow it seemed to twist Jule's misery, turning it into something more like determination. She was pregnant. She would have an orc-son. And her son's father was entirely unacceptable. She needed an escape.

"Baldr," she said, too quickly, glancing over her shoulder. "You were raised apart from your father, were you not? Do you know of any places, any possibilities, perhaps far away from here, where a woman may safely raise an orc-son? Away from both orcs and men?"

Baldr's black eyes blinked, and his mouth opened, and then closed again. "You said—you wished to return to Lord Norr."

What? Jule blinked back at him, and then realized he would have overheard her say that to Grimarr, when skulking about in the corridor. "Of course I don't want to return to Astin," she snapped at him. "Especially not with an orc child. Only the gods know what he would do to me. To both of us."

The words felt strange coming out her mouth, and Jule looked down at her flat belly, put a tentative hand over it. *Both of us*, she'd said, as though this—*scent*—inside her was a foregone conclusion, a soon-to-be-lived reality. Was it? Truly?

Her heartbeat seemed to skip erratically—gods knew what would happen, anything could happen—but her other hand had gone to widen beside the first, almost as though to protect, or embrace. Her son. An orc-son, yes, but still *hers*.

"Baldr?" she demanded, advancing a little toward him. "Do you know what I could do? You *must* know."

Baldr's eyes were darting between her and the curtained door, and he took a short step backwards. "I—should not speak," he said. "The captain—he would not wish you to raise his son elsewhere."

The determination surged up again, sudden and overpowering. "I do not want my son to be raised in this," Jule said, and she meant it. "I *will* run, Baldr, for his sake, if nothing else. And it is in your best interests to tell me where I can go, so I am not caught by humans, and my son needlessly *murdered*!"

The look on Baldr's face was undeniably fearful, and he took another step backwards. "The captain would follow you. He would bring you back."

Of course they were back to Grimarr, because of course he would have no compunctions about imprisoning the mother of his child, what else would Jule expect? However he would be obliged to give her food and sun and fresh air now, he would wish for the health of his son, and that gave Jule some power back, did it not? Had she not seen Grimarr's face, heard his words, when she'd so much as spoken ill of his son?

She was breathing hard, staring at Baldr's wide eyes, because yes, he knew it too. This was power. This was something women had over these orcs. This was the foundation on which Jule would build her escape, and her revenge.

"Then you may tell your captain," she said slowly, deliberately, "that if he *dares* to try and keep me here, I will personally ensure that his precious son is never born."

## 16

Jule knew her words were a threat. One of a blatant and provocative nature, sure to be ill received—but even she didn't anticipate the look of shocked betrayal on Baldr's face, or the sudden, heart-stopping appearance of a good half-dozen huge orcs, rushing into the room all at once.

The orcs growled and loomed over her, circling close around her, and where the hell had they even all come from? A few looked familiar—one of them was Drafli—and though Jule should have been terrified, she felt strangely distant, detached. Inured, perhaps, to the constant threat of these orcs, since there was no way they would hurt her now, not with their captain's child inside her.

There was some loud shouting black-tongue—Baldr, Jule distantly realized, as he shoved through the circle of orcs, elbowing particularly at Drafli before planting himself firmly by Jule's side. And then there was more shouting behind them, because—Jule felt her heartbeat stutter—of course, here was Grimarr, stalking through the doorway with pure fury in his eyes, his deep voice booming so loudly the floor seemed to shake under Jule's feet.

The orcs finally backed off, muttering and growling in black-tongue, giving dark looks over their shoulders as they slunk out the door, with Baldr close behind. Jule only gazed after them, realizing vaguely that the room had begun to sway, and somehow she managed to sink to the floor, to rest her dizzy head on her knees. Next Grimarr would yell, and threaten, but she would wear her mask, and ignore it all.

She had power now. She had one of their sons. And as much as she hated to admit it, her threat wasn't an empty one. She would spare her son entry into the world before she would raise him in a hell like this.

She waited for Grimarr's yelling, but it hadn't begun yet, even though Jule knew he was still there. She could smell that telltale scent of him, wafting through the room, and could even hear his breath, panting in and out.

"Well?" she said, raising her head only briefly toward the sound of him, the blurry sight of his bulk crouching on the floor before her, almost close enough to touch. "What do you choose, orc? Will you keep me here, and lose your son? Or vice versa?"

Grimarr made a sound much like a growl, and Jule felt herself give a grim smile as she looked up again. "Yes, go ahead and yell and threaten all you wish, I'm not going to change my—"

But then the words stopped, catching in Jule's throat, because Grimarr was—weeping. Staring at her with huge, miserable molten eyes, with streams of wetness streaking down his scarred grey cheeks. An orc, *weeping*.

It was an unsettling, unnerving sight, and Jule forced her eyes away from it, back down to her knees. "Your self-pitying tears aren't going to work on me, orc," she said. "I've made up my mind. I'm not going to tolerate you abusing me or my son."

Grimarr didn't speak, though his throat made another of those strange-sounding sobs, and a quick glance up showed him looking truly miserable, and wretched. The sight almost grotesque, somehow, and Jule squeezed her eyes shut, took a breath. No. It wasn't working. It wouldn't.

"You are right to say this, woman," his voice said, finally, so low it was almost a whisper. "I wish my own mother had said this."

He had never before mentioned his mother, and it was unexpected enough that Jule opened one eye to look at him. At where he was staring down at his huge hands, clenching and unclenching them as those tears kept streaking down his cheeks.

"I hear my father's voice in the words I speak to you," he said, just as quiet. "I hear the words he spoke to my mother. From him, I learned to speak to her thus also."

Jule swallowed, but didn't speak—she wasn't giving him a way out of this, no matter what he said—and she watched the tears drip from his face, down onto the stone floor. "I ought not to have said this today, about burning your clothes, or taking you before my brothers," his low voice continued. "This too I learned from my father. To search another for weakness, and use it to bring them shame in the eyes of others."

Jule kept watching, not speaking, and she saw those big shoulders rise, and fall. "This is good for an enemy," he said to the floor. "It is what I have done to Lord Norr, with you. But it is not good for a mate."

Jule heard herself take a breath, in and out—she still was *not* falling for this orc's seemingly appropriate words—but like always, the mention of Astin seemed to twist up a strange, lonely bitterness in her thoughts. "If you think I'm Lord Norr's weakness, orc," she snapped, before she could stop herself, "you're sadly mistaken."

Those liquid black eyes angled up to hers, twisting something deeper in Jule's belly. "You are not Lord Norr's weakness," he said, the words quiet but certain. "His weakness is pride. He thinks himself strong and virile and safe. When I take you from his house, and fill your empty womb with my son, I strike at his pride for all to see."

It was true, almost disturbingly so, and how odd was it that this orc, of all people, should have such insight into Astin's soul? Perhaps—Jule drew in another breath—it was that they were so much the same. Like knowing like.

"I too have weakness," Grimarr's voice continued. "And now you strike at mine, as I have struck at yours. I have begun this between us."

He sounded almost regretful, those shining black eyes steady and bare on hers, his big fingers now folding tight together. "You wield my son," he said. "You wield my wish for you to yield to me before my brothers. This flaunts you as my weakness. It risks all I have sacrificed."

Now this was familiar ground, making it all about him, and Jule clung to that, glared at those strangely appealing eyes. "Oh, what have you sacrificed, orc?" she demanded. "Your own power, your own pride? You poor *beast*."

Those eyes briefly narrowed at her, but then he looked away, his heavy jaw clenching. "I have given much more than this," he said. "I have sacrificed my kin, my own home, all my father's wealth. I have given my pain, and the pain and the lives of many of my brothers. I have given years of study and care and planning to make myself captain, and then to become the first captain in three hundred years to unite all five clans under him. I am the first to call all my brothers equal, no matter their skill with a blade, and to keep them housed and fed without bribe or favour. I have not lost one orc to cold or hunger. I will not."

Jule's eyes seemed caught on his face, on the strained rawness in his voice, and it occurred to her that she knew so very little about this orc, about his family or his past or his goals. About why.

"So what's your aim in this, then," she said, her voice flat. "If you want to keep your orcs alive so much, and you also provoke Astin to destroy you? That seems entirely counterproductive."

Grimarr's eyes glanced to hers again, and he shifted in his crouch, leaning a little closer. "It is not," he said. "It unites my brothers. It brings them hope and purpose. It gives them a home where they are safe. Where their women and sons could be safe."

There was still that strange fervency in his voice, in his eyes looking at her, and here was another realization, far too late. "So I'm not only a means to provoke Astin," Jule said slowly, "but also a personal demonstration to your orcs. A vision of the domestic bliss that could be theirs, if they stay in line, and follow you."

It was a strangely lowering thought, another way this cursed orc was using her for his own ends, but that cursed orc's mouth actually quirked, his big hand reaching out to briefly brush against Jule's knee. "You are a clever woman," he said. "You are indeed all this. But you are also my mate. I do not wish to lose you."

The words, that voice, that touch, were doing strange things inside her, and Jule closed her eyes, turned her head away. "You don't wish to lose your son, you mean."

That hand was on her thigh now, lingering with far too much presumption against the hem of her shift. "Ach, this is true," he said, his voice soft. "I have long wished for a son. But I have long wished also for a woman like you."

He was doing it again, using his voice and his touch and his smell, and Jule scooted herself away on the floor, and tried for a glare at those black eyes. "You barely know me, orc," she snapped. "The only part of me you actually care about is my body, and what it can do for you."

It was true—it had to be—but those eyes blinked again, looking almost wounded this time. "I care for you, woman," he said, his voice so quiet, so wronged. "Oft these past days I cannot breathe but for thoughts of you. I cannot look away when you are near. I care so much it is pain."

Jule's stomach plunged, and she made herself look away again, breathe in deep. "Then you will let me leave," she managed, "and raise our son elsewhere."

Grimarr growled, vibrating the air between them, and again here was his hand on her leg, lingering warm and gentle. "No," he said. "I have placed too much weight upon you to my brothers, and to Lord Norr. If you go, this will bring danger upon you, and upon our son. I will not be able to protect you."

"I don't care," Jule countered, still without looking at him. "I don't want to stay here."

That hand was still so gentle on her leg, sliding up slow, soft, while that scent of musky sweetness filtered through the air. "Is it only my angry words that have pushed you away?" he asked, quiet. "Or is it more than this?"

The fact that he was doing this, as he was saying these things, was preposterous enough to bring a true glare to Jule's eyes, true heat to her voice. "Of course it's more than this, orc," she hissed. "It's *everything* you've done."

His hand briefly stilled, his eyes dark and searching on hers. "I do not understand this," he said. "I have given you food and a guard and a room and a bed. I have asked my lieutenant to meet your every wish, and answer your every question. I have shared unmatched pleasures with you. I have given you my son. What more do you wish?"

Jule stared at him, and then dropped her eyes to where his hand was still halfway up her shift. "Are you serious?" she demanded. "Honestly, orc?"

His eyes had dropped too, following hers, and Jule trembled at the sight of his other hand, coming to join the first.

Sliding slow, heated, against her other thigh, and now—Jule's breath caught—spreading them gently apart.

"Yes," he murmured, as one of those hands moved to crumple her shift, guiding it upwards to expose her. Making Jule's heartbeat thump erratically, but she didn't try to close her legs, not even at the telltale feel of the seed he'd left there last time, now slipping out warm and slick before his eyes.

"What would a man give you," he murmured, his gaze lingering there, dark and hungry, "that I do not."

Jule's mouth barked out a high-pitched laugh, and Grimarr slid her shift up further, yanking it out from under her arse, and pulling it deftly off over her head. Meaning that Jule was sitting naked and spread-eagled on the floor, while an orc crouched between her legs, watching his thick seed slowly seeping out of her.

"Tell me," he murmured, his voice almost a purr as he leaned in and downwards, took a slow inhale. Making his eyes flutter, his lips part, a heated quiet rumble from his throat. "Please, woman."

For some reason Jule still wasn't arguing, wasn't even trying to resist this, and when Grimarr's head turned, his lips brushing hot and sensuous against her thigh, she actually gasped, her leg stuttering a little under his mouth. Tell him. What a man gave her, that he did not.

Those warm hands spread her legs a little further apart, giving him a sight that was thoroughly obscene, especially when—Jule gasped again—his big hand moved to press, soft but heavy, against her lower belly. Enough that she could feel the wet seed still inside spurting out faster, thicker, pooling below her onto the stone floor.

His eyes on it were hungry, satisfied, but his hand lingered there, fingers spreading wide, almost protective. On where— Jule felt her belly constrict—he'd filled her. Filled her with his seed, and now his son.

The thought should have been shocking, horrifying—perhaps it still was, somewhere—but here, like this, it was almost something else. With Grimarr's hand over it, his eyes intent upon it, his whole body kneeling bowed before it, almost as though in worship of it. Of her.

And as Jule stared, her breaths heaving through her chest, Grimarr lowered his mouth to her belly, and kissed it. His eyes closed now, his lashes dark against his cheeks, a bead of wetness streaking from his eye as he kissed her again, again, again.

The kisses were quiet, reverent, whispering of supplication, of devotion. Sliding a little downwards, into her coarse dark hair, tongue and lips and heat as those hands slid her legs apart wider, his body crouching closer between them.

He kept moving downwards, sending sparks and light all through Jule's skin, and the first thrilling touch of his lips against her spread-apart wetness made her groan aloud, her eyelids fluttering, her betraying legs spreading wider, begging for more.

Grimarr gave it, putting his tongue there, deep into his own mess. Licking and lapping at her now, sucking and slurping, clearly not caring in the slightest that he was drinking his own seed, and the truth of that seemed to ramp the pleasure even higher, tighter. Because at the moment, this audacious, obnoxious orc was entirely in Jule's thrall, slavering between her legs like the vicious beast he was, and she let herself lean back onto her elbows to watch, to drink in the sight of it. Of his weakness, his humiliation, his repentance.

The movement only seemed to encourage him, driving his long wicked tongue ever deeper. And a strange, twisted part of Jule wanted more, more, and she groaned aloud at the sight of her trembling thighs moving downward to close around that dark head, pushing it in closer, harder, hotter.

There was the distinct feel of a growl, rumbling straight

into her core, and Jule gasped again, and felt her hands skittering down to his head, pulling him even closer. Needing his face, his mouth, his tongue in her, craving it with a strange, lurid desperation. Her thighs clamped tight around his dark head, her fingers tangled deep in his hair, her breath panting and eyes staring as a twisted, fucked-up part of her shifted one of her legs, bringing it so that her foot was on the back of his head. Shoving him against her, needing him to drown in his worship of her, to plead her forgiveness and truly fucking *mean* it—

Her release came with a shout, a sharp surging blast of wild, pent-up pleasure. Wringing her out around his still-delving tongue, dragging him so tight her whole body was shaking with it, making him earn it, deserve it, fucking furious *hell*.

When the pleasure had filtered away again, leaving Jule feeling weak and rubbery all over, Grimarr was still there. Still kneeling, kissing her softly now, his entire face a shiny, slippery-looking mess. And though Jule should have been repulsed—what the *hell* had that meant, why the hell had she fallen for it—her hands were still in his silken hair, feeling the warmth of it, looking at the truth of it in those black eyes.

Whatever he had said, whatever he'd done, there was—something. Some long-lost part of him, perhaps, that had spoken truth. That meant this.

"You did not say, woman," Grimarr whispered, through those slick-wet lips. "What a man gives you, that I do not."

Both his hands had come to her belly again, fingers wide and reverent, and Jule blinked at the sight, and dragged in air. What had Astin given her, that Grimarr did not, why was it so difficult to think of this, to speak...

"Astin gave me little that you do not," she said finally, and perhaps it was a bitter relief to say that, to accept that Astin had in fact treated her no better than an orc. "But a good man—a good lord—would treat his new woman like a partner, or a friend. Or even a guest, if nothing else."

Those black eyes kept watching—listening—and Jule felt her belly rise and fall under the weight of those hands. "A good lord would show his woman her new home, and explain her place in it," she continued. "He would properly introduce her to his brothers. He would make his expectations clear, and inform her about his daily activities, and his priorities. He would eat with her and converse with her and spend time with her outside the bedroom. He would give her patience and consideration. He would provide clean clothes and rags and baths and even a proper fucking *latrine*."

Her voice had cracked, her eyes darting toward that still-present chamber-pot, and she could feel Grimarr rising a little, pulling up to his knees. He was still wearing his trousers, but no tunic, and in a swift, strange rush of movement, he was here. Or perhaps Jule was there, caught in those strong arms, tucked up close against that broad bare chest, against the slow thump of his heartbeat within it.

"I will alter this," he said, his voice quiet, perhaps even regretful. "I have not before had a woman who wished for these things. My own mother did not wish for these things. Apart from the mating, women wish for their orcs to leave them be."

Jule pulled away briefly, enough to glare up at those eyes. "No, those women were probably all too terrified of you to demand any better," she snapped back. "Luckily for you, I just have more experience than most in dealing with your particular brand of tyrant."

Grimarr's eyes blinked, but then his still-slick mouth twitched up into a slow, sharp-toothed smile. "Ach, this *is* luck," he murmured. "You shall teach me to please you, and I shall teach this to my brothers. Together, we shall bring back the women, and our sons."

*Together.* As if they were partners in this, rather than Jule being a prisoner who'd worked all day in shackles, and she looked away, gave a tight shake of her head. "That's a lovely sentiment, orc," she said thinly, "but I don't believe you. Why in the gods' names would I, after all the things you've said and done?"

She could feel his eyes on her, his chest filling and emptying against her, his big hand smoothing against her hair. "Then I shall make you another vow, woman," he said finally, quiet. "Grant me time to make amends to you. Forty days. And if I fail to please you in that time—then—I shall give you leave to run."

What? Jule's heartbeat skipped, and she lurched back to stare at his grim face. He looked serious, like he did mean it, but he wouldn't possibly truly mean it—could he?

"Rubbish, orc," she said. "Let me guess, you'll 'let me run' like you did last time, when I was too distracted to think properly? Or you'll dump me out on top of your mountain with shackles on, until I beg you to take me back so I don't freeze to death?"

Grimarr's heavy eyebrows furrowed, and he shook his head. "No," he said, and it sounded like he meant that, too. "I will—take you to the safest place I know. Or, if you wish, back to your home. To Lord Norr."

He spat out the last, the distaste almost palpable on his mouth, and Jule couldn't stop staring, blinking at those somber eyes. Back to her *home*, he'd said. "But," she managed, "but what about—"

She couldn't even say it, but her gaze had dropped to her waist, to Grimarr's big hand still spread protectively over it. His claws had come out at some point, black and sharp and deadly-looking, and Jule's finger absently traced against one, waiting. "Well?"

A glance up at his face showed it looking contorted, almost pained. "I would hope and beg that you will do all you can for our son," he said, thin. "I would pray that you will meet him and see his face. I would have you followed, and if you no longer wished for him, I would wish you to leave him for me. I would make no other claim on you beyond this."

The words sounded appallingly true, his face almost painfully bleak, enough that Jule had to look away. "How do I know you're not lying to me," she said. "Or just trying to keep me here until your orc-bond grows too strong to let me leave."

Grimarr let out a harsh breath, enough to flutter her hair. "I will not betray you in this. I give you my word as an orc, as a captain, as your mate. I swear this to you."

His hand over her belly was twitching—trembling, Jule realized—and she looked at those bleak black orc-eyes. Forty days, staying willingly with an orc. Forty days to watch, and wait, and learn. Forty days to plan her revenge, perhaps. To see what Astin would do next.

And it wasn't as if Grimarr was about to just let her escape anyway, was it? And even if she did escape, would she easily find human help nearby? Would this not be far safer for her, and for—her eyes cast down again, to Grimarr's huge hand on her waist—for whatever came next?

"Very well, orc," she said, whispered, to that hand. "Forty days. And if you do betray me on this"—she glanced up to glare at his face—"I assure you, you will live to regret it."

That hand clenched against her belly, knowing far too well her meaning, but his other hand pulled her closer into his arms, into his warm, strong heat. "It will not come to this," he said firmly. "I will show you. There shall be no regret."

"Rubbish, you great prick," Jule snapped back, but it came out muffled, against the warmth of his chest. And in reply he gave a quiet, rolling chuckle, rumbling deep into her, while those arms pulled her tighter, warmer, safe.

"Speak all you wish, woman," he said. "You will see."

# 17

When Jule awoke the next morning, she was once again naked in Grimarr's bed. But her legs were unshackled, there was a scratchy blanket covering her, and beside her on the bed sat Grimarr himself, giving her a wide, slightly alarming smile.

"You wake," he said, with satisfaction. "I have brought you gifts."

*Gifts.* Jule rubbed her bleary eyes and sat up, not missing how Grimarr was again wearing trousers but no tunic this morning. And how his big hand had been resting on her thigh over the blanket, and now slid up to briefly skim, not inconspicuously, against her belly. Still flat, for now, but...

"Clothes," Grimarr said, as his other hand thrust a pile of fabric into Jule's lap. "Washed. Clean."

Clean clothes? Jule couldn't deny the spark of interest as she picked up the topmost item, something made of grey linen—but then she blinked, both at it, and at Grimarr.

"This is a man's tunic," she said. "And"—she grasped at the other item—"men's trousers."

"Yes," Grimarr replied, his brow furrowing. "Clothes. Clean."

Of course, Jule thought darkly, orcs would have no conception of civilized dress, and she shot a brief, helpless look toward where her clothes were—or rather, had been—hanging on the end of the bed. "Where did you take my dress? And my shift?"

"Washing," Grimarr said, still with that frown, though perhaps more confused than annoyed. "You wished for clean."

He had a point, Jule supposed, and she sighed as she picked up the tunic again, and inspected it. It was well made, clearly intended for a smaller man, and indeed smelled clean, its only imperfection a neat little tear in the front. A tear which—Jule pulled it closer, eyed it with slowly deepening revulsion—was new and sheer at the edges, like it had been recently made by a slim, sharpened blade.

"These are clothes from the men you killed the other night?" she said, her voice cracking. "You took these off those dead men's *corpses*?"

"Yes," Grimarr said. "They are spoils of battle, bravely won."

Jule couldn't help a shudder, and she kept fingering the tear, trying not to imagine which of those men had worn this, what he'd felt as the orc-blade had sunk through his skin. "What did you do with their bodies?" she heard her wary voice ask. "Afterwards?"

"We set them aflame," Grimarr said flatly. "With honour. We do not do as the humans say."

A sideways glance at his face showed him glowering at the wall, and despite herself, Jule felt her shoulders relaxing. She'd heard the lurid tales of what orcs did with dead bodies, men's and women's both, and though she hadn't quite been able to picture Grimarr doing those things, she also knew firsthand the things Astin's men had done with orc-corpses. The things Astin had approved, and encouraged, and laughed at.

So she reluctantly stood and pulled on the tunic, and then

the trousers. She'd worn trousers a few times before, but never since she'd married Astin, and they felt oddly tight, and close against her legs. Though she had to admit that the drawstring at the top was highly convenient, especially if her waist was soon to expand, and—

"They seem to fit, at least," she said, swiftly cutting off that disconcerting trail of thought, and glancing downwards. "Though now I really do look like a man."

That was in reference to the kinds of pointed comments Astin would sometimes make, in regards to Jule's height or breadth of shoulder, and Jule was briefly gratified—and not nearly as annoyed as she should have been—when Grimarr scoffed loudly from where he still sat on the bed, and reached to cup one of her breasts through her new tunic.

"No orc could mistake this, woman," he said firmly, as his other hand came round her back, and pulled her still-standing body closer between his spread legs. "Naught is altered that I see."

The words made Jule's stomach flip, her eyes held to where he was looking lazily up at her under black eyelashes. His right hand was still on her breast, giving it a proprietary little squeeze, while his other hand drew her still closer between his thighs. "Though in truth," he murmured, "I hope that one day you shall lose your care for clothes, and walk about bare and shameless before all my brothers."

This was really a thing with him, the flagrant arrogant bastard, but Jule could only seem to roll her eyes, and let him pull her even closer. To where his head was on a level with her waist, and as she watched he leaned in and softly kissed her belly through her new tunic, breathing in deep.

"It would give me deep joy to flaunt you as you flower," he whispered. "To show your belly ripening with my son, your teats leaking out my good milk. Your full womb, dripping with my fresh strong seed."

Jule's breath caught in her throat, and she watched as he kissed her belly again, and again. "You would still wish to—to mate," she heard herself say, "even once the, uh, objective has been achieved?"

Grimarr's glance up at her was mulish, with a trace of surprise. "Yes," he said. "I must bathe my son in good seed each night. It will grow him fat and hale, and keep you ready and soft for his birthing."

"That's not how it works, orc," Jule countered, but Grimarr only gave her another sharp look, and leaned in to kiss her belly again. Again with something almost like reverence, perhaps even genuine tenderness, and Jule had to forcibly tell herself that it was just yesterday—yesterday!—that she'd worked all day under his orders, shackled and exhausted. And the day before he'd killed all those men, and exposed her to his friends. And several days before that he'd threatened her with imprisonment and starvation, and Jule was only tolerating this for forty more days, and that was *all*. Biding her time, planning revenge. Right?

She shoved herself away from his hands and his mouth, far too late, and ignored the almost hurt look in his eyes. He was an *orc*. He'd kidnapped her. Lied to her. Gotten her pregnant with his *child*.

It was still far too alarming to think about, and perhaps Grimarr recognized that, because he abruptly stood to his feet, and reached around the foot of the bed, and picked up a small oil lantern Jule hadn't seen before, already burning with a steady flame. "I have more to show you," he said. "Come, and see."

Jule hesitated, but then followed him a short distance out into the corridor, down to a little curtained opening in the stone wall. And once Grimarr had raised the curtain, she stepped inside, and found a small, clean, windowless room. There was a large metal wash-basin hanging on the nearest wall, and next to it was a wooden shelf, holding a bowl of clean-looking water, and a neat pile of rags. And across the room was what appeared to be an actual proper toilet, with proper drainage, at the proper height, even with a cover, and another pile of rags beside it.

"This is for you, woman," Grimarr said behind her. "If you wish to fully bathe, ask Baldr, and he shall send for warm water. If you wish for washing, leave your clothes and rags on the floor, and they shall be cleaned."

*Really*? Jule glanced disbelievingly at Grimarr's face, but his eyes were oddly inscrutable in the dim light. "Oh," she said. "And—uh—when am I permitted to come here?"

"Whenever you wish," came his reply, and Jule felt her eyebrows rising, her eyes darting again around the small room. He'd brought her clothes, and set up a latrine, and while it was still the bare minimum—a tiny stone hole in an orc mountain for basic bodily functions—it was—something.

"Does this please you?" his voice asked. And blinking toward him in the lantern's glow, Jule made the disconcerting discovery that she couldn't seem to say no. That she was, perhaps, pleased.

"Could I have a moment, then, please?" she said instead, and thankfully Grimarr didn't argue, and stepped outside. Leaving Jule blessedly alone to manage her morning business, and when she walked out into the corridor again, fresh-faced and clean-feeling, she couldn't help a quick, relieved smile at Grimarr's watching eyes.

"What next, orc?" she asked, sounding far more chipper than she intended, and earning in reply a skeptical tilt of a black eyebrow.

"We shall eat," he said. "In the Ash-Kai common-room. Come."

He'd already turned to go, and Jule followed him down the corridor, looking all around as they went. This was the first time she'd seen the passageways in any kind of proper light, and they weren't nearly as rough-hewn, or as low-ceilinged, as she'd imagined. In fact, the walls and floors were smooth and well-polished, and here, at least, the corridor was broad enough for several orcs to walk abreast.

"Why will we eat there?" she asked at Grimarr's back, once they'd made multiple twists and turns, and she'd lost all hope of trying to gauge their direction. "I thought you orcs mostly ate in the kitchen?"

"The kitchen makes one meal a day, for all orcs in the mountain, if they choose to eat it," Grimarr replied, without looking back. "All else is the task of the orcs' clans. Each clan has its own likes, and its own food stores, and its own common-room to eat in."

Oh. "And the Ash-Kai"—the word sounded strange on Jule's tongue—"is your clan?"

"Yes," Grimarr said. "And thus, it is yours also, and our son's."

Oh. As though that son were already fully in existence, and Jule put a hand to her waist, even as she sought to thrust the thought clear of her head. "Right. Um, what are the Ash-Kai like?"

Grimarr's brief glance over his shoulder looked surprised, and perhaps even pleased. "The Ash-Kai have long served as the orcs' leaders and captains. We are strong-willed and cunning and proud. We fight to win."

Jule couldn't help a dubious glance downwards, toward where her fingers were still spread wide against her waist, and she hurriedly dropped her hand back to her side. "How very fortunate for you," she said. "Are all the clans in agreement regarding your obvious superiority?"

Grimarr stopped abruptly ahead of her, that telltale tension snapping back into his shoulders, but when his voice spoke, it was carefully steady. "No. There have been many rifts over this.

We Ash-Kai have oft shown ourselves to be aloof and hard and cruel. We have forced our will on others, and quelled those who questioned it, or suffered by it."

Jule didn't seem to have an answer for that, and followed Grimarr in silence until he halted outside what appeared to be the entrance to another room. One that had a not-insignificant amount of noise emanating from it, suggesting the presence of many unfamiliar orcs, and Jule found herself shrinking back, giving an uneasy glance up at Grimarr's watching eyes.

"Come," he said, with a brush of his warm hand to her back. "They know to expect you. They will be kind."

There was a determined grimness on his mouth as he spoke—a demonstration of his Ash-Kai high-handedness, perhaps—but Jule felt herself giving a tentative nod, and she allowed him to guide her into the loud, bustling room.

It was larger than she'd expected, with a crackling fire at the far end, and scattered about were a variety of stone and wood furnishings—tables, benches, even chairs. The floor below Jule's feet was soft, and a glance downwards showed it covered with furs and animal skins. More of these covered the walls, lending a warmth to the room that would have been surprisingly cozy—if not, of course, for the presence of probably twenty huge orcs, stopping their talking and carousing all at once, to look at her.

Some of the orcs had been eating, sitting on the furs around the low tables, and others had been playing what appeared to be a dice-game of some kind. In the corner stood a set of hide-covered drums, all different sizes and heights, and behind them an orc had been using his hands to pound out some kind of elaborate, ear-jarring rhythm. And on a couch—Jule's eyes darted toward it, and quickly away—a slim, bare-chested orc was casually lounging against another orc in what appeared to be a pose of undeniable intimacy, especially given that the first orc was nibbling on the other's bared, reddened neck with sharp white teeth.

Grimarr, of course, seemed entirely undaunted by all this, and guided Jule toward the nearest orcs, the ones playing the dice-game. "Come," he said again. "I wish you to meet my brothers."

And thus, Jule embarked upon a good half-hour of introductions to strange, unnerving orcs, all with entirely unpronounceable names. Most of their faces were vaguely familiar, though, thanks to Jule's day spent serving supper, and while their eyes were almost universally wary, Jule had to admit that Grimarr had been right, and most of them were, to her genuine astonishment, kinder than not.

"Ol' Grim here hasn't scared you to silence yet, then?" said one of them—the shirtless neck-biting one, in fact—in flawless common-tongue, with a saucy grin toward Grimarr's forbidding face. "Death and dismay all the way, right, brother?"

Grimarr replied with a growl, but to Jule's surprise he didn't look truly angry, and there was an almost-tolerant twitch on his mouth. "Woman, this is Kesst," he said. "The most idle orc in the whole of this mountain. Ignore all that he says."

The orc replied with a laugh and a lewd gesture toward Grimarr, which Grimarr pointedly ignored, as he instead nodded at the more typical-looking orc whose throat Kesst had been ravaging. "And this," Grimarr said to Jule, "is Efterar. He is my Chief Healer. Of far more worth than his mate."

Jule blinked, first at the realization that Grimarr was making a *joke*, and then, at his easy use of that word *mate*. As if the two orcs were, in fact, *mated*, and as the second orc—Efterar—blinked up at Jule with hazy eyes, it occurred to her that he looked just the way she always felt when, well—*mating*—with Grimarr.

"All rubbish, Grim, as usual," Kesst cut in, with a dismissive wave toward Grimarr's bulk. "If you think Eft here would be of the slightest use on the field without me sucking his prick—and thereby helping to ease his brain of the constant shit your orders clog it with—you're full of rotten bilge."

He concluded with a smug smile, and a waggle of his arched black eyebrows toward Jule. "Perhaps you'll do the same for this one," he said in a fully audible whisper, as he jerked his head toward Grimarr. "Gods know he needs it almost as much as Eft does."

With that, he promptly returned his attentions to Efterar's neck, all but sprawling himself over his mate's pliant form, while Efterar leaned his head back, his eyes sliding closed. Leaving Jule to stare at them in disconcerted fascination, until Grimarr nudged her away toward the fire, and beside it, a table laid with various items. "You must hunger, woman," he said. "Come, eat."

A closer look at the table showed it arrayed with a haphazard variety of food, ranging from a half-eaten porcupine carcass—with the quills still on—to a selection of roots and greens and seeds. Much of it entirely inedible, to Jule's mind, but her stomach was indeed growling, and she carefully picked out some greens and berries, and then blinked when Grimarr reached into the fire, bare-handed, and pulled out a large, delicious-smelling package wrapped in greased paper. "Here," he said, "we have cooked you a duck."

There was no way Jule was eating an entire duck—or so she thought—but once she'd sat on a bench with Grimarr, and he began pulling the duck apart and handing her pieces to eat, she found that she was, in fact, ravenous. And that not even the sight of Grimarr lustily eating the duck's usually inedible bits seemed able to diminish her hunger, or her sudden, inexplicable curiosity about all this.

"So do orcs really mate with each *other*?" she asked as she chewed, since it didn't seem worth the effort to fret about table

The Lady and the Orc

manners, when the orc beside you was ripping a duck into shreds. "And you're all *fine* with this?"

There was a loud *crunch* from Grimarr's mouth—he was eating the *bones*, too—and a shrug from his big shoulder beside her. "Why should we not welcome this?" he replied. "Humans do this also, do they not? And with so few women, what aught are my brothers to do?"

Jule gave another quick glance across the room, to where Kesst's hand was now openly stroking a visible, lengthy bulge in Efterar's trousers. "Well," she said, fighting to ignore the sudden heat in her face, "go somewhere private, perhaps, at least?"

"Why?" Grimarr countered, as he handed her another delicious-smelling hunk of duck-breast. "I have told you, there are no secrets in this mountain. We all know when Kesst is on his knees, why must he hide this from our eyes? And does this mean he must also deny Efterar relief if there is no place to hide it, as on the field? That is where Efterar must oftenmost be."

Jule shot another furtive look toward the couch—Kesst's hand was now well inside Efterar's trousers, and sliding deeper—and she took a too-large bite of her meat. "Um, well, what if it makes others uncomfortable? Or jealous?"

Grimarr's brow had furrowed, almost as though he were considering her point. "Ach, I follow how you think this," he admitted, to Jule's vague surprise. "You think of the orc who wishes for a mate and has not yet found one. But this way"—he paused to bite another bone in two with a loud *crack*, while his other hand waved toward Kesst and Efterar—"their joy belongs to all of us. If I do not have a mate to suck my prick, I can see and smell Kesst sucking Efterar, and now I am part of this."

He really meant it, Jule realized—his whole exhibitionist thing was actually the *orcs'* collective exhibitionist thing—and it took far too long to find a plausible counter-argument in her thoughts. "Well," she said, "what if—what if one doesn't *want* all the other orcs to be part of one's pleasure? What if Efterar wants Kesst to be only *his*?"

"Kesst *is* only his," Grimarr replied, in a tone that suggested this was obvious. "And why should he not wish to flaunt his mate on his knees, if it pleases all his brothers? Do *you* not wish to see Kesst suck his prick?"

Jule twitched, and then blinked over at where Grimarr was watching her with knowing, heavy-lidded eyes. "Efterar's prick grows taller than most orcs'," he said, his voice a slow, smooth purr. "Do you not wish to watch Kesst swallow this?"

What? It was ridiculous and audacious and *deeply* offensive, and Jule felt her mouth opening and closing, her eyes darting again across the room. To where Kesst had, in fact, finally taken Efterar's swollen bulge out of his trousers, and where it did, indeed, appear to be nearly the length of a cooking-ladle, tall and slim, jutting up through Kesst's slowly sliding fingers.

"I—" Jule began, but couldn't quite continue, her eyes trapped on the appalling, enthralling sight of it, and beside her Grimarr gave a low, husky chuckle. "Look upon this with me, woman," he murmured. "If you wish to leave, only speak, and we shall go."

Jule should have protested, for multiple excellent reasons, but found herself rooted in place on the bench, her mouth oddly dry. While her eyes held on the preposterous scene across the room, Efterar lying back on the couch with spread knees and dazed eyes, while Kesst bent his silky-haired head, and gave a soft, open-mouthed kiss to the wet, darkened head of that long, swollen cock.

Jule could just hear Efterar's sharp hiss of breath, and his legs fell open wider, allowing Kesst room to sink to his knees between them. But still on an angle, enough that Jule had an unbroken, shocking view as Kesst again took that slick head in his lips, and hollowed his cheeks. And then slid his mouth slowly, steadily, inexorably downwards, deeper and deeper, until that impossibly long prick disappeared entirely from view, vanished deep into Kesst's mouth.

"That's impossible," Jule protested, in a strangled whisper, and beside her Grimarr gave a low chuckle, and slid an over-familiar hand close behind her waist. "He has worked long for this trick, to please Efterar," he whispered back. "He swallows it deep down his throat. Mayhap you can learn this, woman."

Jule gave a sharp elbow into Grimarr's side, but he only chuckled again, and settled his arm closer around her. Watching with her—watching, *with her*—as Kesst slowly pulled all the way off again, his throat reflexively bobbing, his slim chest heaving. And then, as Efterar gave a harsh, guttural groan, Kesst sank all the way down again, until his mouth was once again concealing the whole of that preposterous prick, pressing flush to the black hair at the base of it.

Perhaps half the orcs in the room were watching, now, half seeming not to even notice, but beside Jule Grimarr had casually settled his hand over his own swollen groin, echoing the pose of more than one other orc in the room. Hinting that he was actually *into* this, actually turned on by his own orc sucking another orc off, and Jule felt oddly stung, and perhaps almost a little cheated, for reasons she couldn't at all explain.

"Wait," she hissed at him. "You *like* this? You're actually getting *off* on this?!"

The glance Grimarr shot her was openly surprised, and perhaps guilty, too. "Yes," he murmured back. "Why should I not?"

Jule stuttered uselessly, mouth opening and closing, her face feeling flushed and hot. "You—you *like* other orcs," she ground out. "Other—*males*. You've—*done* that, before."

She gave a helpless wave toward the goings-on on the other side of the room, and she could see the confusion in Grimarr's eyes as he glanced toward them, and back to her again. "Yes," he said. "For pleasure. But I have only taken women as mates."

That did *not* help, and Jule found herself sputtering uselessly, her face hot, her eyes trapped on the impossible sight of Kesst once again sucking Efterar's full length deep down his throat. She would never be able to do that, and Grimarr *liked* that, took *pleasure* from that, what the hell did that mean—

"Woman," Grimarr said, as he abruptly stood, grasped for his lantern, and pulled Jule up after him. Guiding her toward the door, and down the corridor, until they were tucked into a little dead-end alcove off the main passageway, with the lantern's light flickering faint from the floor behind them. "You now have this—*uncomfort*—you spoke of. Yes?"

He'd actually noticed? Jule was taken off guard enough to nod, and here was the scent of Grimarr curling through the too-small space, the big black shadow of his body far too close. "Yet, you wished to watch them," he said slowly. "You wished to see Kesst suck Efterar's prick. Yes?"

Jule couldn't seem to reply—gods, why was she even having this discussion, with an *orc*—but Grimarr seemed to take that as a yes, leaning in further, and putting both big hands to the wall beside her head. "But you did not like to think of an orc sucking *my* prick," he said slowly, and how did he notice these things, why were orcs so damned observant, when it suited them? "On what grounds is this, woman?"

Jule was not answering, she wasn't, but he was yet closer, his breath hot and steady on her ear. "This disgusts you?" he asked. "That I have thrust my prick into my brothers' mouths, and spilled my seed down their throats?"

The traitorous gasp from Jule's mouth betrayed her shocking lack of disgust, as did the convulsive clench between her legs, and Grimarr knew it, the bastard, giving a heavy exhale against her neck. "Then you think me less lusty, less powerful," he said, his voice flatter than before. "Even though I have already sired a son upon you."

"No," Jule said irritably, without at all meaning to, and why was she even talking, damn it, giving this self-absorbed orc his way once again? "It's just—if you like *that*, if that's what you prefer for pleasure, I am obviously not *that*, am I?"

Grimarr's body against hers seemed to relax all at once, and he gave a low, husky laugh into Jule's neck. "Ach," he said. "You think I yet long for this, and this you cannot give me."

It was an abominably succinct summary of Jule's darkest thoughts, and when she didn't reply Grimarr laughed again, warm and heated and hungry against her skin. "Then I shall show you what I truly wish for," he said. "Kneel, woman."

The heat was suddenly alive, racing all over Jule's skin, and she blinked up at the shadow of his face, and inhaled deep. "Why," she whispered, a flimsy protest that he cut off with a warm, delicious brush of his lips to hers.

"Because I wish for this," he murmured against her mouth. "Please, woman."

It shouldn't have felt like that, like furious frenzied hunger swirling through the air around them, like this damned orc saying *please* was the height of bliss attained. But it was, perhaps, in this instant, and perhaps Jule had been craving him since she'd first seen Efterar's hazy eyes, and only more and more with each passing moment...

So she sank heavily to her knees before him, and found with a shocked thrill of pleasure that his cock was already out, already hard. And already—her gasp broke off with a choked moan—seeking and finding her hungry lips, and thrusting itself slow and smooth between them. Flooding her mouth with its slick, swollen, leaking heat, sinking deeper and deeper, until it nestled hard and huge and shuddering against her throat.

"This," Grimarr purred, as he circled his hips, gave Jule her first full pulse of his delicious sweetness, "is what I crave. This is what I thought on, whether I had an orc on his knees, or my own hand on my prick."

Jule could only seem to suck harder, keep drawing out that sweet seed, those luscious words, and he gave a hard, guttural moan, his hand sliding warm and wide against her head. "I should never fault my brothers who care for only orcs," he breathed. "But I have always wished for the mouth and the touch of a fair woman like you. I wish to fill you so full of my seed that you shall never run dry."

Gods, why did that sound so good, taste so good, and his growls were steady, rising, thrilling. "I wished to fill you with my son," he groaned. "I wished to light your empty womb with new life. And now that I have done this, I long to watch you swell and bloom and flower, until my son bursts forth. I long to do this again and again, even the bare *thought* of this is joy beyond compare, woman, *ach*—"

The seed spilled hard and unexpected into Jule's mouth, making her twitch and shudder and swallow, and she kept sucking, drinking it in, with eagerness that she couldn't dismiss or deny. He tasted so good, he felt so good, his voice was like a flame in the darkness, she would do this, would do any and everything he ever wished…

He pulled out with a slow hiss, leaving Jule blinking, dazed, wanting. Needing him to pull her up and kiss her, and then gasping when he did, his tongue soft and languid and comforting in her mouth. While her hands curled tight into the silkiness of his hair, pulling him closer as she kissed back, as her whole body seemed to melt against his warm solid strength.

"Next time, we shall watch," he murmured, soft, between kisses. "And you shall know that it is your mouth I think of."

Jule couldn't help another harsh gasp against him, earning a husky chuckle in reply. "Cursed orc," she whispered back, pushing herself away from him, far too late. "Manipulative exhibitionist *beast*."

But he only chuckled again, the bastard, and it made it easy, too easy, to smile back toward him, and curl her hand around his. To let him guide her out and away again, into the main passageway, which was again filled with the sound of the Ash-Kai's drums.

"Where to now, orc?" Jule asked, sounding almost appallingly eager, and she bit her tongue, hard. "I mean, what shocking, uncivilized sight are you going to subject my unsuspecting eyes to next?"

But Grimarr only smiled at her, his mouth wry and warm in the lantern's flickering firelight. "Stubborn woman," he said. "Come, and see my home."

## 18

G rimarr's home was... unnerving.

"How far down does this place go?" Jule heard her high-pitched voice ask, a good two hours later, as Grimarr led her ever deeper through the mountain's maze-like corridors. His lantern was casting uneasy shadows on the smooth stone walls all around, illuminating the many side doors and connecting passages, and Jule was once again completely and hopelessly lost.

"As far below as above," came Grimarr's reply, sounding entirely unconcerned. As though the mountain were not well over half a league in height, and Jule stared at his broad bare back, at that curved scar bisecting it. "*Really*?" she demanded. "It can't all be in use, surely?"

"No," he said, as he led her around a corner, down yet another indistinguishable dark corridor. "But I shall alter this. Here"—he marked an invisible line behind them—"is for the Ka-esh."

The Ka-esh were another of the orc clans, Jule now knew. In addition to the Ash-Kai, there were four more—Grisk, Skai, Bautul, and Ka-esh. Baldr was apparently Grisk, from the largest and most sociable clan, and Drafli from Skai, the smallest and scrappiest. And, as Grimarr had informed Jule, his principal engineer was Ka-esh, and several of his battle-captains Bautul.

The clans were a theme that had been regularly repeated throughout this little tour, as Grimarr had taken Jule through sections of the mountain dedicated to each clan's members. Even Jule's untrained eyes and ears had been able to note similarities in the wary-eyed orcs inhabiting each area, and it seemed as though Grimarr had made a concerted effort to recognize each clan's unique preferences, and accommodate them accordingly.

"Ka-esh wish their home to be deep and dark," Grimarr explained, as he led Jule into what appeared to be a meeting-room, currently empty of orcs, with a large low table in it, and strange white scratchings all over the stone walls. "Bright sun pains their eyes. They are gifted with mines and tunnels and forging."

Jule silently filed that away—after her forty days were up, all of this could be very useful information, could it not?—and followed Grimarr to another Ka-esh room. This one featured what appeared to be carved-out stone bunks in the walls, several of them inhabited by blinking, silent orcs.

"Come, brothers," Grimarr said to them, as he dropped the lantern by the door, and stepped inside. "I wish you to meet my mate."

The orcs obediently rose to their feet and padded over, and Jule noted that she hadn't yet encountered these three, either in the corridors, or when she'd been serving supper. In fact, with this tour had also come the lowering realization that there were plenty of orcs she hadn't yet encountered, perhaps into the hundreds, and that the entire mountain was truly an orc-filled death-trap.

"Lovely to meet you," Jule said, for what felt like the fiftieth time so far today, and tried to ignore the feel of Grimarr's hand giving an approving little pat to her back. "I'm Jule."

The orcs had come closer, their faces now visible in the lantern's dim light, and Jule blinked, and then found herself blatantly staring. Because unlike the other orcs she'd met so far today, these ones were remarkably smooth-skinned, with straight unbroken noses, silken black hair, and elegant pointed ears. Looking not unlike the elves from the old tales, but for the sheer size of them, and the greyish tint to their skin.

"Uh," Jule said, with a helpless sideways glance at Grimarr, but he was smiling at the three orcs, with genuine warmth in his black eyes. "Tell me, Salvi," he said to one of them, who was carrying—Jule blinked and stared again—an honest-to-gods *book* in his hand. "Have you yet found a way to mine your seam?"

"Not yet, Captain," replied the orc, in excellent common-tongue. "But I have a few more ideas."

Grimarr gave a grunt of approval, a light clap of his hand to the orc's shoulder. "Good. And you, Tristan? John?"

Tristan? *John*? He had to be referring to the orcs standing beside this Salvi, because one of them answered Grimarr in kind, something well-articulated but perfectly unintelligible about casting some tunnel three degrees to the northwest, to allow for the more efficient extraction of the ore therein.

"Good," Grimarr said again, with satisfaction. "I trust you will speak with Fror about this."

The orcs nodded, looking abashedly pleased, and Jule was still blinking as Grimarr ushered her out of the room, and into the next. This appeared to be a kind of storage-room—each clan apparently had their own collection of supplies and items, presided over by an orc of their choosing, and this room was sparsely but neatly stocked, with a small shelf of yet more books, a little pile of what appeared to be paper and charcoal, and a variety of vaguely food-like items.

Grimarr was introducing Jule to the room's custodian, a more typical-looking, scar-faced orc, but Jule was admittedly preoccupied throughout, and once they were in the corridor again she grasped Grimarr's hand, and pulled him to a halt. "Grimarr," she said, "what in the *hell* were those orcs back there?"

Grimarr had willingly hesitated, frowning down at her in the lantern's flickering light. "Who?"

"Salvi," Jule replied, exasperated. "And Tristan, and *John*."

It was so ridiculously preposterous—an actual orc named *John*, not to mention the books, and all those calculations about ore-seams—but Grimarr looked entirely nonplussed. "They are Ka-esh," he said. "Mining and studying pleases them. And John was given his name by his mother. Many of our Ka-esh brothers are named thus."

Oh. Grimarr made to move again, but Jule still hadn't quite digested this, and pulled him back again. "But how they *looked*," she said desperately. "Unblemished, and handsome. Like—like *elves*."

Grimarr's eyes suddenly, visibly darkened, and he gave an erratic jerk of the lantern in his other hand. "They look thus because I have brought them here, and kept them safe," he said flatly. "They have not yet needed to arm for battle or face humans who wish to kill them."

He abruptly began walking again, and Jule rushed to follow him, and listened as he curtly pointed out the busy Ka-esh forge. This was the third forge Jule had seen today, all of them bright and loud and bustling, though this one was dimmer inside than the rest, and the orcs within wore masks against the firelight.

"Do they only make tools and weapons?" Jule asked, squinting toward where an orc was pounding out one of the distinctive curved scimitars, glowing bright orange in the darkness. "Or do you make other goods, too? Rings and brooches, that kind of thing?"

"The orcs of ages past made these jewels and trinkets," Grimarr said, with a frown. "But now, we fight against the end of our own kind. We do not have time or ore to waste on trinkets."

That seemed rather a shame—Jule had heard people say, with misgiving, that orcs were better metalsmiths than any men, and even now, old orc-forged jewelry still fetched a high price at market—and she studied the pounding Ka-esh orc, the sheen of the fire against his sweaty skin. "Not even for your mates, or your sons?" she asked, without thinking. "Wedding-rings, and the like?"

Grimarr replied with a snort, a contemptuous curl of his lip. "Why should I need a ring to claim my mate," he said, "when she reeks all over of my scent?"

Jule felt her face flushing—she hadn't meant for *her*, of course, she would never want an orc-forged ring, especially from *him*, would she? Even so, she couldn't seem to help glancing down toward her now-empty left hand, still lacking Astin's wedding-ring, because Grimarr had gone and *eaten* it.

"Right," she said, too quickly. "Well, what next?"

Next proved to be a large, echoing muster-room, and then a series of smaller, empty rooms, "For the Ka-esh women and sons, when they return," Grimarr said, with an odd tilt to his voice. After that were more sleeping-rooms with carved-out bunks, and finally what appeared to be a shrine, with several orcs silently kneeling before a collection of surprisingly well-shaped stone figures.

Jule watched them with interest—Grimarr had said, when showing her the more cheerful-seeming Grisk shrine, that each clan had its own ways of worshipping—until one of the kneeling Ka-esh orcs looked over his shoulder toward Jule, and gave a visible flinch. Elbowing at an orc beside him, who also looked, eyes wide and almost afraid, before they both edged away, further into the darkness.

It wasn't the first time Jule had experienced that reaction to her today, and indeed, the orcs' responses to her presence had varied wildly from clan to clan, and orc to orc. The Ash-Kai had been the most accepting by far, no doubt due to Grimarr's high-handed orders, and the Grisk had been wary but friendly, perhaps because, according to Grimarr, they generally had the most success with human women. In contrast, the Bautul had been curt and dismissive, while the Skai had greeted Jule with openly leering looks and barely concealed contempt.

There had also been several more instances of the orcs' outrageous exhibitionist ways, scattered across all the clans. So far, Jule had been subjected to the sight of multiple orcs in various states of undress, many with either their own hands, or someone else's hands, on their huge orc-pricks. There had also been several more memorable instances of orcs using their mouths on each other—though none quite so impressively as Kesst—as well as the very vivid, thoroughly shocking moment when they'd walked into the Grisk training-room, and found one naked orc fully seated atop another, legs spread, head thrown back, his mouth crying out as he sprayed white seed across the room.

Thankfully—or perhaps disappointingly—there were no such sights to be seen in this particular room, especially with nearly all the Ka-esh inside it now sending furtive glances over their shoulders toward Jule. Hinting not only at unease, but at actual genuine fear, and Jule belatedly stepped out of their view, back into the corridor.

"Why are they afraid of me?" she said to Grimarr, once they'd travelled upwards again, and he'd shown her some larger rooms shared by all the clans: a trading-post, a small arena, and a set of spring-fed baths, currently boasting several naked soapy orcs that Jule didn't even blink at, after the day's many similar sights. "What do orcs think *I* could possibly do to them?"

Grimarr had led her into what was clearly another training-room, this one featuring a wall hung with weapons, and a rather alarming mass of shouting, swinging orcs. They hadn't stopped their fighting as Jule and Grimarr had entered—in fact, it had almost seemed to become even more brutal, and Jule winced at the sight of blood spraying from one of the brawling orcs' noses.

"Most orcs carry fear of humans," Grimarr said, his eyes narrowing on the fighting orcs. "Some just hide this better than others."

There were no other lanterns lighting the room beyond the one in Grimarr's hand—the orcs had been brawling in pitch-blackness—and Jule frowned at the hard profile of his face in the faint light. "I could see them being afraid of *men*," she said, "but I'm a woman. They could all snap me in half, if they tried."

"This matters naught," Grimarr said, his gaze still intent on the mass of orcs before them. "Both men and women bring death to orcs, from both your weapons and your words. You are why we must do this."

He meant the fighting, the brutal bloody hollering mess in front of them, and Jule wanted to protest, to say *No, this is just who you are, who you have repeatedly shown yourselves to be.* But the words were trapped in her mouth, caught behind thoughts of the Ka-esh, with their fearful faces, and names like Tristan and John. And even this entire cursed mountain, full of real homes and baths and trading-posts, and not at all the filthy animal-den Jule had expected it to be.

"*I* don't want—" Jule began, but before she could finish Grimarr let out a bloodcurdling yell, and hurled himself into the fray before them, fists swinging. Sending all the orcs scattering backwards but two, and before Jule had quite caught what happened, Grimarr had hauled up one of them, and snatched out what appeared to be a small, gleaming knife-edge from the orc's clenched fingers.

"What is this!" he roared at the orc, sending a chorus of uneasy mutters all around, and Jule realized, glancing again at the wall of weapons, that these were blunt training-weapons, not intended to be deadly. While the knife-edge, small enough to be hidden in a closed fist, most certainly could be deadly, and perhaps soon would have been, had Grimarr not noticed it.

"He is Skai, brother," the guilty orc said, casting a look of deep dislike toward his opponent, a hulking, hideous orc with mottled greenish skin. "He insulted us. He said you stole the place of captain—"

Grimarr cut him off with a growl and thrust him away, into the mass of watching orcs. "We are beyond this!" he bellowed at the orc. "I care not what he says of me, but what he does, and what you do. And in this"—he brandished the blade in the orc's face—"you betray Ash-Kai honour. You hide a weapon like a coward and a *man*."

The orc muttered his disagreement in black-tongue, making what must have been a rude gesture toward his greenish opponent, because half of the watching orcs laughed, while half were silent. They were from different clans, Jule realized, but all their eyes remained on Grimarr, who turned to the mottled green orc, blade in hand.

"Our brother insults you unjustly, Simon," he said, his voice carrying through the room. "You will fight again. You with this blade in hand this time, and him with none, until he yields. I care not if you slit his throat."

The room erupted in chaos all around, with the green orc's shrill, bloodcurdling yell rising above the rest as he lunged, the knife glittering in his huge fist. While a furious-looking Grimarr turned away from it all, strode back toward Jule, and all but shoved her out of the room.

"Will he actually *kill* him?" she asked his stiff back, once she'd followed him halfway down the corridor. "I thought you said you didn't want to lose your orcs?"

Grimarr didn't turn around, and kept walking, lantern still in hand. "It will not come to death. The others will stop it."

It still seemed a far too indifferent approach to excessive brutality, and Jule kept frowning as she followed him into a wider corridor, large enough that she could move up beside him, and catch his still-glaring eyes. "Was that orc telling the truth?" she asked. "*Did* you steal the place of captain?"

"It hinges upon whom you ask," Grimarr replied, short, but he didn't elaborate, and turned down one corridor, and then another. Taking her to gods knew where else, and Jule was suddenly far too aware of the tiredness in her legs, and deep behind her eyes. And also, the fact that she hadn't been out of this mountain in days, and how much she longed to see the sky, and breathe in fresh, clear air.

"Is there any chance we could go outside for a while?" she ventured, toward his sharp profile. "You haven't shown me any exits yet."

There was a slight shift in his expression—Jule was, unnervingly, finding this orc easier and easier to read—and he kept his eyes forward as he shrugged. "There are not many of these," he said, too casually. "We keep most of them blocked against men. The ones that are yet open are too steep for humans to use, or too far to easily reach."

The bastard. Jule felt herself short of breath, suddenly, staring at his face, and she stopped walking, right there in the middle of the corridor. "What you actually *mean*, orc," she said thinly, "is that you don't *want* to take me outside. And that maybe you'll *never* take me outside. Am I right?"

He turned to look at her, his eyes undeniably shifty in the lantern's light, and Jule gave a hard laugh. "Of *course* I'm right," she said, as a startling surge of fury seemed to flare and burst open in her gut. "I should know better than to actually believe your empty orc promises. Do you think I would have ever agreed to give you forty days of my life if I knew you were still planning to *imprison* me here, and refuse to give me basic necessities like *sunlight* and *fresh air*?! Don't you realize that humans need these to *survive*?!"

She was yelling by the end, her shrill voice echoing against the stone walls, and Grimarr stared at her, his shoulders square and stiff. "Calm yourself, woman," he said. "My brothers hear you."

Of course, he was concerned about *them*, and not his mate who he was still keeping a *prisoner*, and Jule laughed again, loud and brittle. "No," she said. "I want you to take me outside. Or our agreement is *off*, orc. *Immediately*."

Grimarr's stiff shoulders seemed to go even tighter, his face a hard mask, his hands in fists at his sides. "I cannot take you outside," he said. "Not now."

"Why," Jule snapped back. "Because you still think I'll run."

It should have been the right answer—of course it was— but that look on his face, in those eyes, spoke of something different. Of how he was—he was *hiding* something.

"Why," she said again, but then awareness dawned, bright and bitter, and far too late. The men. The war. *Astin*. And Jule had just agreed to forty days with this cursed orc, what the hell had she been *thinking*...

"You expect the men to come back for me," she said, breathless. "Don't you?"

For an instant, she thought Grimarr wouldn't answer, his eyes hard and blank, but then he let out a slow, heavy exhale.

"No," he said. "The men are already here."

## 19

The men were here.

Jule stared at this orc, this lying deceiving *bastard*, and found herself struck entirely speechless. The men were here. Already. Walking around above them, perhaps even fighting to get in, while Jule had been cooking dinner, and going to bed with Grimarr, and agreeing to forty entire *days* in this cursed mountain with him...

"Whose men," she finally managed. "Astin's?"

Grimarr's mouth tightened, but he nodded. "Yes," he said. "But Lord Norr is not with them."

Of course he wasn't—it would be a wonder if Astin had even emerged yet from whatever rock he'd crawled under— and Jule shook her head, tried to think. "And they're new men? How many? What are they doing?"

Jule fully expected Grimarr to refuse to reply, or spew even more elusive orc rubbish, but he let out another heavy breath. "There are now more than fifty new men. They climb over our mountain, seeking a way in."

Gods *damn* it. "And you haven't killed them yet?" Jule

demanded, shrill. "Isn't that what you orcs *do* when men come to your mountain?"

She could see the distance hardening, slipping further over those eyes. "No," he said curtly. "If I killed every man who walked upon our mountain, I should never stop fighting. For now, I wish to pay heed elsewhere."

*Elsewhere*. He meant her, Jule realized—he'd spent the day with her, rather than fighting off the men on his mountain— and she felt her anger deflating, sinking into something flat and cold. "And you didn't think you needed to tell me any of this?"

Grimarr's eyes looked at her, through her. "No," he said finally. "I did not think you would wish to know."

"Well, I do!" Jule burst out, too loud again, but she didn't care who heard, or what they thought. "If you expect me to give you forty days of my *life*, then I expect you to be honest with me. How the hell am I supposed to trust you with my health, my time, my entire *existence*, when you keep crucial information from me? When you think I wouldn't care to know that my own *husband* has sent even more of his men to rescue me?!"

Something flared in Grimarr's eyes, but it vanished just as quickly, leaving only that deadened flatness behind. "If this is truly what you wish," he said, clipped, "then come. I meet soon with my scouts and battle-captains. You shall know all that I know."

With that, he abruptly turned down the corridor again, leaving Jule to trail after him around countless twists and turns before reaching another unfamiliar room. This one large and open, with a square low table in the middle, and a small fire crackling at the opposite end.

"Not all my brothers know your human speech," Grimarr said, as he strode toward the table, and dropped himself down to seated on the floor beside it. "If you wish to understand their words, you will ask me after. Here, you will not ask questions, lest you shame me before my brothers. Sit."

All of it rankled—especially that last bit, complete with a snapping gesture toward the floor beside him, as if Jule were a *dog*—but after a moment's deliberation, she finally went, and sat. Noting, reluctantly, that sitting was in fact a welcome relief, even if it was next to a deceitful and infuriating orc, who was glowering at the door as though it had personally affronted him.

The first orcs to arrive were Baldr and Drafli, followed by several more orcs that Jule now recognized, thanks to the day's endless introductions. Two of them were Grimarr's Bautul battle-captains, Olarr and Silfast, and another Ka-esh orc named Abjorn, who, Jule now noted, despite his scars and pockmarks, still looked more elf-like than the rest.

Several more orcs were entirely new, and Grimarr quickly introduced them, still with that hard edge on his voice. Joarr, his chief Skai scout, a tall, long-limbed orc with glittering black eyes; Eyarl, his chief Grisk scout, grey-haired and light-eyed; and Valter, a relatively small-looking Grisk carrying, oddly enough, what appeared to be several rolled-up vellum scrolls.

"Welcome, brothers," Grimarr said, once they were all seated around the low table. "My mate joins us today, to hear news of Lord Norr. Now, show me what ground you have crossed these past days."

Valter was already unrolling his scrolls, which turned out to be maps of the lands all around the mountain, extending out for leagues to all sides. Covering no less than seven provinces, and all the estates within, including Norr Manor in Yarwood, and Jule's father's old lands in Salven. And it felt uncomfortably odd to see the notations there in common-tongue, *Norr* and *Otto*, while the orcs around the table gestured and pointed toward those very places, their voices speaking in thoroughly unintelligible black-tongue.

The discussion seemed to move from the areas the orcs' scouts had covered—a range which seemed surprisingly large—to where they would cover next. And then, perhaps, to where they would attack next, the names of the various towns and merchant caravans still all too clear in the black-tongue. And here, suddenly, was the disconcerting realization that Grimarr was choosing to ignore the men currently climbing over his mountain, in favour of causing chaos in several far-off towns, and no fewer than four merchant caravans.

It was utter foolishness, or was it, because it would make the orc forces seem larger than they were, the orc threat more ever-present. And, Jule noted with a wince, one of those towns was directly on Astin's most distant border in Sakkin, ensuring that he would need to split his resources to deal with the orcs there, or be publicly vilified for ignoring his town's plight in favour of his wife's.

"Has Lord Norr yet returned home to lead his men," Grimarr said, finally switching to common-tongue, as his eyes glanced brief toward Jule. "Or does he continue to swive through Wolfen's brothels while his home falls to chaos."

What? Jule started and blinked at him, and then felt her face flush sudden and hot. Grimarr was lying, was he lying?—but Joarr's mouth spread into a sharp-toothed, not-so-nice smile. "He ride last eve," he said, the words careful but smug. "Three painted women in wagon behind. Reek of his fresh scent."

Jule's eyes dropped to the table, and a jolting, flattening wave of nausea roiled hard in her stomach. Oh. Of course Astin was up in Wolfen, taking advantage of all the pleasures the realm's northeastern capital had to offer. A regular activity of his, to be sure—but one that was usually spoken of with furtive whispers and sympathetic glances, rather than smug, taunting smiles.

"Lord Norr received the news yestermorn of his first band's

defeat," cut in Eyarl, the Grisk scout. "After this there was a meeting of men in Wolfen's Citadel. Lord Otto and Lord Culthen rode out after also."

It was appalling to think of how the orcs had gained such detailed information—had they been *inside* the capital's massive Citadel?—but behind their words, Jule could easily fill in the chain of events. Astin had heard of his wife's abduction, but had stayed put in the city, expecting the Talford regiment to quickly recover her. Underestimating the situation, as he was often wont to do, and being roused to action only after the news of the regiment's thorough defeat, and at the express public urging of his fellow lords.

"Lord Otto and Lord Culthen are Lord Norr's allies," Grimarr said beside Jule. "They will swell his bands with their own men."

Jule gave an unwilling flinch, because Frank, Lord Otto—being her cousin, her father's heir, and the current holder of those lands in Salven—would therefore be compelled to defend Jule's honour against the orcs. And while Jule had already given far too much to support Otto, he was a decent man, and she'd never wished him ill, much less a brutal death at the hands of orcs on her behalf.

"You will tell me when these men reach their homes, what plans they make, how many more men they rouse, and when they ride again," Grimarr said. "We will work to swell our own bands here, and be ready to meet the men on our terms."

The orcs collectively seemed to agree, nodding heads and murmuring assent, but beside Jule Grimarr hesitated, his eyes narrow and intent on the maps before them. "At this meeting of men in the Citadel," he said, "was there any talk of terms. Of peace."

Eyarl shook his head, short and curt, and Grimarr nodded, and abruptly stood. "Your good work honours us all, brothers," he said firmly. "We meet again tomorrow."

The orcs filtered out, Valter taking his maps with him, until it was only Grimarr and Jule remaining. Jule still sitting, staring down at the table, and feeling oddly unable to move. There had been no talk of peace. Grimarr was attacking towns and caravans all over the land, while Otto and Culthen came to attack the mountain with Astin. And Astin had lounged about in the capital with women paid to fulfill his particular whims, while his own wife had been kidnapped by orcs.

"Was it your intention to humiliate me, with this?" Jule heard herself ask into the silence, her voice hollow. "With your talk of Astin and his—chosen entertainment?"

Grimarr had already stood, and she could feel his watching eyes, prickling at the back of her neck. "No," he said. "But you yet call Lord Norr your husband. You should know what this man truly is."

"I already know perfectly well what that man is, thank you very much," Jule replied, as coldly as she could. "I have no need of instruction or mockery on the subject from orcs. As if *you* lot have the right to judge *anyone!*"

She could almost taste Grimarr's stiff disapproval, lurking strong behind her. "Why do you say this," he said. "Because my brothers do not hide their pleasure as humans do? Because we take it in the open with others who are willing, and not in secret with those who must sell their bodies to feed their babes?"

"No, because you're starting a *war!*" Jule burst out, as she leapt to her aching feet and stalked away from him, toward the still-crackling fire. "You're attacking innocent towns all over the land, dragging in more lords and more men, sitting here sending good men to their deaths! If you have your way, this foolishness will soon consume the entire *realm!*"

She knew the words were unfair even as she said them, borne perhaps of tiredness and fear, but Grimarr seemed to take them at their full value, his growl rumbling deep through his chest. "You do not listen, woman," he hissed, as he stalked over to stand beside her. "I do what I must to save the last of my kind. The blame is not mine, and not my brothers', but it is—"

His voice broke off abruptly, his hard mouth twisting into a grimace, and he turned away from her, as if making to leave. To just stop, and cut her out, and an inexplicable part of Jule grabbed for his arm, glared at his scarred back. "But what?" she demanded. "Whose blame is your war, then? Astin's? And if so, why not just kill *him*, and be done with it? Especially if you orcs are apparently close enough to be counting the women in his wagon, and listening to private meetings at the capital's gods-damned *Citadel*?"

It should have been unnerving, to hear how easily those words of murdering her husband rolled from her tongue—but if Jule thought Grimarr would be mollified by them, she was wrong, because his shoulders only tightened further, his anger curdling in the air. "I should not speak," his stiff voice said. "I have sworn to show you only kindness. I wish you to stay."

Oh, so *now* he was all about being conciliatory, or honourable, or whatever the hell this was supposed to be, and Jule scoffed loudly at his back. "And you think your kindness will help cover the fact that you're *killing* innocent people? And pretending as though you're *justified* in spreading war and death across the entire *realm*?!"

She had no idea why she was pushing this—of course these orcs would think they were justified, wouldn't they?—but she was almost gratified when Grimarr whirled around, his body looming, black eyes crackling with suppressed anger. "Very well, woman," he growled. "Yes. I have just cause. This war, and the blood it will shed, is on the humans' hands. On *your* hands."

Jule scoffed again, glared up into his hideous face. "You're delusional, orc," she snapped. "Yes, you can go ahead and blame men like Astin all you like, but most humans are entirely innocent in all this. I, for one, have done *nothing* to warrant *any* of this aggression from you!"

"And here you speak lies *again*, woman," Grimarr said back, eyes contemptuous. "You are human, you are part of this, you are at fault. You call that fool Lord Norr your husband. You lived in his house and rode his prick and strove to give him sons. You built his lands and his pride and his wealth and his strength. And again and again, he turned and unleashed this strength in full upon my brothers!"

An unpleasant shudder raced down Jule's back, but she pulled herself tall, snapped in a deep breath. "I *had* to do all that," she retorted. "I didn't have a *choice*."

"More lies," replied Grimarr, clipped. "You chose to wed Lord Norr. You chose to wear his ring and share his bed. You *yet* call him your *husband*."

Jule's hands were gripping tight together, and they felt oddly clammy, despite the nearness of the crackling fire. "I married Astin for my father," she said, and there was an uneasy, tilting refuge in those words. "For his people's safety. I *had* to."

"No," Grimarr growled back. "Again you lie. Your father did not carry you to this wedding in chains, did he? No. He failed to sire a son to rule after him, so he made a plan to build his strength—the humans' strength—upon his death. You agreed to this."

Jule blinked at him, at the memories blurring fast and hard through her thoughts. "We were protecting our people," she said, and that was true, that was fair, wasn't it? "It was my father's *job* to make sure everyone in Salven stayed safe after his death. He was a good lord."

Grimarr's mouth made a sound like a laugh, but with no mirth in it. "No. I knew your father. He made many rules and laws against us. He made peace with men he hated to better fight us. When I was a young orc, I once watched your father rip an orc babe from its mother's arms, and cut it to pieces before her eyes."

Jule's head was shaking back and forth, her stomach heaving, because yes, her father had worked hard to rid the land of orcs, she'd known this, hadn't she? "He was protecting his people," she insisted again, though the words suddenly felt hollow on her lips. "He was a good lord. A good father."

Grimarr's eyes glittered, and he advanced even closer, towering over her. "No," he said again. "He butchered my brothers and our sons. And then he went home with bloody hands, and spoke lies and sweetness to his own petted daughter, so you would agree to sell your troth to the strongest man who swore to further your father's name, and carry on his cruelty to my brothers!"

Jule stared at Grimarr, at that furious contorted orc-face, while his words swung increasingly painful circles in her head. None of this was true, of course not, but her father *had* been a clever man, and ruthless when he'd needed to be. And of course he'd had to make plans for after he'd gone, it had been the single major aim of his later years, and Jule had *promised* to help carry them out, and...

And even as Jule's head was still shaking, saying no, her knees had gone strangely unsteady, and she sank down by the small fire, staring blankly into its flickering depths. *Had* she been used by her father? *Had* she helped Astin wreak his cruelties on these orcs? *Did* she carry any guilt for what Grimarr did now?

"Your father was no fool, woman," Grimarr said now, echoing far too close to her own unsettling thoughts. "But he was a harsh and cruel man. Even my own father did not sell me as a slave to a master who cared not if I lived or died."

There seemed no words to speak, only emptiness and exhaustion remaining, and Jule curled into herself on the hearth, pulling her knees close to her chest. Her father had been a good man. He'd done nothing wrong. *She'd* done nothing wrong. Had she?

"Yes, and then *you* came along and *kidnapped* me, and trapped me here," she said finally, bitterly, because at least that was truth, a mooring to cling to in the madness. "*You're* the monster here, orc."

But in the silence that descended over them, it occurred to Jule that even that might not be truth. Because if this endless day had shown her anything, it was that Grimarr was a good leader to his orcs. A better lord than Astin, or perhaps even her father, and what did that mean? Where did it leave her, trapped here in this mountain, with Grimarr's babe in her belly, and revenge in her heart?

It left no truth to be found, just the scraping exhausted misery, and finally Jule pressed her stinging eyes to her knees, and sobbed.

## 20

J ule stayed by the fire far longer than she meant, her head on her knees, her hand curled over her belly. Sitting in a silence that should have been welcome, but felt like a shroud.

Grimarr was still behind her—she could feel his lurking bulk, standing there, watching her—but he hadn't spoken another word. Not that she couldn't almost feel him thinking them—how could any woman be so gullible about her own life, how had she never properly considered what her father had done with her, what she had in turn done to others.

It still felt wrong, the thoughts a creeping cold sacrilege to her father's memory, to the suffering hell of his death. To how he'd loved Jule—he *had* loved her—and yes, then sold her, to the highest bidder. To Astin.

Gods, this orc was fucking with her head, and Jule was almost grateful when she was confronted with the sudden presence of another orc, shuffling across the room toward them. It was the filmy-eyed orc again, the old one. Sken.

"Stand, woman," he croaked, reaching out a wizened hand

toward her, and Jule instinctively recoiled, arms clenching against her torso.

"No," she said, and then belatedly wiped at her damp eyes with her palm. "Why."

The old orc said nothing, just looked at her with those unnerving clouded eyes, and now here was Grimarr's voice again, a low rumble behind her. "I wish for Sken to look at you each day, woman. He sees what is hidden."

The words sent an odd quiver down Jule's spine—their hidden son, was what Grimarr meant—and she clambered up to her feet, almost as though compelled. This orc could see her son. That wasn't possible. Was it?

But the orc—Sken—had reached out that hand again, slowly enough that Jule could have backed away, but didn't. Just stood and looked as those gnarled, shaky fingers came to rest on her still-flat belly.

"Yes," Sken said, the word a strange startling relief in Jule's thoughts. "Your son knits together as he should. He is lusty and cunning and strong."

He was? Jule blinked at Sken—surely he was lying, there was no way of knowing such things—but behind her she could hear Grimarr's heavy exhale, the way it broke off at the end. "Can you yet see our son's face," his voice said, sounding odd, strained. "His name."

Sken's eyes closed, his deep forehead-wrinkles furrowing, but finally he gave a slow shake of his white head. "Not yet. He must grow more first. Woman must have sun, rest, exercise, kindness, pleasure. Must eat good food and drink good orc-seed."

The fire felt very warm, suddenly, and Jule fought back the illogical urge to look back at Grimarr, to see what he thought of all this. Surely Sken was just saying these things to please him, especially the orc-seed bit—but then again, would it really please Grimarr to have to give her sun and kindness, too?

"I will see to this," said Grimarr's still-strained voice behind Jule. "I thank you, Sken."

Sken nodded and turned away, but Jule's breath felt tight in her throat, her hand reaching out uselessly after his hunched form. "Wait," she said. "Could you see when our son should be born? And if I"—she swallowed hard—"if I will survive it?"

Sken hesitated, and turned his filmy eyes back toward her. "In the spring," he said. "And should you not survive it, it shall not be your son who kills you."

Jule blinked at him, and then back at Grimarr, who looked as nonplussed as she felt. "Explain this, Sken," he ordered. "Who do you speak of."

Sken replied with a shrug, a noncommittal wave of his wizened hand. "It is not yet clear," he said. "Not you, boy. Stand down."

Grimarr's eyes were glinting, his right hand clenching uselessly at the non-existent sword-hilt on his belt, but he spoke nothing further, and Sken tottered away, and out the room's open entrance. Leaving Jule and Grimarr alone, standing in front of the crackling fire, looking at each other.

"You will not come to harm, woman," Grimarr said finally, into the silence. "Not by our son, or aught else. I will not allow this."

Jule could only seem to stare at him, distantly marvelling at the words, at the seeming intensity behind them. This ridiculous warmongering orc, who not a quarter-hour ago had accused Jule of *selling* herself to help destroy the last of his kind, was now swearing with all sincerity to *protect* her?

She could see Grimarr following that—for all his faults, he was clearly not stupid—and his shoulders sagged slightly, his breath coming out slow. "I ought not to have faced you so harshly with these truths," he said, quiet. "You thought your father a good man."

Jule should probably have argued it—her father *had* been a

good man—but she couldn't seem to muster the willpower, or even the words. Because yes, despite being a good man, her father *had* used her for his own ends, hadn't he? And he *had* killed orcs. He'd openly worked to rid the world of them, as all good lords were expected to do.

And Jule had never truly spared it a thought. Had never truly considered that there might be orcs like Baldr, or Kesst, or John. Orcs who were eager and kind, or lazy and laughing, or shy and scholarly. Orcs who just wished to live in peace under their mountain.

"My father did what the world around him expected, I suppose," Jule said finally, to the fire. "I did so too. I didn't think to question it."

There was an instant's stillness, then the feel of Grimarr's big body stepping closer beside her. "I cannot fathom this, woman. You question me at every turn."

Jule's eyes darted toward him, expecting to see judgement, or censure—but instead, there was an almost-genuine warmth in his eyes. Almost—tolerant, or affectionate, and Jule blinked hard, looked away. He was an orc. He was starting a war. She would give him his forty days, and then...

"Ach, I should welcome your questions, woman," his voice continued, still quiet, still wry. "I must learn to hear dissent. I must learn to quell my anger at those who bring it."

"But you're angry at me for more than that, aren't you?" Jule replied flatly, because that was what he'd meant earlier too, wasn't it? "You're angry with me for marrying Astin, for going along with my father's plans for me. For being *human*."

There was another instant's silence, and then a sound from Grimarr much like a sigh. "Yes," he said finally. "And yet, no. It is as you said to Baldr. You can love my son and hate me. Yes?"

Jule nodded, silent, and beside her Grimarr sighed again. "We orcs need women," he said slowly. "We crave women. Our sons weep in the night for the lack of you. Yet women run from us. You kill our babes. You serve and abet the men who seek to destroy us. We must steal you away even to *speak* with you."

Jule kept watching the fire, listening, the entire world slowly going still, but for this orc's quiet, raw voice beside her. "And when we steal you, of course you are afraid. You think our faces loathsome, our ways fearsome and lawless. You fear how you crave us, and you suffer in the birth and raising of our sons. And when you run, you proclaim your fear and suffering to your men, and they seek to avenge and protect you, and bring us yet more pain and death. It is"—his breath drew in—"sorrow beyond speaking."

Jule's mouth was dry, her eyes trapped on the flame, its crackling heat far too close. "In a just realm, I would have come to you with kindness," Grimarr continued, his voice almost too soft to be heard. "I would have wooed you and honoured you and proven my strength. I would never have taken you thus."

Jule didn't reply, couldn't, and he sighed again, his regret almost palpable in the air. "I wish I could alter this," he whispered. "For you, mayhap it is too late. But in all that I do, in this war I fight, I seek for the day when an orc might walk up to a woman, and speak, without fear of death."

His words rattled in Jule's thoughts, their truth far too clear, their grief real enough to be her own. And in them, somewhere, was the need—the blind, inexplicable compulsion—to turn. To finally look at those bleak black eyes, and to reach out a shaking hand, slow, and put it to this orc's hard, heaving chest. To say, perhaps, that in all this miserable mess, he *could* speak. To her.

Grimarr looked down at Jule's hand touching him, and then up at her face. And the sudden snarl from his throat was fury and fire and breath, straight from his mouth to hers, lighting her aflame like a flintlock to tinder.

They tumbled to the floor together, her pulling him pushing, his big body heavy and hard over her, pinning her to the stone below. Her own body arching up, her trouser-clad leg hooking behind his, her hands gripping desperate and fervent around his broad bare back, against the scars etched into it.

His replying growl felt like her own, rumbling powerful and deep into her chest, and perhaps she even growled back as she yanked on his hair, pulled his head down. Finding his hot, angry mouth, feeling for the first time the true strength of its tongue, the bite of its sharp teeth. And then hearing him hiss with pain, or perhaps pleasure, as she bit him back, pulled him harder, scratched at his back with fingernails that should have been claws.

His own claws were out, for the first time in this, scraping light over Jule's skin as he shoved up her new tunic, baring her heaving, jiggling breasts to the room. And to any orc who happened to walk past its unobstructed door, but Jule couldn't have cared less, because those clawed hands were gripping her, caressing her, surging hot craving all through her skin.

His tongue was still deep in her mouth, curving slick and strong into her throat, almost enough to make her gag, while his bulging hardness below shoved close and powerful against two damned layers of trousers. And with a series of desperate squirming kicks Jule was out of her trousers altogether, her legs widening around him on their own accord. And now he was the one fumbling below, his big hand shoving downward, the scent of his bare cock suddenly heady and mouthwatering in the air, so close—

He drove into her so hard, so deep, that Jule's entire body flailed up, her mouth actually shouting around his tongue. But there was no escaping it, not his invading tongue or the deep piercing invasion of his prick, or the scrape of his sharp, angry claws against her still-shuddering breasts. There only feeling it, revelling in it, in being pinned and taken and impaled within a breath of her life by a huge, vicious, furious orc.

His first full thrust was like a hammer slamming between her legs, all hard steel and raging pounding agony, and Jule cried out even as she pulled him harder, sucked that tongue deeper. Yes, he had to do this, had to fuck her like the orc he was, show her she deserved this, he deserved this. Had to pump her full with the seed she could already feel drenching her, slipping out slick around that driving prick.

Fuck, it hurt, and fuck, it was good. It was anger and revenge and hunger brought to life, in clashing bodies and brutal invasion, in conquer and surrender and craving. It was this orc saying, for perhaps the first time, that he feared her too, he hated her too, and perhaps even more because of the life he'd made inside her.

The truth of it was thick and choking, as much as his tongue down her throat, and suddenly Jule was fighting back in earnest, biting as strong as she could against it. Tasting the tang of his blood in her mouth, feeling the hard, furious growl as he reared back, as he kept pounding her, jolting dizzying pleasure with every driving thrust.

"Cursed woman," he hissed, mouth smeared with red, eyes glittering, hair hanging down over his face. Hands flat to the earth on either side of her head, his broad bare chest heaving, streaked with rivulets of sweat, every muscle stark and corded and beautiful in the firelight. "*My* woman."

And without warning, without comprehension, he'd yanked his invading heft out of her, leaving her legs splayed wide, her wetness quivering, leaking, bereft. While her jolted eyes stared at where he'd brought that slick, dripping prick upwards, hovering it over her face, and she opened her mouth to protest. A crucial mistake, because that huge orc-prick took it, and shoved itself hard and shocking between her lips, and slammed deep down into her throat.

Jule twitched and spasmed and gagged, even as her mouth sucked desperately, gaining its first glorious taste of that succulent leaking seed. But he wasn't being kind or gentle this time, just kept pummelling into her throat, taking his pleasure from her, so brutal and powerful that her eyes watered, her body flailing, couldn't breathe, an orc's prick was choking her throat—

She bit down, hard, and the raging orc pounding her gave a howling, bloodcurdling scream. And then yanked himself out, his huge hand and sharp claws pressing flat against her neck, holding her there, helpless, trapped, screaming—

And then his swollen, pulsing cock sprayed its pleasure, straight down into Jule's red, gasping face. Burst after burst of slippery, stringy white clinging to her cheeks, her nose, her chin, coating her all over with hot orc-seed. While one of his hands kept her there, pinning her helpless, and the other pumped even more white out of that prick, aiming himself, making sure she was covered all over with her humiliation, and his pleasure, and his rage.

When it finally stopped Jule was shaking all over, and perhaps he was, too. His hand moving unsteady from her skin, his eyes blinking down at the mess he'd made of her face, and she could only seem to stare back, too stunned, too used, to speak.

"Ach," he said, eyes closing tight, and again here was that pain, filtering familiar across his face. Almost as though he couldn't bear to look at her, as though he were about to back away, and for some inexplicable reason Jule's hands grasped at him, at his waist and his arm, saying, *Wait, don't go.*

Those eyes blinked open again, looking at her, and she could see them dilate at the sight of her, still hungry, even as his mouth winced, and his head shook back and forth. Saying, *No, I should not have done this*, all the stupid orc-apologies that didn't speak to the real truth, the true bitterness hovering between them that had gone unspoken, until now.

"Don't," Jule's voice croaked, her eyes held to his still-blinking ones. "You have every right to be angry. You should be."

Grimarr stared down at her, and she could see his throat jump as he swallowed. "What if I have hurt you, or our—" he began, but Jule stopped him, her fingers coming up to press against his still-bloody mouth.

"Stop," she said. "It's fine. Kiss me."

He blinked again, and then obediently lowered his head, and kissed her. Quiet this time, gentle, and almost painfully sweet. Speaking truth too, now, just as true as the anger, and Jule desperately kissed him back, tasting him, needing him. She loathed this orc. She craved this orc. Was it any wonder that he would feel the same?

Grimarr was still blinking as he pulled back, and then his hand—without claws, now—reached down for Jule's tunic, which was still bunched up around her neck. And then he gently, carefully, used it to wipe up her face, cleaning off what seemed to be copious amounts of his mess, even in her eyelashes, and her hair.

"That's my new tunic," Jule pointed out, for lack of anything better to say, and above her Grimarr twitched, and let out a small, choked chuckle. "I shall have it washed. And give you another one."

"And find a way to take me outside, afterwards?" Jule asked, tentative, thinking back to Sken, to that tiny little life—lusty, cunning, strong—inside her. And Grimarr above her was thinking of it too, so transparent, this orc, weighing the future health of his son, against the likelihood that Jule would run, or try to betray him to Astin's men on his mountain.

Jule still wasn't about to say that she wouldn't—this hadn't changed that much, right? Or had it, because Grimarr above her gave a heavy sigh, and a slow nod of that shaggy head.

"Yes," he said, his voice weary. "I shall seek to find a place at the top of the mountain to take you, away from the men."

Something flipped in Jule's gut, and she couldn't seem to stop her mouth from curving up at him. A true, genuine smile, borne of true gratefulness, to this impossible orc, who'd just done unspeakable things to her.

It made no sense, it was appalling and inexplicable and utterly ridiculous, she was a *lady*—but Jule couldn't stop smiling, all the same.

## 21

The top of Grimarr's mountain was *glorious.*

It had taken some time getting there, and the intensive efforts of a handful of Ka-esh orcs, who Grimarr had tasked with opening up a long-blocked passage to a specific location he had in mind. Watching the Ka-esh pound away at what looked like solid rock with awls and pick-axes had been a fascinating—and deafening—sight, but it was one Jule entirely forgot once Grimarr finally led her through the new rough-hewn passage, out into the open evening air.

"Oh *gods* in *heaven*," Jule gasped, as she slowly turned in place, inhaling, drinking it in. The sun was just setting, painting the western sky in vivid reds and blues, and the air was cold and clear, the open world around them beautifully, breathtakingly vast after all those days in the mountain. "You might have the most spectacular view in the *world*, Grimarr."

And not only that, but this place on the mountain was a clever marvel, too. It was a flat, grassy little bluff, with even a few scrawny bushes scattered about, and sheer stone walls going up on three sides. The last side was open to the west, dropping off steep and treacherous below, and showed nothing but the huge, stunning sky.

"Where are the men you spoke of?" Jule asked, stepping a little closer to the cliff, and peering down at the sharp, jagged wall of rock below. "Camped for the night at the bottom?"

"Yes," Grimarr said, his eyes suddenly wary on hers. "On the plain to the east. These men are not yet fool enough to wander my mountain at night."

With the words he came another step closer, no doubt in case Jule tried to run, or yell for the men, or pitch herself off the steep cliff to her death. But she didn't even want to think about any of that, in this moment, not with the cool air filling her lungs, and the stunning sunset unfurling across the sky.

"So why this mountain?" she asked instead, looking again at the yawning expanse of jagged rock below, seemingly absent of warmth or life. "There's no place to grow or pasture anything, there's barely any vegetation for cover, it's so close to human settlements, and your lake..."

Grimarr's face visibly spasmed at the mention of the lake, and he stared past her, toward the reds and purples of the setting sun. "This mountain is our home," he said. "It has been our home since the earliest tales. There is power in this."

Jule watched him, waiting, perhaps knowing he would say more, if she were patient. "And we must needs be near humans," he added, quieter, again with that strain of bitterness tainting his voice. "For the women. And for all the goods and knowledge that have been lost, and now must be taken back."

He meant the raiding—they'd in fact just encountered a returning Skai raiding-party in the corridor, dripping blood and rolling stolen barrels—and rather than pointing out the cruel, shortsighted barbarism in this, Jule remained silent, considering, and followed Grimarr back inside. And then, back in his bed, she rode him quiet and careful in the dark, her hands on his chest, his hands warm and powerful on her hips.

When she awoke late the next morning Grimarr was gone, but there were no chains to be seen, and a new, rather larger tunic was neatly draped over the end of the bed. Jule was admittedly sore, and somewhat scraped up, from the incident by the fire the day before, but it was nothing worth fussing over, and once she'd dressed she stood and looked at Grimarr's awful tapestry. Orcs raging and pillaging, innocent men running in fear. Telling, perhaps, only one side of the tale.

It wasn't an easy thing to think about, and Jule was still considering it when she stepped out into the corridor. Finding a silent, glowering Drafli standing there, with his huge scimitar in hand, but then, much to Jule's relief, here was Baldr, striding up the corridor toward them. "Hello, woman," he said, with a nod, and a flash of white teeth. "How fare you this morn? And your little one?"

Jule's hands instinctively went to her stomach—still flat, but feeling decidedly uneasy this morning, and perhaps—perhaps?—just slightly thicker than it should have been. "Fine, thank you," she said, over that thoroughly disconcerting thought. "Where is Grimarr?"

Baldr and Drafli exchanged glances, and Baldr smiled at her again, rather less genuine this time. "If you come," he said, "I will take you to him."

Jule nodded her agreement, and carefully followed Baldr through the dark corridors, tilting downwards. Going toward the Bautul area, she now knew, and though she still couldn't pinpoint where exactly they were, it was disconcerting to realize, after several moments, that she was walking steadily and easily, with only a hand trailing against the wall. Despite the fact that it was pitch-black all around, and that her only guide was the sound of Baldr's padding feet up ahead, and the slight clank of his sword.

"The captain meets with Silfast and Olarr, and with three Bautul captains from the south," Baldr said, unexpectedly, as he led Jule through a complicated set of connecting passages. "He seeks their support for the coming conflict."

Jule's thoughts flicked back to the meeting the day before, to Grimarr's mention of swelling his ranks. "Wouldn't he have their support already?" she asked. "I thought he was the first captain to bring all the clans together in three hundred years. Or whatever."

"The captain has support from a *majority* of orcs from each of the five clans," Baldr replied, with heavy emphasis on *majority*, "but there are still those with power in the clans who do not wish to be bound to his rule. Their allegiances must be courted or bought."

Right. It was always so with men too, as Jule knew far too well—though why Baldr was telling her this now, she couldn't fathom. "How many orcs do these captains represent? And how does Grimarr aim to earn their allegiance?"

"These captains boast hundreds of orcs," Baldr said, slower now. "They are the largest bands to resist the captain's quest for unity. We cannot spare extra goods to pay them, with a siege so close at hand, so he seeks to sway them through a display of cleverness and strength. He seeks to show a clear path to victory, and their own rewards when it is achieved."

It made sense, again, though Jule felt a twisted little chill down her back at the word *siege*. Of course that would be where all this was headed, with the mountain being as impenetrable as it was, in every way a fortress with massive stone walls. But a prolonged siege meant hunger and filth and disease, misery for both those inside and out.

"So does Grimarr mean to fight the men, instead of waiting out a siege?" Jule asked, and there was an instant's silence from Baldr, broken only by the sound of his steady footsteps.

"His plans are not fully set yet," he said finally. "But if he can draw all of Bautul to our side, we will have more options to choose from. The path to victory will be far easier to find."

Jule considered that, and then felt her eyes narrow toward where she knew Baldr to be. "If this is such an important meeting," she said, "why do you so willingly take me there? We both know Grimarr barely tolerated me at that meeting yesterday, and that was with his own orcs."

She could hear Baldr's steps slowing to a halt, so she did the same, feeling an unwilling flicker of pride when she successfully avoided bumping into him. "You are a clear sign of the captain's strength," Baldr said, careful, suddenly almost strained. "If you would—if you could consider—feigning your deference to him, perhaps, or showing yourself as a woman— take your hair down, perhaps—or—or something—the captain, we all, would be greatly appreciative, and—"

His voice had gotten more high-pitched as he'd spoken, and Jule interrupted him with a hand to his arm, a wry laugh from her mouth. "Grimarr put you up to this, didn't he?" she said. "You need not speak further, Baldr. I follow your meaning."

Baldr made a sound very like a relieved chuckle, though he remained unmoving in the darkened corridor. "But will you? Please, woman? Last I knew, it was not proceeding well."

It was an unsettling thought, an unsettling request, and Jule wasn't in the least obligated to these orcs, was she? Particularly not in helping them raise more forces to fight her own—yes, still her *husband*—but the thought of a siege, orcs like Baldr and Kesst and John gone hungry, the very slight swell in her own belly, lusty, strong, cunning—

Baldr was walking again, leading her toward the welcome sight of slowly brightening light, filtering from a door at the opposite end of the corridor. This had to be where the orcs were meeting—the sound of arguing voices was rapidly rising—and Baldr abruptly turned to look at her in the dim light, his face drawn, almost pleading.

"Please, woman," he whispered. "I will remind the captain to take you outside again, after."

It was so ridiculous, and preposterous, and even more preposterous was the fact that Jule gave a heavy sigh, and rolled her eyes, and then—did it. Reached for her braid, carding her hair out into loose waves, and then, for good measure, undoing the top button, or two, of her clean new tunic.

Baldr's relief was almost palpable, his eyes now locked to her chest, and Jule rolled her eyes again, and stalked away, toward the lit room. Striding inside, into welcome light and heat, and into—she blinked, and halted in place—the unfriendly staring eyes of nearly a dozen watching orcs.

Baldr had said there were only three captains, but Jule belatedly realized that of course they would not travel alone. And that Grimarr had his own Bautul captains there, Olarr and Silfast, and also Valter with the maps, and of course there was Grimarr himself, sitting stiff and angry-eyed at the far end of the long, rectangular table.

"Woman," he said, his voice hard and disapproving. "Why are you here. I did not ask for you."

Jule hesitated in place, realizing with a chill of horror that Grimarr hadn't put Baldr up to this in the least. That this was all Baldr, the sneaky green beast, and now she was trapped here, in a room full of hostile, unfamiliar orcs. Many of which—she shrank back slightly toward the wall—were huge and glaring and breathtakingly hideous, just the type who haunted children's dreams.

"Um," she said, to the room full of watching eyes, and then found the relative safety of Grimarr's face, angry and suspicious as it was. "I, uh, wished to see you."

The room had gone deathly silent, but for the crackling fire, with every orc's attention fully on her. And Jule could see the moment when Grimarr realized the power of it, his narrow eyes flicking from her hair, down to the too-low opening of her tunic, and then back up to her face.

Grimarr said some harsh, rolling words in black-tongue,

eyes sweeping over the rest of the watching orcs, and in reply several of them shrugged, and one of them laughed. To which Grimarr nodded curtly, and then jerked his head toward Jule, in a movement that clearly meant, *Come.*

"You may stay for a spell, woman," he said flatly. "But you will be silent, and obey."

Jule nodded mutely, with genuine relief, and sidled around the room toward him. He was seated on a low bench beside the table—this was the first meeting-room she'd seen with benches—and he glanced sideways at her as she slipped in beside him. His eyes watchful, perhaps uneasy, and she saw his throat swallow in the room's flickering firelight.

It was a sudden, startling reminder of the day before, of being held down and taken before the fire, and looking at those eyes, lingering on those memories, had suddenly set the world tilting toward absurdity, or perhaps madness. Why should Jule not play the part? With every set of eyes in the room held to her face, caught in her thrall?

And Grimarr had said to be silent, but he hadn't said to be still. So Jule inched a little closer to him on the bench, her shoulder nudging into his arm, until he was obligated to raise the arm, and settle it heavy and warm around her shoulders.

He abruptly began speaking again, his mouth full of loud tangled black-tongue, perhaps to distract from Jule's imposition. But the orcs weren't watching him—they were watching Jule—and she felt herself slowly leaning in toward him, and inhaling the musky warm comfort of his chest.

He was wearing a tunic again today—Jule had rather preferred it yesterday, when he hadn't bothered—but it wasn't long enough that she couldn't slip her hand up inside the back of it. Feeling ridged muscles and smooth scarred skin, and she let her fingers linger there, while her eyes wandered from his chest up to his still-speaking mouth.

Grimarr wasn't really a terrible-looking orc, she thought,

disjointed, with a swift, furtive glance at the rest of the table. Despite all the scars, his face was strong, symmetrical, his mouth well shaped, his ears still pointed and whole. Though his hair—Jule frowned, and reached up to stroke at it—clearly hadn't been touched since she'd braided it, days before, and was rapidly approaching the state of a tattered birds'-nest.

Grimarr hadn't stopped speaking—in fact, he hadn't even looked at her since she'd first sat down—so in a bizarre burst of daring, Jule shrugged off his arm, and twisted herself sideways. Planting one leg on either side of the bench, as she began combing at his hair with her fingers. Tugging out the knots piece by piece, and then smoothing her fingers through the silken strands, and finally plaiting them into a new, neat braid.

She still had the ribbon from her own braid, tucked into her trouser-pocket, so she pulled that out, and tied it on. While Grimarr just kept speaking, pointedly ignoring her, even as she nudged at his arm, and he obligingly lifted it again, settling it back around her shoulder.

The orcs continued their debating—some were clearly arguing with Grimarr, from the sound of it—but it was still all in black-tongue, so Jule paid it no heed. Instead, she felt her hungry hands begin their wandering again, one of them trailing down and up Grimarr's hard thigh against hers, until she discovered—oh.

She stared at it for an instant, the bulging shape of it far too clear under his trousers, a small spot of growing wetness just visible at the head. And why was she staring, why was she so transfixed, it shouldn't be at all surprising that Grimarr would be fully aroused in a room full of arguing orcs, was it?

But he was still arguing too, still paying Jule not even the slightest attention, and there was an inexplicable, compelling heat in that, perhaps even a challenge. Enough that she held her eyes to his face, and slowly, gingerly slid her hand upwards, trailing lightly over that bulge in his trousers.

His speech didn't hesitate, his eyes unwavering on whatever orc he'd been talking to, but the hard bulge under Jule's hand had leapt against her fingers, swelling even further. He liked this, she thought, with a strange, stilted breathlessness, so she let her fingers wander there again, more intently this time.

His face again didn't flinch, didn't betray even the slightest acknowledgement, though again that hardness under her fingers pressed itself up, strong, into her palm. Willing Jule to touch it, and curse her but she wanted to touch it, her fingers circling carefully, willingly, around it.

In reply it gave a long, sustained shudder, even as Grimarr kept on speaking. And Jule's face felt very hot, suddenly, and even more so when she glanced at the table, and found nearly all its eyes still staring at her, with one hideous orc actually giving a slow, gratuitous lick of his lips as he watched.

They couldn't actually see what Jule was doing, behind the protective cover of the table, but her fingers had halted all the same, going slack against Grimarr's trousers. Against Grimarr's wishes, perhaps, because even as he kept speaking, his big hand slid down to hers, and closed her fingers back around him.

Fuck. Jule couldn't help a shuddery exhale, eyes fluttering, and when Grimarr's hand let off, and moved back up to gesture at a map on the table, she couldn't seem to stop herself touching, exploring. Feeling his hard heft twitch and dance eagerly under her fingers, because of course he would love this, wouldn't he, the bastard? And what would he do if she were to just—perhaps—tug at the trousers' loose drawstring, and slip her hand inside?

Her answer came with a deep growl from his throat, aimed not at her, but at whichever orc he was arguing with, while his finger jabbed at a hazy point on the map. And gods, he was such a transparent prick—*had* such a transparent prick, now jutting out huge and straight and quivering from his slack trousers, all but begging for Jule's touch.

The other orcs had to know—of course they knew, from the way they were still staring—but they still wouldn't be able to actually see, and none of them had seemed to raise the slightest protest. So Jule dropped her eyes and watched, brazen and breathless, as her appalling hand curved around the base of Grimarr's bare cock, and slid up.

The movement brought another growl to his throat, cleverly disguised as part of his ongoing argument, and Jule couldn't hide a furtive, unwilling smile as she did it again. This time bringing a silken bead of white orc-seed to the tip—and when she pumped up again, harder this time, that bead grew until it burst, running down the full length of him in a thick rivulet of mouthwatering white, pooling hot and sticky against her fingers.

Jule swallowed hard, staring, but Grimarr was still speaking, still entirely ignoring this. And he wouldn't notice—surely he wouldn't notice—if she left off for an instant, and surreptitiously brought her fingers to her mouth?

But his voice had abruptly broken, in what seemed to be mid-sentence, and when Jule looked up, he was finally looking back at her, his eyes dark, speculative, crackling. And so were all the other eyes at the table, a sea of staring hungry orcs, and Jule froze in place, her finger still halfway between her lips.

"Woman," Grimarr's heated voice said, in common-tongue, "your deeds mislead us from our work."

Jule remained still, caught in the web of his voice and his eyes, both finally intent upon her. "Forgive me, Grimarr," she murmured, her voice sounding strangely husky to her ears. "Do you wish me to leave?"

Those eyes looked at her, all hot hungry thwarted power, and in that instant, Jule was distantly, thoroughly aware that of course he didn't want her to leave. That this was a show he very much wanted to continue presenting, to his own current and future benefit—but that Jule also *was* distracting the orcs, none of whom had seemed able to look away for the past quarter-hour. And as the meeting's instigator, Grimarr couldn't afford to be seen as a selfish host, or inconsiderate of his guests' needs.

"Perhaps," Jule said, and she could not be thinking this, *not* saying this, "if I were to hide from your guests' view, perhaps under the table, and be very quiet, you would allow me to stay?"

Grimarr's astonishment wasn't the least put-upon, his eyes gone wide and shocked on hers, but he recovered quickly, and spoke again, this time in black-tongue. Clearly asking indulgence of his fellow orcs, because several of them nodded, several shrugged, and several others leaned closer over the table, eyes alight.

So Grimarr shrugged too, his big shoulder rolling, and then gave Jule a dismissive wave toward the table. So casual, so uncaring, and it only seemed to fuel the fire of Jule's lurching hunger as she obeyed, sliding off the bench to her knees, and ducking herself below the table.

It was dark, and the stone floor was hard, and above her Grimarr's voice was speaking again, seemingly having fully resumed his meeting. But his thighs had nestled a little around her, drawing her closer into their safety, and—Jule's gasp had to be audible, above—toward where he had his slick length full in hand, and was aiming it straight toward her face.

It wasn't an invitation, but an order. And one that a twisted, wanton part of Jule couldn't seem to refuse, as she moved a little closer, inhaling, watching, longing.

But she couldn't seem to go that last distance—she couldn't suck off an orc in the middle of a meeting, could she?—and finally, thankfully, Grimarr decided it for her. Gripping his big hand around the back of her head, and drawing her forward, even as his other hand slowly, purposely guided that huge, dripping hardness between her lips, deeper and deeper, until her mouth was stretched tight all around, his slick head nestled full into the back of her throat.

Jule's mouth had let out an audible, undeniable groan, setting that prick fervently twitching, and when her desperate eyes looked up under the edge of the table, Grimarr's were looking back down. Intent, hungry, powerful, pleased.

"Silence, woman," he said, the words a taunting, breathtaking thrill. "Else I may ask you to suck each of my guests in turn."

Fuck, had he truly just *said* that, but his eyes on her were smug, insolent, dazed with pleasure. And the threat had worked, because Jule was sucking desperately on him, in perfect silence, drawing out long, succulent draughts of that sweet, delectable orc-seed, and swallowing it hard down her throat.

Grimarr replied with a swift, approving smile, all sharp white teeth, and then settled himself a little deeper inside, his hand still on the back of her head. And then, he just started talking again, his voice perfectly steady as he argued with this orc and then that, while Jule desperately sucked him off under the table.

It was deeply, inexplicably arousing, feeling that hardness leak and shudder between her lips, that big hand clenching on the back of her head, while the rest of him blatantly and thoroughly ignored her. As if getting his cock sucked during an important orc-meeting was an entirely expected occurrence, one that he was fully entitled to, without question or consequence.

It only made Jule suck harder, dragging him deeper, craving him draining him, and when her tired, stretched-out lips began to make slurping sucking noises, he didn't seem to notice that either, thank the gods. Only swelled wider and wider, his hips bucking just slightly as he delved deeper, his fingers hard and powerful and demanding against the back of her head—

He blasted into her without warning, with only the slightest inflection in his still-speaking voice, even as his cock shuddered and pumped out its seed down her throat. Flooding her mouth with it, spilling and dripping out her lips, marking her and filling her, even as he still outwardly took absolutely no notice of her, the complete and utter bastard.

The sheer, shocking truth of it finally set Jule's own body convulsing and shuddering, wringing out its pleasure between her legs in furious, long-denied relief. Until she was left shaky and gasping, and she had to pull away from him, put her hands to her hot face, try desperately to breathe. Fuck. What in the bloody everloving *fuck*.

But Grimarr just kept on speaking, his voice noticeably more even than before. While his hand on Jule's head had switched to petting, gentle and almost affectionate, like she was a good hunting-dog who'd just made a kill, and not an actual woman who'd actually sucked him off in an actual company of orcs.

The chagrin kept growing as he kept speaking, as the orcs around finally shoved back their benches, and stood. All the better to look under the table, perhaps, and Jule curled herself up closer into Grimarr's thigh, into the safety and the shame.

When Grimarr's hand finally tugged her up to her feet, the room was blessedly empty, but for him. And Jule suddenly couldn't stand to look at him, at the cursed orc who'd taken such pleasure—for the second day in a row—in her blatant, humiliating degradation.

"Woman," he said, as his hand tilted her face up—but Jule kept her gaze safely beyond him, on the stone wall, and the flickering firelight upon it.

"You have honoured me, my fair one," he continued, his

voice quiet, with a trace of triumph in it, or perhaps wonder. "You have earned me my brothers' swords."

Jule darted a furtive look toward him, and then away again, her face heating at even the sight of him. "They agreed?" she managed, her voice thick. "To join you?"

"Yes," Grimarr said, and he gave her a twitchy little shake, drawing her gaze back to his face. "I know not why you did this. It was"—he swallowed, his throat convulsing—"a gift beyond compare, woman."

His eyes were so intent on hers, drawing yet more heat to her cheeks, and Jule had to look away, shake her head. "Baldr suggested it. He thought you needed help."

Grimarr barked out a choked, hoarse laugh. "Ach, I did," he said. "I did not grasp that half of them only wished to see you. To find proof that I have gained a lord's woman, and made her my own."

There was pride in his voice, and still perhaps that trace of wonder, and Jule gave another uneasy glance toward him. "You—you threatened to *offer* me to them," she said, the truth of that sounding breathtakingly awful on her lips, far more than all the rest. "To—to ask me to—"

She couldn't finish, her body giving a hard, all-consuming shudder, and Grimarr's hands on her face were suddenly strong, compelling, holding her eyes to his. "No," he said, quiet, fervent. "Those were only words. Only the power I wished to show. I could never do this. I should tear to pieces any orc who touches you, or my son."

The conviction in his voice felt real, one of his hands coming down to spread flat and possessive against her belly, and Jule frowned at it, and then back up at his face. "Well, what if," she managed, and why was she asking this, why did she care, "what if someday you did find another woman you liked more. Or multiple women. Like Astin. What then."

There had been whispers of this back in Yarwood, of orcs

sharing their hapless, helpless women with one another, or even keeping multiple women at once for their own. And from the look in Grimarr's eyes, it suddenly felt—possible. Like there *were* orcs that did such things, and what if Grimarr was one of them, dear gods, Jule hadn't even *considered*—

"No," he said again, still with that strange fervent intensity in his voice, his eyes. "I would not do this. You are *mine*, woman."

Jule couldn't believe this—Grimarr's own face had betrayed it—and she could see the power of his exhale, the sudden hollowing of his chest. "I shall not speak false," he said, quieter. "There are orcs who have done this. My own father did this. But it oft brings only envy and strife and pain, for both the women, and the sons they make. And most of all, for the orcs who watch from outside, and possess no mate at all. It poisons the brotherhood from within."

Jule felt her mouth twitch, into something perhaps resembling a smile. "How typical of you, orc," she said. "It's always all about your pet project, isn't it? Your planned future utopia of domestic orc bliss."

Grimarr frowned, and he gave a hard shake of his head. "It is not just this," he said. "It breaks the bond of a mate. It mocks the decree of the gods."

Jule's eyes searched him, not following, and he absently raised a hand, and smoothed it against the new braid she'd made in his hair. "When an orc and a woman mate," he said, "it binds them. My scent shall never fully fade from upon you, nor yours from me. I shall long for you in the night, and you for me, for as long as we walk together. It is hard to break this. It is cruel."

Jule considered that, and far too easily found the unsaid weight behind those words. "So you're telling me," she said, "that when—if—I decide to leave, after our forty days are up, your orc-magic will still—"

She couldn't quite seem to finish, because here, suddenly, in her thoughts, was the incongruous vision of Astin. Of herself, perhaps, alone in a room with Astin, obligated to touch and caress and kiss Astin, while knowing— remembering—this.

"It is not magic," Grimarr said, stubborn as ever. "It is as the gods decree. And if you wish to please the gods, you will stay."

"Oh, so now me staying is all about pleasing the *gods*," Jule made herself say, with a roll of her eyes, but for some stupid reason her mouth had quirked up, too. "Nothing to do with pleasing *you* in the least, orc."

"No," he agreed, also with a faint smile, and here was his hand, settling big and warm against her waist. "And if you wish to please the gods even further, mayhap you shall henceforth come to all my meetings."

"Not a chance in hell, orc," Jule said back, but there was no real heat in it, and when Grimarr pulled her closer she didn't resist, just breathed in the warm, musky scent of his chest. Strong enough to shove away those last lingering images of Astin, and the cold, uneasy disquiet they'd left behind.

"I would wish you to stay safe here with me," Grimarr's low voice whispered, into her hair. "This will please you too, woman. You shall see."

Jule couldn't seem to refuse, and instead just closed her eyes, and breathed. Thirty-eight days. She would see.

## 22

The next band of men arrived five days later, wearing the bearing of seasoned fighters, and the colours of Jule's cousin, Lord Otto.

"Will we kill them, Captain?" asked a hungry-looking orc named Skirvir, one of the first new recruits to arrive from the southern Bautul bands. "My blade thirsts for human flesh."

He'd flashed Jule a malicious grin as he spoke, but beside her Grimarr growled, and gave a reassuring squeeze to her hand. "Not here," Grimarr said. "There shall be no men killed on this mountain until I order it. If you wish to fight, go ask Silfast if you may join his raid to the east."

It had been Grimarr's consistent refrain these past days—ignore the men currently crawling all over the mountain, in favour of looting food and supplies from multiple far-off towns and caravans. It was a clever strategy, Jule had to admit, especially with her increasing knowledge of the mountain, and the true power of its built-in defenses. The ascents were steep and treacherous, the hard rock resistant to fire or digging, the exits now reduced to far-off tunnels below, except for that unreachable alcove near the top. Even the water supply wasn't an issue,

Jule had learned, since the orcs had cleverly engineered several plentiful streams to run inside the mountain, well away from possible poisoning or sabotage.

"Will you *ever* actually engage the men here?" Jule asked Grimarr, once Skirvir had loped away. "Not that I would at *all* condone this, but wouldn't it be to your benefit to pick off the men as they arrive, rather than waiting for their numbers to grow into the thousands?"

Grimarr was still frowning after Skirvir, and gave her a brief glance downwards. "I gird for many outcomes. I wish to wait and watch what the men do, and be ready."

It wasn't a real answer, Jule knew very well, and though it rankled to be kept in the dark, she found that she couldn't even fault him for that. She was still technically an enemy, after all— the men now traipsing about the mountain had been sent by her cousin—and for all Grimarr's lack of real information, he seemed to have no qualms allowing Jule to follow him from his meetings to the training-room and back again, as if she were his besotted pet lap dog.

In truth, it wasn't an objectively unpleasant way to spend her time—the meetings had remained safely uneventful, and Grimarr's prowess in the training-room was really rather diverting. He had also taken Sken's instructions for their son's health with grave seriousness, and after his own daily sparring sessions, he had begun insisting that Jule spend time training each day as well.

"This is ridiculous," Jule complained, that first day, after he put a wooden blade into her hand, and ordered her to try and stab him with it. "Surely when Sken said exercise, he meant a nice little stretch, or a stroll? A walk around the mountain, perhaps?"

But Grimarr only flashed her his sharp-toothed smile, and shook out his huge, bare-chested form with distracting ease. "I watched you oft ride and hunt before you came here," he said.

"You must not become a weak woman while you carry my son. I wish you to stay strong and hale. I will be gentle."

By gentle, Jule soon discovered, he meant utterly infuriating, and exacting as well. Making her chase and kick and swing at him, while he easily avoided every one of her attempts, calmly pointed out all her errors and missed opportunities, and ordered her to try again, and again, and again.

By the end of it, Jule was all but drenched in sweat, and Grimarr mercifully swept her bodily up into his arms, and strode toward the door. "Your mettle pleases me, woman," he said, as he carried her back to their room. "But your skill shows much to be learned. I am glad Sken drew me to this."

Jule didn't even bother trying to protest, because it was so damned typical, and she proceeded to sleep for half the following morning—but the next day it was easier, and the next, even more so. And soon, she almost found herself enjoying their daily sessions, and revelling in Grimarr's proud praise at even her slightest improvements.

There was also something compelling about the activity—about actually *doing* something with her time, and being busy, and learning new skills. Rather than just following Grimarr about all day, sitting in endless meetings full of incomprehensible black-tongue, while he planned a war, and she accomplished nothing.

"You know, I should like to make myself more useful," she said to him, several days later, during their daily stint outdoors. He'd continued taking her out for an hour or so each day, always to that tiny, unreachable bluff near the summit, and today it was bright and clear, just the kind of day that made one want to accomplish things. "Perhaps I could do work around here that needs being done. If you would allow it."

She was becoming more accustomed to the sight of Grimarr's face in the bright light, all lines and scars in sharp relief, and didn't even flinch when he turned and fixed her with a ghastly frown. "Why would I not allow this?" he demanded. "I thought you did not wish to work. After this time in the kitchen, and with the candles."

Of course he would bring *that* up, and Jule frowned straight back at him. "That was different," she snapped. "That was you shackling me and making me a drudge in your kitchen. And, I'll have you know"—she lifted her chin—"being chained to a kitchen is many women's worst nightmare. I had *servants* for this."

Grimarr's thick eyebrows went up, and his frown faded slightly, in place of something almost approaching amusement. "So you still will not make candles, then."

Jule made a face at him, and then flopped herself down on the nearest flat rock and leaned back, eyes closed, head tilted up to the sun. And then, rather self-consciously, because she *knew* Grimarr was watching, she tugged up her tunic a little, exposing her slightly thickened belly to the sun's soothing heat.

"Fine," she said irritably, keeping her eyes closed. "If it matters that much to you, I'll make your damned candles."

There was a brief chuckle, and then the sound of Grimarr's big body lowering to sit beside her. "I thank you, woman," he said, and with it was the feel of his hand, settling light on her torso's warm, exposed skin. "Ask Baldr to help you. After this, he can guide you to other work also, if you wish."

Jule opened an eye to look at him, but his gaze was intent on her bare stomach, and on his hand spread wide upon it. And as she watched, he leaned forward, until his mouth was barely a breath from her skin, and then—he spoke. In quiet, rolling waves of black-tongue, not unlike a purr, or a caress.

It made Jule's heartbeat stutter uncomfortably, her breath catching close in her throat, and Grimarr glanced up, the hard furrow returning between his eyes. "What," he said. "I cannot speak to my own son?"

Jule swallowed, tried for a shrug. "You never speak to me

that way," she said, stupidly, and then felt her face flush hot and crimson. And then even hotter when Grimarr's mouth broke into a slow smile, white teeth sharp and gleaming in the sunlight.

"This would please you?" he murmured, as he moved his body up closer, his eyes locked to hers. And then immediately launched into a low, smooth, inexplicably thrilling string of black-tongue, all dripping honey and pooling hunger in her ears.

"Cheating orc," she managed, but he only laughed, and the sound of that made it even worse, sending ripples of heat all through her groin. And when that hand touching her moved upwards, sliding the tunic with it, she could only seem to arch into it, and gasp.

It led to Grimarr taking her right there, out on a rock, in the open air. Playing straight into his exhibitionist streak again, Jule well knew, but there was only sky and rock all around, and she had to admit it felt wonderful like this, bright and clean and joyful in the sunlight.

"You again baffle me, woman," Grimarr said, once they were both sated and breathless, and he'd wiped up the requisite mess. "First you suck me before my brothers, and now you welcome my prick in the sun. I thought you wished to hide these things."

Jule cast an uneasy glance around—there was still no way anyone could possibly see, right?—and tried for a shrug. "It's not that I wish to hide," she said. "I only wish to have a proper choice in the matter."

Grimarr seemed to consider this, his mouth pursing as he tucked himself back into his trousers. "Ach. So my prick is like the kitchen, then."

Jule blinked at him, once—and then burst out laughing, despite herself. "Yes, Grimarr," she managed, between chuckles. "Your prick is just like the kitchen."

He only looked at her, bemused, but as she kept giggling, she could see the smile slowly tugging at the corner of his mouth. His eyes warm, tolerant, so damn expressive, and in an odd, unguarded moment Jule leaned in, and brushed a brief kiss to his scarred cheek. "Better than the kitchen," her betraying voice murmured. "Obviously."

He did finally grin at that, making Jule's stomach flip disconcertingly. "I am glad of this," he said back. "And if you truly do not wish to make candles, woman, then do not."

Jule couldn't seem to reply, and instead gave a noncommittal shrug, her face strangely hot. But once they were back inside again, and Grimarr had headed off to yet another meeting, Jule found herself standing with Baldr, in the damned kitchen, and conferring about candles.

"What do you mean, you have no string?" she demanded at him. "You orcs stole all the wax from my cellar, but didn't think to bring the string?"

Baldr only shrugged, and cheerfully pointed out that he recalled seeing some string in the Grisk storage-room. This led to a trek over to the Grisk wing, where Ymir, the cranky storage-room porter, informed her that he would only trade it for the Ash-Kai's bowls. And thus, Jule embarked on an afternoon-long quest around the mountain, ever followed by an increasingly amused Baldr, who had seemingly decided against giving Jule directions, in favour of letting her find her own haphazard way about.

"Woman?" said Grimarr's voice, when she very nearly strode straight into him in the Ash-Kai wing, several hours later. It was still pitch-dark in the corridors, and Grimarr was with several other orcs, but Jule was disconcerted to discover that she knew where he stood among them, both by sound, and by the distinctive, musky scent of him. "Why do you wander about so?"

"I'm *trying* to make your candles," Jule said irritably, "if

Ymir actually keeps to his word, and gives me his damned string, the old codger."

With that, she stalked off toward the Grisk storage-room—or what she hoped was the Grisk storage-room—followed by the sound of Baldr laughing behind her. "You women are strange creatures," he said, once he caught up to her again. "Why must you suddenly do this now, when you promised it to the captain many days past?"

Jule didn't deign to answer that, and after yet more negotiation at the Grisk storage-room, she finally gained possession of her string. And then she and Baldr did the hot, tiring work of actually making the candles, by the hundreds, until all the wax and string was gone. Just in time, it turned out, as a Grisk orc named Varinn, one of Baldr's friends, popped his head in to announce that Grimarr had just ordered all the fires but the kitchen's and the forges' to be doused, in order to prevent the men's trying to block or dig out the smoke-holes.

"What other kind of work needs doing around here, Baldr?" Jule asked, as she mopped the sweat off her forehead, and eyed their makeshift racks of drying candles. "Grimarr said you could line me up with a few things. After I go have a nap, that is."

Baldr, unnervingly, and no doubt at Grimarr's request, seemed to have already developed a comprehensive mental list for just such an inquiry. And so it was, that over the next few days, Jule found herself doing a variety of curious, unrelated tasks that she herself would never have thought orcs needed doing. Showing the Skai tailor how best to expand a shirt. Identifying a disconcerting quantity of old human items in the Grisk storage-room. Using chalk to draw a landscape, "human style", on the Ash-Kai common-room wall. And down in the bowels of the mountain, helping the smooth-faced Ka-esh orcs interpret an impressive variety of human texts and maps, and explaining the contexts to which they referred.

"Why is this land owned by Lord Rikard, and not Lady Scall?" John asked one afternoon, in regards to a map he'd spread open on the table of the Ka-esh common-room, which was dimly lit with one of Jule's candles. "As Lord Scall's wife, should Lady Scall not take it when he dies?"

Jule couldn't help a grimace, and in reply John sidled a little away, his eyes lingering uneasy on her mouth. She was the first human he'd ever directly interacted with, Jule had learned, and it was odd to realize that he found her just as unsettling as she'd first found the orcs.

"They changed the law when I was a child," she replied, with as bland an expression as possible. "So instead of a man's wife or daughter inheriting, the property now defaults to the closest male relative. Women can no longer hold title."

John's black eyebrows drew together, a sharp white tooth chewing his lip. "What if there are no male relatives left?" he asked. "As with Lord Norr?"

"Then the wife's closest male relative inherits," Jule said thinly. "In Astin's case, that would be my cousin Frank. Lord Otto."

"This does not seem logical," John said, and Jule couldn't help a roll of her eyes, to which John gave a slight but noticeable flinch.

"It isn't logical," she replied. "It's yet another way for men to protect themselves and their positions, at everyone else's expense."

John was watching her carefully now, his head tilted. "Why do you women tolerate this? Why do you cling to your men so?"

*And refuse to consider orcs in their stead*, was the unspoken question, and Jule had to think about it, her eyes held to John's smooth face, his lovely pointed ears. "It's all we know," she said finally. "It's difficult to accept one's life as a prison, when one has spent an entire existence in its walls."

John kept studying her, his quill absently tapping on his scroll. "Yet you seem to have accepted this. Why?"

Jule had to think about that, make herself speak truth. "I think, perhaps," she began, "I have seen more than many women. Many women have good husbands, or at least, husbands that they themselves chose. My husband, Lord Norr"—she swallowed—"was not my choice. And he is not a good man."

"Lord Norr allowed you to be taken," John said, nodding, as though that settled the matter. "And he has not yet come for you."

It was true. Jule's forty-day deadline was already somehow down to twenty-two, and while there were now multiple regiments of Astin's men camped outside, there was still no sign of Astin himself. Or of Otto or Culthen, for that matter, who, according to Grimarr's scouts, were each now ensconced at their own holdings closest to the mountain, still multiple leagues away. Directing their forces from a distance, rather than in person, and while Jule could easily understand their motivations for this—coming here themselves would give the whole situation even more legitimacy and attention—it still hurt, more than she wanted to admit.

"If Lord Norr comes," John said now, "would this change your view of him? Or of us?"

His eyes were watchful, almost suspicious, and Jule knew by now that these orcs saw humans as short-sighted, fickle, self-absorbed. That many of them would expect Jule to return her affections to Astin, no matter what happened here, or what Astin did.

"Actually, no," Jule said, short. "It wouldn't change a thing."

John seemed to accept this, moving on to his next question, but in the hours and days following, Jule's thoughts seemed to linger and brood on it all. Comparing the life she'd spent with Astin, to this one.

And the truth was, this life—the one where she was most certainly an actual prisoner in an orc-mountain—felt *better*. It felt far freer, and far less like a prison, than her old one ever had.

And if Jule had her way, she could admit, perhaps, it might be best if Astin never came at all.

## 23

A week later, there was still no sign of Astin.

Many more men had come, however, steadily trickling in from the three lords' southern fortresses, and several bands of mercenaries had arrived from the northeast. There were even miners, now, men who specialized in tunnels and digging, commanding teams of burly workmen with pickaxes.

Before coming to live in the mountain, Jule would easily have given the situation's full advantage to the men—they certainly had more resources, and access to far more soldiers— but now, she fully understood that the truth was quite the opposite. That laying siege to a human-constructed fortress was one thing, when one could climb or dig under walls, or fire catapults, or poison wells. But laying siege to a huge, impenetrable, fire-forged mountain, complete with a secure water supply, was another matter entirely—especially when said mountain was full of clever orcs with considerable tunnelling and mining skills, who'd clearly spent years, if not decades, planning for just such an event.

At first, it seemed that the men's main strategy had been to crawl over the mountain, setting its little remaining brush afire, and seeking new ways in. In general, this had been a failing proposition—most upper areas of the mountain were entirely inaccessible, even with ropes and ladders and teams of men— and Jule had winced at the word of the injuries, and worse, that had so far befallen the climbing men.

Of late, the men seemed to have abandoned their climbing efforts, in favour of attempting to laboriously dig out the most promising paths into the mountain. In return, Grimarr had only filled in the tunnels nearest the digging, and arranged for convenient new rockfalls over the dug-out areas each night. It seemed easy enough work for the orcs, supported by incomprehensible calculations from the Ka-esh, and Grimarr's only real challenge, as far as Jule could tell, was keeping his increasingly irritable orcs in line.

"Are you *ever* planning to meet the men in combat here?" Jule had asked him, more than once, but Grimarr only continued to reply with vague, noncommittal answers.

"I watch, and wait," he would say, with a grip of his hand to her arse, or a thrilling nip at her throat. "We shall see what comes."

It was far too easy to sink into his offered distractions and easy words, enough that Jule almost—almost—believed him. But at the same time, Grimarr was barely sleeping, he was sending off multiple raids each day, and the forges kept burning at all hours of the day and night. And most telling of all, many more orcs had continued to pour into the mountain, not only from Bautul, but from across all five clans, all primed and armed and ready to kill—if not for Grimarr's orders, holding them back.

The rising tensions within the mountain soon led to several brutal fights, including a vicious, impromptu brawl between Grimarr and one of the new Bautul captains in the kitchen, while the room full of orcs watched. It finally ended with the

Bautul captain suffering a badly broken arm, and screaming bloody murder on the floor while Sken and Efterar set it straight again.

"Did you really have to break his arm?" Jule asked Grimarr afterwards, once she'd followed him to their room, and pulled off his torn, bloody tunic. He was still furious, all but vibrating with rage, and he paced in a swift circle, all prowling deadly anger.

"Yes," he snapped, "I did. I needed a wound that would heal, but slowly, so that the others will see."

It was so damned calculated, as he always was, and Jule couldn't help a tolerant smile at his twitchy pacing form. "For all your high talk of civilization, orc," she said, "you are as brutal as the whole of Bautul and Skai combined."

He replied with a low growl, a sharp glare toward her. "I must needs be so," he shot back. "I do this so our son will not need to."

Their son. Jule still couldn't hear the words without twitching, but Sken's daily examinations—now sometimes supplemented by Efterar—had continued to prove their son's existence, as did Jule's decidedly thickened waist, and increasingly tender breasts. Sken had said, again, that the babe would most certainly arrive in spring—not a dissimilar time frame as with human babes, that—but already it seemed further along than a human babe should be. *Cunning*, Jule kept thinking. *Lusty. Strong.*

"You wish for our son to succeed you?" Jule heard herself say, her voice gone rather high-pitched. "As the orcs' *captain*?"

"Yes," Grimarr said back, in a tone that suggested this was obvious. "He shall be captain, and his world shall be better than mine."

Oh. It was a thought Jule hadn't yet considered in this, and she added it to the growing swirling mass in her head. The idea of building a better world not for themselves, whether orcs or humans, but for their children. For her own son.

"And you think war with Astin will accomplish this?" Jule asked archly, and in reply Grimarr gave a hard grunt, and stalked over toward her. Putting his big hands to her, and then bodily flipping her down and over, so that she was on hands and knees on his bed, her arse facing out toward him.

"I know," Grimarr said, as he unceremoniously yanked down Jule's trousers, and exposed her bare behind to the room's cool air, "that heaping shame upon Lord Norr will do this. I know"—oh *hell*, because that was the feel of that familiar hardness, prodding just *there*—"that no man, and no orc, wishes to follow a shamed lord. And a shamed lord"—he bore down, deep, while Jule bit back a scream—"is one whose woman craves his enemy's prick."

Jule could only gasp, trapped, impaled on that thrilling huge orc-prick, and behind her Grimarr laughed, low and dark. Like he knew exactly how cold that was, the calculating plotting fiend, but in this moment—in too many moments, these past weeks—Jule had found that she didn't quite care.

"Craving is putting it a touch too strong, orc," she said, over her shoulder, between her gasping breaths. "Mild interest, perhaps, more like."

He replied with a delicious growl, deep enough that it rumbled into her through his invading cock, and then he drew himself out, so abruptly that Jule twitched and gasped. And when she tried to push back and find him again, he was far too strong, the bastard, easily holding her whole body off with one hand, and laughing.

"Stubborn woman," he murmured, as she felt that hardness just nudge inside her, again, and again. "Speak truth. You crave this. All women do."

Jule might not have fought it, if not for the last bit, and she gave a growl of her own, even as her eyes fluttered with the rising galloping hunger. "Arrogant *beast*," she hissed back, over her shoulder, toward where his eyes were intent on his cock, as he nudged it in and out. "It's all the orc-magic. The bond, or whatever. Not you."

It was enough to snap his eyes back up, narrowing hard and disapproving on hers. "You lie, woman," he hissed. "So much from your mouth is lies. You are human through and through."

Jule resented that, deeply, and she strained again to push back onto that torturous heat, just out of her reach. "And you are an orc," she shot back. "Brutal and aggressive and deadly, all you care about is your power and your pleasure and your pride, and appearing stronger than you truly are!"

The words should have struck deep, true as they were, but Grimarr only curled his lip, and raised his black eyebrows. And then he held Jule still, his powerful hands digging into her hips, pulling her apart—and then he slammed himself deep inside, strong and shocking enough that Jule actually shouted with it, full of him, full of shrieking clawing pleasure.

"Lies again," he breathed, and now he was pummelling her in earnest, driving inside in stroke after breathtaking stroke. "This is power, woman. Lord Norr's wife screaming upon my prick, and carrying my son in her belly!"

Gods, he was awful, and gods, he felt good, and Jule kicked and squirmed at him, to no avail. Being thoroughly and brutally fucked by an orc, stabbed again and again with a huge slick orc-prick, feeling the seed spurt and drip, *please…*

"Please," she heard herself say, and in reply there was a harsh, taunting laugh behind her.

"Please, orc," he corrected her, ordered her. "Please, Grimarr. And then you shall have your seed."

There was no use arguing, Jule well knew by now, and this time the craving was too strong to even try. "Please, orc," she gasped, as he punched inside, again and again. "Please, Grimarr. Fill me."

His groan behind her was deep, guttural, agonized, as he gouged inside one last time—and then sprayed her full of him, pulsing out again and again with hot, sticky, glorious pleasure.

He stayed there, gasping, for several breaths, while Jule gasped too—and without warning he pulled out, and stepped back. Releasing the pent-up flood of his seed inside her, and Jule groaned helplessly as she felt it spurt out of her in sticky rivulets, running down her still-spread legs while he watched.

"Stubborn woman," came Grimarr's voice, quieter now, and here was the feeling of cloth, mopping her up, before the mess fully soaked her trousers.

"Stubborn orc," Jule replied, still a little shaky, and Grimarr's big hands turned her back over, gently this time.

"Yes," he murmured, as he wiped up her front with the rag—one of the ones they'd begun keeping in their room, for just this purpose—and then tossed it aside, and pulled her trousers back up. "Are you well?"

His hand had spread wide over her belly, nudging up under her tunic, his eyes asking the question he really meant. Was their son well, and Jule ignored the odd twist in her gut as she dropped her eyes, and nodded.

It was perhaps the fourth or fifth time they'd done it like that so far, rough and raw with unanswered truths, and each time afterwards Grimarr had stopped, and asked. *Are you well. Is this pain. Do I hurt you, or our son.*

Perhaps it was a sign that they should have given it up, but Jule's inexplicable, traitorous body seemed to crave it, whenever he offered it. Just as it craved the sweetness, the daily suckling of his seed, the way his big body spoke softly to her in the dark as it moved above her, her legs tight around him, his cock buried deep between.

"You?" Jule asked, quiet, following on his question to her, and Grimarr nodded, looking down as he tucked himself back in his trousers.

"Yes," he said, short. "For this, I thank you."

He glanced brief toward her, and then away again, and Jule felt herself swallow, her eyes held to his face. He meant because it had helped with the anger, even she could see that, and it had done so each other time he'd taken her like this, too. Taking the anger, letting it out, putting it back in its place again.

"The Ash-Kai raid shall soon leave," he said now, angling toward the door. "I must go see it off. Meet me here again at dusk."

The words weren't an order, Jule now knew, but a kindness. Giving her free rein of the mountain, doing whatever she'd like to do, making herself at home in his home. Like a good lord, a kind lord, would do. Like she'd asked.

"Wait," Jule said, already halfway across the room, her hand to his arm. "Grimarr. I have—a question."

He turned, waiting, eyebrows raised, and Jule looked at him, at those watching black eyes. It didn't matter if she asked. The answer meant nothing. Right?

"If I were to leave here," she began, tentative, "would you take another mate? Another woman? Once our forty days are up?"

She hadn't mentioned that ever-encroaching deadline in several weeks, now, but she had been carefully counting each day as it passed. And it was now down to ten—*ten?*—which suddenly, for some reason, felt like no time at all.

"Do you aim to leave here?" Grimarr asked back, his voice just as careful as hers. "In ten days?"

So he'd been counting too, then, and Jule tried for a casual shrug. "I don't know," she said. "It depends."

"On what does it depend," came Grimarr's immediate reply, his eyes gone narrow, and Jule sighed, searched for an answer. On what did it depend? Really? Him? Their son? Astin? The war?

"I want to see what you decide to do with these men," Jule

said, finally. "I want to know how far you'll go with this war. I want to see if you"—she swallowed, lifted her chin—"if you'll order a massacre or not."

The words felt true—they *were* true—and Jule marvelled at that, at what it meant. It meant that this thing, between them, wasn't the question anymore. The question, instead, was how brutal this calculating orc truly was. How many lives and families he would destroy.

"I have no idea what the hell you're planning out there," Jule continued, with a helpless little wave in the direction of the men's camps. "But if you were really just trying to humiliate Astin, you wouldn't have worked so hard to bring on all these extra fighters, and make all those weapons. So are you really planning to wait until all the realm's armies are here, and then dump an avalanche on them, or annihilate them in the night? Or maybe you'll start burning down all those towns you're raiding? Or, maybe you're just biding your time until Astin finally shows up, and then you'll drag him in here and torture him, or threaten to throw me off a cliff while he watches?"

Grimarr's mouth thinned, but he didn't speak, and Jule took a step closer to him, studying those black eyes. "You have *something* planned beyond hiding away in here and seeing what happens, orc," she said. "You *always* have a plan. And this plan is probably awful, and I want to know what the hell it is before I commit to making a *life* with you. And, as part of that"—she had to stop, draw in a long breath—"I'd also like to know how replaceable I am to you."

His face was oddly inscrutable, but he still didn't speak, and Jule couldn't seem to stop herself from filling the silence. "I'm already your third mate, aren't I? And we both know I'm a convenient pawn in your war, your principal means of shaming Astin. And then there's how hard I worked to support Astin and my father, and perhaps you'll never really forgive me for that. And you think I always lie, and yet you keep these huge secrets from me, and I just—"

Her voice had been rising, going louder and shriller, until it broke off in her throat entirely. Leaving her blinking back the inexplicable prickling behind her eyes, the inexplicable hurt behind her words, the almost desperate need for him to say that he did care, that he truly was a good lord, that he was worth whatever this was, tangled deep in Jule's chest.

"Woman, I—" Grimarr began, but then broke off too, and looked away. Making Jule's heart plummet even further, because he so rarely hesitated, he always had an answer, and this meant—it meant—

"You know what, never mind," Jule managed, as she spun on her heel, and strode toward the door. "Clearly you still won't tell me, and therefore all my worst suspicions are probably true, and this is going to be an utter disaster. You'll kill all these men, their children will grow up to hate you, and your war will never, *ever* end!"

She was already out in the empty corridor when Grimarr's big hand caught her waist, and pulled her to a stop. Lingering against her belly, like he so often did these days, like he was caressing both her, and their son.

"Woman," he said. "Listen to me. I do not wish for this."

Jule looked, found the glint of his black eyes in the dark. "Then what do you wish for, orc."

There was the sound of a sigh, of his other hand coming to join the first on her waist. "What I wish for," he said slowly, "what I wait for, what I plan for—is peace. With men."

His hands against her clenched on the words, like the very thought was painful, but he'd said it. He'd said he wanted *peace*. Had he?

"What?" Jule said blankly. "No. That's not possible. You're gathering an *army*."

"Yes," Grimarr said, his voice quiet but firm. "I do gird to fight. But also, each night, since the men have come to our mountain, we have left them a letter. In this letter I ask to meet, and set terms. And three times, since this has begun, I have sent this same letter to Wolfen. To the place you claim as your Citadel, and its lords and magistrates. And once to each town and caravan we have raided, before the raid has begun."

"*What*?" Jule said again, gaping at him, because he didn't—he wouldn't—would he? He was gathering an army. He hated Astin, and men. Didn't he?

But his eyes and his hands were steady, true, and Jule couldn't stop staring, couldn't even think. "*Why*?" she demanded. "What are you asking for? Who are you asking to meet with? And *why* in the gods' names didn't you *tell* me?"

Grimarr hesitated, his gaze briefly shuttering, like there was yet more he was hiding. And suddenly Jule wanted to shake him, or yell at him, or throw her arms around him, because he was offering *peace*, and he was hiding it, and *why*?

"I ask to meet face to face with your human lords, in a safe place," he said finally. "And when we meet, I will ask to own these lands around our mountain. I will ask for rights to trade, and rights to wed women who wish for this. I will ask for an end to all raids and killing, on both sides. I will ask for safety for orc sons."

Jule was shaking her head, still staring at him, but she felt the comprehension dawning, spreading its way through her thoughts. All this time, Grimarr had been proclaiming the orcs' strength, flaunting it very clearly, while also very publicly asking for peace. While making sure he absolutely could not be ignored, with Lord Norr's wife still trapped inside his mountain, and whispers and rumours no doubt swirling all over the realm.

It was brilliant, it really was, and despite herself Jule felt her mouth twitching up, her head giving a funny little shake. "You sneaky conniving *bastard*," she breathed. "You were planning for this all along, weren't you. Even fighting those first men who came here—letting some of them run—making sure word spreads that I'm here, and how thoroughly you've humiliated Astin. And now you're gathering an army of orcs, from all over the realm, and no doubt letting *that* be known too, while you also raid all over the countryside, and throw around peace proposals, and show that your mountain can't be touched. And the men still think there are thousands of you orcs in hiding, all over the realm. You *bastard*."

Grimarr didn't deny it, but his eyes briefly, almost imperceptibly, flicked down toward Jule's belly. And that was part of it too, of course it absolutely was, and Jule felt like the wind had been knocked out of her, like the world had suddenly turned sideways.

"So I really am just a pawn," she heard herself say, her voice almost painfully thin. "Just a means to an end, for you."

Grimarr's black eyebrows furrowed, his hands spreading wider against her waist. "This is not so, woman," he said, but his voice was thin, too. "I chose you. I have told you this. I watched you ride and hunt and trade. You are strong and fair."

"But I'm not what you really would have chosen, if all this hadn't been your plan," Jule said, almost a whisper. "Right? So if I left, you *would* take another mate. Maybe one you really wanted."

Those eyes looked at her, that dark head tilting, and she heard him give a heavy sigh, felt it under her skin. "I wish for you, woman," he said, soft. "I wish for you to stay. You have brought me great joy."

But it wasn't a denial. He would have chosen someone else. And he would take another mate. He *would*. And Jule couldn't quite hide her flinch, her eyes dropping to the floor at their feet.

"Oh," she said, with a wretched twist of a smile. "Well. Perhaps if I do leave after all, and your top-secret peace proposal works out, you'll find another woman who'll both bring you joy, *and* be worthy of sharing your plans with, as well as your bed. Someone you'll actually like, and trust, and respect, and care about."

"Woman," Grimarr said, perhaps a plea, or a reproach, but suddenly Jule just felt sick, and alone, and exhausted.

"You don't trust me," she said. "And clearly I can't trust you. So just—go. Please."

He didn't speak, or even try to argue, and Jule waited in silence, eyes on the floor, until he turned on his heel, and left.

## 24

J ule spent the rest of the day moping about the mountain, feeling off-kilter and out of sorts.

She'd known she was part of Grimarr's plan. She'd *known*, since the start. But she had, perhaps, allowed the strength of that to slide. She had, perhaps, wanted to believe he truly cared. That she mattered.

It was abominable, on its face, and deeply shameful, too. Jule had had all those grand plans of revenge, and she'd meant to follow through with them, and somehow, these past weeks, she'd almost entirely forgotten them. Instead, she'd been lured into the novelty and the freedom of life with these orcs, and abandoned her purpose here entirely.

She was a pawn. Replaceable.

Gods, it hurt, and how in the gods' names had she been so stupid? How had she not spent all this time learning black-tongue, or creating a secret map of the mountain, or attempting to communicate with the men outside? Why hadn't she tried to escape, or to show the men a way in?

But this was why, because even the thought of it almost made her feel sick to her stomach. Men in the mountain, killing the orcs, perhaps wiping them out for good. And no matter what Grimarr did or said, the truth was, Jule didn't want that to happen. She *wanted* peace between humans and orcs. And what the hell did that mean for her now?

"Oh, hey, Jules," said a voice, and Jule blinked up, and found Kesst standing over her, giving a cheerful smile. "What's up?"

Jule had been sitting on a bench in the candlelit Ash-Kai common-room, which was currently otherwise empty, thanks to Grimarr's raid. "Nothing, really," she said, as she tried to wipe a surreptitious hand across her too-wet eyes. "Just—sitting."

But Kesst was a curious, clever orc—he'd become something of a friend, these past weeks—and he dropped his lean, ever-shirtless form down onto the bench beside Jule, and gave a lazy, catlike stretch. "Ol' Grim giving you grief, then, is he?" he said. "Shooting off his mouth instead of his prick?"

Jule couldn't help a half-smile, and a twitchy shrug of her shoulder. "Something like that," she said, and in reply Kesst raised his eyebrows, folding his arms over his chest.

"C'mon, Jules," he said. "Me and Grim go so far back, I know how *all* his shit smells. Out with it."

Jule made a face, but then let out a heavy sigh. Why not tell him? Grimarr didn't *really* care about her, so what did it matter, anyway?

"Grimarr's been keeping secrets from me," she said, with an involuntary little sniff. "He doesn't trust me. He might not even really *like* me. He's using me to get what he wants from all this, and he basically told me that if I ever leave, he'll replace me with another woman. A *better* one."

Kesst gave a low laugh, a roll of his dark eyes. "And what did you say? Please tell me you told him to stop spewing rubbish?"

Jule blinked, and shook her head, and beside her Kesst

stretched again, this time folding his arms behind his head. "Because he is," he said firmly. "That overstuffed oaf is obsessed with you, and that little orcling you're growing. Brings you into every second sentence he says, runs off after you at the first opportunity, and laughs at the stupidest shit. He hasn't been this happy in *years*."

Jule couldn't help a snort, because if this was happy Grimarr, she'd hate to see the unhappy one, and Kesst gave a smug nod, as if fully following her sentiment. "So naturally, he's terrified of losing you," he said firmly. "And being a right bastard about it."

Oh. "He doesn't seem very terrified," Jule said doubtfully. "And he *has* had two mates before me, so I'm sure that part is true, isn't it?"

Kesst dismissed Grimarr's previous and future women with a contemptuous snort. "Probably," he said. "He's bound and determined to make himself into the greatest captain of all time, and having a woman is all part of the show, isn't it? But I can assure you, it's *you* he wants, Jules. He wants a woman who'll fuck his brains out, and suck his seed out, and also come in here and do *this*"—he gave a little wave at him, the room, the mountain—"without running away screaming, or blubbering at him every night, or plotting to kill him in his sleep. You're a revelation, Jules."

Jule winced, because she had indeed thought, at first, about doing all those things, hadn't she? "But Grimarr's never once said that to me," she replied, quiet, to the floor. "He's kept this huge secret from me, all this time. He doesn't *trust* me."

She could feel Kesst's gaze prickling on her skin, searching and speculative. "If you want the truth, Jules," he said, "I don't think Grim trusts anyone."

Jule couldn't help an uncertain glance up—surely Grimarr trusted Baldr, at least, or Sken, or Kesst himself—but Kesst was frowning at the wall opposite, chewing his lip with sharp teeth. "I don't suppose Grim's told you about his family?"

"He's mentioned them," Jule said uneasily, casting her thoughts back. "It didn't sound like it was good."

Kesst snorted, and kicked his clawed foot at the fur-covered floor. "No," he said, "it wasn't. I mean, most of us orcs have some fucked-up parent issues, but when you've got *Kaugir* for a father—"

Wait wait wait. "*Kaugir* was Grimarr's *father*?" Jule demanded, her voice gone shrill. "The horrible captain who you all left chopped up in a *field*?"

Kesst nodded, and gave a jerky shrug of his usually graceful form. "Not *we all*," he said, his voice a little stilted, now. "Just Grim. And thank *fuck* for it."

Jule's mouth had fallen open—Grimarr had killed his own *father*?—but suddenly, somehow, it all made perfect, appalling sense. All his reluctant, seemingly disparate comments about the cruel Ash-Kai, about stealing the place of captain, about sacrificing his father's wealth. Even his assumption, so easy, that their own son would become captain after him. As though he were—Jule swallowed hard—the orcs' *prince*.

"Oh," Jule said numbly, blinking at Kesst's knowing eyes. "But—but *why*? Why would Grimarr do such an awful thing? And why would he hide *that* from me, too?"

"Do you truly wish to hear the tale?" Kesst countered, his eyes gone oddly flinty. "Do you truly wish to listen?"

Jule gave a fervent nod—she did, she *had* to know—so finally, with his voice carrying a stilted, unfamiliar cadence, Kesst began to speak.

He told of Kaugir the Iron-Claw, Captain of Ash-Kai, Grisk, and Ka-esh for nigh unto forty summers. He told of many victories and women won, and of a certain young woman named Mary, who birthed Kaugir his first live son. Grimarr, of Clan Ash-Kai.

He told how Kaugir saw the strength granted by his lusty young son, and wished for more. How he stole more women not only from the men, but from his fellow orcs as well. And how in punishment for this sin against his brothers, the gods stole away all Kaugir's sons, save for the first alone.

Mary, too, brought forth two more sons, but neither lived to grow, and the bearing of the second of these left her near death. But Kaugir did not heed his mate's suffering, nor the pleas of his son for her care. And when his son sought to bring a faraway orc with strong magic to help his mother, Kaugir struck his axe upon his half-grown son's back, and thus brought him near death also.

Jule's eyes had squeezed shut by this point, visions of Grimarr's scarred back parading across her eyelids, but Kesst kept speaking, still with that odd, formal cadence to his voice. Telling how Kaugir's fair mate died a cruel death, alone and in pain in the mountain, without even her loyal, beloved son by her side. And how after this, no orc dared to again bring a mate or a son to the mountain. How instead they learned to keep them secret in dens and camps, well away from Kaugir, and other orcs who might wish to follow the path he had shown them.

But this only made the orc-sons easier for men to find, and only brought the orcs more death and suffering. Kaugir saw the power of this suffering, and used it to strike back at the men who killed the orc-sons. This only led to more war, and yet more suffering.

Kaugir's son watched all this, and he learned. He learned that war only winnowed his brothers, and did not sate their thirst for revenge. He learned that his brothers' bloodlust was borne of grief and loneliness. He learned that the war and the women were two sides of the same blade.

And from this, Kesst's lilting voice continued, Kaugir's son learned wisdom. He learned to be quiet and wise, to fight and kill, to search for strength away from his father's cruel eye. He worked in secret to save the hidden orc-sons, and to build up his weaker brothers, both in battle, and in the forgotten ways of service and learning and magic and home. He earned the fealty of many, and trusted no one.

And when Grimarr of Clan Ash-Kai, the Prince of the Orcs, had gathered his strength, he fought his father Kaugir before all his brothers. He killed his father by his own hand, under the open sky, and left him to rot in dishonour. He did this to avenge his mother, and his blood brothers, and all they had lost.

Kesst's hypnotic voice halted there, but his silence almost seemed part of the story, somehow, spiralling off toward the guttering candle-flame. Leaving Jule staring blank and heavy toward it, almost as though she were caught in a trance, or a spell. As though through Kesst's strangely spoken words, she'd seen all that had happened, with her very eyes.

"I'm—so sorry, Kesst," she heard her muffled voice say. "For you, and for Grimarr. For all of you."

Kesst shrugged beside her, bumping her shoulder with his, and suddenly it felt like the spell had broken, snapping apart into dust. Leaving Jule sitting there, wiping at her oddly wet eyes, while Kesst stretched his arms over his head again, and gave her a wry, bitter little smile.

"So you see, Jules," he said, "Grim can't afford to trust anyone. He certainly can't trust a human he's only known for a month. But that doesn't mean he doesn't care, all right? Or that he doesn't *want* to trust you. Surely you can see that, in how he talks to you? How he looks at you, and touches you?"

Jule felt herself nodding, wiping at her eyes again, and Kesst huffed a wry chuckle. "I mean, ol' Grim refuses to even leave the mountain," he continued. "Says it's to keep a presence, a watch on the men, but we all know better. Even today, instead of going with the rest of our Ash-Kai brothers on that raid, he's skulking around below, barking out orders at anyone who'll listen, and making a right nuisance of himself."

Kesst was now giving Jule a very pointed, almost expectant look, and as she wiped away at the last of the wetness from her face, she found herself eyeing him with slowly increasing suspicion. "Wait. And you expect *me* to do something about this?"

Kesst nodded, still with that expectant look on his face, and Jule groaned aloud, even as she gave a shaky, reluctant laugh. "You damned underhanded orcs," she snapped, though there was no heat in it. "You came here and told me all this just to cajole me into rescuing you, didn't you? Let me guess, Efterar's caught up in whatever Grimarr's doing down there?"

Kesst didn't even look slightly ashamed, and instead winked, and stood gracefully to his feet. "See, this is why we like you, Jules," he said. "C'mon, I'll take you."

Jule threw her hands up, but followed him out of the room, and down to the Skai barracks. Where Grimarr was, indeed, standing over the long, apparently sleeping form of one of his scouts—the slim, snarky one named Joarr—and shouting in black-tongue at Efterar, who had his arms crossed and chin raised, and a bottle in his hand.

"No, I am not waking him up," Efterar finally replied, in flawless common-tongue, once Grimarr had stopped for air. "He sustained this injury bringing you this information this morning, and you need to leave him the hell alone. And yes, I know he's our best scout, and that's why he's not dead. So fuck *off*."

They were both entirely ignoring Jule and Kesst, though of course they had to know they were there, and beside Jule Kesst gave an irritated sigh. "Right then," he said, and then lazily stretched out his arm, and settled it lightly over Jule's shoulder.

It was barely a touch, but immediately both Grimarr and Efterar broke off their arguing, and turned to stare. Both looking suspicious, and increasingly disapproving, and after an instant's stillness Grimarr stalked over and knocked Kesst's hand away, growling something at him in black-tongue.

Kesst only smiled and raised his hands, palms out. "I'm doing you a favour, brother," he said lightly, with a pointed glance toward Jule. Earning yet another bark of black-tongue from Grimarr, who then snatched Jule's wrist, and all but dragged her out of the room.

"Where are we going?" Jule asked at his back, finally, after being pulled upward through the Bautul wing, and then the Ash-Kai. Grimarr didn't stop, or answer, but his hand flexed almost painfully around her wrist, pulling her closer behind him. Moving so fast now that Jule was almost jogging to keep up, her feet sliding on the cool stone, her thoughts twisting and curdling and shouting all at once. He didn't trust her, he'd killed his father, he was her mate a good lord a murderer a *prince*—

"Grimarr," she gasped at him. "Stop. Please."

He immediately halted, so swiftly that Jule careened straight into his back, her hand pressing flat against the solid powerful warmth of it. Her fingers sliding into that awful scar, he'd tried to save his mother, he'd been so young, gods Jule's head was a pure and utter *mess*—

"What, woman," he said, but he still hadn't turned around, and Jule swallowed hard, and felt her hand slide gently down the length of that scar. "Kesst," she began, "he—told me a story, just now."

Grimarr's back only seemed to go tighter under her touch, the muscles flexing against her fingers. "Yes," he said. "I can smell his skald-magic upon you. And?"

Jule blinked in the darkness, her head tilting. "His skald-magic?"

"Ach," Grimarr said curtly. "He carries the rare skill of

galdr-telling, when he chooses to wield it. It is a gift beyond price, and bears much power."

Oh. Jule's scattered thoughts had followed that for an instant, was *that* why he allowed Kesst to lounge about the mountain as he did, rather than sending him off to raid with the rest—and she gave a hard, bracing shake of her head. "Right," she said. "Well, um, he told me about—*this*."

Her hand was still tracing against Grimarr's scar, and if possible his back went even stiffer against her. "He told you that," he repeated, his voice wooden. "All of it?"

Jule nodded into the darkness, but somehow Grimarr must have sensed the movement, because his back twitched against her, and then jolted away, out of her reach. "Then speak, woman," he said flatly. "Will you now leave me for Lord Norr, in ten days? Now that you know what I am, and what I have done?"

Dear gods, this *orc*, and Jule's eyes were inexplicably prickling again, blinking toward where she knew him to be in the darkness. "Of *course* I wouldn't leave you for that," she said, her voice wavering. "You only did what you had to do, to protect the people you loved. And to tell the truth, Grimarr, if I'm going to leave you for *anything*, at this point, it'll be for lying to me like you have! Not telling me the truth about your family, or your motives, or your plans. Not telling me that you've actually spent your whole *life* working for *peace*!"

And that was perhaps what hurt most of all, that he'd lie to her about something so gods-damned *pure*, as though maybe he thought Jule was base enough, human enough, to still prefer this stupid war, after all. And she could only seem to stand there, sniffing and wiping at her eyes—until suddenly Grimarr was here in the blackness, all around her, folding her into his warm safe arms.

"Ach," he said, soft, his voice close in her ear. "Woman. I am sorry. I ought to have told you all this. I did not mean to bring you grief. I did not wish you to think"—he breathed out, heavy—"that I do not hold you dear."

They were the right words, kindling something deep in Jule's belly, but her body still felt stiff in his arms, her eyes blinking hard against his chest. "But you *didn't* tell me," she said. "And for all your talk of orc honesty, you *lied*. And *why* would you lie to me about all your plans for peace, when I'd have been so *happy* to hear the truth?"

Her voice cracked on the words, and Grimarr's hands on her back pulled her closer, so tight it was almost painful. "Because here is truth, woman," he said, his voice very quiet. "I did not wish to give you this hope of peace. If peace truly comes, this makes it easier for you run away with my son, in ten days. And I *do* wish for this safety for our son's mothers. I ask and fight for this, with these men. But"—he hesitated, his fingers convulsing on her back—"I did not wish this for you. I wished you only to see fear, and a life alone, without me."

Of course. The *bastard*. And *this* was the Grimarr Jule knew, making it all about his wants, and his way—and she should have yelled at him, or pushed him off, or demanded that he escort her out to the men this very moment. But instead she just stood there, breathing heavy in his arms, while her thoughts swirled useless and stilted through her head.

"I ought not to have wished for this," his voice said, so soft that the sound of it ached in Jule's chest. "But yet I do. Still."

His hands were sliding up and down her back, silently pleading with her to listen, to understand. And curse her, but Jule *did* understand, and she felt her body wilting against him. Grimarr did care. He wanted her for his own. He wanted her to *stay*.

And despite everything, maybe this meant she wasn't just a pawn, a means to an end, after all. It wasn't like with Astin, or even her father. She *mattered*.

And suddenly, somehow, that was *all* that mattered. This

orc was a self-serving lying beast, but he was a good lord, he
*cared*, and somehow Jule's hands were around him, clawing at
him, pulling him close. Needing him, desperate and frantic,
and with a hard, guttural groan he yanked her bodily up off the
floor, one hand under her arse, the other carded deep into her
hair. And in a breath he kissed her, hot and luscious, while she
wrapped her legs tight around his waist, and sucked his tongue
deep into her mouth.

His replying growl was life, shuddering and sparking under
Jule's skin, and it was echoed by the long, thrilling shudder of
that familiar hardness, pressing between her spread legs.
Feeling so good, *gods* so good, and even better when Grimarr
began striding easily through the corridor, up in the direction
of their little outdoor alcove, while that hard bulge ground up
against her with every rolling step.

"Wish to see you," he whispered, against her lips, as he one-
handedly thrust away the boulder that blocked the exit. "In the
sun."

And suddenly there *was* sun, though it was dim and rich,
lowering in the sky, and scattered across with deep blue clouds.
But it was glorious to see it, to breathe in the cool air of an early
mountain evening, and Jule only wrapped herself closer
around Grimarr's bulk, her hands deep in the mess of his hair,
her mouth drinking up the taste of him. Of an orc, yes, but one
that cared. One that truly wanted *her*.

And he did want her, his hands already yanking off Jule's
tunic, exposing her skin to the still-warm sun, while she did the
same to his. Not caring if he was scarred and hideous, because
he was also huge and muscled and gorgeous, and strong
enough that he was still holding her up one-handed as he sank
down to seated on a boulder, shoving down his own trousers as
he went, and grinding his bare, leaking cock just *there*, between
Jule's still-clothed spread legs.

It left her breathless and craving, squirming over him as

she kissed him, desperately needing to get closer, to take him inside. But her own damned trousers were still in the way, and Grimarr let out a low, throaty laugh as he bodily lifted her off him, stood her on her feet before him, and yanked her trousers to her ankles.

"Thanks," Jule gasped, as she swiftly stepped out of them, fully naked now, and went to climb back aboard—but suddenly his strong hands were here, on her hips, holding her there. While his eyes looking up at her glittered in the light, his face a mass of scars and shadows, and still so stunning that it took Jule's breath away.

"My fair, ripe woman," he murmured, his smile lazy and sharp. "I wish you to flaunt to me what is mine."

As he spoke, he moved one of his hands to Jule's, and guided it up over her bare breast. Which felt heavy in her hand, tender, already fuller than it used to be, swelling out between her fingers.

Grimarr actually licked his lips as he dropped his own hand and stared, and somehow the need, the craving firing compulsion, had taken over all sanity, and replaced it with—this. With Jule's own hungry hands caressing her breasts, pinching at her hard jutting nipples, while the watching, gasping orc put his own hand to his huge, dripping cock, and slid up.

Fuck, it was hot, his eyes glittering and his lips parted, his gaze firm on her hands, which had abandoned her breasts, in favour of sliding downwards. Now caressing her slightly rounded belly, perhaps jutting it out even more, even fuller, for his eyes—and earning in reply a harsh, helpless groan from his mouth.

"More," he gasped, so Jule gave him more, arching her back as she kept one hand on her belly, and began to slide the other lower. Down to the liberally dripping wetness between her legs, which was already swollen and slick, and she swirled a slow finger against it, feeling it—and then watched as her trembling, dripping finger reached back up, toward Grimarr's parted lips.

He sucked the finger loudly and eagerly inside, his eyes scorching and commanding on hers. Saying, *Give me more, now*, so an unthinking, appallingly wanton part of Jule stepped closer, stepped her legs wide around his seated form on the rock. So that her groin was on a height with his mouth, and she put both hands down to her slick wetness, pulled it wide apart for him. Showing him everything, while his greedy black eyes stared, and stared, and stared.

"Kiss me," she breathed, and with a hard, spine-tingling growl, Grimarr leaned in, and did it. Put his hungry mouth to her dripping heat, right where Jule most craved it, and at his first sweet, suckling kiss she cried out, far too loud, but it didn't matter, nothing mattered, but this.

"Oh *gods*," she gasped, as that hot, clever mouth licked and sucked, that glorious tongue sliding deeper, harder between her legs. "Oh fuck, Grimarr, oh please, don't stop."

But then of course he did, the prick, his face already wet with her, his breath heavy and gasping. But instead of taunting her, or making her beg, he bodily spun her around, so she was facing away from him toward the sun. And then he pulled her hips back again, so that she was once again straddling him, but this time with her bare arse exposed to his face.

"Ach, yes," he gasped behind her, and those were his huge hands, gripping hard at her arse-cheeks. "Now bow for me."

Fuck, *fuck*, but there was no resisting it, only doing it. Bending herself over double, her hands grasping at a nearby rock for balance, until her most private, most secret parts were wide and naked and exposed to a watching orc. An orc whose big hands were only pulling her apart further, showing everything, his breath tickling just *there*, oh gods.

"For what do you wish," his voice purred, hot breath against her trembling wetness, and Jule gulped for air, felt her exposed heat clenching for him, putting on the most obscene of all possible displays for his eyes. But he only laughed, making it even worse, and Jule could scarcely think enough to find words, or speak.

"Kiss me," she managed again, finally, and oh, sweet mercy, he did. Not only kissing, but licking and suckling and delving all up and down the crease of her, putting his tongue any and everywhere it could reach, and while Jule should have been humiliated—her bare arse was grinding helplessly back onto an orc's eagerly slobbering face, outside, in the open air—the sheer, shocking pleasure was too much, too desperately powerful, to even pretend to resist.

"Fuck," she moaned, as his slick, hot tongue curled inside, ever deeper, into a place it was most certainly not supposed to go. "Fuck, Grimarr, you, you're not—"

That slick tongue pulled away, curse him, even as his hands pulled her wider, more open—and there was the thrilling, outrageous feeling of a slick finger, pressing there instead. "Ach, why should I not," his breath murmured, hot against her skin, "If it brings you pleasure?"

Jule was not justifying that with an answer—she wasn't quite that far gone yet—and there was another soft, shameless kiss, his tongue twisting slow and purposeful inside before pulling out again. "You are mine," he whispered, as one of his hands slipped lower between her legs, brushing familiar into her swollen wetness. "Both this"—his hand slid backwards, further up, to where he'd been kissing—"and this."

Jule's heartbeat was thundering in her ears—she knew what he meant, she'd heard other women giggle and whisper about it—but she shook her head, fought for the last vestiges of sanity. "A lady wouldn't," she gasped, "allow such things."

But Grimarr only laughed, as his fingers lingered there again, one now slipping just slightly inside. "But you are my mate," he whispered. "And now that I have taught your womb and your mouth to welcome my prick, next I must teach this."

Jule's answering groan was helpless, ravenous, her entire body quivering against him. Fighting him, or begging him, and he gave that laugh again, spread her apart wider. "You are ready to learn," he whispered, with another slow, wicked lick. "I will be gentle."

And that, maybe, more than anything, was what tilted the earth under Jule's feet, tilted the hunger into reckless depravity, because her head actually, somehow, nodded. Making Grimarr give a sound that was half-laugh, half-growl, and already he was guiding her trembling body down and back, so that she was almost seated on his lap—except.

The first, slightest nudge of his smooth, hard cockhead against that tight hole was thoroughly, desperately shocking, and even more so was the realization that Jule *wanted* it there. Wanted its tapered head to keep nudging against her like that, slick and strong and careful, searching for a way in.

And she could let it in, she could—she'd let his tongue in, hadn't she?—and with a deep, shaky breath, she willed herself to relax, and push down a little harder. Crying out as he sank in a little deeper, tighter, oh fuck she was doing this, she was really, really doing this—

"Good woman," Grimarr whispered in her ear, his hands gently caressing her arse, supporting most of her weight, giving her the freedom, the space, to do this. "Fair woman. Brave woman. You honour me. You please me. You give me—*ach*—"

The words broke into a guttural moan, his chest heaving hard behind her, his face pressing into her neck. And it was enough, somehow, that Jule could keep going, keep pushing, taking that thick, ramrod cock inside her. It felt strange, and wrong, and impossibly wonderful, like Grimarr was all that existed in the earth, Grimarr was everywhere, everything, growling into her neck with strangled, desperate black-tongue while she pushed deeper, harder. Impaling herself on him, offering herself up to him, sacrificing the last of her innocence and her dignity on the altar of his rock-hard orc-prick.

It was like her body was crawling all over with it, the invasion going far beyond her arse into her very being. Like this orc had found the most fundamental part of her, and filled it with himself, and Jule gasped and choked and sobbed as he finally sank all the way inside, locking them together. Pinning and impaling her fully on his lap, the whole back of her sweaty and flush against his front, with his face still in her neck, one of his hands spread wide over her belly, and—Jule shook, and whimpered—his other hand coming down her front, and finding her still-slick, spread-apart wetness. And then, while Jule gasped and sobbed, he slowly, surely slipped his long, thick middle finger deep inside, all the way, until the rest of his hand pressed close and flat and protective against her.

It was impossible to thrust, or think, or even speak. There was only gasping for air, writhing and shuddering over him, into him, surrendering to his rule, his mastery, his rising, whirling pleasure. While he gasped and growled close behind her, just as lost as she was, his face on her neck given way to hungry mouth and sharp teeth sinking into her skin, but Jule arched into it, giving him more, didn't care, couldn't, only more, more, *more*—

The pleasure crashed over her like a flood, like a thundering blast of ecstasy, ripping her from the inside out. Escaping her mouth in an unstoppable scream, and behind her Grimarr's body arched, tightened, and fired. Pumping her body full of his seed, her soul with pleasure beyond words, beyond thought, wild and beautiful and shameless and free in the fiery light of the slowly setting sun.

When Jule came to herself again, she was sprawled sated and limp over Grimarr's hot, sticky body. Which was still invading hers, in multiple tender, messy-feeling ways, but at the moment it was the most glorious, most peaceful feeling of perhaps Jule's entire life.

"Curse you, orc," she croaked out, her voice sounding strange and unused, and behind her Grimarr gave a short, guttural chuckle.

"Why must I always have curses," he murmured. "And never thanks, or praise."

Jule managed a snort, and somehow moved her still-tingling hand to touch at her neck, where his mouth had been. And when her fingers came away, they were indeed slick and red with blood. *Her* blood.

"Because you *bit* me, orc," she said back, though it came out sounding warm, perhaps even tolerant. "And drew *blood*. I thought you were supposedly above such a barbaric thing."

"No, I only did not wish to alarm you," he replied, soft, and though Jule should have been appalled by that, or enraged, she couldn't even seem to dredge up mild annoyance.

"Leave it to you to hide something like *that* all this time, too," she said. "You are *such* a scheming degenerate *beast*. It's a miracle any woman would let you touch her at *all*."

She could feel his silent chuckle, his face nuzzling into her hair. "Mayhap," he murmured. "And yet, here you sit upon my prick, with my son in your belly."

Jule tried for a growl, but it came out more like a moan, and Grimarr chuckled again, spanned both his hands against her thickened waist. "This pleases you," he purred. "*I* please you. Admit this, woman."

Jule's beleaguered thoughts were suddenly surging in all directions at once, and she swallowed, and felt herself blinking toward the sunset's deepening light. "You *kidnapped* me, Grimarr," she said, quiet. "You don't trust me. And you've kept the truth from me. A *lot*."

The words hung there, undeniably true, but also—unfinished, somehow, and behind her Grimarr exhaled, pressed a soft kiss into her hair. "Ach, it is not just this," he said. "Speak the rest. Please, my fair one. Jule."

Gods damn him, and his honeyed orc words, and his big, warm hands against her, his big body still inside her. Whispering, promising, that she was safe, their son was safe, he was a good lord. There was nothing to fear, either outside or within. She could choose to trust him, even if he didn't trust her.

"Fine," Jule said finally, with a sigh. "Fine. You're—you're a good lord, Grimarr. You're clever. And strong. Determined. You protect those you care about. You take the time to understand them, and recognize their strengths. And you fight for their freedom and safety. To make their lives better. To give them a *home*."

Grimarr's hands tightened against her belly, his face pressing now into her shoulder, and Jule sighed again, held her eyes to that setting sun. "And I just—I *like* you," she said, quieter. "I like your hands, and your voice, and your smell, and your taste. I like it when you smile, when you laugh. And"— she drew in air—"I love how you feel inside me. I love how you can make me forget everything else in the world, but you."

His breath behind her had seemed to come deeper, heaving in and out of his chest, but he didn't gloat, as Jule might have expected, or goad her into saying more. And when she finally angled her head to look back at him, his eyes on the sky seemed strangely bright, his mouth hard and set.

"What is it?" she asked, and she realized that her hand was stroking against his bare thigh under her, fingers spread on silken skin. "Is something wrong?"

His eyes belatedly flicked down to hers, and she could see him swallowing, could almost taste his unease. "You honour me, woman," he said, almost a whisper. "But there are more truths I have not yet told you."

Oh. "Such as?" Jule asked, feeling her body suddenly go taut against him. "Grimarr?"

He felt tense now, too, his hands clenching on Jule's belly. "I was brought," he began, "tidings today. From the north."

"From Joarr?" Jule asked, carefully, and at Grimarr's replying nod, her heart shuddered, kicked into speed. Tidings from Joarr, from the north. "From Astin."

The words came out in a whisper, and when Grimarr didn't reply, she knew she had the truth of it. "What kind of news?" she asked, through the odd choke in her throat. "He's finally riding out?"

"Yes," Grimarr replied, the single word a punch straight to Jule's gut. "Within two days' time, Lord Norr will be here."

## 25

J ule dressed in stilted, rushed silence, keeping her eyes on her trembly hands. Astin was coming here. Within two days.

It shouldn't have been a surprise—it *wasn't* a surprise—but it was odd to realize just how unsettling it was. That perhaps, deep inside, Jule had expected that Astin would never come. That she had, in fact, been glad of it.

And now, even the very thought of Astin—his voice, his tall body, his handsome face—was sending jolts of jagged ice down Jule's spine. She didn't want to see Astin. She didn't want to speak with Astin. In truth, if she had her way, she never wanted to think about Astin again.

"Are all three of them coming?" Jule asked, her voice scratchy in the silence. "Astin, and Lords Otto and Culthen as well?"

"Yes," came Grimarr's reply, quiet. "All three ride together."

"And what do you think their goal is?" Jule heard herself ask. "I don't think Astin's ever actually led a real battle in his life, so—?"

Grimarr made a sound that was half-snort, half-sigh. "From

what Joarr was able to learn," he said, "they wish to meet. With us."

Jule felt herself startle, her eyes finally darting back up to Grimarr's face. The men wished to meet. To discuss terms. To perhaps even implement the peace Grimarr wanted, but instead of looking pleased about this, his eyes were shadowed. Uneasy.

"Well, that's great, isn't it?" Jule made herself say, as brightly as she could. "It's what you've been working toward all this time. You must be thrilled."

Those eyes were watchful, careful, on hers, but she could see his shoulders relax, just slightly. "It is still very far from done," he said. "But it is good. I have hope of this."

Jule eyed him for another moment—perhaps he was thinking of those ten days again, how peace might make it easier for her to leave—and she shoved that thought back, and tried for a smile. "Great," she said again. "I'm truly so pleased for you, Grimarr. So what are your next steps? I'm sure you've already got it planned down to the second?"

His shoulders relaxed a little more, his mouth giving a faint twitch up. "Come inside with me," he said, "and you will know all that I do."

Jule followed him inside, and soon found herself ensconced in yet another meeting with Grimarr and his captains. One which, after a blur of black-tongue from Grimarr, was held entirely in common-tongue, clearly for Jule's benefit, and perhaps even her participation.

"We will ready the bands to attack from here, here, and here," Grimarr was saying, pointing to a variety of locations on Valter's map of the mountain. "And we shall only agree to meet here or here"—he jabbed at two spots low on the mountain—"so we cannot be ambushed. If the men refuse our terms, or do not offer more meetings or counter-terms, we will strike at midnight."

There were now thousands of men camped around the mountain, Jule knew, and perhaps only six hundred orcs inside. But in the dark, in close combat, on their own territory, the orcs would have every advantage—the men would be tired, perhaps unarmed, unable to see, unable to tell friend from foe. And here, suddenly, was the understanding that Grimarr could have done this at any point this past month. Could have attacked at night, and built a pyre of bodies by morning.

The weight in Jule's stomach had seemed to sink even deeper throughout all this, as the orcs argued through the intricacies of what band would come from where, which tunnels would be used, whether they would use fire or not. As if the planned peace-meeting with these men would accomplish nothing, and perhaps from the orcs' experience, it couldn't. Except.

"You need to keep Lord Norr out of your talks," Jule cut in, at the first break in the orcs' conversation. "You need to make every possible effort. If you truly want to negotiate for peace, he absolutely cannot be there."

All the orcs were looking at her, some with clear disapproval in their eyes, but the certainty was growing, sharpening, in Jule's thoughts. "Grimarr has humiliated Lord Norr so thoroughly that the whole realm knows it," she said. "And Lord Norr will never, *ever* forgive you orcs for that. He would happily sacrifice thousands of his own men to uphold his honour. If you haven't yet considered how personally he will take this affront"—she took a breath, met Grimarr's eyes—"you've miscalculated."

Olarr began to speak, but Grimarr raised a hand, cutting him off. "How do we then face this," he said, his eyes hard on Jule's. "What do you say."

Jule blinked, and suddenly felt warm all over. What did she say. Grimarr was asking her. Grimarr *cared*.

"You need to keep Lord Norr out of the talks in a way that

doesn't come back to implicate you," Jule replied firmly. "Sabotage his carriage. Maim his horses. Poison him if you have to. Or"—she took a breath—"you have me write a letter to Otto, and ask to meet with him and Culthen alone, without Astin. I'm not sure Otto will agree, but"—she took another breath—"he owes me. In a major, *major* way."

It was true, and the added distance from it all had without question given Jule a far greater understanding of the true sacrifices she'd made on Otto's behalf. Her marriage with Astin had kept the peace between the two men, had averted what would have likely been a brutal feud between them for Jule's father's fertile, profitable lands. It had kept Otto his inheritance and his reputation, and the chance to raise his two small sons in safety.

Grimarr's eyes had a distinctly disbelieving look in them, his fingers drumming on the table. "You would truly call this debt to help us, woman?" he asked. "You would meet with Lord Otto on our behalf, and offer our terms? You would speak for us? For *orcs*?"

It sounded ridiculous, or did it. Jule didn't owe these orcs anything—they'd kidnapped her, Grimarr had lied, he didn't trust her—but looking at her mate's watching, wary eyes, there was nothing else to say.

"Yes," Jule said. "I would."

## 26

T he next night and day passed in a dizzying blur of meetings, battle preparations, and back-and-forth communications between the orcs and the men.

And rather than sitting on the outside, like she always had before, Jule somehow, suddenly, found herself caught straight in the middle of it all. Helping to write out letters and proposals, conferring with Grimarr and his captains on plans and alternatives, and providing as much context about Astin and his forces as she possibly could.

It was truly an active betrayal of Astin at this point, well beyond anything she'd done so far—but once again, Jule found that she didn't seem to care. Astin was a petty, cruel, vicious man. He'd been petty and cruel and vicious to the orcs. The least he could do was face them, and hear out their offer of peace.

Jule's disdain was only reinforced when Astin finally made his grand entrance to the men's camp, late the following morning. He was flanked by an entire armed regiment, and while there was no visible sign of his actual person, there was no mistaking the opulent, brand-new carriage, drawn by a team of four beautiful, high-bred, perfectly matched new horses.

"Did you see those *horses*?" Jule demanded at Grimarr, once they'd gone back inside, from the hidden little ledge they'd been observing from. She hadn't known said observational ledge even existed—another one of Grimarr's many secrets—but in all the ongoing hubbub, there didn't seem time to be angry. Especially when Grimarr had finally relented so thoroughly on his secrets and his plans, allowing Jule firsthand access to every new piece of information as it came—including this.

"Yes, I saw," Grimarr replied, his brow furrowing in the light of the lamp he was carrying. "Why must I see these horses?"

He was, of course, thinking only of the regiment, and Astin's arrival, and what this meant for their meeting. Lords Otto and Culthen had already arrived, with far less fanfare than Astin, and the orcs had accordingly left out Jule's carefully written letter, requesting a meeting with only Otto and Culthen. The letter had been taken to Otto's tent, and he had ostensibly read it, though as yet there had been no apparent reply.

"Because horses like those cost a *fortune*," Jule said scathingly. "For their price, he could have kept his household fed and guarded for *years*."

Grimarr's eyes darkened with clear disapproval, or perhaps contempt. "Lord Norr is a fool. If I did not have this peace to think of"—his fingers clenched on the hilt of his scimitar at his side—"I should kill him now, and grant these horses to you."

Jule couldn't help a laugh, a brush of her hand against his muscled arm. "Such a generous orc," she said lightly. "And perhaps you'd come riding with me, after?"

It was odd to think how appealing that idea was—of everything she'd left behind in her old life, riding was probably what she missed the most—but Grimarr fixed her with a deeply disgruntled look. "Orcs do not *ride horses*."

"Well, not horses like *those* ones, true," Jule replied. "They're built for speed, not riding, especially with any weight. But perhaps a different horse? Something more your size? It would be quite the sight, you know."

She was teasing him now, and Grimarr knew it, his irritation fading into something almost tolerant. "I do not wish to spoil your dream, woman," he said, "but this horse would throw me from its back at once, and you would laugh until you wept."

Jule grinned at him, and put her hand back to his arm, lingering longer this time. "Only a little," she said. "But in all seriousness, Grimarr, if all this goes through—perhaps we could consider acquiring a few horses? I could teach you to ride."

Grimarr blinked down at her, and abruptly pulled her close, his arm settling heavy over her shoulder. "I shall think on this, woman. For now, if you truly wish to ride a beast"—he gave her a curving, wicked smile—"my prick awaits to serve you."

Jule elbowed him hard in the side, but he had a point, didn't he? And once they'd started walking again, past the door of an unused Grisk barrack, Jule elbowed him again, steering him inside. And then put both hands to him, sliding up under his tunic, finding his shifting hard muscle and warm silken skin.

"Now a good time?" she murmured, and in reply Grimarr gave a heated growl, dropped the lamp to their feet, and yanked her close. "Yes," he breathed. "Ride me. Sheath me. Show me what is mine."

Jule could only gasp in return, pulling his face down to hers, and tasting the delicious musky sweetness of his mouth. Gods, it was good, and she only drank deeper as Grimarr bodily picked her up, and carried her over to one of the room's low beds. Deftly pulling off her trousers in the process, and dropping himself back onto the bed with her on top, so that she was straddled wide over him, his swollen leaking hardness already nudging up against her hungry wet heat.

"Such an efficient beast, too," Jule murmured, eyelashes fluttering as she settled her weight deeper onto him, felt that smooth, silken head begin to split her apart. "And as strong as any horse."

Grimarr gave a low chuckle, showing her his sharp teeth. "And you shall never fall," he said, "with a prick like mine to hold you safe."

Jule made a sound that was partly a laugh, and partly a sigh. And as he slowly, surely sank inside her, she unthinkingly put her hands to his scarred face, and smiled into his black eyes. Watching him as he took her, his eyes hazy with pleasure, affection, safety.

It was enough to make Jule lose her breath, trapped in the strange, stilted lurch in her chest. She cared for this orc. She respected this orc. She wanted this orc.

She wanted to *stay*.

He kept driving deeper, slow and delicious, until he'd settled himself all the way inside. Where he belonged, Jule's thoughts whispered, and when he shoved up at her tunic, she yanked it off over her head, and put those big warm hands to her thickened waist, where *they* belonged. His. *Hers.*

"Ride, my fair one," Grimarr whispered, his voice so soft, his eyes so expressive on hers. So Jule did, slowly rocking herself back and forth against him, as that huge cock circled and throbbed inside. Holding her safe, sparking her full of pleasure and warmth and life.

Jule only vaguely heard the orcs passing by the room's open door, and then, perhaps, pausing to look. To see her naked and exposed in the flickering lamplight, seated full upon their captain's prick, riding it harder, deeper. Feeling it now swelling even fuller inside her—there was nothing this orc loved like an audience—and Jule loved *him*, and even as that thought twitched and protested, it seemed to unfurl deep under her skin. Enough to make her arch her back and moan aloud, her breasts full and peaked and heaving, her cheeks flushed, her body on fire.

"Oh, Grimarr," she gasped, shameless, desperate, depraved. "Fuck. You feel so *good*. I *love* you."

His answering growl was more like a roar, his hips suddenly bucking up, slamming into her, like the untamed beast he was. And Jule could only hold on and ride, bouncing and jolting on his powerful body, there was nothing like this, no truth or pleasure like this, she was his, he was hers, she wanted to *stay*—

He went taut all over, suddenly, locking hard beneath her— and then he shouted as his seed sprayed, gushing hot and liquid deep within. Enough to finally strike that tinder, set Jule aflame, and her own release crashed over her in a furious swarm of wild, surging ecstasy.

"*Damn* it," she breathed at him, once the pleasure had faded, his hardness softening just slightly inside. "*Curse* you, orc."

His hand came up to palm at one of her bare breasts, enclosing it in his fingers. "Always with the curses," he murmured, but his eyes and his voice held so much warmth, it almost felt like Jule would burst. "One day, you shall thank me."

Jule couldn't help a choked laugh, her body clenching close around his. "Don't hold your breath."

Grimarr only grinned up at her in return, all sharp teeth and breathtaking approval. "Is this a challenge, woman?"

Jule grinned back, opened her mouth to reply—but she was interrupted by the sound of a not-so-subtle cough, from the open doorway. And when she glanced over, there were in fact a handful of orcs, including Baldr and Varinn, standing there looking at them—at Jule, still seated naked on their captain's cock. And though her face went hot, Jule didn't move to cover herself, because Grimarr liked it, and Grimarr was *hers*.

"Yes, brothers?" Grimarr said under her, not making the slightest move either, except to caress a warm, approving hand over Jule's belly. "Is there news?"

"Yes, Captain," said Baldr, his voice a little odd, and when Jule studied him more closely, his eyes were odd too, wary and sparkling. Like fear, almost, and like... hope.

"Lord Otto wishes to meet with you, Captain," he said. "Today."

## 27

They agreed to meet on the south side of the mountain, on a low little outcropping that offered easy access to the men below. Grimarr had also agreed to a tent, to protect from possible arrows on both sides, and he had sworn to the men, in writing, that it would only be him and "Lady Norr" at the meeting.

"Lady Norr?" Jule asked afterwards, wrinkling her nose, and Grimarr grimaced as he pulled his tunic off over his head. They were getting dressed in their room, preparing for the meeting, and someone had brought back Jule's dress and shift, from wherever the hell they'd been all this time. The dress had been shabby but clean, and Jule had been rather shocked to discover, first of all, that wearing a dress again felt distinctly unnatural, and also, due to her ever-expanding belly, that it no longer fit. In the end, she'd had to leave it open at the back, and put on a cloak to cover it.

"I wish for the men to see I have not harmed you, or altered you," Grimarr said now, his back to her as he pulled on a new tunic. Jule had never seen this tunic before—it was spotless white linen, perhaps never before worn—and when Grimarr turned around to face her, wearing it, Jule felt her heartbeat skip. It was actually cut to fit him, unlike all of his other clothes she'd seen, and it flawlessly showed off his broad shoulders and chest, made him look like a brutal, beautiful orc prince.

Which, in truth, he was. Wasn't he?

Jule felt strangely shy, suddenly, her voice trapped in her throat, and she reflexively put her hand to her belly, to the odd safety of it. "Well," she said thickly, "they'll see this, won't they?"

Grimarr's hands were carding distractedly through the mess of his hair, though his eyes were very intent on her waist. "That," he said, stubborn, "could not be helped. But mayhap you will"—he grimaced as he tugged at a knot in his hair—"defend him, to Lord Otto."

Jule gave a silent nod, and then stepped closer, absently swatting Grimarr's hands away from his head, and reaching for the comb Baldr had brought. And then using it to pull through Grimarr's silken black hair, brushing it shiny and smooth.

"Is there anything else I should be aware of, for this meeting?" she asked at his back as she worked. "Beyond the details of your proposal?"

Grimarr's shoulders looked stiff, suddenly, but one of them gave a dismissive shrug. "Naught more than we have yet spoken of," he said, which was fair, because combined they had already spent hours talking about this, deciding what Jule would say, what points were most important, what Otto and Culthen were likely to say or do. Jule knew Otto far better than she knew Culthen—Culthen and her father had always been on polite but distant terms—and Grimarr had grilled her on every detail of Otto's history, every interaction with him she could remember.

Those memories had mostly been good—Jule and Otto had been frequent playmates as children, and over the years she had always considered him a friend, an ally. And looking back over it all, Jule had wondered, more than once, if perhaps she should have gone to Otto after her marriage, and made her situation clear, and asked for his help escaping it.

*Astin manipulates and humiliates me*, she could have said. *Astin is irrational and unpredictable. Astin keeps his household in poverty, because it pleases him to have the upper hand.*

*Astin makes me fear for my life.*

That one, perhaps, was new, risen out of the changed perspective this distance, these orcs, had given her. And by this point, Jule could freely admit that the reason she'd settled so well into orc life—better, by all accounts, than so many of the women before her—was because she had already been so trained to work and live in fear. That her initial experience with this life—being trapped by powerful, terrifying males in an inescapable prison—had, in truth, been little different from her old one.

And now—Jule finished braiding Grimarr's hair, and tied it off with a ribbon—it had become inescapably clear that this life was, in fact, a marked improvement over her old one. That despite his faults, Grimarr had in fact proven himself a far better partner, and lover, and friend, than Astin could have ever hoped to be.

And—Jule turned Grimarr around by the shoulders, met his eyes—damn the deadline, damn Astin to hell. She would stay.

"Very handsome," she said, thickly, as her hand gave a light little flick at his braid. "You look every bit the striking, ruthless, powerful captain."

Grimarr's eyes seemed to glint, his hand coming up to cradle her face. "Thank you, my fair one," he said. "I shall never forget this."

It sounded almost—regretful, somehow, and Jule blinked at him, her forehead furrowing—but he had already grasped her hand, and pulled her toward the door. And then back out into the corridor, where orcs were already waiting, asking questions all at once in black-tongue, and Grimarr barked out orders as they walked. Preparing his bands for battle, Jule knew, if this all-important meeting failed. If she failed.

But she wouldn't, and she squared her shoulders as they neared the mountain's exit closest to the meeting tent. The exit had, of course, been previously filled in, but the orcs had dug it out again with astonishing speed, and there were only a few rocks for Jule to climb over, Grimarr's guiding hand steady on hers.

The midday sun was blinding, the air fresh and cool, and Grimarr helped Jule pick her way down the mountain toward the tent. Their path was protected from the men's view, almost entirely obscured by jagged walls of rock, and once again Jule appreciated the effort Grimarr had put into this, how every last detail had been considered, and dealt with.

The tent was larger up close than it had appeared, and there were men already there, standing guard outside it. Catching sight of Jule and Grimarr seemingly at once, their hands snapping to the hilts of their swords—but they didn't draw their weapons, thankfully, and that boded well, didn't it?

"Good afternoon, fellows," Jule said to them, pleasantly, once they were close enough to speak. "Lovely day, isn't it?"

The men's staring eyes were exclusively on Grimarr's bulk behind her, and Jule could feel his coiled tension, without even looking at him. The men were tense too, their eyes wide and almost horrified, and Jule realized that perhaps none of them had seen an orc up close before, and that the sight would, of course, be rather alarming. Especially when—Jule gave an uneasy glance between Grimarr and the men—the men were almost half his size, their faces so smooth and bland and unmarked. Almost as though they were children, rather than men.

"This is Grimarr of Clan Ash-Kai, the orcs' captain," Jule

said now, gesturing between him and the men. "And as we agreed, he is unarmed. Shall I prove this to you?"

One of the men gave a curt nod, and after a quick confirming glance at Grimarr's blank face, Jule proceeded to run her hands close over his hips and legs and chest. Proving that there were no weapons or steel hidden anywhere beneath, and even going so far as to turn him around, and lift up his lovely new tunic, and show that there was nothing hidden on his back.

The man visibly blanched at the sight of Grimarr's scarred back, but accordingly waved them toward the tent with a shaky hand. And that was one success achieved, and Jule felt almost cheerful as she lifted the tent's flap, and stepped inside.

There were more armed men in the tent, perhaps ten or twelve of them, but Jule only had eyes for the one standing in front. Tall, slim, with warm blue eyes, and brown hair that was prematurely greying at the temples. Her cousin Frank, Lord Otto.

"Cousin," Jule said, with relief, and a swift, genuine smile. And in a breath she was in his arms, briefly embracing his slim form, and breathing in the light sweaty scent of him. "It's so *good* to see you."

She meant it, and Otto seemed to feel the same, grasping her tightly by the shoulders, his eyes crinkling at the corners. "You too, Jule," he said. "I can't tell you how damned relieved I am to find you alive and in one piece."

His words were perhaps betrayed by his pointed glance to her waist, and then up toward Grimarr behind her. Grimarr, who suddenly looked supremely huge and dangerous and out of place, his scarred grey face giving a spectacular scowl toward where Otto's hands were still on Jule's shoulders.

Luckily, Otto had never been a foolish man, and he immediately dropped his hands from Jule, and held one out toward Grimarr. "You must be the orcs' captain," he said. "I am Franklin, Lord Otto, of Salven. And this"—he gestured toward another nearby man, this one with a pot-belly, and a bushy grey beard—"is Lord Culthen, of Tlaxca, whose lands border mine to the east."

Grimarr shook Otto's hand with visible care, and then did the same with a narrow-eyed Lord Culthen. "I am Grimarr, of Clan Ash-Kai," he said, his voice deep and carrying. "I am here on behalf of this realm's five orc clans, to seek peace with men."

The men in the tent immediately began to shift and murmur, several of their hands going to their sword-hilts, but Otto silenced them with a look. "Leave us for now, fellows," he said. "We'll signal if we need you."

The men accordingly shuffled out, leaving only Otto and Culthen, and Jule and Grimarr. And as Otto turned back to face Jule, crossing his arms over his chest, suddenly he looked tired, older than his years.

"What's going on with all this, Jule?" he asked. "The truth, if you please."

Jule took a breath, let it out, met his eyes. "The truth is, Frank," she began, slow but careful, "the orcs are tired of fighting with humans. They want to be left alone, to live in peace. And there's absolutely no reason not to agree to this. It would benefit both us and them, and prevent many unnecessary deaths."

Otto's eyebrows had gone up, and he reached over to Culthen, and took a scroll from the older man's hand. "So you actually *endorse* this," he said. "And you actually believe these orcs are negotiating in good faith? And that they can hold to what they promise?"

He shook out the scroll as he spoke, and Jule briefly glanced toward it. It was the list of terms Grimarr had had written out, in Tristan's beautiful hand. End of all aggression, with severe consequences for those who disobey. Ownership of the mountain. Payment of taxes. Freedom for the orcs to trade, to marry, to walk free without fear of death.

"The orcs will keep their word," Jule said, lifting her chin. "Grimarr is the first captain to bring the five clans together in three centuries, and he has devoted his entire life to accomplishing this. The orcs hold him in high regard, and have willingly followed and supported him in this. He is a good lord."

Otto's eyes flicked toward Grimarr, who was standing there immobile, his face an unreadable mask. "Perhaps you've forgotten, Jule," Otto said, "that this supposedly good orc invaded your home, killed two of your servants, and *kidnapped* you. And then—"

He gave a furtive wave toward Jule's thickened belly, and she put a reflexive hand against it, fingers spreading wide. Searching for truth, and for the courage to come out and say it.

"Grimarr hasn't forced me in this, in any way," she said slowly. "I wanted this. I want his son. I have longed for a child for many years now, and this"—she shot another glance at Grimarr's oddly flat eyes—"has given me great joy. Grimarr has given me joy."

There was an instant's silence, during which Otto's increasingly skeptical gaze went from Jule, to Grimarr, to back again. "Are you truly certain of that, Jule?" he asked. "Forgive me, sir"—there was another cursory glance toward Grimarr—"but orcs have repeatedly proven themselves to be crude, violent, uncivilized, and morally bereft. Any gently bred lady should, by rights, find an experience like this deeply traumatizing. Have you considered the very real possibility that this orc has used some kind of magic to bewitch you?"

Jule felt herself frowning back at Otto, but she took a careful breath, weighed her words. "Of course I've considered it," she said. "But I have learned to better examine my own prejudices and assumptions. And from what I have seen, yes, the orcs' customs differ from humans' in many ways, but they are not by nature cruel or corrupt. They are"—she took another breath—"people. Individuals. Just like us."

Otto's eyebrows had gone up, and behind him Lord Culthen looked deeply dubious as well. Downright disapproving, in fact, as though Jule were most certainly parroting orc lies, so Jule squared her shoulders, and brought up more truth. Her truth.

"*You* perhaps forget," she said firmly, "that I have spent the last five years living in Lord Norr's household. And in comparison, I assure you, the orcs are by *far* the more civilized. If you want to condemn someone for traumatizing hapless women, why not try looking over your own damned shoulders!"

Her voice had risen at the end, carrying through the tent, and perhaps even beyond it, to the men outside. Leading Otto and Culthen to exchange uneasy looks, and Jule sighed, pulled a distracted hand through her hair.

"Look, I know peace won't be easy," she continued. "But you *must* see that it's the most productive way forward, and works to all your benefit. You'll receive increased income in the form of taxes, you'll be able to assure your people of their safety, you'll free up your resources to focus on more important things. You will give your children a safer, better world."

Otto's head was tilted, his eyes thoughtful. Perhaps even considering it—*were* they considering it?—and suddenly Jule felt her heartbeat pounding faster, her breath coming shallow and hopeful in her chest. "The orcs will not betray you," she said, with as much conviction as she could muster. "I fully believe this. They have the strength to gain this peace by force, but instead they have sought it through letters and proposals and warnings and offers. They want this war to end. It is the only way forward."

Otto still didn't speak, instead glancing back at Culthen again, and Jule took a step closer to him, drew herself to her full height. "There is no logical reason for you to refuse," she said. "Except for perhaps shallow prejudices, and petty revenge. And I know, Frank, you are better than that. Do this for your sons. Give them a life where they never have to worry about orcs again. *Please.*"

Otto gave a heavy sigh—he was considering it, he *was*—and his eyes flicked behind her, toward Grimarr. And when Jule looked too, she blinked, and felt her whole body go still. Because Grimarr looked ghastly, suddenly, his face pale and drawn, almost as though he were in pain. And it made no sense, this was going well, perhaps better than they could have anticipated. Wasn't it?

"Look, Jule, I'll be honest," Otto said, drawing Jule's eyes back to his face. "At the moment, I'm just as eager to end this miserable business as you are. But Norr needs to have a say, and right now, his only interest is this."

With the words, Otto pulled open the scroll in his hand, and jabbed a finger at a line of Tristan's script near the end. A line Jule couldn't recall seeing before, and she squinted toward it, her heartbeat picking up speed. It wasn't—it couldn't—was it?

"Lord Norr wants you back," Otto said. "Now."

## 28

L ord Norr wants you back.

The words shouted and rattled in Jule's head, and the earth beneath her feet seemed to stutter sharply, and then tilt sideways. *Lord Norr wants you back. Now.*

And Jule's only saving grace, whirling hope soaring through her thoughts, was Grimarr. Grimarr, standing here, strong and powerful and determined, her protector, her mate. He would *never* allow such a thing, not in a thousand years. Would he?

But when Jule turned to stare at him, the world dipped and swirled again. Because Grimarr was only looking at Otto, and not at her, and that look on his face, she'd never seen him look like that, like all the world had turned to ash.

"Not yet," he said to Otto, his voice slow, flat, deliberate. "First you will sign and proclaim this peace to all your men, and all villages within two days' ride of here. We will watch to ensure you have done this. Only then"—his eyes shuttered—"do we return Lady Norr to you."

What? *What*?! Jule stared at Grimarr, but he didn't look at her, his flat eyes held to Otto's. Which meant—he meant—

Without warning Jule's footing seemed to stagger, the tent

spinning strong and fast in her vision, and it was Otto, not Grimarr, who caught her by the arm, and held her steady. "Are you well, Jule?" he asked, but she could barely hear through the rushing in her ears, the sudden comprehension screaming deep inside her skull.

Grimarr had negotiated to give her back. Grimarr was *trading* her, like chattel. Grimarr had lied to her, and manipulated her, and betrayed her. Grimarr would sacrifice—Jule's shaking hands went to her swollen waist—he would give up—he would—

"Jule?" Otto said, with obvious concern in his voice, and Jule fought desperately for air, for composure. She had to keep it together, had to think, how could Grimarr have done such a thing, *how*.

"I just—had a dizzy spell," she gasped, and she couldn't bear to look at Otto, or Grimarr. "I think I—need to sit—a moment—"

Culthen was already striding toward the door of the tent, barking an order at someone, and somehow, here was a small three-legged stool, from somewhere. And Jule couldn't look up, couldn't speak, could only sink onto the stool, breathing hard, her hands tight over her belly. Her son. She had to think of her son. Had to think...

She could feel the eyes on her, all three sets of them, waiting. And gods, she had to pull herself together, force back the fear and the galloping misery, breathe, *think*.

"Much better, thank you," she heard her shaky voice say, as her head lifted up, and she fixed her eyes to Otto's hazy form. "My apologies, Frank. Now—you were saying?"

She didn't look at Grimarr, couldn't stand to see him, but she could hear him speaking, once again reiterating their terms. His voice sounding oddly thick and choked, but perhaps that was the rushing in Jule's ears still, the chaos shouting in her skull. Had to think. Her son.

Otto spoke back, some kind of counter-offer that Jule didn't hear, and when Grimarr didn't reply Jule lifted her chin, held her eyes on what she knew to be Otto's face.

"Excuse me, Frank," she said, her voice wavering only slightly. "But what if I do not wish to return to Astin? Could we perhaps consider other options? Perhaps I could stay with you, or leave altogether? I could move west to Osada, or beyond?"

The words sounded abominable, coming from her mouth—living alone in a foreign country with an orc-son would be a sure and certain hell—but what else was there, beyond Astin, beyond Grimarr. Her mate, who she loved, who wanted to trade her away...

"I'm sorry, Jule," Otto said, his voice sounding truly regretful. "But if you truly want this treaty to have any chance of happening, you have to go back. It's the only way Norr will agree. I'm sure you can appreciate the strength of his will around this."

There was a wealth of meaning behind his words—he had no doubt had to spend sickening amounts of time in person with Astin, debating this very point—and Jule swallowed hard. "Could we then," she said, "perhaps include a concession—*please*—that Astin will not hurt my son?"

The silence seemed to ring through the tent, louder than any shouting, until finally it was broken by Otto's slow, weary sigh. "I'm so sorry, Jule," he said. "But no. Not if you want Norr to accept this. He would never stand for an orc child to be birthed under his nose, even if you gave it back to the orcs afterwards. And let's be honest, you don't want to live with Norr under those circumstances either. Do you?"

Jule's breath seemed to be lurching in her lungs, threatening to escape in strangled, sobbing gulps. And finally she was desperate enough to look up at Grimarr, at that ashen stricken face, the orc she loved, who was throwing her away to the wolves.

"You would allow Astin to kill your son?" she heard herself say, her eyes pleading, begging on his. "Truly, Grimarr?"

But his hard jaw was set, his hands in fists, his eyes flat and glittering in his drawn, pale face. "I must," he said, his voice hollow. "I must give all to save my brothers. I must end this endless war."

The pain was like a lance, straight through Jule's chest, because of course Grimarr would do anything for this, give anything. And that included her, and their son, and she should have known, should never have given him her time, or her trust, or her heart. Even—the pain ricocheted again, deeper this time—even his promised forty days would have been a lie, to gain him time to negotiate this. All his affection, all his honeyed words, for naught.

"So what do you say, Jule?" asked Otto's careful voice. "Do you in fact agree to this? Will you return to Norr, to give these orcs their peace?"

It was a horrible question, made all the worse by the images suddenly parading through Jule's skull. Baldr and Drafli, Kesst and Efterar, Tristan and John and Sken, every damned orc in that mountain. Their lives, their futures, perhaps their own sons, all hanging in the balance. Hanging on her.

And if Jule didn't agree, would there ever be another opportunity again? She knew how much thought and effort Grimarr had poured into this, she knew how deeply he and the orcs longed for this. And Grimarr was going to attack tonight if the men refused, and how many orcs and men would die?

And how could Jule go on, knowing she could have prevented it?

"Yes," she said, though the word was a choked, miserable sob. "I'll go."

## 29

Grimarr walked Jule back to the mountain in silence, without so much as a kind word, or an apology. And perhaps Jule should have expected as much, because what could one possibly say, after one had sold away one's mate, and one's son?

It wasn't a done deal, yet—Otto had agreed to take the proposal back to the rest of the men, and had promised to give it his strong personal recommendation. And if Jule hadn't felt so dead inside, she might have rejoiced at Otto's clearheaded foresight in this, at the much-needed reminder that there were still good men in the world, after all.

But instead there was only this numb, heavy emptiness, growing heavier with each unsteady step. This mountain had never been home. This orc had never cared for her. These orcs now lining the black corridors, looking at Jule as she passed, had never been her friends.

At least it was quiet, with no jeers or whispers or laughter, and Jule kept her head down as she followed Grimarr's silent form through the corridor. Toward his room, of course—she would likely be held here until the men returned their decision—and once Grimarr had pulled back the curtained door for her, she went numbly to the bed and sat down, her head bowed, her hands folded tight together.

There was nothing for it. Nothing left. Only waiting, and waiting, and then death.

Grimarr had not yet moved, still standing there in the middle of the room, and Jule could hear his breath, coming out harsh through his mouth. And why didn't he leave, he was only making it worse, so much dread and misery that Jule didn't know how to bear it.

"I am sorry, woman," his voice said, finally, low and cracked. "I did not wish to do this."

Jule's nose gave an involuntary sniff, and when she wiped at her eyes her hand came back wet and shaking. "But you did," she heard her thick voice say. "You planned it all along."

He didn't deny it, and Jule felt those lurking sobs rising closer, fighting to escape out her throat. "You might have," she managed, between gulps of air, "told me."

There was a thin, strained silence, broken only by the sound of those heavy breaths. "I thought," he said, slow, "you would know this. When men steal a noble, they oft seek terms for their safe return."

The hurt flared again, now tilting at humiliation, or perhaps rage. "Yes, *men*," Jule choked out. "You are *orcs*. And you have been telling me, all this time, how you are different. But you are exactly the same. You trade me away, just like my father did, for your own gain. You condemned my father for doing such a thing to his own child, and yet—"

She couldn't speak the words, but her hands had gone to her belly, curling helpless around it. What her father had done had been wrong, yes, she saw that now—but at least he had discussed it with her, planned it with her, explained why. But this—

"He's your *son*," she heard herself say, her voice sounding like someone else's. "I can understand, maybe, why you would throw *me* away, but you said you wanted him. You said he would be captain after you. You *said*."

The words sounded desperate, pathetic, because of course nothing Grimarr had said had been true. But it had felt so true, at the time, he had said it with so much beyond only words, with his hands and his touch and his eyes.

"I was greedy," Grimarr's slow, strained voice said. "I wished, for my own sake, that the men would say no. I gave myself leave to cling to this. To you, and our son."

That almost made it worse, somehow, and Jule gulped for air, blinked at the floor. "And if the men *had* refused," she said, "and I stayed, and bore your son, would you have ever told me the truth?"

He gave a heavy sigh, almost a groan. "No," he said, so quiet, now. "I would never have wished for you to know I would do this."

Jule's mouth gasped out a sound that was half-laugh, half-sob. "Of course," she said bitterly. "You would lie. You have lied to me ever since I came here, why would that ever change? You lied about the forty days. You lied about your past, about your plans, about your proposals to the men. You swore you wouldn't betray me, you manipulated me into trusting you and helping you and sleeping with you. You probably even lied about that too, all your 'as the gods decree' rubbish—"

And the thought of that—the prospect that he'd deceived her in that, too—was suddenly making her breath come short, her heartbeat thundering in her ears. No. He wouldn't have. Would he?

There was a strange, guttural noise from Grimarr's throat, and suddenly he was here, kneeling on the floor before Jule, his face on a level with hers. And it was the first time she'd looked at his face since coming in here, and his eyes were black shadows, his skin deathly pale, his mouth contorted with something not unlike pain.

"Woman," he breathed, and his hands were on hers, covering hers, hot and sticky and twitching. "It was not all lies. I would not lie to you about the pleasure we took together. I did not lie when I spoke of my care for you, and for our son. I have"—his throat convulsed—"I have known more joy with you than ever I thought could be within my grasp. I have *loved* you, woman."

There were streaks of wetness running down his cheeks, and Jule felt her head shaking, no, no, *no*. "But if you loved me," she said, her voice so hollow, "how could you do this to me?"

Grimarr's mouth was a thin line, his eyes both dark and bright in his pale face. "Ach," he whispered, "I have naught other choice."

There were nothing else to say, nowhere to go from here, and Jule wiped at her face with her hands. "Then we're done here, aren't we?" she whispered. "Please, just go."

He didn't move, his glittering eyes almost exquisitely painful to look upon, and Jule shook her head, pushed blindly at his hands. "Please," she said again, pleaded. "Go."

Another strange noise escaped from Grimarr's throat, but he nodded, and stood. Still waiting, hesitating, but after a frantic, desperate wave of Jule's hand, he turned and left.

And finally Jule was alone, in the blessed empty silence of the room, and she buried her face in her hands, and wept.

## 30

The rest of the day felt interminable, and so did the evening following it. Empty, endless hours with no Grimarr, no news, no light or life or warmth.

It only became worse at nightfall, once the cursed mating-bond began gnawing at Jule's thoughts. Whispering that she could easily find Grimarr, wherever he was, and bring him back here, and he would not refuse her pleasure, would he? But then, the thought of that—his beautiful body making love to her, while he himself had traded away her and their son—was almost visceral in its painfulness, and finally Jule clung to the bedpost, and spoke to the only other being she could trust. Her son.

"I am so sorry, my sweet little one," she whispered, looking down at the proof of him, that slight swell in her belly. "I should have done more to protect you. I should have thought more of keeping you safe. I should have run, when I had the chance."

There was no judgement, only a listening silence—cunning, lusty, strong—and Jule swallowed, put a hand against it. "I wished," she whispered, "to believe that I was safe. Cared for. Protected. I let myself believe this, and I gave up all my plans of revenge, and escape. I trusted when I should not have. I was a fool, little one, and now it is you who will suffer."

She had been fighting not to think of the specifics of it, of what Astin would order done, but it was sure to be swift, and humiliating, and agonizing. And Jule had to face this, her son had to face this, and she gulped for air, for words.

"You are brave, little one," she said. "I know you are. I know you will face this with strength. I only wish"—she dragged in a gasping breath—"I had been able to see your face, or hear you speak. I wish I could watch you grow up strong and proud and beautiful. I would have loved you so, little one."

The wetness was streaking from her eyes again, the sobs far too close, and finally Jule just let them wash over her, wringing her out again and again with the gasping, choking grief of it. She was going to lose her son. She was going to lose everything.

When the sobs had finally faded again, sunk back into the quiet, dreadful emptiness, there was a furtive little knock on the doorframe. Jule blankly looked at it, not speaking, and finally the curtain lifted, showing Baldr's greenish form, illuminated in the light of the small lantern he was carrying. He was also carrying what looked like a packet of meat, a bunch of fresh-looking berries, and a waterskin.

Jule wasn't hungry, or thirsty, but when Baldr handed them to her, she took them, and set them on the bed beside her. "Thank you," she made herself say, her voice wooden. "You're very kind."

Baldr's bulky form seemed to twitch in the lamplight, and Jule felt another wave of dull realization wash over her. Of course he had known too. They had all known, all this time. And Baldr had listened to Grimarr lie to her, again and again, and he had never once even hinted at the truth. He had let Jule believe they were friends.

He seemed to follow her thoughts, his big hands twisting

together on the lantern's handle. "It grieves me to see your sadness, woman," he said finally. "I hoped it would please you to go back. You and the captain have been so often at odds these past weeks."

Jule gave an unwilling sniff, a clench of her hand against her belly. "We have not truly been at odds lately," she said, quiet. "Not since our son."

Baldr grimaced and then nodded, his lantern swaying in his hand. "I know," he said. "I should have told you the truth. It was just this hope, of finding peace—and with it women, and sons of our own. And the more we saw this, between you and the captain, the more we all wished for this. I am sorry."

Jule couldn't even seem to find anger toward him, only the dull, yawning emptiness. "It wasn't your fault," she said. "You have always been kind to me, Baldr. I am glad to have met you."

He made an awful face, his eyes briefly dropping to the floor. "We do not know for certain yet that you will need to leave," he said, with a false-sounding brightness. "The men could yet refuse. Or return with counter-negotiations. It could yet take weeks, or months."

It was a fair point, but Jule had already had too much time to think, and to fully comprehend just how thoroughly Grimarr had planned all this. *This is power, woman*, he'd said that day, betraying perhaps more than he'd meant. *Lord Norr's wife, carrying my son in her belly.*

"No," Jule said, wearily, toward Baldr's feet. "Now that so many people have seen the proof of my son, Astin will want this dealt with as soon as possible. If word spreads of my pregnancy, it would be the ultimate shame, the worst possible smear upon his name. As your captain well knew, when he planned all this."

Baldr didn't argue, thankfully, and after another mumbled, stricken-sounding apology, he slipped back out again. Leaving Jule alone in the dark silence, where she numbly tried and failed to sleep, and instead stared at nothing as the endless hours passed, and endless thoughts of Grimarr shouted and clambered in her head.

She didn't move again until morning, when the thoughts of Grimarr somehow turned to truth, with his big body striding through the curtain. Here, so close, and the whispering hunger in Jule's thoughts leapt up, the smell of him almost overpowering in the small room—but no, no, he'd *sold* her, and she pressed her hands to her eyes so hard it hurt.

"What," she managed, even as her betraying tongue came out to lick her lips. "You have news, I presume."

He didn't speak, but when Jule dropped her hands and looked at him, the truth of it was there, in his eyes. News, from the men. And it was all too clear, suddenly, what that news was, and when had Jule learned to read this orc so well, how had any of this even happened, why.

"They've accepted your terms," she heard her wooden voice say. "Haven't they?"

"Yes," he said. "It is done."

## 31

---

J ule had known it was coming. But even so, Grimarr's words seemed to open a fresh, gushing wound, straight through her heart. *It is done.*

"Congratulations," her flat voice said, her eyes intent on the floor at his feet. "You must be pleased."

Grimarr didn't speak, only stood there, and Jule fought for breath, for strength. "When am I to go. Soon?"

"Yes," came the reply, his voice just as flat as hers. "They have already spread word to their men, and the men break camp now. The riders have gone also to the towns, and we wait only for the magistrates to sign this word into law."

Well. He'd done it. All this orc's grand plans had actually achieved the unthinkable. And if it had been two days ago, Jule might have broken into giddy laughter, thrown her arms around his neck, and told him what a brilliant calculating beast he was—but at the moment she could only sit here, and watch the waves of fear and dread as they passed.

"Mayhap you shall yet have a good life, after this," said Grimarr's voice, low and halting. "You will go back to your servants and your horses. I know you have missed your home."

The words were strangely, shockingly painful, cutting through the haze in Jule's thoughts like a knife, and her head finally snapped up to look at him, her eyes gaping at his pale, drawn face.

"My *home*?" she heard her shrill voice say. "With *Astin?* With a man who will murder my son against my will, and then never let me forget he existed? Have you not yet noticed, orc"—she had to pause, gulp for air—"that I hate Astin just as much as you do?!"

Something spasmed on Grimarr's mouth, and his eyes briefly closed. "I knew," he said, quiet. "But I hoped I was wrong."

Gods curse this orc, and his twisting everything to suit himself, and Jule felt her hands clench tight and clammy together. "Well, you weren't wrong," she gritted out. "And now that you have provoked Astin beyond imagining, you walk away, and throw me under his feet."

Grimarr's hand came up to rub at his mouth, and dropped again. "Will Lord Norr hurt you," he said. "For this."

Jule thought about lying, but why would she protect this orc, after all he had done to her? "Yes," she said, wearily, while the sickening vision of Astin's horsewhip hurtled through her thoughts. "He will."

There was no question of it—at this point, it was really only a matter of degree—and Jule felt her heartbeat rising, her eyes squeezing shut. She would face it. She would be brave. Like her son.

"You should run," said Grimarr's voice, fervent and low. Like he was actually *suggesting* this, and Jule felt herself gape at him again, her heartbeat thundering in her ears.

"No, I can't run," she managed, "and you of all people should know that. If your treaty is built around my safe return to Astin, and then I run away, everyone will think I've come back to you. Astin would happily encourage them to believe so, and they will trample your peace to bits. Thanks to you, orc, I am now trapped with Astin for *life*."

But Grimarr already knew that, of course he did, and his exhale was slow, heavy, resigned. "Ach, woman," he whispered. "I would not expect this from you."

Jule pulled her knees up to her chest, and hugged them close. "Well, I didn't expect this from you, either," she said. "But here we are. And at least this way, you can get a"—she had to swallow, make herself spit out the words—"a new mate. A better one. Like you really wanted, all along."

There was an instant's awful, looming silence, the misery rising and waiting to fill it—and suddenly there were hands, alive, warm, on Jule's skin. On her face, tilting it up toward his, and here was his forehead pressing to hers, the smell of him filling her lungs with its warm succulent sweetness.

"Ach, woman," he whispered. "Do not speak thus. Do not think thus. You have been a better mate than ever I deserved. You are fair and brave and strong and proud. You freely defended us to your own people, and now you"—he took a hard, shuddery breath—"you give your own life for that of my brothers. You face the fate I have thrust upon you with honour, and not once have you begged, or fought, or sought to run. Instead you speak comfort to our son and give kind words to Baldr and heap shame upon my head."

Jule didn't reply, couldn't, and he came closer, breathed her in, cradled her face like it was something precious. "You are a true mate," he said. "A rare prize, who proudly bears the son I have craved all my life. And I have *sold* you. I have sold you to one I loathe more than any on this earth, but for myself."

His hands were shaking against her skin, his breath now coming in strange high-pitched gasps, and Jule realized he was weeping. This awful orc, who'd so thoroughly betrayed her, lied to her, thrown her away, was weeping in her arms.

"You are right to say," he breathed, between gasps, "that I am worse than your father. I have betrayed both my mate and my own son. I have never cared for anyone how I have cared for you, and now I must give you over to certain harm, and my son to certain death. I am sick to even *think* of doing such a thing, but I have, I *must*—"

The words shattered and broke, lost in the strength of his sobs, shuddering his big shoulders, curling his body in on itself. While Jule stared at him, felt the wetness welling again in her own eyes, and streaking down her cheeks. He didn't deserve sympathy. He most certainly didn't deserve forgiveness.

But, perhaps, he had cared.

"Grimarr," she said, choked, helpless, and somehow her hand was touching him, spreading against his heaving chest. Snapping his blinking eyes up to hers, and they were pleading, miserable, desperate. Speaking of the unthinkable years he would face after this, forever tainted with a guilt that would never stop gnawing. He had achieved a life of peace, over the death of his own son.

But he *had* achieved it. And he should be rejoicing, because by doing this he had accomplished what no other orc had ever done, and saved his people, his entire race, from destruction. He was a hero, a visionary, the father of Jule's doomed child, and she hated him, and loved him, and would never, *ever*, forgive him.

"Just—kiss me," she whispered, the words appalling and unconscionable on her lips—but this was it, this was farewell, forever. And like always, Grimarr *knew*, he understood, black eyes hard and bright—and suddenly he was here, his mouth hungry and desperate on hers, the taste and the scent and the feel of him exploding all at once, firing every nerve behind Jule's skin with sparkling, blazing light.

His big body shoved her down to the bed, pinning her onto

it with breathtaking force, and all Jule could do was gasp, cling to him, fill her mouth and her breath with the strength of him. Her mate, still, in this moment, even after everything he had done.

His groans into her mouth were fierce and guttural, and already his hands had yanked off the dress she'd been wearing, and found her bare body beneath it, spreading her legs wide apart. And at the first touch of that familiar, beautiful hardness against her willing wet heat, Jule gave a ragged sob into his mouth, against the swirling strength of his tongue.

It seemed to catch something, change something, and he pulled his mouth away, his liquid eyes held on hers. "Please, woman," he breathed, "may I have you, one last time, I know I should not even ask this, you ought to spurn and mock and curse me, but—"

But Jule had caught his mouth back in hers again, fervent and desperate, while her clinging, grasping hands drew him closer, harder. And he willingly obliged, pressing that swollen cock deeper against her spread-apart clenching wetness, until finally it breached her. Plunging slow and purposeful and powerful inside, filling her up with him, until he was sheathed all the way, skin to skin. Impaling her to the hilt of his massive, leaking orc-prick, pulsing with life and seed inside her.

"Speak to me, woman," he whispered, pleaded against her mouth. "Tell me I have not failed you in this. Tell me I have brought you joy with my prick, if naught else. *Please.*"

And of course this cursed bastard was making it all about him again, but the wetness was still dripping from his eyes onto her face, the touch of his hand almost painfully tender on her cheek. And this orc deserved nothing, this orc was a gods-damned *hero*, and Jule's legs seemed to spread wider on their own accord, her heels digging hard into his back.

"You have," she gasped. "Brought me joy. With this. It's—"

She couldn't seem to finish, and his hips rocked against hers, his mouth kissing soft and hot against her neck. Making her whole body arch up, pinioned on the hard pole of him, his movement hers, her movement his, as one.

"Speak," he groaned, into her skin. "Tell me you shall not forget this. Please."

Jule's mouth cried out, her body clinging to him, rolling against the crashing waves of his powerful hips. "I won't forget," she gasped, her eyes trapped upon the sight of him, a hideous beautiful orc ravaging her, his claws scraping against her skin, his huge cock driving in deep below. "Can't. Ever. You've been—"

The words choked off in her throat, and when Grimarr pulled back up to look at her, blinking at her with those beautiful dark eyes, Jule's entire body beneath him seemed to quiver in reply, strung tight like a string, vibrating to meet his light. Her swollen body stretched out around his invading prick, thrust full of his leaking seed. Her belly filled with his child, lusty and cunning and strong. And her eyes, her breath, her entire *being*, caught and consumed, exposed and displayed, pushed to its utter limits, for him. Because of him.

And it occurred to Jule, distantly, that perhaps—perhaps *this* was why this orc had always wanted others to see. This was why he wanted to flaunt this to the world. Because this—when Jule was pushed, exposed, flayed bare, split apart on an orc's driving prick—*this* was who she was. She was brave. She was powerful. She was lusty and cunning and strong.

She just—*was*.

Her mate was still looking at her, still drawing out her truth with only the heat of his eyes, and suddenly, somehow, the words were just there, spilling from Jule's lips. "You've changed *everything*, Grimarr," she whispered, as her hands carded deep into his hair, held on tight. "You've shown me a whole world I never knew existed. You've taught me to face my fear. To test my limits. To find deep joy, and take it for my own. You showed me—*home*."

Grimarr's face spasmed, his eyes squeezing shut. "You honour me beyond compare, woman," he whispered. "I shall never forget you, as long as I live."

And perhaps that was all that mattered, in this moment, and Jule drew his head up, swirled her tongue into the sweetness of his lips. Bringing an almost feral-sounding growl to his mouth, guttural and powerful, vibrating deep and true inside.

"Then fuck me, my love," she whispered. "Please. Give me something to remember."

It was like Grimarr's big body over her coiled as she spoke, drawing up tight—and then sparked to raging, burning life. Pinning her arms above her head with one huge, powerful hand, while the other hand roughly grasped her face and tilted it, burying his face against her neck. And then sharp teeth clamped down, as that huge cock slammed inside, so brutal and powerful that Jule actually screamed.

But he only did it again, his teeth sinking deeper, his cock pummelling inside, again and again. Harder than he'd ever done before, enough that Jule's teeth rattled in her mouth—but she was clinging, begging, pleading for more, even as her mouth gasped, or perhaps sobbed.

"Please, Grimarr," she choked out, "please. Give me. Show me. Don't let me forget. My mate. My *love*."

And with that, the raging body above her stilled, his lips suddenly soft and trembling on her neck, his prick hard, huge, swollen thicker than Jule had ever felt it. And then his seed surged out inside her in a flood, battering itself into her, filling her so full she thought she might break.

When it finished, his body seemed to go quiet over her, and hers beneath his, but for their shuddering breaths. And when

Grimarr finally pulled back from her neck, his cheeks were wet again, his mouth and chin smeared with red, his eyes raw and pained on her face.

"Ach," he said, his voice cracking, and Jule put her shaky hand up to his mouth, covered his lips with her fingers.

"No," she whispered. "No regrets, for this. And"—she paused, tried for a smile—"thank you, Grimarr. That was very lovely."

She kept smiling, blinking hard through watery eyelashes, but he didn't smile back. If anything, he looked even more drawn and haggard than before, and he pulled his big body up to kneeling, and drew himself out of her. Bringing forth the inevitable spurting mess, and his eyes on it were like those of a starving man's, greedy for something that was no longer his.

His hands felt the same, coming up tender against Jule's face, and sliding down over her neck, her shoulders, her arms. And then coming to squeeze at her breasts, lingering there before moving down to her curved belly.

His breath was coming in strangled little gulps, his fingers spreading as wide as they could go, and he slowly, carefully bent to kiss the slight swell of their son, his mouth murmuring in soft, choked black-tongue. Until his voice broke off altogether, and he pulled away and hid his face in his hands, his big shoulders shaking with the strength of his sobs.

"I am sorry," he whispered. "I am so sorry."

And he didn't deserve it, but all the same, Jule's body pulled up too, seemingly on its own. Her arms circling tight around his waist, pulling him close, and in a jerky movement he did the same, pressing her ear against the rapid thud of his heartbeat.

"I shall seek you and our son in the afterlife," he said, his voice low and halting into her hair. "And there, should you allow it, I shall show you the ways of a true mate. I shall cherish and protect and honour you. I shall regain your trust and bring you greater joy than ever you could *dream* of."

He was weeping again, gasping into Jule's ear, and Jule was sobbing too, her hands so tight around him that perhaps they could never let go.

"Until then, orc," she said. "Farewell."

## 32

I n the end, it was the next morning before all the orcs' terms were met. Every town within two days' ride had been notified, and the provincial magistrates of Sakkin, Yarwood, Tlaxca, and Salven had agreed, in writing, to grant the orcs land rights, marriage rights, trading rights, and legal rights. Recognizing the orcs as people, for the first time in known history.

Of course, it wouldn't in fact be that easy—those four provinces didn't comprise even half of the entire realm, and it would take decades, if not centuries, before all the old bitterness and grudges were forgotten. And it would take considerable luck and cunning to safely navigate the orcs through those first tenuous months and years, which were bound to be full of mistrust and protests and rebellions on all sides.

But if anyone could pull off such a feat, it would be Grimarr. And after spending the entire night held close to her mate's big body, hearing him whisper broken black-tongue to their doomed son, Jule felt a curious, resigned acceptance of him, and of what he had done. He had sacrificed her, their son, his own wants, for his people. It was noble and heroic and single-minded and breathtakingly cruel, and that was, perhaps, just who he was. Who he had been, this entire time.

And even if Jule could never forgive him, she could, perhaps, understand. And once she'd washed and dressed, for the final time in this mountain, and Grimarr silently held out his hand, she took it. And allowed him to lead her out of the room, and into the black corridor. Toward the exit. Toward Astin.

Jule felt her heartbeat rising—she had been trying, quite desperately, not to think of Astin these past hours—and perhaps Grimarr felt it too, because his hand clenched on hers, his steps briefly hesitating in the darkness. "My brothers," he began, his voice oddly tilted, "wished to say farewell. They await in the large muster-room, if you will see them."

Jule silently nodded, and allowed Grimarr to draw her around a corner, changing their path. As if she didn't know her way to the muster-room by now, and she swallowed hard as she reached and trailed her hand against the corridor's smooth, cool stone wall. She had somehow come to appreciate this mountain, in all its tricky meandering forbidding coziness, and this was goodbye to it too, to a home that had never truly been hers.

There were voices coming from the muster-room as Jule and Grimarr approached, but then utter silence, suddenly, as they stepped inside. And there, lit by the huge crackling fire at the far end, was a mass of dozens of orcs, standing there, and staring at them.

"I didn't think it possible for so many orcs to be so quiet," Jule heard herself say, with genuine astonishment, and in reply there was a smattering of chuckles, and the room's tension seemed to vanish at once. Replaced with the murmur of rising voices, and the sight of multiple orcs coming forward to greet her.

"Thank you, woman," said one young Ka-esh, named

William, hand in hand with a new orc that Jule didn't recognize. "We are indebted to you."

Jule tried to smile, and speak kindness in return, and she felt her smile becoming more genuine, and perhaps more tearful, with each orc that spoke. Baldr, Joarr, Silfast, Olarr, Afkarr, Salvi, Tristan, John, Eyarl, Kesst.

"You deserve better than us, Jules," Kesst said, his usually saucy eyes gone rather flat. "And most certainly better than *him*. To wit, was *that* really necessary at this point in the game, Grim?"

He'd pointed at Jule's neck as he spoke, prompting her to raise her hand to it, and realize—oh. It was where Grimarr had bitten her last night, and it felt inflamed and tender still, and was certain to be very visible to anyone who looked at her. And especially, of course, to Astin.

Grimarr hadn't replied—he had said very little so far in any of this, his body a solid, forbidding presence beside Jule—and Kesst made a clucking sound, and reached behind him to drag a tired-looking Efterar over. "Can't you do something about this?" he demanded toward him. "This prick"—he waved irritably at Grimarr—"is hell-bent on giving that awful man of Jules' even more of a complex than he already has. No offense, Jules."

Jule waved it away, and Efterar stepped closer, frowning at Jule's neck. "Mind if I touch you?" he asked, and once Jule shook her head, he carefully put his hand to her neck, and closed his eyes.

"Please tell me you haven't fucked her this morning, too," Kesst continued toward Grimarr, as his own hand stroked up and down Efterar's back. "Because it sure as hell smells like you did. But you wouldn't be *that* much of a jackass, would you?"

Grimarr didn't reply, his face gone even more forbidding, and Jule felt her own cheeks heating. They *had* done it that morning—they had, in fact, done it multiple times last night after the first time, quiet and desperate in each others' arms—and she realized, far too late, what Kesst was referring to. If Astin were to take her to bed, immediately or even within the next day, he would find her body chock-full of viscous, leaking orc-seed.

"I'll put Astin off," Jule said, into the rising panic, and she felt Efterar's hand on her neck twitch, and then his other hand coming up beside the first.

"Make sure you do," Kesst said firmly. "Step on him, if you can. Though perhaps you'll be best served by avoiding him as much as possible, at least until..."

His voice trailed off, his eyes flicking down to Jule's too-visible belly, and she felt herself flinching, her arms curving protective around it. Kesst was right, of course, that avoiding Astin would be the ideal strategy—but Jule knew there would be no avoiding him, after this. No possible escape.

"Shut it, Kesst," Efterar said now, carefully pulling his hands away from Jule, and frowning at her neck. "You're upsetting her. And sorry, but that's the best I can do."

Jule touched a tentative hand back to her neck, and found that the tenderness had been replaced by smooth, raised scars. Still unquestionably better than having fresh marks, and she tried for a grateful smile. "Thank you," she said. "I'll miss you both."

Efterar nodded, and after an instant's awkward silence, he pulled a regretful-looking Kesst away. Leaving Jule standing alone and uneasy next to Grimarr's still-silent form, and was that it, was it over now?

But perhaps it was, because she'd spoken with almost every orc here, and she felt her head bowing, her eyes blinking. It was over. She didn't belong here, these orcs weren't her brothers, this mountain wasn't her home. She had to go.

She numbly turned toward the door, and the safety of the

dark corridor, but then Grimarr gripped her hand again. "I wish to hear from Sken, once more," he said. "Before you go."

Jule's heart seemed to skitter in her chest, but she nodded, and allowed Grimarr to draw her into another room. This one dark and quiet, but for Sken rising creakily to his feet from a rocking-chair, and coming to stand before them.

"Tell us, brother," Grimarr's halting voice said. "What you see. Before he is gone."

Jule felt her body flinch, her hands touching to her swollen waist, her breath coming short. But she nodded too, because she desperately needed to see, to know, to remember.

Sken came a step closer, and reached his wizened hand to rest beside Jule's on her belly. His gnarled fingers spreading wide as his head tilted, his hazy eyes gone distant and vague.

"Your son swims and dances inside you," his thin voice said. "He is lusty and hungry and strong. If he is given leave to grow, he will test you and try you and laugh with you. He will speak the words of both orcs and men, and fight for truth without fear."

The words echoed and spun in Jule's head, so loud she almost didn't hear Grimarr's low voice beside her. "A worthy son," he said, his hand coming to rest heavy on Jule's shoulder. "Do you yet see his name."

Sken's eyes were closed now, a deep furrow between them. "He is called Tengil," he said. "For he is a king."

Tengil. A king. A worthy son, who would fight for truth, speak with both orcs and men. And Tengil was here, suddenly, bright and alive in Jule's body, Jule's blood, Jule's thoughts and mind and future. Her son. This one. Here.

"But he will die," Grimarr's voice said, so quiet, his hand clenching tight on Jule's shoulder. "At the hand of Lord Norr."

Sken's slow, answering nod was like a slap to the face, a streak of agony from Jule's head to her feet, and she had to close her eyes, find her balance, choke down the lurking sob in her throat. He would die. Tengil. A king.

The urge to run was almost overpowering, screaming in Jule's thoughts, and it was only Grimarr's hand, heavy on her shoulder, that kept her in place. She had to do this. She had to go. For her mate, his brothers, their sons. She would do this. She would.

Even so, she couldn't stop the wetness from streaking down her cheeks as they began walking again, through the still, silent corridor. She'd so longed for a son, for a mate, for a home. And for just a moment, it had been hers, here in this mountain, so close within her grasp.

And when Grimarr's big body came to a halt before her, just inside where she knew the exit to be, she put her hand to his scarred back, and leaned her wet cheek against it. Taking just one more breath while she could, breathing in this cruel brave beautiful orc she loved, before everything was lost forever.

"I would have stayed," she whispered, into the aching silence. "Forever. You know that, right?"

There was a hard twitch of those shoulders against her, and then those arms were here, tight and strong and safe around her, one last time.

"I know," he said, into her hair. "But no matter where you are, you shall always be my mate, my fair one. I shall always be with you."

There was nothing left to say, only that wetness slipping steadily down Jule's cheeks, and she gulped for air as Grimarr slowly, reluctantly pulled himself out of her arms. And then, before them, was the sound of crunching rock, the blinding light and heat of sun. The awareness, suddenly, of air and earth and men, and the last, lingering caress of her mate's hands against her skin.

"I am sorry," his voice whispered, so quiet she could barely hear it. "My fair Jule."

"Grimarr," she breathed, reaching—but his touch had already vanished into nothing, and Jule's blinking eyes saw only his stiff back, growing smaller and smaller as he walked away. Back into the tunnel, leaving her behind and alone, until he entirely disappeared into the blackness.

He was gone.

## 33

When Jule stepped out of Orc Mountain, it was into a world that was too bright, too open. Too foreign, suddenly, full of dread and fear, scratching strong and reckless behind her blinded, blinking eyes.

"Jule?" said a vaguely familiar voice, and Jule twitched, shading her face with a shaky hand. It was—a man. Frank. Lord Otto.

His eyes were creased with concern, his face otherwise so pale and featureless, and Jule blinked at him, and forced herself not to grimace. Lord Otto. A man. Come to take her away.

"Hey, you're all right," he murmured, his voice low and soothing, the kind of tone one would use on one's horse, or one's dogs. "It's fine. You're back with us again. We're going to take you home."

*Home.* Jule felt herself twitch again, harder than before, but Otto's eyes were kind, and his proffered hand spoke of kindness too, of a courtesy long ago ingrained in Jule's being. A lord, kindly, helping, taking her away to—

To Astin.

Jule's blinking eyes were already searching, scanning the rocky plain around them. There were fifty-odd men standing about, dressed and armed for travel, and with them all their assorted wagons and horses, already hitched and waiting. These were the last of the men who'd been camped around the mountain, the lords' personal entourage, and there, on the far side of them all—there was Astin. Lord Norr. Standing beside his costly new carriage, and looking at her.

He was beautifully dressed, of course, his military uniform perfectly tailored, buttons and gilt gleaming, tall boots buffed to a spectacular shine. His wavy brown hair was longer than usual, giving him a decidedly rakish look, and even now, Jule still felt her heartbeat stutter at the sight of him, all sheer, breathtaking perfection, outwardly a lord in every possible regard.

But Jule had changed, these past weeks. Everything had changed. And now, somehow, it seemed easier to look past Astin's handsome face and bearing, to the truth hidden behind it. The way his arms were crossed over his slim chest. The square set of his shoulders. The hard jut of his chin, the glint in his eyes, the whiteness around his mouth. And the barely visible handle of that coiled horsewhip, clenched tight in his pale fingers.

He was furious. Dangerous. Deadly.

The old, familiar fear had lurched up, wild and briefly uncontrollable, and Jule snapped her gaze back to Otto, who was still standing beside her, waiting. "May I please ride back with you, Frank?" she heard her voice ask, coming out more composed than she felt. "I would much prefer not to be alone with Astin, at the moment."

Otto's eyes followed hers toward Astin's stiff, watching form, and he gave a regretful shake of his head. "I'm sorry, Jule," he replied. "But Norr's been expecting you for some time."

"Yes, I can see that," Jule said back, through clenched teeth. "But I can also tell you, Frank, that it is not safe for me to be alone with him right now."

She could see the unease rising in Otto's eyes, but he shook his head again, grimacing. "Look, I thought you agreed to this," he said, quiet. "And if you refuse to go to him now—to your own *husband*—before all these witnesses, you know what will happen. Don't you?"

The fear surged through Jule's body again, deeper this time, because of course she knew what would happen. The end of the orcs' treaty, the end of peace, the peace her son's father had worked so hard for, given so much for, horrible cruel brave orc, a hero, her mate, *always*—

Jule had to drag in a breath, square her shoulders, squeeze her eyes shut. She had agreed to this. She could survive this. She would be brave.

Otto had held out his arm again, his eyebrows raised, and Jule's hand barely shook as it reached out, and clasped his. Agreeing, finally, and she could see the relief in his eyes, could feel it in the slight clutch of his fingers to hers.

"It'll be fine," he said, under his breath, but Jule didn't dignify that with an answer. Just held her head high, and allowed Otto to escort her through the cluster of watching men and waiting horses. Closer and closer to Astin, who had been watching all this with glittering eyes, and that telltale tightness on his mouth.

He didn't speak as Jule approached, but his gaze flicked down to her waist, once, and then back to her face. His mouth thinning even further, and this close Jule could see the new shadows under his eyes and cheekbones, the spidery red veins in the whites of his eyes.

"Your wife, Norr, as promised," said Otto beside her, with a perfunctory bow. His eyes not quite meeting Astin's, nor Jule's, and instead seeming to fixate on Astin's beautiful new carriage behind him. "Perhaps we can all meet for dinner tonight in Agayan?"

Agayan would be the obvious stopping-place, a mid-sized town perhaps a third of the way back to Yarwood, but Astin gave a brief shake of his head. "No, once we reach the main road this afternoon, we'll make our own way home," he said. "Won't we, wife?"

Astin smiled at Jule as he spoke, thin-lipped and terrifying, and she felt the fear lurch again, almost enough to make her retch. She would be alone in a carriage with Astin, for days, trapped entirely at his whim, please, gods, mercy—

"Trot along now, Otto," Astin said, with a meaningful flutter of his fingers. "I'll take things from here."

Otto didn't quite hide the disapproval on his mouth, but he gave Jule's hand one last squeeze, likely meant to be reassuring, before backing away. Leaving her standing here, facing Astin, alone.

Or not alone, perhaps, because—Jule's breath caught, her hand coming brief to her belly—had that been a twitch, inside? Perhaps?

Astin was still smiling, but his eyes had narrowed even further, darting down to follow Jule's hand. And when he looked up again, she could almost feel the rage, snapping to life in the air around them.

"Get on your knees," he said under his breath, though his mouth remained wide, in that farce of a smile. "And beg my forgiveness for getting knocked up by a foul beast. *Loudly.*"

But Jule hesitated, her hand flat against her belly, while the revulsion coiled and surged in her head. She'd expected this, she knew this was how it would be, but—

But there was another flutter against Jule's hand. Her son. Here. Alive. For now.

And suddenly, surging in her thoughts, there was a strange, startling clarity. She had to think. She had to save her son. She was cunning and brave and strong. She *was*, and that meant she could outsmart Astin. She had to.

"But what if the child is yours," she breathed. "Wouldn't it be wiser to—"

"No," he hissed back, his nostrils flaring. "I haven't fucked you in half a year, and my whole household knows it. Now, get on your knees, before"—his fingers flexed meaningfully on the whip handle—"we do *this*, while they watch."

It was probably an empty threat, but Jule still flinched at the vision of it, had to take a hard, gasping breath. She couldn't risk Astin doing that, not here, not where Grimarr might see. Gods only knew if Astin was trying to provoke something, to destroy this peace before it even began...

"Very well," she heard her voice say. Had to think, had to comply, for now, and she looked down, and breathed. And then knelt, carefully, on the earth before Astin, and gazed at her pale-faced reflection in the high gloss of his black boots.

"Forgive me, Lord Norr," she said, her voice carrying clear but for a slight break at the end. "I ask your mercy upon me for my misdeeds."

A brief glance upwards showed Astin's lip curling, his eyebrow arching—meaning he wanted more from this, he wanted begging and sobbing and heartfelt promises, the old familiar script Jule had blindly followed so many times. But she was not giving Astin that, not anymore, and she held her eyes steady to his, waiting.

Astin's hard slap to Jule's face came without warning, sending her reeling sideways, crying out with pain—and his second strike was even worse, the whip's solid wooden handle crashing against her cheekbone. Leaving her gasping on her knees before him, fighting and failing to breathe.

"Get up," came Astin's thin voice. "Now. And smile."

The pain was still radiating through Jule's skull, and her first attempt to get up failed, leaving her on her hands and knees in the dirt. But another breath, focus, *think*, and she tried again, and rose back to her feet. Her body still swaying, her face still shouting with pain, her eyes smarting and hot.

Their audience was still standing there, Otto included, fifty men watching in silence as their lord assaulted his pregnant, kneeling wife. And suddenly Jule's resolve had condensed, hardened, into something much like hatred, and she looked straight at her husband, and did not smile.

"What now," she heard herself say, quiet. "Do you have more to show them?"

Astin snarled in his throat, but it sounded more like a squeak, and Jule couldn't quite hide the scorn on her mouth, in her eyes. A sight that Astin clearly didn't miss, because without warning he lunged forward, and clutched at her arm with slim, taut fingers. "Get in the carriage," he hissed. "Now. And wipe that smirk off your face."

Jule replied with the blandest look she could muster, and accordingly made for the carriage. Its lacquered door was being held open by an unfamiliar, red-faced driver, who carefully averted his eyes as Jule climbed up inside, with Astin close behind her.

The door slammed shut with a deafening bang, shaking the whole of the carriage, and Jule carefully lowered herself down onto one of the smooth leather seats. It was nearly black inside—there were shutters concealing the tiny windows—but after so much time in the orcs' dark mountain, it felt almost like Jule could finally see again. And as the carriage slowly began to move, taking her away from the mountain for good, she drew up her courage, and looked at the seat across. Meeting the full force of her husband's waiting gaze, burning with hatred and contempt.

"Explain yourself," Astin hissed, leaning forward toward her, pulling the whip taut between his pale hands. "*Now*."

"What am I supposed to explain?" Jule heard herself reply,

her voice surprisingly calm. "That your house was attacked by orcs, when there was no guard assigned, and you *knew* it was a target?"

"No, you tedious bitch," Astin snapped back. "Getting yourself knocked up by a fucking blackmailing *animal*. Telling Otto that you didn't want to come back to me, within full hearing of all his men. And putting me in a position where I had to publicly sign a fucking *peace-treaty* with a horde of uncivilized *barbarians* who live in the fucking *dirt!*"

He was hollering by the end of it, leaning far too close, and Jule could smell the familiar scent of alcohol, lurking strong on his breath. "And then *that*," he said, and without warning, his hand grasped a handful of Jule's hair, and yanked her head to the side. Exposing those scarred bite-marks on her neck, while the disgust rose and flared in his bloodshot eyes.

"Fucking *vile*," he said. "And where the *fuck's* your wedding-ring?"

Her wedding-ring. There was a sudden, wild bubble of laughter, lurking in Jule's throat, and she managed to cover it with a loud sniff, a surreptitious wipe at her eyes. "The orc stole it," she made herself say. "And wouldn't give it back. I'm sorry, I know how expensive it was."

That seemed to mollify Astin somewhat, because he dropped back onto his seat, his eyes narrow and assessing, his arms crossing over his chest. "It was that big ugly beast who brought you out, wasn't it," he said. "The one pulling the strings behind this whole farce. Their so-called *captain*."

Jule didn't reply, didn't move, and Astin gave a hard, high-pitched laugh. "Yeah, I thought so. So how was it, wife, having a monster like that take you? What was it like being fucked by a brute who publicly hacked his own fucking *father* into *pieces*?"

Jule felt her mouth give an unwilling spasm—Grimarr had *had* to do that, he'd been protecting the people he loved—but perhaps Astin had read her expression as revulsion, because he only laughed again, the grating sound echoing through the carriage.

"Yeah, even for an orc, that one's a real fucking prize," he said. "Those subhuman shits have tainted this realm for far too long. And believe me, their day is *coming*."

Astin was giving a decidedly smug smile, one that Jule knew into her bones, and her heart was pounding again, her sweaty hands gripping tight against the swaying carriage's seat. "What do you mean?" she asked, as steadily as she could. "Didn't you just sign a *peace-treaty* with the orcs?"

Astin laughed again, and his hand had gone, perhaps unconsciously, to his waist. To where there was strapped a dagger Jule hadn't seen before, its silver hilt jewelled and gleaming out the top of its smooth leather scabbard.

"Sure we did," he said, but his voice and eyes were entirely unconvincing, and Jule stared, and thought, and stared. Astin had a plan. The men had a plan. A plan to somehow attack Grimarr, to attack the orcs, and betray their peace.

The men had *lied*.

The air suddenly felt far too thin, the carriage deathly close and constricting, and Jule had to hold her body still, think, *think*. She could face this. She could outsmart Astin. She had to...

"Why bother signing the peace-treaty at all, then?" she heard her voice ask. "Why not just refuse? Tell the orcs to go fuck themselves?"

Astin shrugged, and as Jule watched, he pulled out that dagger from its scabbard. It was bright, sharp, and new, and he touched a light, casual finger to its glinting, deadly point. "We need to get inside that mountain," he said. "Root them out from the bottom up, every last one of them. Force hasn't worked yet on the sneaky buggers, so it's time to try diplomacy."

Gods curse Astin, curse Otto, *curse* every lying male who had ever *lived*, and Jule stared at this odious, reprehensible man, who was somehow her husband. "And who all knows?" she managed. "The towns? The magistrates? The public?"

"No, of course not," Astin said dismissively, as he inspected the dagger's sharp edge. "You can't trust any of them to keep a secret like that. Only the important people know."

Jule could only seem to stare, her hands still clenching hard at that seat. Did the orcs know? Had Grimarr known? No, he couldn't, because he wouldn't have given her back if he had, would he? But then again, Grimarr had lied about so many things, hidden so many things, she couldn't trust him, couldn't trust anyone...

"We're stopping as soon as we can, by the way," Astin continued, his voice still cool, conversational. "At the first surgeon we can find. I don't care if he's a fucking *butcher*. We're getting that thing dealt with, *today*."

His eyes had glanced purposefully down at Jule's belly, his lip giving a revolted little curl. "If it's big enough," he said, "I'm sending it back to the orc in a box. You can write your name on the card."

Jule's breath was scraping out her mouth, her thoughts screaming in her head, her stomach roiling with nausea. He couldn't, he wouldn't, there had to be something, anything, appeal to his better side, please, placate, praise—

"Oh, come now, Astin," she said, as smoothly and lightly as she could. "That's a bit much, don't you think? Do you really want to give away to the orcs that you're going to betray them? Also, you don't want to lower yourself to *that* level of barbarism, do you?"

The look Astin shot her over his dagger-blade was entirely unreadable, accompanied by a vague shrug of his shoulder. "Don't I?" he said. "When it comes to a nasty bit of orc-spawn that belongs in the *dump*?"

Jule felt the wince on her mouth before she could stop it— and gods *curse* her for it, because Astin's eyes on her shifted, changed. Turning into something dark and cold and far too familiar, and now here was that smile, lighting up his face in almost a parody of what a handsome laughing lord might look like.

"Wait," he said, tapping the dagger on his finger. "Wait wait wait. You *want* this orc's leavings?!"

Jule tried to speak, find some kind of response—but Astin was already laughing, his shoulders shaking as he leaned back against the leather seat. "You're fucking *kidding* me," he said, between chuckles. "Though I suppose there's a certain logic to it, isn't there? A barren, stubborn bitch who can't give a son to her own *husband*—a fucking *lord*, at that—wants to whelp an orc brat. 'Cause that's what it apparently *takes* to get a babe in you. A fucking *orc*-prick."

His laughter had faded at the last, his eyes hardening again, turning cold, speculative. "Pretty fucking insulting, though," he said. "You should hear the shit they're saying in Yarwood about you. About *me*."

Jule's thoughts were flashing, shouting warnings, no, no, *no*—but Astin was leaning forward again, something new glinting in those hard eyes as he tossed the dagger from hand to hand.

"So you know what?" he said. "Maybe we don't need to wait for the surgeon. Maybe we can do this right here, right now. And the official story—listen very carefully, wife—is going to be that you couldn't stand to have it inside you anymore, so you did it yourself. You understand? I tried to stop you, but you refused."

Jule stared, aghast, because even Astin wouldn't be possibly be so cruel, would he? But the dagger had flipped to point toward her now, its sharpened tip only a hands-breadth away from her, and Jule cringed back into the seat, oh gods, oh *gods*.

"You can't," she gasped. "That's *madness*, Astin."

But of course that was the wrong thing to say, the *worst*

thing to say, because he only smiled again, mocking and awful and horrifying. "Oh, *I'm* mad?" he asked coolly. "You're the one who let an orc fuck you, you're the one who said you wanted to stay with him over me, you're the one who comes in here and tells me you want to give birth to a fucking orc's *filth!*"

The dagger's sharpened point came closer and closer as he spoke, backing Jule flat into the seat, her arms curling protective over her belly, her eyes fastened to that deadly dagger-tip. Astin was going to kill her, Astin was going to kill her son, *no—*

And without warning, there was another flutter against Jule's hand. From inside.

Her son. Tengil. He was lusty and cunning and strong. And he was here, because Jule and Grimarr had made him. And Grimarr had killed his own *father* for peace, while Jule had placated hers, placated Astin, did what was expected, looked the other way...

But Jule had changed. She had learned. She had been mated to an orc, she had tasted home, she had loved. She was lusty and cunning and strong.

She just—*was.*

And suddenly the world seemed to slow all around, the carriage's darkness close and quiet. And Jule swallowed, and raised her chin, and looked her husband in the eyes. A man she had enabled, a man she had helped, a man she knew had done unspeakable things. A man who would continue to do unspeakable things, if allowed to do so. A man that no one else had ever had the strength to stop. Not even Grimarr.

And here, in this carriage, in this moment—it was only her.

"Oh, *fine,*" she made herself say, with an exaggerated roll of her eyes, and it came out calm, almost easy. "If you're that determined, Astin, at least let me do it. You can watch, even get yourself off, if you want."

Astin blinked at her, looking briefly, genuinely astonished, and then grimly, coldly satisfied. And when Jule reached for the dagger-hilt, his slack hand let her take it, and circle her fingers around it. Feeling the heft and strength of it, pointing toward her belly, her waiting, brave son.

And with one choked, gasping breath, Jule spun the blade toward her husband, and plunged it deep while he screamed.

## 34

It did not take long for Lord Norr to die.

He had never tolerated pain well, despite his complacency inflicting it upon others, and his attempts to push and swat Jule away were weak, useless. And Jule had spent weeks learning to fight and spar with a huge, brutal orc, and she knew how to pull up and twist the blade, tearing apart muscle and flesh.

Astin kept screaming, but the carriage hadn't slowed in the least, and there was the distant, grim understanding that he must have either arranged to have the carriage insulated for sound, or ordered his driver not to stop at any commotion. And when his screams finally faded, his blood pooled thick on the floor around Jule's feet, the carriage was still moving, bumping along as if nothing at all had occurred.

"I'm so sorry it's come to this, Astin," Jule heard her shaky voice say to the limp body before her. "I'm so sorry. I wish there had been another way."

There was no reply, of course, and Jule had to turn her face away, gasping desperately for air, for composure, for anything. She'd—done that. She'd been the cause of that. She'd committed the unthinkable. She'd killed Astin, and saved the orcs, and her son, and herself.

"Help," she heard her shaky voice gasp, into the harrowing silence. "Someone, help."

The carriage didn't slow, and Jule desperately scrabbled at the window, and found a knob, and twisted it. Thrusting out the pane of glass just slightly, and she braced herself, dragged in the cool air. "Help!" she screamed, as loud as she could. "Stop!"

The carriage finally slowed, and came to a rattling halt. And then there was light, and voices, as the carriage door was thrust open, its grisly scene lit by harsh sunlight, and here was the unmistakable form of Otto, his face shadowed in the too-bright light.

"He's dead," Jule gasped at him, as his gaze swept over the sight inside the carriage. "Astin's *dead.*"

She could hear the shock in her voice, and the sheer, rising terror of what would come next, whether trials or punishments or executions. And Otto seemed to know it, his eyes giving a brief glance outside over his shoulder—and then, with his body blocking the view behind, he reached a gloved hand, and carefully moved Astin's limp hands onto the dagger.

Jule gaped at him, but he only wiped his gloved hand on Astin's trouser-leg, and then turned to face her, still blocking the view outside. "Listen, Jule," he said, his voice low and urgent. "Here's what happened. He was too humiliated by seeing you. He couldn't handle the shame anymore."

Jule kept gaping at him, gave a hard shake of her head. "But it's not true. He was *fine.* Other than trying to kill me."

"Then it was self-defense," Otto replied, with a grimace. "And if you try and take the fall for it, I'll testify and say you were confused. So leave it. It's better for all of us with him out of the way anyway."

It was surprisingly cold, for someone who had supposedly

been Astin's friend and ally, and Jule couldn't help another swift, horrified glance at Astin's ruined body. He was dead. Her husband, Lord Norr, was dead. She needed air, needed to get out of here, away, *home*—

But Otto was still lingering, blocking the carriage's exit, and studying Jule with careful, assessing eyes. "So will you sue for Norr's lands?" he said, even quieter than before. "On behalf of your unborn child?"

What? Jule jolted all over, staring—and then she heard a choked, incredulous sound come from her mouth. Astin was dead, she had just killed her *husband*, and Otto knew it—and this was all he cared about. The possibility that the child in Jule's belly *could* be Astin's, after all, and therefore the sole heir to Astin's lands and wealth, rather than *him*.

"So that's why you're being so magnanimous," Jule heard herself say back, under her breath. "Getting low on funds these days, I assume?"

Otto didn't even try to deny it, the slimy bastard, and Jule let out another sound not quite like a laugh. "Me destroying myself once over for your benefit wasn't good enough for you?" she hissed. "And then you try to sacrifice me and my child for your own benefit *again*, lying to the orcs about a peace-treaty you have zero intention of keeping? And now you stand here, over Astin's warm body, and ask me for *this*?!"

Otto at least looked slightly ashamed, but his eyes glanced nervously behind them, where Jule could see uniformed men beginning to assemble outside the carriage. "I just want a deal," he whispered. "To your benefit, as well. We *are* family, after all."

Jule couldn't stop staring, her thoughts twisting and curdling, swirling around a rising, sickening comprehension. Grimarr had been right all along. It wasn't just openly cruel men like Astin who were the enemy. It was regular, kindly, well-meaning people like Otto—like her—who looked the other way, thought of their own welfare, and took the easiest path forward.

Jule's eyes had darted toward Astin again, lying so cold and empty across from her, his blood still warm under her feet. She'd been brave enough to face that enemy, her own damned husband. And surely, *surely* she could find the strength to face this one.

"Then here's your deal, *cousin*," she breathed, as she shoved her way past Otto's form, and down out of the carriage. Out into light and fresh air, and—her resolve stuttered, briefly—straight into the middle of a mass of watching men.

It was nearly all of them, Jule's twitching thoughts pointed out, fifty armed and uniformed soldiers in a loose circle around her. Some with weapons drawn, some not, but all with wary, watchful eyes, flicking between her and the carriage behind her.

Otto had just stepped down from the door, revealing the unmistakable, gruesome sight inside, and now here were the rising murmurs, the shifting feet, the accusing, suspicious glances. *Is that blood. Is that Lord Norr. Is Lord Norr—dead.*

It felt hard to breathe, suddenly, the world spinning and sparking white behind Jule's eyes, but no, no, she had to face this. Had to face the truth, her enemies, herself.

And somehow, there was the strength to square her shoulders, and lift her head. To sweep her gaze over the armed men all around, and speak.

"My husband, Lord Norr, is dead," her voice said, wavering but clear. "Just now, in this carriage, he sought to kill me. And when he failed"—she couldn't help a swift look toward Otto, watching behind her—"he took his own life, with his own dagger, before my eyes."

The murmurs immediately rose again, the men giving uncertain glances between one another and the carriage, but Jule sharply raised a hand, and they fell silent again. "Lord

Norr has been unwell for some time," she continued. "He was consumed by responsibilities, and was mistreated as a child. However, his legacy will now be one of peace, and hope for a brighter future for our own children."

Her hand had come to rest on her belly as she spoke, drawing the men's eyes collectively toward it, and Jule drew in another deep, bracing breath. "The killing has to stop," she said. "The death has to stop. We *need* this peace, between orcs and men."

The conviction had risen in her voice, her entire body—but she still twitched at the ugly sound of a snort, from the back of the crowd. "What if we don't *want* peace with orcs," a voice called out. "What if we don't make deals with *monsters*."

There were a few laughs in reply, and many more nodding heads. "Forget the whole deal," another voice called out. "Wipe out the swine for good."

The anger surged down Jule's back, and she glared at the man who'd spoken, at his pale featureless face. "The orcs are *not* swine, or monsters," she countered. "They're people. Just like us."

There were a few more laughs from the crowd of men, a few more pointed slurs, and Jule felt the fear beginning to pulse again, her hands going to clammy fists at her sides. "The treaty's been signed," she said. "By our towns, by our magistrates and lords. It's *done*."

"It's just a piece of paper," another man said, earning a chorus of agreement, and Jule shot a helpless, searching glance behind her, toward Otto. He'd wanted a deal, he'd said they were family, hadn't he?

But there was an odd, distant look in Otto's blue eyes, a strange hesitation on his slim body—and suddenly the truth struck at Jule with blinding, harrowing force.

She'd made a horrible, *stupid* miscalculation. Otto cared about Astin's lands and wealth, yes, likely even enough to honour the peace-treaty—but right now Otto was also Astin's next in line to inherit, and there were other, easier ways to ensure his standing.

And the easiest of all would be for Jule to die.

It wouldn't even have to be today, Jule realized, her eyes darting frantically between Otto and the surrounding men. It could be anytime between now and her son's birth. And it could be a single word in one of these men's ears, a switch of a cup, a silent dagger in the dark.

"Frank," she breathed, searching his impassive face, please gods, please. "Support me on this. You agreed."

But his face, his *face*. Looking at the men, and then at her. Weighing the options, thinking of his own welfare, searching for the easiest path forward. Proving himself Jule's truest enemy after all, after Astin, after everything.

"We're family, Frank," Jule managed. "Like you said. I've already sacrificed so *much* for you."

But he was already betraying her, again, his eyes decided, determined, lingering now on the men. And the horror was flooding Jule all at once, because he only had to say, *She lies, she killed Lord Norr for the orcs*—and the tension would erupt into chaos. And then all Otto's problems would be solved at once, Jule dead, Tengil dead, the orcs' peace, dead...

Jule was trapped. She was doomed.

"Please, Frank," she begged, her voice breaking. "Please. Don't."

But it was too late, oh gods it was too late, he was looking resolutely away from her, his gloved hand moving to grip at his sword-hilt, his mouth opening to speak—

When suddenly, from on top of the carriage behind him, a tall grey blur hurled itself to the earth, and pressed a sharp, gleaming blade against Otto's neck.

The orcs were here.

## 35

For an instant, it was like the world had stuttered around Jule, its visions flashing bright and unreal before her eyes.

There was Otto, with shock and fear etching across his face, while the orc behind him—Joarr—gave a broad, rather demented grin. There were more orcs emerging from the trees all around, their huge scimitars flashing in the light. There were men shouting and jostling, fumbling for weapons, scattered and shaken and afraid.

But beyond all that, there was *Grimarr*.

He'd charged out from the trees at the head of the orcs, his face contorted with rage, his mouth bellowing so loudly it rumbled the earth. He was huge and bare-chested, covered with battle-scars all over, his curved scimitar raised high in his sharp-clawed fist. And he was running with an easy, deadly grace, his boots kicking up earth behind him, his black eyes on Jule crackling with fury and fire and *life*.

Grimarr was here. For *her*.

And when the world had snapped back to speed again, it

was with Jule's mate, here, looming close beside her, his huge powerful body protecting her, *safe*.

"Are you well, woman," he growled, his familiar voice hot surging relief in Jule's ears, and she managed a shaky, twitching nod. Earning a brief, near-painful clutch of his claws against her back, before he thrust her well behind him, and brandished his gleaming scimitar toward the mass of scattered, fumbling men.

"You ask what happens if you do not keep this treaty with orcs," his deep voice bellowed, carrying over the hubbub. "This is what happens. You die."

He'd waved his huge clawed hand toward the advancing orcs, prowling uncontested through the clusters of men. There were Silfast and Olarr, both huge and craggy-faced and terrifying, and close behind them was Baldr, his black eyes flaring with anger, his bare-chested greenish body looking surprisingly coiled and deadly. And there was Drafli, too, swaggering tall and near-naked with his massive scimitar in hand, and behind him Afkarr, Simon, Abjorn, Eyarl.

It wasn't a full fighting-band, Jule knew, and the orcs had to be outnumbered five to one—but even so, none of the men were attacking, not even those with swords drawn. And that, of course, was because of their commander, Lord Otto, who was still scrabbling uselessly against Joarr's tall, smiling form, the flashing knife-edge still pressed to his throat.

Grimarr had given a deep, mocking snort, surveying the scene with glittering, contemptuous eyes. "Speak, little lord," he said to Otto. "Shall you break this treaty you have made with us? Shall you choose death over peace?"

Otto's face was very pale, his eyes desperately darting all around, and Jule felt her own contempt rising, and with it a cold, twitching rage. He was *still* looking for the easiest path forward. He truly *would* choose death—at least for his men—if it were better for him, in the end.

And Jule was not letting him get away with it. Not this time.

"There are more orcs hiding in the forest!" a voice called out—*Jule's* voice, carrying high and clear through the air. Snapping every face here toward her, both orcs and men, the former with confusion in their eyes, the latter with unmistakable fear. And as for Otto, he was looking markedly ill by this point, and Jule bit back the sudden, vindictive urge to smile.

"This orc *always* has a plan," Jule's loud voice continued, her head giving a sideways jerk toward Grimarr. "And it's probably awful. I shouldn't test him, Frank, if I were you."

Otto truly looked as though he were about to sick up on his boots, his eyes darting around at the trees, at the band of huge, vicious, extravagantly armed orcs standing among his shifting, ashen-faced men. And when his gaze found Jule's again, it was wide and earnest, almost as if pleading with her. Asking her for help, for a rescue, even now.

But Jule's jaw was set, her hands in fists, and she gave a slow, purposeful shake of her head. She was done with him, done with the betrayals of every person she'd ever held dear. She stood for peace, for her son, for herself.

"For what do you wish, little lord," insisted Grimarr's voice beside her, deep and menacing. "Peace? Or death?"

There was another instant's stillness, the tension alive in the air all around, every eye now held to Otto's face. Waiting for him to decide.

And surely he could see the easiest path now. Surely his selfishness could be relied upon over all else. Surely...

"Peace," Otto called out, finally. "We choose peace."

Oh, thank the *gods*, and Jule felt the relief flood her all at once, so strong it brought stars to her eyes. There would be no fighting. No death. The orcs' peace was still true, still here, for Jule's mate, and his brothers. For her son.

"Of course we're not going to break a treaty we just signed," Otto continued, his voice coming out impressively calm, despite the knife still pressed against his throat. "This is all just a misunderstanding."

The relief was clear on the men's assembled faces, and already they were sheathing weapons, and backing away. Meanwhile, Joarr had finally let go of Otto, sending him stumbling, and then in two smooth, highly impressive leaps, he was once again crouching on top of the carriage behind them, looking supremely pleased with himself.

In front of Jule, Grimarr had lowered his scimitar slightly, and was fixing Otto with a scowl of purest scorn. "I am glad to hear of this—*misunderstanding*," he said, his voice deceptively even. "Surely no true lord would break his word thus to his people. And most of all to his own *kin*."

He'd cast a telling look toward Jule as he spoke, his hand flexing on his scimitar-hilt, and Jule could see Otto's throat swallow, his uneasy eyes glancing brief toward her. "Of course not," he said, with a pained little smile. "We're family, aren't we, Jule?"

Jule bit back a snort—sure they were family, at least until it became more convenient to *murder* her. And even now, she knew full well that Otto could still kill her, so easily, with just a word, at any moment. He was still her enemy, still a privileged, self-absorbed fool who would always take the easiest path forward.

And that meant—Jule squared her shoulders—she couldn't dare leave here with him now. She couldn't risk it. Not for her son, or herself.

"We *are* family, Frank," she said, her voice cold. "Therefore, I'm sure you'll understand if I don't wish to continue on to Yarwood with you at the moment, under the circumstances?"

She was eyeing Astin's carriage again, the grisly sight inside still far too visible, and already here were the visions, unbidden and sickening, of what would need to come next. Astin's viewing, Astin's funeral, facing Astin's innumerable associates and employees, returning to that cold empty house that had never been hers...

And thank the gods, Grimarr was suddenly here again, his clawed hand clamped solid and warm on Jule's shoulder. "No, she shall not return there," he said, his voice deep, steady. "Now that Lord Norr is dead, we shall return this woman with us to our mountain. She shall serve as proof of your renewed vow, and your goodwill toward us."

The relief again felt like a physical force, swarming at Jule's bones—she could go back, truly?—but she managed to keep her eyes steady, her body upright. "I am willing to serve thus," she said to Otto. "And perhaps, cousin, you will come to visit me on occasion, to ensure that I am well treated, and that our peace-treaty continues unhindered. And to discuss, also, certain family matters."

She meant the lands, and Astin's estate, and she could see the understanding flare across Otto's eyes, the sudden realization that perhaps this could still all come together to his benefit, if he played his hand properly. And his swift replying smile toward Jule was actually a genuine one, warming his face and his pale weak eyes.

"Of course, dear Jule," he said. "I'll return in a week or two, once Norr's funeral arrangements have been settled, and we'll talk."

Jule managed to bite back the sneer on her mouth, and gave a thin, chilly smile instead. "Excellent," she replied. "And as I'm sure you're aware, cousin, my lord father left me certain guaranteed trusts upon his death, which shall soon need to be returned to my control, with their sums fully restored. In the meantime"—her eyes swept over the men's well-stocked supply wagons—"as a gently bred lady, I shall require some additional supplies, to ensure my resumed captivity is a more comfortable one."

Jule didn't miss the flare of irritation in Otto's eyes, but thankfully he wasn't fool enough to argue, and waved a hand toward the supply-wagons behind him. "Naturally, cousin," he replied, with a pasted-on smile. "Which would you like?"

"That one," Jule replied, without hesitation, pointing at the largest wagon at the end of the pack, loaded with flour and salt and pork and ale. "I'll also need those two horses hitched to it, of course. And, did I see Lord Norr's new gelding here as well?"

She was pushing now, she knew, but that horse had deserved better than Astin, and soon one of the men produced him from the back, fully saddled and bridled. He was just as beautiful as Jule had remembered, a tall fine thoroughbred, and she entirely ignored the gasps from the men all around as she yanked up her skirts, and leapt up into the saddle, legs astride.

"Safe travels, dear cousin," she said to Otto, with a cool smile. "I shall eagerly await our next meeting, and look forward to a lifetime of peace."

And without waiting for his reply, she kicked at her horse's sides, and rode away through the trees.

## 36

Jule rode through the forest at a breakneck pace, feeling her horse's powerful body rolling beneath her, while the trees around her raced by.

She was going back, her exultant thoughts whispered. Back to Orc Mountain. Back—*home*.

But was it home, truly? After everything Grimarr had done? He had saved her just now, surely—but even that may have been for his brothers, for their peace. Because when it came to Jule alone, the stark truth was, he had still betrayed her. He'd still sold her. He'd still sent their son to certain death. He'd lied, he'd cheated her, he'd used her for his own ends.

And worst of all, by sending her away alone with Astin, he had signed off on her death. Just like her father, like Astin, like Otto.

That truth, grim and certain, only seemed to rise as Jule rode, closer and closer to Orc Mountain. Its rocky cliffs looming high and deadly over her, its peak piercing up into the low clouds, its base sprawled broad and powerful over the earth.

It was truly a beautiful place, Jule thought, as she pulled the horse up before it, and wiped a hand at her damp eyes. It was a fitting home, for its noble orcs. If only it truly *could* be home. Her home.

She slid off the horse's back, landing hard on her feet beside him, and again she wiped at her eyes, and tried to choke back the rising lump in her throat. Gods, what a horrible, exhausting, endless day. Astin had wanted her dead, Otto would have ordered her dead, she'd killed her *husband*, her own mate had *sold* her, and now here she was, standing before the mountain that had never been her home, and wanting to weep like a child.

When suddenly, without warning, there was clattering noise all around, and the sound of boots, pounding at the earth. And when Jule looked up, blinking through damp eyelashes, once again, the orcs were here.

There were Baldr and Drafli, Olarr and Silfast, Afkarr and Abjorn and Simon and Eyarl. And behind them was the loaded supply-wagon, lumbering pendulously from side to side, being driven by a still-grinning Joarr, standing tall upon the wagon-seat with reins in hand.

But closest of all, striding toward Jule with deadly purpose, was Grimarr, of Clan Ash-Kai. Her mate, her betrayer, the father of her son.

Jule twitched back against the horse—she couldn't trust him, she couldn't, he'd *sold* her—and she could see him twitch back too, coming to an abrupt halt, a few paces away. While the other orcs gathered all around behind him, looking between him and Jule with odd, uncertain eyes. While Grimarr's eyes were pure glittering black, her mate her love he'd *sold* her, and Jule felt something yank hard in her chest, swallowing her breath.

"What," she heard her scratchy voice say. "Should I"—she had to pause, take a gulping breath—"should I not have come back here?"

Grimarr's eyes narrowed, intent and piercing, and she could see those fists flexing at his sides, his claws sharp and black against his palms. "Ach, woman," he said, his voice a slow rolling quiet. "Yes, you should be here. This is your home."

Jule's breath was heaving oddly—it wasn't, he wasn't—and she fought to drag in air, to find words. "But you," she began, "you—"

She couldn't speak, suddenly, pressing her trembling hands to her face so hard it hurt—but before her, there was the hurtling, incongruous sight of Grimarr, of Clan Ash-Kai, Prince of the Orcs, sinking hard to his knees on the earth, and looking up at her, into her, with bottomless black eyes.

"Woman," he said, his voice heavy, his clawed hands straining against his knees. "I was wrong. I have hurt you. I have misjudged you. I have *failed* you."

Jule blinked, but couldn't seem to speak, and Grimarr gave a hard shake of his head, as if to thrust something away from it. "I failed you," he said again, quieter. "In all my plans for peace, I did not think of your wishes, or your happiness. I thought only of my brothers', and my own. I ought not to have done this."

The words sounded raw and pained, like he truly did mean them, but this orc had said so many convincing words, and Jule looked away, fought to ignore the watching eyes all around. "Well, you did do it," she said, her voice tight. "And you would probably do it all again, given the choice."

"No," came Grimarr's reply, sudden, forceful. "No. I would have sought another path. I would never have given Lord Norr leave to touch you, or harm you, as I did today. I should have protected you, as I swore to do, and found a way to kill this man first. You should never have had to do this, in my stead."

Jule again couldn't seem to speak, or look at him, and she could hear his harsh breaths, coming in and out. "I should have shared my plans with you," he continued, quieter. "I should

have made you part of this. And even had I not found a way to
kill Lord Norr, and still needed to trade you to him for peace, I
should have sought your blessing. I should never have trapped
you and hurt you with this before the men, as I did, after you
spoke so nobly to them in our stead. I would have trusted you,
as you trusted me."

Jule's eyes had darted back toward him, catching on the
grief in his face, the single streak of wetness down his cheek.
"I should have begged you," he said, slower now, "to stay true
to me, in your heart, and to seek a way to return to my side. I
should have begged you to meet me in secret, and welcome
me in the night. I should have sought to remind you that
even if you share a bed with another, you are always my
mate, and that I shall always long for you, and welcome you,
and cherish you. That this mountain shall always be your
home."

It was like the words were arrows, piercing deep through
Jule's skin, and she made herself shake her head, hard. "It's just
the bond," she said, her voice hoarse. "The orc-magic. You said
so yourself, before. It's hard to break."

"*No*," Grimarr countered, loud enough that Jule twitched.
"It is not just this. I have had other mates. I know what the
bond does, and does not do. It is far more than hunger with
you, woman."

Jule was still watching, snared in those eyes, in the truth
flaring behind them. "You are brave and kind and lusty and
clever," he said, his voice ringing deep with conviction. "You
did not bow to fear of the mountain or my brothers. Instead
you learned their ways, and made friends of them, and worked
on their behalf. You did not sigh or weep or complain. You
learned to walk the mountain as one born to it."

Jule couldn't help another twitch, and a furtive glance up at
that mountain, watching silently over them. And here,
standing before it, the still-watching eyes of its orcs, witnessing

the sight of their captain on his knees, weeping before his mate.

"You gave me many gifts," Grimarr continued. "Your eager hunger. Your warmth and your laughter. Your way of easing my anger and grief. Even your questions. And then, you gave all for our gain. And even when your own death was at hand, as it was today, you yet defended our peace to these men. You have saved legions of my brothers and our sons, even after all the ways I have failed you. I could not have asked for a more worthy mate, or a truer friend."

The words seemed to linger in the air, drawing tight in the space between them, and Jule could see Grimarr's chest filling, his hands clenching his knees again, almost as if to brace himself. "And you told me," he said, toward his hands, "that you wished to have a choice. Like the kitchen. And so I wish to give you all the choices within my power. You may stay here in your home, and freely partake of all its wealth, as long as you wish. You may choose to bear my son here, or elsewhere, or not at all, as you wish. And"—his mouth contorted, his claws now digging sharp into his knees—"you may choose to keep me as your mate, or you may choose another, or none at all. But should you choose another man, or another orc, I shall uphold this, with all the power at my command."

*What?* Jule felt her whole body flinch, her eyes blinking disbelievingly down toward Grimarr's pained, miserable face. "You would," she managed, and then sucked in air, tried again. "Tolerate another orc? Mating with me, and raising your *son*? Here, in your own *home*?"

The orcs standing around them were shifting oddly, more than one hand clenching at a sword-hilt, but Jule's eyes were trapped on Grimarr, lost in his twisted mouth, his shallow, panting breaths. "It is your home also, and thus your choice to make," his voice said, an oddly strained monotone. "I have many brothers who should treat you with only kindness, and never once dream of hurting you, as I have. Mayhap one of the Ka-esh, I know you have found them pleasing—"

His choked voice broke off there, his huge shoulders heaving, and Jule could only stare at him, her own breaths coming short and harsh. This horrible cruel brave orc, this hero, on his knees before his brothers, offering the unthinkable, offering *everything*. His wealth, his home, his support, his humiliation. His shame.

And that meant, Jule realized, with a shocked glance around at the wide-eyed watching orc-faces, it was Grimarr also risking his hard-won place as captain, his entire life's work. *No orc wishes to follow a shamed lord*, he'd said that day. And for their captain to lose his pregnant mate, and to watch his son raised under another, and to support this with all the power at his command—this was surely shame well beyond what these orcs would bear.

But Grimarr was offering it, for her. He was offering the utter opposite of what his own father had done, the opposite of what Astin and Otto had done—and he was doing it openly, publicly, before all his brothers. And had it only been weeks ago when he'd held Jule out before them, huge and deadly and victorious, *Behold my new mate, smell how she bears my scent and my seed...*

But then, that same night, deep and secret, the old powerful magic fusing to life between them. *I shall pledge you my troth, my fair Jule. I grant you my favour, and my sword, and my fealty. I shall forever mark this night...*

"And what do *you* wish, orc?" Jule heard her shaky voice ask, to those desolate black eyes. "What would be *your* choice, if given one?"

She could see Grimarr's chest expanding, those eyes briefly squeezing shut. "My own wish," he said, so quiet, "is to earn your trust once more. To prove to you that I can be a worthy mate, and a worthy father to our son. I wish to be forever yours, my fair one."

Forever hers. Jule had to squeeze her own eyes shut, draw in a deep, bracing breath. He wanted to earn her trust. Be a worthy mate. Forever hers.

And when her eyes blinked open, finding that dark head still bowed before her, she felt her shaky hand reach out, slow, to brush against that silken hair. Snapping his head up, his glittering gaze searching hers, and Jule traced her fingers down his scarred, wet face, while her heart clamoured inside her chest. Her orc. Her mate. Her prince.

And for all that Grimarr had done, he hadn't lied, in this. He hadn't made himself seem justified, or Jule at fault. He hadn't said, *I rescued you today, I came to your side when you needed me, I saved your life.* Instead, he was giving her this choice. All of the choices. Anything she wanted, here, within her grasp. Him. *Home.*

And even if Jule couldn't offer forgiveness—or even trust, not yet—she could face this. She could be brave, one more time.

She *was.*

"Very well, my fair mate," she whispered, to those molten black eyes. "Then prove your word, and take me home."

## 37

There was an instant's twitching, shuddering silence. Filled only by the sound of one of the horses, stamping and whinnying behind them, and the thick, heavy exhale of Grimarr's breath.

And suddenly, exploding in Jule's entire being, there was— joy. Grimarr's warm powerful arms, circling tight around her. His scent, swirling close and potent into her lungs. His whole body, here, against her, with her, clutching her almost painfully close, while his breath gasped harsh and deep against her ear, as though he'd been starving for air, until this moment.

"Yes," he choked, and that was wetness streaking against Jule's cheek, perhaps his, or hers, or both. "My mate. My fair one. *Ach.* Yes. You are *mine*, you shall stay safe with me for *always*—"

His voice broke off there, but his arms only went tighter, swaying Jule bodily against him, and she belatedly noticed that she was clinging back, both her arms gripped tight around his neck, her legs already clamped around his waist. He was huge and rock-hard under his trousers, of course he was, and Jule felt herself choke out a laugh, or perhaps a sob, into the warm, delicious heat of his neck.

"For now," she corrected him, because she was honour bound to make this clear, before her frantic, grasping hands decided to start tearing his trousers off at once. "You still need to prove this to me, orc. I still don't trust you. I may never trust you *again*."

But Grimarr only buried his face deeper into her neck, that hardness under his trousers pressing strong against her. "Ach, I shall prove this," he said, his voice a deep, thought-swarming rumble against her skin. "I swear this, woman. I shall give you honour and care beyond all your deepest wishes. You shall not regret this."

Jule's eyes were leaking again, her body clinging harder against him, against the feel of his heartbeat, his breath, his big hands running fervent up and down her back. "I pledge you my troth, and my life," he said, his voice quiet but sure. "I am forever yours. My own brave, clever, fair one."

Jule was fully weeping against him now, without at all meaning to, and in reply Grimarr only squeezed her tighter, rocking them back and forth. "I shall please you," he murmured. "I shall bring you joy. I shall feed you and kiss you and plough you until you *scream*."

Even the thought brought an unwilling moan to Jule's already-gulping mouth, and in reply Grimarr gave a laugh that was more like a growl, tinged with unmistakable triumph. "I shall take great joy in this, woman," he said, with a meaningful grip at Jule's arse. "Now that I have had you in all possible ways, your next task shall be to take me *here* with ease, whenever I should wish."

Jule pulled back to glare at him, but that meant that she was looking at his hideous, dear face, at those glittering, too-bright eyes. "Curse you, orc," she murmured, but his delicious clever mouth was so *close*, and within a breath she was kissing him, strong and deep. Their tongues tangling hard and familiar, the hunger whirling up like a raging, thundering storm, Jule's hands on his face in his hair yanking at his shoulders, there was nothing more than this, here, *him*—

At least, until there was a familiar-sounding voice beside her, saying words that didn't at all register in Jule's fogged brain, and when she belatedly pulled back to look, it was—the orcs. Not only the ones who'd been travelling with them, but more from the mountain, Kesst and Efterar, Tristan and Salvi and John, Gegnir and Narfi, dozens of curious faces crowding all around.

And when Grimarr's big hands whirled Jule around to face them, and then bodily raised her up, as if brandishing her to their watching eyes, there was only warmth, pleasure, safety. Her mate was claiming her, honouring her, before all his brothers, before all five clans.

"My mate has returned!" Grimarr called out, his voice echoing against the nearby stone of the mountain. "My mate, who so nobly gained our peace with the men, has now bravely spurned her own kin, and killed Lord Norr in our stead. Not only this, but she has freely chosen me as her mate, above all others, and brought back my son to our home. Tonight, we will celebrate!"

The surrounding orcs cheered, the sound a surging cacophony in Jule's ears, but she found herself actually smiling through the din, and again blinking back the cursed wetness behind her eyes. "And my mate and his loyal orcs rescued me, and kept me safe," she added, her higher voice carrying over the noise. "They bravely faced a band five times their number, and secured our peace-treaty with the men. Not only this, but together we've brought back a wagon, full of meat and ale!"

The noise had swelled even louder, the orcs already surging around the wagon, unloading it with astonishing speed. Carting off barrels and packages toward the mountain, while

Grimarr spun Jule back around to face him, hoisting her onto his hip.

"You honour me, woman," he murmured, into her hair. "My clever, wise mate. Not only did you kill Lord Norr, and trick these fool men who wish to break our peace, but you bring food and drink for my brothers also."

"And horses," Jule said, pulling away enough to give him her most meaningful, teasing smile. "Just like you wanted."

Grimarr groaned aloud, his eyes briefly casting toward the three horses, one of them Astin's lovely gelding, and the two others still hitched to the supply-wagon. They were both strong, solid workhorses, better suited for hauling than riding, but still more than capable of carrying an orc rider's weight.

"If I'm staying, I'm setting up a stable," Jule said firmly. "And you're learning to ride with me. So next time you go off on a deadly mission like that, you can at least have the option to steal their horses, if you need to."

Grimarr groaned again, but there was no malice in it, only a hungry teasing warmth, his face turning to bury deep against Jule's neck. But Jule was still considering that point, suddenly, her thoughts catching up far too late to what exactly the orcs had done today, and why.

"What *was* your plan today, anyway?" she asked Grimarr, pulling back to look at him. "When you attacked the men? Where were the rest of your orcs?"

Because they hadn't been hiding in the trees, Jule had known that very well, and Grimarr gave an over-casual shrug, a wry twitch of a sharp-toothed smile. "I did not truly have a plan," he said. "Not this time. Only to do all that I could to keep you safe."

Oh. "And how long, exactly, were you planning this non-plan plan?" Jule asked, eyeing him with a steadily increasing suspicion. "All your strongest and most loyal fighters, fully armed, right there in the woods? Joarr hiding on top of the damned *carriage*?"

"For some time, mayhap," Grimarr said, with an expression of blandness that was fooling no one, and Jule gave an incredulous huff of laughter, a hard scratch of her fingernails against his bare back.

"You are such a complete conniving *bastard*," she informed him. "Why didn't you *tell* me?"

But here, moving brief but unmistakable across her mate's eyes, was why he hadn't told her. He still hadn't trusted her. He still hadn't been sure. He'd still thought, perhaps, that Jule would see Lord Norr, be alone with Lord Norr, and change her mind.

He'd been afraid. And today, perhaps, Jule had taken those fears, and finally destroyed them, for good.

"I did speak this, a little," Grimarr said now, with a grimace. "When you told me you would have stayed. I said, in turn, I should always be with you, no matter where you were."

That was true, he *had* said that, and after everything else today, Jule could only seem to sigh, and put her hands to his dear beautiful face, while an odd, shaky relief seemed to stutter through her thoughts. Grimarr *hadn't* truly given her over to death, after all. He *wasn't* like her father, or Astin, or Otto. He never, ever had been.

"I did not know what would come of this," Grimarr continued, quiet. "I did not know if I should ever speak to you or our son again, or if I could keep you safe amongst all these men, without destroying this peace for my brothers. But I wished to do all within my power to be near to you, and give you what help I could, if you yet wished for this."

"I did wish for this," Jule whispered, to those eyes. "Thank you, Grimarr."

But he gave a hard shake of his head, his mouth tight. "I indeed failed you in this, woman," he said. "I yet gave you over to Lord Norr, and watched this scum strike you, while my brothers and I crept into our places in the trees. And when you were in this carriage with him, I ought to have broken in and slit his throat—but Joarr would not allow this, and knew we must wait. He has a touch of the old magic, you see, in kenning such things."

Jule blinked, following that, pulling the pieces together. "So was me killing Astin actually part of your plan, too?" she asked, carefully. "What with all that time we spent together in the training-room, with you teaching me how to fight and kill?"

But Grimarr had fixed Jule with one of his ghastly scowls, his eyebrows furrowing, his lip curling with deep disapproval. "*Ach*, no," he said, voice flat. "What kind of weak orc should I be, to place my mate and son in such danger? You are not to make my kills for me, woman. You are to stay *safe*, away from these fool men who all wish to kill you. And beyond this, you are to grow my son, and ride my prick, and suck my seed, and find peace and purpose in your new home. And this is *all*."

Jule couldn't help a roll of her eyes at his scowling face, but she leaned closer into him anyway, into the warm strong safety of him. "Such a stubborn orc," she murmured. "But I must admit, after today, that does sound quite lovely."

"Good," he said, but it came out absently, his eyes still searching hers. "I am sorry I did not trust you, woman. I am sorry I hurt you, and failed you."

Jule could only shake her head, breathing in his close, familiar, beloved scent. "I should have trusted you, too," she whispered. "I should have known you'd keep me safe. You always have."

There was a low, sustained growl in her ear, almost more of a purr, inviting her to relax, to revel in this glorious moment—but there was more to say, one last truth between them, and Jule took a bracing breath, and held those eyes.

"And I should have thanked you," she said. "Long ago. For

taking me away from Astin, and that awful house, in the first place. For rescuing me, when I so desperately needed it, even when I couldn't admit it, or accept it. And thank you"—she swallowed hard—"for giving me the space and the freedom to accept the truth about my old life, and my old beliefs. Thank you for challenging my ignorance, and doing it with so much patience and kindness. Thank you for giving me so many opportunities to make this my home."

Grimarr's head had tilted, studying her, but he didn't yet speak, and Jule drew in more breath, more honesty. "You're such a good lord, Grimarr of Clan Ash-Kai," she whispered, with a twitchy little smile. "I'm honoured that you chose me as your mate. I hope to bring you much joy, and bear you as many sons as you might wish."

His eyes looked bright, suddenly, his black lashes blinking hard against his cheek, and without warning he yanked her closer, pulling her so tight she could scarcely breathe. "Ach, woman," he rumbled, into her ear. "Do not tease me thus. Else you shall bear me a whole *brood* of orclings, and your womb shall never lie fallow again."

The hunger surged without warning, so powerful it brought a groan to Jule's mouth, and in reply Grimarr pulled back, and gave her a slow, sharp, wicked grin. Her favourite smile, from her favourite orc, and Jule could only blink and smile back, warm, tearful, true.

"We shall welcome what comes together," Grimarr said now, his voice gruff, his hands spreading wide and strong against her back. "Now rest, my fair one, and be content. I shall carry you home."

## 38

That night in the muster-room, before a huge, snapping, blazing fire, the orcs held a party unlike any Jule had ever seen in her life.

It was full of ale and food and shouting and music and dancing, and hundreds of orcs, some familiar, and some entirely new. All seeming to be moving and talking at once, beating drums and playing games and starting fights, and calling out congratulations and ribald jokes with equal frequency as Jule and Grimarr made their way through the crowd.

There was also an astonishing amount of nakedness and cavorting, taking place on couches that had been thrust to the centre of the large room, so that any orcs who wished to could watch, or join in themselves. Jule recognized Narfi, the small orc from the kitchen, riding upon Simon's shockingly massive prick while also eagerly sucking Drafli's, and Kesst was once again giving an impressive show, swallowing Efterar to the base while the surrounding orcs leered and cheered.

It should have all been appalling and overwhelming, and perhaps it might have been, if not for Grimarr's heavy arm around Jule's shoulder, his voice close and warm in her ear, answering the sudden deluge of questions currently filling her thoughts. How had Joarr stayed hidden atop that carriage, what had been the odds of the orcs actually defeating those men in battle, wherever were they going to put the stable, and Narfi and Simon—or Narfi and Drafli—weren't *mated*, were they?

"Ach, no," Grimarr said, with a chuckle, into her ear. "This is just for pleasure. It is not like Kesst and Efterar, or me and you. If another orc should touch Kesst, Efterar should throttle him, as I should with any orc who touches you. One must speak these vows, you see, to fulfill this bond. As I did, with you."

Jule curled closer against the warmth of him, and couldn't help a furtive smile up at his watching eyes. "Right," she said. "And now, with this peace-treaty, you can have weddings too, right? Who's going to be the first, do you think?"

That distance that passed over Grimarr's eyes was so familiar, and so infuriating, but Jule waited for his answer, and finally it came, careful and halting. "I hoped," he said, "that some day, we might do this. You and me."

The heat unfurled down Jule's back in a flood, and she couldn't help another smile, disbelieving this time. "Are you—*proposing* to me, Grimarr?"

The look in his eyes was tellingly wary, now, and his lip jutted out in what should have been a hideous scowl, but the sight only sent another surge of warmth down Jule's back. "I have already spoken the vows of a mate to you," he said. "I have already given you my seed, and my son, and my home. Why should this—*proposal*—amaze you?"

Jule's eyes had glanced reflexively down toward her left hand, still lacking any adornment, and she could feel Grimarr's eyes following her gaze, an odd awareness filtering across his face. "Ach," he said. "You humans, and your silly wedding-rings."

There was an equally odd note in his voice, enough to make Jule pull him entirely to a stop, searching his inscrutable face. "*Grimarr*," she said, exasperated, even as her hand stroked up against his broad bare chest. "What? Tell me."

His hand had twitched toward his trouser-pocket, reaching inside, and then bringing out something small, that glittered in his fingers. And it was—Jule choked, and stared—was a ring.

A *wedding-ring*.

It was made of gold and silver beaten together, sparkling in the light, and inside it, Jule could just make out the tiny, exquisite lines of script, circling around it. Script not unlike what she'd seen in some of the old Ka-esh books, all curling, strangely elegant black-tongue.

"I stole your wedding-ring from you," Grimarr said, his voice almost too quiet to hear in the noise all around. "I scorned you when you asked why I did not give you a new one. So in these days past, when I was parted from you, I made you a new one, in the Ash-Kai forge, to right this wrong."

Jule couldn't seem to stop blinking down at it, an orc-forged wedding-ring, made by her mate's own hand. And it was so like him, like *them*. All hard-looking shards of gold and silver, different at first glance, but so beautiful when fired together, created into something whole and new.

"What does it say?" she asked finally, her voice hoarse, and those black eyes darted up to hers, and away again.

"It reads," he said, "'I pledge you my troth, my fair Jule.'"

Oh. It was the vow of a mate. The vow he'd made to her in the candlelight, their first night together. *I grant you my favour, and my sword, and my fealty...*

"You must not needs take it, or wear it," Grimarr said, his voice rather rushed. "You must do naught you do not wish for. But I wished to give you this choice, with all the rest."

The prickling was back again behind Jule's eyes, and she felt herself give a jerky shrug. "Well," she said, "in our human tradition, I would make the choice, but you have to ask first. Properly."

She had no idea if Grimarr even knew what that meant, and his black eyes blinked at her, once—but then, in a sudden rush of movement, he was half-guiding, half-dragging her toward one of those benches, in the middle of the room. Thrusting her down to seated upon it, while he dropped to both knees before her, his fingers still holding the ring, glinting gold and silver and beautiful in the firelight.

"Jule," he said, his voice deep enough that it seemed to reverberate the air around them, dulling the nearest voices to a low murmur. "Woman. You are my mate. The mother of my son. You are brave and kind and lusty and clever. You gave all for me, and for my brothers, when I did not deserve this. You gave me many, many gifts."

The voices around them had seemed to fade even further, Jule's sole focus on Grimarr's voice, his eyes, the way that ring was trembling slightly in his fingers. "I could never have thought that you would be all this, when first I took you," he said slowly. "I would not have dreamed that any human would do all this, least of all a woman who was daughter and wife to my enemies. But you have shown me that I was wrong. You have taught me that humans can be true mates, and true friends. You are worthy of honour. You are worthy of trust. And I wish"—his breath was audible, in, out—"I wish to show you that I can be worthy of your trust, in return."

The words felt true, his eyes felt true, his hand now reaching for hers, closing it in its warm safe heat. "I wish," he said, quieter now, only him only her, "to pledge you my troth as both your mate, and your husband. I wish to wed you, my fair one. Will you"—his eyes flicked to the ring, and then back to her face—"accept this vow, from me?"

Jule could hear her heart beating, the silence spreading wide, but for the weight of Grimarr's breath against her skin.

An orc, her mate, on his knees before her, with those words in his mouth, that ring in his hand, shimmering truth in his eyes—

"Yes, Grimarr," she whispered, to those eyes. "I will."

It was like the room exploded all at once, shouts and cheers rising all around, but Jule could only look at Grimarr. At the single tear streaking down his scarred cheek, at the rueful, relieved smile on his mouth. At the way his shaky fingers had found hers, and were now sliding on that beautiful new ring, in the place where Astin's had been. A new ring a new home a whole new *life*, and when Jule flung her arms around him he was there, here, warm, alive, *hers*.

"Ach," he breathed, choked, into her hair. "You honour me, woman. Thank you, for this."

But Jule was done with words, suddenly, done with her mate's sadness and regrets. And instead, she dragged him up, dragged his face close, and desperately, frantically kissed him.

He growled back into her mouth, all heat and power and triumph, and in a whirl of bodies and limbs he was sitting on the bench, with Jule straddling him on top. Her hands were already carding deep into his silken hair, pulling him closer, drinking up the glory of his hot mouth, his sharp teeth, his swirling, powerful tongue. While his hands were roaming strong and shameless over her back, her arse, her breasts. Spreading, brief, over the ever-growing swell of her belly, while he groaned dark and guttural into her throat.

Jule could only seem to gasp and grind against him, her hungry heat already finding the hard, twitching ridge of him through their multiple layers of clothes. And the craving for it, for this, was suddenly so powerful she couldn't breathe or think or follow. Could only thrust her desperate hands against his powerful bare shoulders, his broad bare chest, the hard ripples of his abdomen. And this was all hers now, for good, and Jule broke their kiss long enough to watch her greedy hands race over him, grasping and stroking, plucking at his nipples, tracing the strength of his shoulders, fluttering up against his warm lips.

"Beautiful orc," she heard herself say, her voice shaky and appalling, but those eyes only flashed with pleasure, that mouth parting, that long tongue curling against her fingers.

"Fair woman," he purred back, his voice a swelling vibrating heat. "I wish to see you. I wish to touch you."

The words tugged at something low in Jule's belly—it was him asking, like he'd always done, since their very first night together. And the reason he was asking—she blinked at him, fought to orient her whirling thoughts—was because they had an audience. Because it wasn't only him and her, two hungry bodies on a bench, but it was hundreds of orcs, hundreds of eyes watching them. And a swift glance behind Jule showed that they *were* watching, the room gone far quieter than it had previously been, with rows of orcs standing around them, staring at them with greedy black eyes.

But Grimarr knew that—of course Grimarr knew that—and his eyes on Jule's were waiting, too. Giving her the choice in this, even though she knew how much he craved it, how this was almost all his fantasies brought to life, in this very moment.

And Jule loved him, she wanted him, and what the hell did it matter if anyone else knew that, or saw it? Because that was who she was. A lusty, hungry, brave woman with her own glorious gorgeous mate, and she wanted him so much she was damn near shaking with it.

"Yes," she breathed. "Please, Grimarr."

The disbelief rose first, swarming bright in those eyes—and then the understanding, and the hunger. So bare and hard and potent, like the look of a long-starved predator, ravenous and ready to kill.

"Brave woman," he rumbled, his hand come up to cradle brief and reverent against her face. "*Good* woman."

But his other hand had already come down to the front of her dress, claws out—and with a single powerful stroke, he tore both the dress and the shift beneath it, straight down the middle. Exposing Jule's bare breasts and belly to the warm open air, and then he hurled the remnants of her clothes powerfully away, leaving her entirely naked upon him.

The room had seemed to go even quieter all around, and Jule could almost feel all those watching orc eyes, prickling against her bare skin. Following the line of her back, the curve of her arse, the swell of her heavy breasts, the jut of her hardened, flushed nipples. And, too, that curve of her belly, with an orc-son inside it, and that was where Grimarr's warm hands went first, fingers spreading wide, claws brushing both gentle and sharp.

"My woman," he murmured, into the surrounding silence, and it was enough to wash away the remnants of the tension, the whispering shame. "My own fair one. My mate."

Jule shuddered over him, her entire body seeming to streak to life with pleasure, with the words his voice his powerful hands on her skin. And those warm hands were sliding, now, slow and proprietary, up her belly, curving warm and protective over the swell of her breasts, squeezing gently against them—and then over her shoulders, down her back, until they were gripping strong and possessive against her arse. Drawing her spread legs a little closer against his still-clothed, still-swollen hardness, and drawing an audible, uncontrollable gasp from Jule's mouth.

"You hunger for me, my fair one," he murmured, so soft, his voice a vibrating thrill of pleasure. "You long for my prick, and my seed."

Jule couldn't help another breathless groan, a convulsive circle of her hips against that tantalizing, unreachable hardness, and Grimarr's low laugh was another thrill of heat, of colour, of life. Even as those big hands on her arse tugged it up slightly, drawing her hungry wetness away from him, and— Jule gasped with shock, even as she moaned with pleasure— tilting her bare arse up and out, straight toward their watching, captive audience.

His hands had pulled her slightly apart as he'd done it, and it meant that all those orcs could see—*everything*. Jule's spread-apart arse, her swollen lips, her dripping-wet core, clenching desperately and greedily against the open air.

"You must needs be filled," came Grimarr's heated voice, setting that clenching even stronger, harder, for those watching eyes. "You must needs be seated full upon a good strong orc-prick, and pumped full of good seed."

Jule could only seem to gasp and nod, begging for this lost in this, and when that infuriating, mouthwatering orc raised a black eyebrow, there was only more hunger, more longing, pleasure rising and soaring and gorging with life.

"Yes, Grimarr," Jule gasped, to those beautiful black eyes. "Please, do this for me. Please, fuck me. Fill me with your orc-prick. Pump me full of your good seed."

The surge of pleasure in those eyes was a joy all its own, as was the slow, warm, wicked grin that tugged up that mouth, showing her all those sharp white teeth. "Good, brave woman," he whispered. "I shall do this."

And then, thank the gods, one of those hands dropped to his still-fastened trousers, and—Jule nearly choked—drew out that huge, swollen, leaking orc-prick.

It was larger than Jule had ever seen it, already spurting white from the tip, his bollocks below almost straining with their bounty. And fuck it looked good, smelled good, and Jule could feel her own body dripping for those watching orc eyes behind her, while her tongue licked her suddenly-parched lips, and her hungry fingers fluttered down to coat themselves in delicious white.

Grimarr gave a hard, heated chuckle, watching with warm, indulgent eyes as Jule brought her wet fingers to her mouth and sucked them off. Moaning at the impossible, succulent taste of it—and then going for more, and more, her thoughts wildly wondering if she could just get on her knees, suck him back, and start drinking—

But Grimarr's strong hands were both on her arse again, guiding her back toward him, and yes, yes, *this*, her body dripping and clenching and starving for him, almost, almost—

The first touch of that hard wet cockhead against her brought a shout to her mouth, astonishingly loud in the strange silence, but Grimarr had moaned too, the sound thick and guttural, his fingers trembling warm against her skin. Still guiding her downwards, guiding that hard hot cock slowly up inside her, and gods he felt huge and gods it was *spectacular*, her body grasping and craving for it, her breath coming in harsh, high-pitched gasps.

"Oh gods, oh *gods*," she breathed, or perhaps chanted, as that huge hardness spread her apart, drove inside, stretching her around it, impaling her on its powerful heft. "Oh gods, oh gods, Grimarr, *please*—"

He was slowing slightly, meeting resistance now, so impossibly thick and full inside her. And so *alive*, too, twitching and swelling and leaking, bringing more indecent gasps and groans to Jule's mouth, and even more when those hands on her arse tilted her up again, spread her open. Showing all the watching orcs just what this looked like, Jule's pink, swollen, straining body, stretched open wide around his huge grey orc-prick, jutted now halfway up inside her.

And perhaps it was the bond, it was hunger it was madness, but Jule *was* this, she *was*—and she tilted herself back a little further, showing them even more of her stretched, quivering, dripping body, with their captain's prick halfway up inside. She was lusty and hungry and strong, she was being fucked by the orcs' captain before all five clans, and why should they not see its being done? Why should they not see their captain's hunger for her, his honour and regard for his mate? And should she not show them her own pride, her own hunger, as well?

Grimarr's breath was coming out in sustained groans, his eyes half-lidded and half-wild with pleasure, and when his big hands on Jule's arse spread her apart even wider, she moaned aloud, and did it. Opening her hips and her legs, tilting herself back, taking deep, heaving breaths, showing them all he wanted to show them, all he wanted them to see. And willing herself to relax, to accept this, to take this gift he offered, to swallow his huge, powerful cock inside her, before all his watching brothers.

She wriggled down a little harder, bringing another guttural gasp to his mouth, and in reply there was more heat, more pressure, pushing hard and powerful against her. Sliding deeper and deeper inside, breath by breath, heartbeat by heartbeat, she was his, he was hers, they were one, before all five clans, signed and sealed and witnessed—

And with one final, jolting push, he was in. Jule's groin pressed flat and hard against his, his swollen bollocks wedged against her crease, her body pierced and filled and violently trembling, stuck and stretched and conquered by an orc captain's prick, while all his orcs watched in bated, breathless silence.

"Oh," she gasped, into him, against him, her eyes her hands caught on his face, fingers clutching against the strength of his jaw. "Oh. *Grimarr*. My *love*."

His replying moan was dark liquid ecstasy, his cock swelling even fuller inside her, his big hands suddenly pulling her close into a tight, powerful embrace. All bare skin to bare skin, inside and out, impaled on an orc's lap, crushed in his arms, filled with his prick and his son.

And it was almost too powerful to bear, suddenly, and even more when that warm mouth kissed quiet and reverent against her hair, her ear, her neck. His claw carefully drawing her hair out of the way, and Jule arched her neck for him, arched her whole body for him, yes, yes, *yes*.

When his teeth bit down, and his hips drove up, Jule heard herself scream, all pure flaring euphoria, while Grimarr's own groan roared against her very bones. Tearing her open, ripping her apart from the inside out, that prick driving while that hungry throat swallowed, her hungry orc her hungry self, and it was all Jule could do to hold on, to breathe, to *be*. To take this invasion, this gift, to be flayed and rammed and bared so mercilessly, stretched and scratched and soaring, bright and alive and exalted with joy—

Jule's release came with a gouge and a scream, her body wrenching and writhing around him, while the ecstasy kicked and jolted, wringing itself higher with every breath. And then Grimarr was the one shouting, his whole being claiming her marking her filling her, firing and flooding her full of his liquid surging power like a long-blocked cannon, fusing alive inside her.

The world seemed to be beating around her, against her, but when Jule blinked awake again it was only her heartbeat, or perhaps his. Pulsing through his big hands on her face, tilting it up to where he was blinking at her, his mouth red, his eyes dazed and clouded with pleasure.

"Ach," he whispered. "My fair, brave, generous mate. You are all an orc could *wish* for."

Jule couldn't seem to speak, suddenly, and found herself feeling almost shy, perhaps both of him, and the watching orcs all around. And Grimarr seemed to see that, thankfully, and his big arms circled closer around her, drawing her into the safe, solid heat of his embrace, while one of his hands stroked soft and reassuring against her back.

"You bring all my dreams to life, woman," he murmured, quiet, into her hair, as the voices seemed to rise again around them, the watching orcs finally returning to their party. "And those of my brothers, as well. Most of them have never seen a woman take an orc-prick, or welcome it with such eagerness. I wish to show them how this should be done."

Right. Jule couldn't help a short, sniffly laugh against him, into the warm heat of his shoulder. "It's still all about your planned orc utopia, isn't it?" she mumbled. "Teaching them how not to be terrible lovers, so they can lure unsuspecting mates of their own?"

Grimarr replied with a husky growl, a slight clench of his claws on her bare back. "It is good, that they learn this," he said, voice harder than before. "But this joy is ours, woman. I have longed to take a woman like this all my life, and you have given me this gift. This, and so many others. My love for you, my thanks to you, it is"—he pulled back again, met her eyes with his—"it is like you made a sun, inside me. One that shall never fade, or burn away. I shall forever cherish this, woman. I shall forever cherish *you*."

Damn this orc, and his hands and his eyes and his beautiful honeyed words, and despite everything there was wetness streaking down Jule's cheeks again, far too strong to blink back or ignore. "You cursed orc," she whispered back. "I love you, too."

His replying smile was almost painfully tender, lighting up his entire face. "We shall build this new life, from this love, and this light," he whispered. "You shall see."

Giving birth, it turned out, was a more harrowing, exhausting experience than being kidnapped by orcs, living trapped in a strange mountain, and killing one's husband combined.

It dragged on for nearly an entire agonizing, miserable day, during which Jule became increasingly, desperately certain she was nearing inevitable death. But her attendants—Sken and Efterar, as well as an initially nervous, but very well-paid, human midwife—remained patient and unconcerned, spouting platitudes that were as empty as they were infuriating. *It'll be over soon. You're doing fine. Almost there.*

In the end, the only actual comfort came from Grimarr, who'd firmly planted himself close beside Jule, and proceeded to bark and growl at Sken and Efterar with gratifying ferocity. All the while touching and caressing Jule with strong certain hands, filling her breath with his scent, and flooding her ears with his voice.

"Brave woman," he said, again and again, between every contraction, holding Jule's desperate gaze with his glittering black eyes. "Strong woman. You honour me. You shall do this. You *are*."

Jule could only gulp and shout and sob, worse and worse as the hours passed, but finally, *finally*, a full eternity later, somehow, it was done. And into Jule's trembly, exhausted arms, Efterar placed a sticky, floppy, grey little bundle.

It was—Tengil. Their son.

The world seemed to fall silent all around, caught in the sheer dazed wonder of this sight, this moment. A tiny, wriggly new being, come to life, brought to life, here, in Jule's arms.

And one of her secret, nagging fears was already laid to rest, because gods, Tengil was *beautiful*. His body a smooth, pearly grey, utterly unmarked, with teeny clawed hands and feet. His little features even and balanced, his ears delicately pointed, his nose an adorable, pointed little snub. And his eyes were pure bottomless black, blinking up at Jule's face, and she could only seem to stare, and stare, and stare.

Beside her she could feel Grimarr staring too, and now here was his big hand, coming to spread wide and reverent against Tengil's grey skin.

"Tengil," Grimarr said, quiet, drawing the babe's blinking eyes toward him. "Our son. A king."

The words sent a powerful shudder down Jule's back, and then again when Grimarr kept speaking, now in rolling waves of black-tongue. And while some of the words were still unfamiliar to Jule, after spending the better part of a year mated to this orc, she now knew enough to at least follow his voice's meaning.

*I am Grimarr, your father*, he said. *This is Jule, your mother, who has carried you and brought you forth with strength and bravery. You are an orc. You are Ash-Kai. You have been born into an age of peace, thanks to the love your mother has given us.*

Something seemed to swell in Jule's chest as he spoke, as the babe blinked at his father with intent black eyes, almost as though he understood every word. And then, once Grimarr had fallen silent, Tengil immediately turned his tiny head, and started bonking it with impressive force against Jule's bare chest.

Jule's tension seemed to break all at once, coming out in a hurtling, high-pitched laugh, and beside her Grimarr was chuckling too, his big hand stroking Tengil's back with clear approval. And after a few moments' help from the midwife, Tengil was happily nursing at Jule's breast, his tiny eyes squeezed shut, his little fist clamped firmly around Grimarr's finger.

"He is indeed our son," Grimarr said, with immense satisfaction. "Look how hale and lusty he is. I am most pleased, woman. I am glad I chose to mate with you, above all others."

His grin at Jule was proud and hungry and dangerous all at once, sending a disconcerting thrill down her thoroughly exhausted body, but she managed a roll of her eyes at him. "You're glad *I* chose to mate with *you*, you mean," she corrected him. "Let alone giving actual *birth* to your actual *offspring*."

She'd meant it as a joke, but Grimarr's eyes on her had sobered, his free hand coming to cradle gently against her face. "Yes," he said. "I am glad of this, woman. I thank the gods each day for this. You are my light. I love you so."

He followed the words with a slow, lingering kiss to Jule's mouth, speaking just as clearly of his warmth, his devotion. And she kissed back, hard and suddenly desperate, so grateful for him, for his generosity and strength, for all he had done these past months to make her pregnancy not only tolerable, but enjoyable. Daily massages and lovemaking, tasty cooked food and regular exercise together, challenging and fascinating work together each day. Building toward their new life, their new world, together.

And while there was still much work left to do, and with it innumerable obstacles to overcome, so far, the peace between orcs and men had continued to hold. Surviving not only multiple new human laws that restricted the orcs' newfound freedom and activities, but also several outbreaks of violence, mostly attacks on innocent orcs. But Grimarr's deft handling had so far kept the situation under control, helped in part by Jule's regular communication with Otto, who, to his credit, had continued to publicly and enthusiastically support the peace-treaty, from his highly profitable new lands in Yarwood.

And that peace-treaty, tenuous as it was, had already changed the orcs' world beyond imagining. The mountain now legally belonged to them, with land multiple leagues all around. They could now trade away newly forged jewels and trinkets, in exchange for food and clothing and supplies. And though most humans still avoided orcs at all costs, orcs were free to walk the roads, and visit the humans' towns and establishments, and approach humans to speak, if they wished.

And thanks to that last point, several orcs had found new mates, and over the past few months, two more women had actually decided to move into the mountain. One was a clever blonde wisp of a girl named Rosa, who had apparently fallen in love with John in a human library, and whose belly was already gently rounding with his son. And the other was a plump, dreamy brunette named Stella who—if one could believe Silfast's tale—he had found prostrated on the Bautul goddess' altar, deep in the northern forest. Their worship together was quite something to behold, with far rougher handling on Silfast's part than Jule had ever received from Grimarr, but they certainly both seemed to enjoy it, with Stella taking clear satisfaction in meekly provoking Silfast to ever more drastic measures.

And though Jule still found it rather peculiar to be so aware of such intimate things, it was lovely to have other women in the mountain to talk to, and laugh with, and just be human with. Making and enjoying human meals together, reading and discussing whatever books Rosa had gotten from the library, and pulling together a cheerful little playroom—without any deadly weapons—for their soon-to-be orc-sons.

It was all legions better than Jule could have ever expected, especially in a year that also included being kidnapped from one's home, and killing one's husband, and giving birth to an orc's son. An orc Jule was still kissing, in fact, their tongues tangling together, his fingers twining tight into hers.

When Grimarr finally pulled away Jule felt shivery and breathless, her eyes locked to his. Staring tiredly as he brought up their joined hands, and gently kissed her fingers, his mouth lingering on first her wedding-ring, before moving to the thick gold band on his own finger. A ring Jule had made herself in the Ash-Kai forge, with much assistance, and had then given to Grimarr before a human priest at the base of their mountain, with hundreds of orcs cheering all around.

And while it still wasn't perfect between Jule and Grimarr, and their ongoing trust in one another was still a daily choice, Jule held no reservations, no regrets. She wanted to be here. She wanted this peace. She wanted this orc, stubborn and calculating and enraging as he was. Her beautiful, powerful, brilliant mate. Her own choice.

"And I love you, Grimarr," she whispered, quiet, to those still-watching eyes. "So much."

Her voice cracked slightly as she spoke, her eyes blinking, but both his hands were already here on her face, wiping the wetness away. And his mouth was already here again, kissing with warm, heady, familiar hunger. And with just a touch of his delicious sharp teeth this time, dragging up an undeniable, whirling heat through Jule's dazed, blunted thoughts.

"Wait, wait, hold on, you two," said a voice, Efterar's voice, sharper than it had been yet today. "None of that. She just gave *birth*, for gods' sakes. No sex. For *weeks*."

Grimarr abruptly pulled back from Jule, and fixed Efterar

with a ghastly scowl. "Do I look like I am—*sexing*?" he demanded. "I only tend to my own fair mate. My *wife*. The mother of my own *son*."

An unmistakable warmth had crept into his scowl, his big hand gently caressing Tengil's downy head, but Efterar only glared back, arms crossed. "You aren't having sex *yet*," he said flatly, "but we've all seen enough to know *exactly* where it goes from here."

He was referring, of course, to the fact that Jule and Grimarr had blatantly continued their ongoing public activities, in the mountain's common-rooms and meeting-rooms and beyond, on a near-daily basis. And after so long, Jule no longer found any shame in it, but only a powerful, fundamental pleasure. Being openly ravished, exposed, filled, and fucked by her own chosen mate, living their truth and their joy without reproach or regret.

"I should never risk harming my mate with this," Grimarr said, fully frowning again. "But what harm is this kissing? Or what harm is there if she might wish to suck my prick for a spell, and regain her strength by my good seed?"

The hunger seemed to swirl all at once, soaring through Jule's muddied exhausted thoughts with an unrepentant compulsion, but Efterar gave an exasperated groan, and now it was Sken who stepped forward, poking a wizened finger into Grimarr's broad chest.

"No, boy," he said. "Your brother is right. You don't do this until you're sure you can control it. Else your mate will *never* bear you another son."

The fear flared across Grimarr's eyes, but then he scowled again, even more ferocious than before. "You lie, Sken," he said flatly. "Do not pretend I do not know this now. Not after you said my son would be killed, and he was not."

Sken's filmy, remorseless gaze glanced briefly toward Tengil, who now seemed to be falling asleep against Jule's breast. "I know best what I see, boy," he said, "and you know to heed my words as truth."

Grimarr sighed, but Jule could see him relenting, his broad shoulders sagging. "For how long must we forego this?"

"Forty days," said Efterar promptly, with a meaningful wink at Jule. "And then we'll see."

Grimarr shot Efterar another ferocious scowl, but then turned his back on him, and settled his bulky form down beside Jule's tired body on the bed. Pulling her close into his warmth, his big arm embracing both her and Tengil at once, and the pleasure of that, the fundamental rightness of that, seemed to spark and flare behind Jule's exhausted eyes.

"Ach, my fair one," Grimarr murmured, close into her ear. "I have been again punished for my past sins. Forty days I must not have you. Not even your *mouth*."

He sounded genuinely mournful, and Jule turned her face toward him, and felt herself give a choked chuckle. "Like hell," she said thickly, "am I going forty whole days without *that*."

Grimarr blinked at her, but then his mouth twitched up, warm and approving. "Hush," he said, with a wary glance toward where Efterar and the midwife were now tidying up the messy bed-linens. "Do not let our keepers hear this, woman."

Jule gave another chuckle, and nestled closer into Grimarr's warm strong arms. Sinking into the perfect, precious truth of this, of her family, her mate, her own tiny sleeping son. They'd done it. They'd changed the world, and created new life within it.

"Sleep now," Grimarr whispered, as he pressed a soft, quiet kiss to Jule's hair. "I will hold you."

Jule knew he meant it, and as she closed her eyes, inhaling the scent of him, the world around her only seemed to grow brighter, rich with beauty and warmth and life.

She was home.

## THANKS FOR READING
AND GET A FREE BONUS STORY!

Thank you SO much for joining me for Jule and Grimarr's story!

If you'd like to spend more time with our orcs, sign up to my mailing list at www.finleyfenn.com for some fun extra content, including delicious Grimarr artwork, and a free Orc Sworn story. I'd love to stay in touch with you!

### FREE STORY:
### OFFERED BY THE ORC

**The monster needs a sacrifice. And she's naked on the altar...**

When Stella wanders the forest alone one fateful night, she only seeks peace, relief, escape. A few stolen moments on a secret, ancient altar, at one with the moon above.

Until she's accosted by a hulking, hideous, bloodthirsty *orc*. An orc who demands a sacrifice—not by his sword, but by Stella's complete surrender. To his claws, his sharp teeth, his huge muscled body. His every humiliating, thrilling command...

But Stella would never offer herself up to be used and sacrificed by a monster—would she? Even if her surrender just might grant her the moon's favour—and open her heart to a whole new fate?

### FREE download now!
www.finleyfenn.com

# ACKNOWLEDGMENTS

I'm so grateful for my readers, and especially my brilliant beta readers and advance reviewers. I could not do this without you!

Special thanks to Jesse for your much-needed insight and ridiculous editing skills (and the unforgettable new head-canon!). And Amy, thank you SO much for all the ongoing encouragement, guidance, and support. I can't tell you how much it means to me.

Finally, my utmost gratitude and adoration to my own bonded mate, who consistently outdoes any hero I could dream up. I love you, my dark one.

## ALSO BY FINLEY FENN

### THE HEIRESS AND THE ORC

*Once, he was her dearest friend... but now he's a brutal, terrifying monster.*

In a world of recently warring orcs and men, Ella Riddell is determined to ignore it all. She's the wealthiest heiress in the realm—and soon, she's to wed a lord, and become a real lady.

Until the night her engagement-party ends in utter *disaster*, and Ella runs for the forest—**and straight into the powerful arms of a hulking, deadly orc.**

And it's not just any orc. It's *Natt*. The orc Ella made a secret, foolish pledge to, many years past...

He's huge and shameless and vicious, not at all the gangly, laughing daredevil Ella remembers. **And he's here with one shocking, scandalous aim: to wreak vengeance on Ella's betrothed. With *her*.**

With her hunger.

Her surrender.

Her undoing.

Ella knows she should run, even if this deadly enemy was once a friend. Even if his scent drags up a dark, forbidden longing. Even if his kisses are the sweetest, filthiest thing she's ever tasted in her life...

But will Ella truly risk her perfect future, for an orc? Will she face the bitter truths of the past, and brave the terrifying Orc Mountain, before more war rises to destroy them all?

## ALSO BY FINLEY FENN

### THE LIBRARIAN AND THE ORC

*He's a fierce, ferocious, death-dealing beast. And he's reading a book in her library...*

In a world of recently warring orcs and men, Rosa Rolfe leads a quiet, scholarly life as an impoverished librarian—until the day she finds an *orc*. In her library. Reading a *book*.

He's rude, aggressive, and deeply terrifying, with his huge muscled form, sharp black claws, and cold, dismissive commands. But he doesn't *seem* truly dangerous... at least, until night falls. **And he makes Rosa a shocking, scandalous offer...**

Her books, for her surrender.

Her ecstasy.

Her enlightenment...

Rosa's no fool, and she knows she can't possibly risk her precious library for this brazen, belligerent orc. Even if he *is* surprisingly well-read. Even if he smells like sweet, heated honey. Even if he makes Rosa's heart race with fear, and ignites all her deepest, darkest cravings at once...

**But surrender demands a dangerous, devastating price.** A bond that can't easily be broken. And a breakneck journey to the fearsome, forbidding Orc Mountain, where a curious, clever librarian might be just what's needed to stop another war...

## ALSO BY FINLEY FENN

### THE DUCHESS AND THE ORC

*He's a massive, mocking, murderous monster. And there's only one thing he wants from her...*

In a world of recently warring orcs and men, Maria is desperate for escape. She's trapped in an opulent prison, tainted by rumours of madness, and wed to a cold, vindictive duke who hungers only for war.

But with no family, no funds, and no hope, there's nowhere left to run—except for the one place even a duke can't reach. The place where women almost always meet their doom...

**Orc Mountain.**

It's a grim, deadly fortress, filled with fierce, bloodthirsty beasts—**and the first orc Maria meets is the most terrifying of them all.** A huge, hostile, hideous brute, hardened by hatred and war, who instantly accuses her of foul trickery, and threatens her with death—

**But this orc also wants something.** Something that kindles deep in his gleaming black eyes, in his rough, rugged scent, in the velvet heat of his voice. Something that just might grant Maria his safety... but only if she grants him *everything* in return.

Her defeat.

Her dignity.

Her devotion...

And surely, a duchess wouldn't dare make such a shameful deal with the devil—or would she? Especially when surrender might spark yet more war... **or bring the mighty Orc Mountain to its knees?**

# ALSO BY FINLEY FENN

## THE MIDWIFE AND THE ORC

*Orc Mountain needs a midwife. And this devious, deadly orc is determined to find one...*

In a world of recently warring orcs and men, Gwyn Garrett is a lord's daughter on a mission—to escape her lord father, dump her cheating betrothed, and pursue her true calling as a plant-obsessed midwife.

**Until the night her brand-new house is invaded by an *orc*.** A tall, taunting, treacherous monster, with sharp teeth, vicious claws, and gleaming black eyes. And worst of all, a blatant, brutal mission of his own...

He's come to court her.

Claim her.

*Compromise* her.

But Gwyn is far too clever to fall for this sneaky orc's schemes—right? Even if he moves like a graceful god, if his voice is sweet syrup in her ears. If his low, mocking laugh sparks something hot and reckless, deep in her soul...

It's hunger, it's *home*, it's everything Gwyn never knew she needed—but in its wake, there's only devastation. Defeat. And the realization that she's forever linked with this horrible orc, and his horrible plans...

And with the war. The fates of hundreds of women like her. And the truth that **Orc Mountain desperately needs her, and maybe this proud, lonely orc does too...**

# ALSO BY FINLEY FENN

## THE MAID AND THE ORCS

*She's fallen for an angel... but he's mated to a monster.*

In a realm of orcs and powerful men, housemaid Alma Andersson is drowning—in grief, debt, and drudgery. And when her awful employer makes his darkest demand yet, she flees for the forest, and tumbles toward her doom...

Until she's snatched to safety by a **huge, vicious green beast.**

**An** *orc*.

He's utterly terrifying, with his towering bulk, sharp teeth, and deadly black claws—but his touch is gentle, and his eyes are kind. And his scent is a deep, decadent sweetness, sparking a furious flame between them...

But it's only more disaster, because **Alma's shy, soft-hearted rescuer is already mated... to another** *orc*. A tall, silent, snarling monster named Drafli, who loathes Alma on sight, and clearly longs for her death.

Yet Drafli will do anything for his sweet mate, even if it means tolerating a weak, worthless human. So he makes Alma a cold, calculated offer: **he'll share his mate with her... but only on his terms.**

He wants her silence.

Her surrender.

Her servitude.

And with Alma's fate firmly in Drafli's ruthless hands, how can she face her own dark desires—or all the secrets hidden behind Orc Mountain's walls? **Can a lost, lonely housemaid come between two orcs... without being crushed?**

# ABOUT THE AUTHOR

Finley Fenn has been writing about people falling in love for as long as she can remember. She creates steamy fantasy romance tales with cranky-but-sexy men and monsters, loads of angst and drama, a dash of mystery and action, and wholehearted happily ever afters.

When she's not obsessing over her stories, she reads everything she can get her hands on, and drools over delicious orc artwork (find her latest faves on Facebook at Finley Fenn Readers' Den). She lives in Canada with her beloved family, including her own cranky-but-sexy husband, and her cranky-and-hungry dog.

To get free bonus content, character illustrations, and news about upcoming books, sign up at www.finleyfenn.com.

CPSIA information can be obtained
at www.ICGtesting.com
Printed in the USA
LVHW032142070323
741161LV00019B/315